BLIND CURVE

TELL ME NO LIES

DEAD RINGER

"Just the ticket for those looking for excitement and romance."

—RT Book Reviews

"An entertaining...exceptional...emotionally taut tale... offers twists and turns that kept me enthralled to the last page."

—Old Book Barn Gazette

"Thrilling and edgy...*Dead Ringer* delivers excitement, suspense, and sexual tension...Highly recommended."

—RomRevToday.com

LIKE A KNIFE

Annie Solomon

Two Lethal Lies

FOREVER

NEW YORK   BOSTON

This book is a work of fiction. Names, characters, places, and incidents are the product of the author's imagination or are used fictitiously. Any resemblance to actual events, locales, or persons, living or dead, is coincidental.

Cover design by Diane Luger

Forever
Hachette Book Group
237 Park Avenue
New York, NY 10017
Visit our website at www.HachetteBookGroup.com.

Forever is an imprint of Grand Central Publishing. The Forever name and logo is a trademark of Hachette Book Group, Inc.

Printed in the United States of America

First Printing: October 2010

10 9 8 7 6 5 4 3 2 1

ATTENTION CORPORATIONS AND ORGANIZATIONS:
Most HACHETTE BOOK GROUP books are available at quantity discounts with bulk purchase for educational, business, or sales promotional use. For information, please call or write:

Special Markets Department, Hachette Book Group
237 Park Avenue, New York, NY 10017
Telephone: 1-800-222-6747 Fax: 1-800-477-5925

ACKNOWLEDGMENTS

I'd like to thank Patrick McNally for his help with the legal system and Dr. Stewart Perlman, Dr. Jeanne Ballinger, and Dr. Peter Jelsma for their help with medical issues. I must extend my apologies to Dr. Perlman as well. He came up with several clever ways to do away with someone, none of which, alas, worked out for the book. All exaggerations, fictions, and mistakes are, of course, my own.

I'd also like to thank Beth Pattillo, who helped pull me out when I got myself stuck in the mud of plot and character. And to Larry, who always reminds me there is a way out, even if I swear there isn't.

TWO LETHAL LIES

1

The man gazed down at the body stretched before him. She'd been a pretty thing. A bit scrawny, perhaps, but with the makeup removed and her face in sleep's repose, she had the bare, otherworldly look of an angel.

Then again, he always saw his brides that way. Sisters of Mercy. Chaste, docile, patiently awaiting the intimate piercing that would join them forever.

He stroked her arm, caressing the limb from the shoulder all the way down to the wrist, watching the play of vein and artery below the soft skin. The sight thrilled him—as much for its own sake as for what he knew was coming.

He tried to prolong the moment, to control his breathing and the rising excitement. Before he'd learned to have power over his impulses, he'd squandered the precious fluid. Even now he could wait only a few seconds. Compelled, he found the blue vein still pulsing in her arm, gently, carefully squeezed the needle in, and began the ritual. As the bags filled with the deep claret blood, his heart filled with a fevered, zealous devotion. In that moment, he would have done almost anything for the creature in front of him.

He crooned a soft hymn as he drained her. Brushed the hair back from her pale, pale skin. Sweet child. Sweet, sacred child.

There would always be things in this world that could not be explained. Just as there would always be people who tried to explain them. A bad childhood. A bad set of genes. God's will. He smiled. Or the Devil's.

But the fact was, the most important things had no explanation. Life and death were true mysteries.

But as humans, we weren't just empty bottles whipped down the road by the wind. We could take action. We could spurt seed into a fertile womb or steal air from healthy lungs.

In this way we became the myth ourselves. The Creator. The Destroyer. The One Who Acts.

Not because we hate or love, but because we can.

There was no better reason for doing what he did.

Because he could. Like God, the ultimate actor.

Just as it has pleased God throughout the ages to slaughter the innocent, it pleased him to watch the life seep out of his silent sacrifice.

When it was done, and her heart had stopped, he secured her gift in the cooler, dating it carefully.

Then he kissed her serene forehead and her bloodless lips, picked up the blade, and carved out her eyes.

2

Some men were born heroes. Mitch Turner wasn't one of them. Heroes, even humble ones, drew the spotlight. And the last thing Mitch wanted was attention.

But when his pickup rumbled over the old wooden bridge that cut the town of Crossroads, Tennessee, in two, the universe had other ideas. So did the eleven-year-old beside him.

"Dad—wait! Look!"

He saw it at the same time. A small form on top of the bridge rail.

"What's she doing?" Jules asked.

But it was obvious. He stopped the truck. "Wait here."

"But—"

He firmed up the order. "Wait here." He dove out the door.

Julia Turner watched the girl on the bridge turn as Mitch raced toward her. For a minute, Julia stopped breathing. Then the air exploded out of her as the girl turned back to the river and did the unthinkable.

Flew into the air.

Julia gripped the dashboard, her mouth hanging open. Then her dad sailed over the rail after her.

Julia yanked off her seat belt and leaped out of the truck. In a heartbeat she was at the railing. There he was, bobbing in the water, turning in every direction. From where she was, Julia had the better view.

"Dad!" She pointed to her right, where several hundred yards away, long strands of scraggly red hair were sinking beneath the water.

In seconds, strong strokes took her dad there. He disappeared below the blackness, and for a few horrible moments it looked like he might not come back.

But he popped up at last, gasping for air and tugging something with him.

He did it! He actually did it!

Julia rushed back to the truck. The keys were still in it, but the engine was off. Just as she'd seen Mitch do a thousand times, she turned the key, and when the engine only coughed but didn't start, she said the same thing she'd heard her dad say.

"Dammit, old girl, don't do this to me."

The charm worked. The engine turned over, and she wrenched the seat as close to the pedals as possible. She still wasn't tall enough to reach them and see where she was going, but by fits and starts, she managed to get the truck down the bridge to the other side where her dad was heading.

She set the brake carefully, then dashed out again and grabbed an old blanket from the truck bed. It was dirty and leaf-strewn because her dad used it to haul stuff, but she snatched it anyway, scampered around the edge of the bridge, and slid down the bank to the river. Her father was approaching, using one arm to swim while the other cradled the small body he'd rescued.

"Over here!" Julia jumped up and down, waving her arms.

At last the water was shallow enough for Mitch to stand. He shifted the girl into both his arms and carried her to the shore. Dripping wet, he stumbled up the bank and laid the girl on the blanket. Julia thought he was going to fall down he was breathing so hard.

"Is she okay?"

The girl's eyes were closed, and she looked all scrunched up and tiny. More like a doll than a person.

Mitch wiped water off his face. "I don't know."

He started pumping the girl's chest and blowing into her mouth and pumping her chest again.

Endless minutes of nothing but the sound of her dad working on the small body. Then ... another miracle—the girl coughed, groaned, and opened her eyes.

"There we go," her dad said softly. "Welcome back."

Mitch's arms trembled with exhaustion. Every muscle ached and he wanted to collapse on the ground for a week. Not for the first time, he wished he had a cell phone. A few buttons and someone else could take over. But phones and credit cards and accounts of every kind were a thing of the past. And any kind of authority—police, EMT— would have questions he didn't want to answer.

"Hey," Julia said. "What's your name?"

The girl startled, seemed to see them for the first time, and started to sob.

He told Julia to wait while he got the truck, but she

thumbed over her shoulder with a triumphant, mischievous look. Their dusty black pickup was already at the near end of the bridge. Half of him wanted to scold her; the other half wanted to pin a medal on her.

He chucked her under the chin. "Good work, soldier."

She smiled happily, like he knew she would, and as it often did, it took his breath away. She would be a mankiller someday. Every inch of her inherited beauty was there in her face. The silky dark hair, the amazing blue eyes. He was going to have a handful if he wasn't careful.

But he was careful. He was always careful.

Mitch hadn't originally planned to stop in town. But the girl had abandoned a backpack when she went into the river. Inside, a wallet told them her name was Sara Jean Blunt and she lived in Crossroads.

The address took them in the direction they were already heading—across the bridge to the better side of town. Her house was at the top of the hill that overlooked the river and the flats, with its sprawl of cramped homes and old warehouses. Mitch stopped in front of a large clapboard house, a well-maintained Victorian wonder, with turrets and angles and a wide, wraparound porch. The geography and the architecture told him everything he needed to know about the girl's family and their position in the town.

Beside him, Sara Jean was shuddering inside the blanket, sniffling and weeping quietly as if afraid to let him hear. He got out, came around, and lifted her off the seat. She shivered in his arms while Julia bounced beside them.

"Is this where you live? Wow, it's so big. Do you have

your own room? Can you see it from here? What color is it? Do you have a TV?"

"Down, girl. Let's get Sara Jean inside. She's tired."

He knocked on the door, and when she saw where they were, Sara Jean groaned. "Oh, God." She looked up at him, her eyes wide and filled with tears. "Don't tell them. Please. Promise me you won't tell them. They'll be so disappointed." She hiccupped. "I'm so...so tired of being a disappointment."

A shard of sympathy struck him. He knew all about disappointing people. "I'm sure you're not a disappoint—"

"Look at me!" She threw off the blanket. "I'm too tall and too skinny, and my hair is this awful red, and everyone calls me Sara Jean Butt!"

Clichés tumbled through his head—kids can be stupid, so ignore them; everyone goes through an awkward stage; toughen up and fight back—but sometimes the only way to protect yourself was to hide the truth. He'd spent most of his life in deep cover, so he should know.

Fortunately, he was saved from replying by a small, trim woman with the same head of burning red hair as Sara's. "Mrs. Blunt?"

She screeched when she saw her daughter. "Oh, my God, Sara Jean, what happened?"

Mitch pushed past her. Made a split-second decision. "She...she fell into the river."

Out of the corner of his eye, he saw Julia open her mouth. He nudged her with his elbow to shut up. Not that Mrs. Blunt was listening.

"The river? Dear Lord, Sara Jean, what on earth were you doing—"

"Where's her room?" Mitch interrupted, turning

around with the wet child in his arms. "You should get her out of these clothes."

With rapid steps, she led the way to a staircase, and Mitch and Julia followed her up to the second floor. "Are you all right?" she asked her daughter. "You didn't break anything, did you? How's your ankle? She broke her ankle last summer," she explained quickly to Mitch.

Sara Jean's room was a flurry of pink and white. Ruffled pillows fluffed up the bed; balloons and teddy bears danced on the walls. It was the kind of room that made a man feel wildly uncomfortable but that little girls everywhere loved. Julia was no exception. He watched in regret as she gasped and gawked at the dolls and stuffed animals—all the trappings of the girlhood she never had and never would.

Mitch laid Sara Jean on the bed. "You'll be okay now."

An unspoken message passed between them. "Thanks," she said.

Mitch nodded, hoping he'd done the right thing. If nothing else, he'd done the convenient thing. The choice that would get him and Julia out of there fast. There was still time to make it to Nashville and from there head south to the Gulf. "Come on, Jules. Let's go."

"Wait," Sara Jean's mother said. She was scrambling around the room, collecting dry clothes and towels from the bathroom. "Please."

"That's okay," Mitch said. "We gotta hit the road."

"No, we don't," Julia said.

"Jules," Mitch warned.

"Don't have a job to go to, no one waiting on us."

"You're out of work?" Sara Jean's mother looked

concerned. A couple of years ago, being unemployed was like having leprosy—only the poor and shiftless caught it. Now, so many people were out of work it was almost a pandemic. "Do you live in town?"

Mitch opened his mouth, but Julia got there first. "No, ma'am. We don't live nowhere."

"Anywhere," Mitch corrected. "And we're *fine*." He emphasized the last word with another meaningful look at Julia. She scowled at him.

Mrs. Blunt seemed to sum up the situation. "I'm sure you are, but I couldn't live with myself if I didn't thank you properly. I've got chocolate chip cookies downstairs." Julia's eyes lit up. "If you'll just wait until I can get Sara Jean dried off..."

Jules took his hand and tugged him away. "Be happy to." She smiled.

But when they were in the hallway, Mitch yanked his hand away. "What do you think you're doing?"

"Nothing."

"You're damn right. Because we're going."

She hopped down the stairs and plopped onto one of the chairs that sat on either side of a table in the foyer. Crossing her arms and setting her mouth, she shot him a "make me" look.

He knew that look. "Come on, Junebug," he wheedled. "You know the rules."

"I hate your stupid rules," she said. "One of these days, I'm gonna be old enough to make my own rules."

"Well, until then you're living by mine. And rule number one is we don't talk about our troubles, and rule number two is we don't get involved in other people's."

"Then why'd you jump in the river?"

"That's different. I couldn't exactly watch Sara Jean drown."

"Well, I can't let her poor mother feel guilty about not thanking us properly."

"Okay, that's it." He pulled her up. She weighed no more than a pea, so it wasn't hard. "We're going."

"I'll scream. I'll tell them you beat me." He dragged her toward the door. "Mrs. Blunt! Mrs. Blunt!"

"Stop that."

"Oh," she groaned at the top of her voice, "I'm sooo hungry. Can't remember when I ate last."

"You little—"

"Mrs. Bluuuunnnnt!!"

Mitch threw up his hands. "Okay, okay." He held up a finger. "One cookie."

"And a glass of milk."

"All right. One cookie and a glass of milk. And no talking about us."

The commotion brought Sara Jean's mother running down the stairs. "Everything all right?"

"Just fine," Mitch said, a wary eye on the kid.

Sara Jean's mother brightened a bit. "I put Sara Jean to bed. She"—the mother's eyes darted away and back again—"she wasn't up to talking. Would you mind?" She gestured for them to follow her into the house, and they walked through the rooms with their heavy farmhouse replicas, the rugs and ceramics, not to mention family pictures. Julia's eyes popped and a look of worshipful awe crossed her face.

The kitchen was large and bright. A dining area was carved out of one corner, where a window looked out on a tree-filled backyard. In lieu of chairs, a wooden bench sat below the window, and Julia bounded onto it, gazing at the yard's October harvest of gold and red leaves.

But Mitch knew her focus was probably on one tree in particular, where a homemade swing hung alone and idle.

Sara Jean's mother made coffee, and while they waited for it to brew, she brought a plate of cookies to the table. Mitch thought it better all around for Julia to be gone for this part, so he let her take a cookie, then gestured toward the window.

"Go ahead," he told her.

She didn't need a second invitation. She whooped, grabbed another cookie, and dashed out the back door. He sat across from the window, where he could keep an eye on her. She leaped onto the swing and was airborne in seconds.

"She's adorable," Mrs. Blunt said with an edge of wistfulness. "You and your wife must be very proud of her."

Mitch nodded, his gaze still on his girl. "I am. But my wife...Julia's mother passed away."

"Oh, I'm so sorry."

"Thank you. It was a long time ago. Julia was just a baby."

"Well, you've done an amazing job with her. I wish... I wish Sara Jean could be that happy again." She brought Mitch his coffee, which he sipped gratefully. He was still wearing his wet clothes, and his skin was icy.

Mrs. Blunt noticed the shiver that went through him. "Good gracious," she exclaimed. "I can't believe I've left you in those wet clothes."

"That's okay. We're not stay—"

"Don't be ridiculous. Let me get you something of

Tommy's, my husband..." She was already pushing him out the door and into a laundry room off the kitchen. "Stay here and I'll bring you something. Then we can just pop this stuff into the machine and be done with it."

She was back in a few minutes with a pair of sweat-pants and a T-shirt, which he dutifully put on, though the shirt barely covered his midsection and the sweatpants reached only to the top of his ankles.

"Well, at least they're dry," she said when she saw him.

He padded back to the kitchen in bare feet and saw Julia still happily ensconced on the swing. A few minutes later, Mrs. Blunt came back, poured herself a cup of coffee, and joined him at the table.

"Now," she said brightly, though there was the glisten of tears in her eyes. "Tell me what really happened at the river."

Mentally, he groaned. The house with its cozy warmth was like flypaper—no matter how hard he tried, his feet kept sticking. But he couldn't bring himself to lie again.

When he was done, tears snaked down her cheeks and she put her hand on his arm. "God bless you," she said. "If you hadn't been there..."

"I promised her I wouldn't tell you. She seems to think you wouldn't understand."

Sara Jean's mother sighed sadly. "She's right. I don't."

"Maybe she needs someone else to talk to."

"Someone else? Oh, you mean a therapist. I don't know. We're not much on that kind of thing here."

Mitch remained silent. Wasn't his problem.

The front door slammed closed. "Bitsy?"

Mrs. Blunt—Bitsy—rose. "In here!"

A worried-faced woman rushed into the kitchen, toting an overstuffed briefcase and an armful of binders. She dropped everything on one of the counters and flew to Bitsy, who burst into tears and rushed into her arms. The two women hugged, the newcomer tall and rangy next to the petite redhead.

"Is she all right?" the newcomer asked.

Bitsy nodded, sniffing and swiping at her eyes.

"What on God's earth happened?" She suddenly seemed to notice they weren't alone. She stopped short, looked pointedly at Mitch. "Who are you?"

"Oh, God," Bitsy said. "That's...that's—" She reddened, and clamped a hand over her mouth. "I don't even know his name," she wailed. "My manners, my head just...just—"

He rose, extended a hand. "Mitch Turner."

"Hannah Blunt," the taller woman said. "Sara Jean is my niece." She looked him up and down, taking in the too-short shirt and pants. "And you are?"

"He saved her," Bitsy rushed in. "He's the one who pulled her out of the river. If it wasn't for him, Sara Jean would be...would be—" She dissolved into sobs, and Hannah put an arm around her.

Another door slammed, and a third person ran into the kitchen. Mitch assumed this was the husband, Tommy. He threw his briefcase on the counter, too, and, as Hannah had done, ran to hold his wife.

The resemblance between the two newcomers was plain, and Mitch judged them to be brother and sister, though the woman—Hannah—was the taller of the two and clearly the one less interested in first impressions. While Tommy looked like he owned Brooks Brothers, she looked like she'd spent the last week in the shapeless black dress she wore.

But if her clothes were dull, her intelligence was not. She gave him a sharp look and took him aside.

"What happened? And tell me exactly. Don't leave anything out."

That intense look, the firm tone, and the intent of the question were all too familiar. "You a cop?"

Her brows rose. "A lawyer."

Cop. Lawyer. Different sides of the same coin. And not one he wanted to get near.

He held up his hands. "Look, all I did was pull the girl out of the river. If Mrs. Blunt hadn't insisted, we'd already be on our way."

"We?"

He thumbed over his shoulder. "Jules and I."

Hannah looked out the window and back at him. He didn't like the suspicion in her face. In fact, he didn't like anything about her.

3

Julia pumped higher and higher, watching the house careen up and down in a breathless, windswept arc. She could be a bird—like in the *Once and Future King,* when Merlin changed Wart into a hawk and they flew high over the kingdom. She closed her eyes to get the full, soaring feel of it, and it made her dizzy.

When she opened her eyes again, something was there that wasn't before. She let the swing slow as Sara Jean backed out a window onto an overhang, crawled to the edge, and then onto a nearby tree limb. She perched there in a long nightgown, swinging her legs and staring at Julia.

"What's your name?" she said at last.

Julia told her. "You can call me Jules if you want."

"That your dad, Jules?"

"Uh-huh."

"I've never seen him before."

"We don't live around here."

"Where do you live?"

Julia never could come up with an answer to that one. "Around."

"Around where?"

"Just...around. In the truck."

"You live in a truck?" Sara Jean's voice was full of awe instead of scorn.

"Sometimes. When he's working, we live in a house or an apartment."

"When he's working? Doesn't he work all the time? My dad does."

"Nah, he only works when he wants to. Or when we need the money."

Sara Jean seemed to find that fascinating. "What's he do?"

"Tons of stuff."

"Like what?"

"Pumps gas. Washes dishes. Fries stuff on a grill. He's built houses, railroad bridges..."

"Wow." The list seemed to overwhelm her. "My dad works in a bank."

"Does he have an office where he hands out money?"

"I guess."

"My dad doesn't believe in banks. Says he doesn't like people knowing his business."

"My dad knows everyone's business," Sara Jean said glumly.

Julia nodded solemnly, and Sara Jean plucked a red leaf off a branch, which she proceeded to shred.

"At the river, why'd your dad...Why'd he do...what he did?"

Julia shrugged. "Why'd you jump in?"

Sara Jean shrugged, too. "I don't know."

They sat in silence for a while. Julia was back on the

ground now, using her feet to turn in a slow circle, twisting the ropes that held the swing.

"Must be cool always going to new places," Sara Jean said. "No one knowing who you are. When I'm older, I'm going to travel all over the world."

"If I had a house, I'd never go anywhere."

"You'd get bored."

"No, I wouldn't. I'd love it."

They looked at each other, each recognizing what the other had said.

"We could switch places," Sara Jean said.

Julia stopped circling. "Like in *The Prince and the Pauper*."

"The what?"

"It's a book my dad read to me. In it, a prince and a beggar who looks like him switch places."

Sara Jean drew her legs up under her nightgown and leaned back against the tree trunk. "You'd have to dye your hair red."

"You'd have to dye yours black."

Sara Jean smiled. "My mother would hate that."

"My dad's eyes would pop out of his head."

They started giggling, but a voice called from the house. "Jules!"

Sara Jean stopped laughing and put a finger to her lips.

Mitch stuck his head out the back door. "You okay out here?"

"Fine."

"You're talking to yourself."

"No, I'm not. I'm talking to Merlin. He wants to turn me into a turtle."

"Not on my watch."

"See? That's what I told him."

Mitch glanced at the twist of rope over her head. "You're going to make yourself sick."

"I know."

He shook his head. "Just don't upchuck all over the Blunts' yard."

"I won't."

"You need me, I'll be in the laundry room."

When he'd disappeared back into the house, Julia gave Sara Jean the all clear.

"I think your dad's right," Sara Jean said when she'd crawled back out. "There's always too many people knowing your business. Especially when you're a kid."

Julia didn't say anything. Truth was, she didn't mind it at all.

"Who's Merlin anyway?"

"A wizard."

Sara Jean laughed again. "You're even weirder than me. So . . . you going to unwind or what? Bet you throw up all over the mums."

"Mums?"

Sara Jean pointed to the flowers edging the patio.

"Bet I won't."

Sara Jean giggled. "Give you ten dollars if you do."

Julia grinned. And let the swing go.

Mitch had hoped his little foray outside would have dislodged Hannah, but she was firmly planted in his way when he came back. Tommy and Bitsy were still hovering together, and it didn't look like rescue was coming anytime soon, so he tried another tactic. "I'm just going to"—he backed toward the laundry room—"see if my clothes are ready for the dryer."

But Hannah followed, blocking the doorway while he transferred the clothes into the dryer.

"On the phone, Bitsy said Sara Jean fell into the river. Is that what happened?"

"Look, you talk to Mrs. Blunt—Bitsy—about it, okay? Up to her to tell you what she wants you to know."

"She's my niece. You can feel free to tell me what happened."

But Mitch had already broken his promise to Sara Jean once. He wasn't going to do it twice. "If it's all the same to you, I'll just let her parents handle that now." He opened the lid of the top-loading washer, turned his back, and buried his arm inside. Maybe she'd take the hint and leave.

She didn't. "So, Mitch Turner, what do you do?"

He hauled out the wet clothes, chucked them into the dryer.

Lie or don't lie? He took the ambiguous route. "Whatever comes my way."

"Got a place to stay?"

"Got my truck 'til we get to where we're going."

"Oh?" She smiled, but it didn't feel as innocent as it looked. "Where to?"

This was all beginning to sound more like an interrogation than a conversation. "South."

"No permanent residence, then?"

"Like I said, we're in transition." He punctuated his answer by slamming the dryer door closed.

"What about your daughter?"

He traded her stare for stare. "What about her?"

"She should be in, what, fifth or sixth grade now?"

"When we have to, we homeschool."

"Don't you mean truck school? Or on-the-road school?"

"We do fine, Ms. Blunt."

"Hannah. And I'm sure you do. But children need stability."

"Yeah? Where'd you hear that?" He took a stab in the dark. "You have any kids of your own?"

"No."

"So your opinion is based on, what, hearsay?"

"Common knowledge."

"Well, you don't see Julia jumping off any bridges, do you?"

He realized his mistake instantly, and she went for the kill. "Is that what happened to Sara Jean?"

Damn. "I told you to talk to—"

She smiled. "I will. You can bet I will. In fact, I'll just go and check on Sara Jean now."

She swept out of the room, and he realized he was sweating. He'd been leaning against the dryer, and the thing was damn hot. Except it wasn't the machine that made him uneasy.

He checked the timer. Thirty minutes. Then he'd collect Jules and they could keep on keeping on.

A head popped into the room. "Mr. Turner?" Tommy Blunt stood in Hannah's place, making Mitch feel like he'd never shake these people.

"It's Mitch."

Sara Jean's father entered, his hand extended. "I don't know how I can thank you."

"No need. I just did what anybody—"

"I don't think so. And I want you to know we're grateful. My wife tells me you're looking for work and a place to live. I'm sure I can hook you up with something. And we've got a small carriage house you and your daughter can stay in until I get things settled."

"That's not necessary. Really—"

"I insist. Won't take no for an answer. We owe you our daughter's life. It's the least we can do. And I'm afraid your daughter's already agreed." He grinned. "You'll stay for dinner, of course, and then we can get you moved in."

He slapped Mitch on the back and disappeared.

A minute later, a loud whoop came from the kitchen. Julia.

His heart sank, and that old saying came back to him a hundredfold: No good deed goes unpunished.

4

After dinner, Tommy mentioned staying in town again, but Mitch insisted on heading back on the road.

"*Why* do we have to go?" Julia asked plaintively as Mitch ushered her out of the kitchen, the Blunts following.

"We'll talk about it later," Mitch told her.

"But I *like* it here," Julia said. "And they *want* us to stay. Don't you?" She appealed to Bitsy, her blue eyes pleading.

"Of course we do," Bitsy said to her. And to Mitch, "Are you sure you won't stay? Even for a few days?"

"Look, you have plenty on your plate right now with Sara Jean." Mitch steered Julia toward the front door. "You don't need two more bodies to worry about."

"They *like* worrying about us!" Julia dug in her heels. "And I won't get in the way, I promise."

"Jules," Mitch said in a quiet way that immediately silenced her. He knelt down, put his hands on her shoulders, looked directly in her eyes, and spoke in a low, emphatic voice. "We are not staying." It was a tone he'd used since she was a baby, and it always got results. "Thank the Blunts for dinner."

For half a second, he thought there was going to be a scuffle, but then she lowered her head. When she raised it back up, she was fighting tears. Mitch knew he was right, but being right didn't mean he also didn't feel like a heel.

"Thank you for dinner," Julia said.

"You're more than welcome." Bitsy bent down and gave her a hug. "Come and visit whenever you want."

Julia nodded and fled out the door.

Mitch shook hands with Tommy.

"You change your mind, we'll be here," Tommy said.

"Appreciate it," Mitch said, and walked into the night.

Back in the truck, Mitch could breathe again. But Julia stared straight ahead, her little face set. Ordinarily, he'd drive a few hours, find a place to pull over, and camp outside. It was still warm enough with the sleeping bags. But he wanted to make things up to Julia, so he shelled out for a motel on the edge of town.

Normally, she would be bouncing up and down to stay in a motel. The height of luxury to her. Plus TV.

But tonight she was having none of it.

"I don't see why this is so much better than a real house."

"Because it's only the two of us, like always."

"And what's so great about that?"

Instead of answering, Mitch took out their backpacks, found her pajamas, and handed them to her. She grabbed them wordlessly and disappeared into the bathroom to change. Marched out, got her toothbrush and toothpaste, marched back in. She brushed her teeth noisily, peed, flushed, then plopped into the bed by the window without turning on the TV.

If he didn't know she was mad before, he knew now.

"Not going to watch TV?"

"That wasteland?" she said, mimicking him.

He fished in her backpack and came out with a book. "Read?"

She groaned loudly, then whipped away from him, burrowing low, and pulled the covers over her head.

He sighed. Hoped the sulk wouldn't last past morning.

Mitch was up with the sun. He rolled over and stretched, saw Julia was already up, and felt relieved. He hadn't been looking forward to a whole day in the truck with a pouty kid.

"Mornin', Junebug!" he called through the closed bathroom door.

No answer.

Uh-oh. Maybe his optimism had been short-lived.

He waited ten minutes, needing to use the facilities himself, and when she didn't come out, he got out of bed, slid on his jeans, and knocked. "Jules?"

Again, no answer.

"Come on, Junebug. You can't stay mad at me all day."

When she persisted in the silent treatment, he'd had enough. "Okay, Julia. That's it. Stay mad, see what I care. But mad or not, here I come." He flung open the door and stopped short.

Everything he'd been, everything he'd done, everything he'd left behind, coalesced into a single moment of pure terror.

Julia wasn't there.

He'd been running away from this moment for eleven years, and now that it had come, he was as unprepared as though it had never occurred to him. His mind blanked; his heart shut down. He froze solid, a rabbit with a hawk circling.

How long it took to get the circulation going he had no idea. Somehow he managed to get his shirt and shoes on. When he came alive again, he found himself running to the alcove with the ice and vending machines, hoping, praying she'd taken some quarters from him and was buying a forbidden Coke.

But it, too, was empty. No one had seen her, either. Not in the motel lobby where he'd signed in and paid cash the night before. Not in the parking lot or the McDonald's across the way.

The clerk behind the desk at the motel offered to call the police, but even now, with catastrophe staring Mitch in the face, he couldn't take the chance. What if this was all a horrible misunderstanding, and five minutes from now she came waltzing in, saying she'd gone exploring?

No, he couldn't risk the police. Not until he knew for certain what had happened. Bad enough he was drawing all this attention to himself. He forced a smile on his face, a shrug into his shoulders.

"Nah, that's okay. You know kids. I'm sure she'll turn up. Here"—he dug into his pocket, found a wad of bills, and handed some to the clerk—"for tonight." He wanted to make sure she had a room to go to if by some miracle she was taking a walk. "And if she does show up, let her into the room, will you? And tell her to stay put."

"Will do." The clerk shook his head in sympathy. "Got two kids myself."

Not knowing what else to do, Mitch got in his truck, inserted the key, and turned on the engine. Of course it would decide on this morning of all mornings not to turn over.

He pumped the gas, tried again, and cursed when the damn thing still wouldn't start. Truth was, he should have had the truck looked at months ago. But he hadn't wanted to take the time or be without wheels in case he needed to get out fast. Now he was paying for that caution.

"Come on, you nasty old road hag," he muttered, and punched the steering wheel when he got no cooperation. If someone had gotten to Julia, where would they have gone? Even if he could get the truck moving, there were miles of country in every direction. Where to start? Nausea swirled in his stomach.

How could anyone have taken her with him in the room? He wasn't a heavy sleeper. And knowing Jules, she wouldn't have gone easily.

Then again, she'd been mad at him. Would she have let a stranger abduct her out of spite? Hardly.

But she was a kid. And kids did things.

He thought back to the day before. Wished to God someone else had been there to see Sara Jean go over that bridge. Then he could have avoided the crazy, impulsive rescue, the house, the meal, the "good" people with their gratitude and their handouts, the shell of normalcy Julia thought she wanted.

The shell of normalcy...

He gripped the wheel. She wouldn't. She couldn't.

He tried the ignition again. Desperate, he wanted to

pound at the gas pedal, but he made himself pump gently. "Come on, baby," he crooned this time. "You can do it. For Jules, not me. Come on..."

And like the damn thing heard him, the truck came to life.

He yanked the gears into reverse, squealed out of his parking space, and careened out of the motel lot.

Fifteen minutes later, he was hammering on Bitsy and Tommy Blunt's front door. It took them a while to answer, and when they did, they were in robes and pajamas.

"Oh, my Lord." Bitsy took one look at him and said, "Something's wrong. What is it?"

Mitch pushed past her. "Where is she?"

"Where is who?" Tommy asked.

"Who? My kid. Who else?" Mitch was already plowing through the downstairs, his chest tightening with each empty room.

"Julia left last night with you," Bitsy said.

"She isn't here," Tommy said.

Mitch ran up the stairs.

"I assure you, she isn't—"

Mitch wrenched open the door to the master bedroom, saw the covers strewn on the bed.

"Why don't we go downstairs," Bitsy said, "get some coffee, talk about—"

He flung open another room. A desk and a neatly made bed.

"Please, Mitch, we'd know if she was—wait, that's Sara Jean's room. I don't think—"

But he'd already opened that door, too.

And snuggled under the covers next to Sara Jean's red head was a smaller, black-haired one.

• • •

"We were going to switch places!" Julia cried, while Mitch glared at her. "Like the prince and the pauper. But Sara Jean was asleep, and I was tired...."

"I'll bet you were," Mitch said. "What in the world were you thinking?"

Julia scuffed a toe against the floor. They were in the empty room with the desk and the bed. "I told you. I don't want to go. And I don't see why we have to."

"Because I said so."

The narrow look she gave him clearly said, "Not good enough, pal."

"We can't stay."

She shrugged.

"What's that supposed to mean?"

Silence.

"Jules..."

Another shrug. "I'll just do it again."

"Next time we'll go too far to walk back."

"Then I'll hitch."

"You damn well won't!"

"I will if you make me."

He wouldn't put it past her, either.

"Come on," she cajoled. "We'll have our own house and everything."

Mitch wanted to shout at her, shake her, force her to understand. But he couldn't. Not without telling her everything, and that was information he'd take to his grave.

"A week," he said.

"A month."

"Two weeks. And that's it."

She thought it over. "'Til Christmas."

"Christmas! That's over two months!"

She gave him that shrug again.

He growled at her. "You're supposed to be meeting me in the middle, not escalating your position. Who taught you how to negotiate?"

She grinned. "You did."

He lunged, pulled her under his arm like a football, and gave her a gentle head noogie. "You're too good a learner."

She giggled, and he released her. She was grinning widely, mischief and laughter in her eyes. His heart clenched, and for some unearthly reason, tears gathered at the back of his throat.

Abruptly, he turned away. DNA was a cruel master.

"Daddy?"

He swallowed. Cleared his throat. "Yeah, Junebug?"

"So, are we staying?"

"I guess so."

"'Til Christmas?"

He had himself under control now, so he turned and wagged a finger at her. "But no promises after that."

"*And* I go to school?"

He eyed her, partly in disbelief for her nerve, partly in horror. "Jesus, Jules. Most kids would do anything to stay *out* of school."

"I'm different."

"Tell me about it," he said grimly.

"Unique."

He grunted.

"That mean we have a deal?" She held out her hand to seal it.

He knew what he should do. Be tough. Resist. Disaster loomed if he didn't.

But the dread of losing her again was still with him. It turned his constant paranoia into mere habit. After all, they'd been free for over a decade. How much would it hurt to give her what she wanted? At least for a little while.

So he slid his large hand around her smaller one and they shook once. And that evening, they moved into the Blunts' carriage house.

5

Mitch set their backpacks at their customary place by the main exit, where they could be grabbed in a hurry if necessary. Bitsy had hired someone to clean the place from top to bottom, so all Mitch and Julia had to do was make themselves at home.

The carriage house was a square brick building tethered to the back of the Blunt home by an alley. The carriage that had once been lodged there was long gone, and the space had been divided into a series of rooms. He had known far bigger homes with many more rooms and many more floors, but Julia walked the space as though she were a farmer tramping a magical pasture somewhere over the rainbow. Every nook, every cabinet, every window ledge, was exclaimed upon and marveled over. He indulged her fascination and used it to dampen his own uneasiness.

That night they had dinner with the Blunts again, and this time, Sara Jean was there. She looked fully recovered from her ordeal, if a little withdrawn, especially around her parents.

Mitch volunteered himself and Julia to do the cleanup, and when Bitsy protested, Julia said, "Oh, no. He's an expert at dishwashing. It's just about the best thing he does."

Mitch could have shaken her, though she was right. But in the midst of this comfortable house, with its professional owner and his family, dishwashing seemed shameful.

"That's what you're looking for?" Tommy asked. "Job-wise, I mean?"

"He fries stuff, too."

Sara Jean added, "Maybe he can fry something for us."

Mitch gave Julia a scolding look. "You've been talking about me?"

"Well," she said, though she knew it was against the rules. "You do fry things."

"I'm a fry cook," Mitch explained to Tommy, who nodded thoughtfully. "But I can do whatever you got. Janitorial, light carpentry, lawn maintenance."

"He makes patty melts," Julia said. "And egg creams."

Sara Jean looked horrified. "Yuck."

Julia giggled.

"Don't worry," Mitch said, "there's no egg and just a little cream in it."

"But there is chocolate!" Julia cried.

"Then why's it called an egg cream?" Sara Jean asked.

Mitch winked. "A mystery for the ages."

The doorbell rang, and Bitsy disappeared to answer it. She came back with a short, stocky bulldog of a woman carrying a nylon bag over her shoulder. Bitsy didn't look very happy, but the newcomer greeted Tommy effusively, then asked Sara Jean how she was.

"Fine," Sara Jean murmured.

"And this must be our hero," the woman said, looking at Mitch.

"This is Mitch Turner," Tommy said. "And that's his daughter, Julia. Mitch, this is Shelby Townsend. She owns the *Crossroads Sentinel*."

Mitch froze. He was allergic to reporters the way some people were allergic to shellfish—even small-town ones were deadly. But there he was in the Blunt kitchen in front of the whole family and Julia. He couldn't exactly take off. So when Shelby stuck out a pudgy hand, Mitch took it. Her grip was tight and the handshake firm, an indication of how she handled the world, which only increased his apprehension.

Bitsy said, "Shelby, I'm not sure we want everyone in town knowing—"

But Shelby overrode her concern. "How's about we get you over here, Mr. Turner." Before he could protest, she had her camera out and was taking his picture. He put up a hand to cover his face and tried ducking his head, but she just kept taking pictures until she got one she liked.

When she tried to question him about the rescue, he said, "I really don't want to make a big deal out of it."

"A modest hero, too." Shelby beamed.

"Really," Mitch protested. "I'm not a—"

"You're a hero to Sara Jean," Julia said.

"Butt out, Junebug."

"I'm just saying—"

"How about you, Sara Jean?" Shelby asked. "No more playing near the river?"

Sara Jean flashed a quick look at Mitch and her parents, then answered Shelby with downcast eyes. "No, ma'am," she said.

"Bet you were scared," Shelby said, fishing.

The normal answer would have been yes. The more likely answer, given the situation at the time, was no. Sara Jean seemed caught between the two, so Mitch threw an arm around her, shielding her from the nosy reporter. "Of course she was. And now I think it's time for Sara Jean to get those...uh...those pajamas for Julia."

Sara Jean looked at him blankly. "Pajamas?"

Thank God for Julia. "You remember," she broke in quickly. "The *pajamas* you were going to lend me." She grabbed Sara Jean's hand and dragged her away.

Bitsy bit her lip. "How did you hear about the...uh, accident?" she asked Shelby.

Shelby winked. "Can't reveal my sources, now, can I?"

Bitsy frowned and threw Tommy a baleful look. "That Emmalyn Mosley has a big mouth."

Tommy's face reddened. "My secretary did not..."

Shelby found something interesting in her camera bag to look at, and the rest of Tommy's words died out. Struggling for what to do or say, he blurted out, "Shelby, join us for banana pudding?"

Bitsy looked like she wanted to clap her husband over the head with a frying pan, but she quickly recovered. "Of course, we'd love to have you. Mitch, would you call the girls down for me?"

But he didn't want either Julia or Sara Jean around while the reporter was still there. "How about we let them have some girl time. They can have dessert later."

"Later?" Shelby asked. "Are you staying with the Blunts, Mr. Turner?"

"Mitch and Julia are in the carriage house," Tommy said as Bitsy began serving out the custard.

"Nice of you." But she looked at Mitch thoughtfully, as though wondering if Sara Jean's rescue had been a clever way to insinuate himself on the Blunts and the town.

"He's looking for work, too," Tommy added. "Maybe you know something?" Without prompting, Tommy ran down the list of things Mitch had said he'd done.

Mitch tensed. The Blunts meant well, but he felt spread-eagled and staked to the ground.

Thankfully, Shelby shook her head. "Can't think of anything at the moment." She dug into dessert. "Don't suppose you know much about computers?"

"Sorry," Mitch said, not sorry at all. "Bit of a Luddite."

Shelby looked as if she never expected him to know, let alone use, that word.

"That's okay," Bitsy said. "I'm sure something will turn up."

That's what Mitch was worried about.

Mitch's picture ran in the *Crossroads Sentinel* along with the story of his rescue of Sara Jean. Both Bitsy and Tommy made sure he had a copy. Julia was thrilled and wouldn't stop talking about it. The chatter was nerve-racking, but it was too late to do anything more than hope the small-town paper didn't have much circulation outside of Crossroads.

Two days later, a grizzled guy named Crick, who was eighty if he was a day, stopped by and offered Mitch a job at a small restaurant he owned in the dwindling down-town strip. His grill man had gone into rehab and wasn't expected back anytime soon.

The hours were good—only breakfast and lunch—so Mitch could pick up Julia from school, and Crick agreed to pay him in cash. Mitch told him he wouldn't be there past Christmas, but the two months would give Crick time to find a more permanent replacement.

They shook hands, and Mitch started work the next day.

The following week, the first murder happened.

6

Three waitresses handled the morning shift at Crick's. The oldest, Loritta, had been there forever and practically ran the operation. A lanky sixty-year old with splayed feet and a pile of graying hair beehived on top of her head, she shared her full-time duties with Denise.

"Neesy," she corrected when Loritta introduced her. "Neesy Brown." She had the fine, milky skin of some lucky redheads, the kind of complexion that radiated from within, innocent and pure. But there was nothing innocent about the expression in those green eyes. Or the way her turquoise uniform sat on those ample hips. And when she caught him looking, she broke into a mischievous grin and extended her hand. "Well, aren't you a welcome addition."

Loritta gave her a light slap on the arm. "Now, don't go eating the boy up before he's had a chance to ripen."

The third waitress, Mary Nell, worked only the morning shift. A tiny blonde with stark Appalachian cheekbones, she was skinny all over except for the big baby bump under her apron. She smiled shyly when they were introduced.

"Nice meeting you," she said.

"Twins." Neesy winked, and Mary Nell blushed.

"Now, we'll all get along just fine," Loritta put in, and gave him a purposeful stare. "Just keep the eggs and pancakes coming and we'll do right by you." The bell over the door tinkled, signaling the first customer of the morning. "Okay, girls." She waved over her head. "Here they come."

It didn't take him long to get into the rhythm. By the time the breakfast crowd slowed, Mitch was practically dancing to the old moves—cracking eggs, flipping pancakes, pressing sausage patties. If someone had asked him fifteen years ago what he'd be doing now, he would never have predicted this. But he was good at it, and that gave satisfaction. Especially when Neesy stuck her head in the kitchen.

"They're liking whatever it is you did to the French toast."

"Cinnamon in the egg batter."

"Clever you." Her face dimpled with her smile, and she disappeared into the hullabaloo behind the swinging doors. But she left behind an impression. Sharp, spicy citrus and a wave of feminine vitality. Not one of those skinny, New York model types. At least, not the kind he knew with their boyish figures and barely there breasts. She harkened to the time when hips were fashionable. Lush was the word that came to mind. And temptation.

Maybe it was the fluff of red hair curling around her pretty face. Or the dimple in her chin. Or the turquoise uniform—cut a little too low and a little too tight.

He warned himself against that uniform. Casual flirtations could be lethal, and that was all he had to offer.

So he'd made it one of his rules to stay away altogether. But every now and again, in the shadows of his heart, he wished for more. For someone to confide in. Someone who could take the past onto her shoulders and share the burden. But in the end, it was always easier alone. Safer and easier. He and his hand had a fine sex life when necessary. And no one got hurt.

At eleven, Mary Nell stopped to say good-bye and grab a few bacon scraps. "You don't mind, do you?" Her voice was high and childlike, and she looked to be around thirteen. "There's a stray in the alley I've been feeding." She blushed again.

"Not my dime." He wiped his hands on his apron and followed her out the back door.

Waiting for her was a skinny black dog, part Rottweiler, part Lab, part he didn't know what. The animal wore an eager, expectant look, and he barked when he saw Mary Nell. She laughed. "Hello to you, too."

She knelt, leaning over her belly to lay the meat on the ground, and the dog lapped it up. She smiled and rubbed the animal behind the ears.

"You shouldn't do that," Mitch said. "Doesn't look like he's had a bath in a while."

"I know, poor thing."

"Why don't you take him home and clean him up?"

"Oh, Boyd wouldn't like that," she answered immediately.

"Boyd?"

"My husband."

"Doesn't like dogs?"

She shrugged her thin shoulders. "Not much."

"Hope he likes babies," Mitch teased.

She grew quiet, and he realized he'd touched a sore spot.

"He will. Once they're here, I'm sure he will."

Mitch was instantly sorry. "Of course he will." He helped her rise, and she gave him another blushing smile.

"Thanks. See you tomorrow." She waved to the dog. "Bye, you." The dog started to follow her, but she stopped and shook her head. "Stay here, now. Go on. You stay here." She took a step and the dog took a step.

She laughed, but the sound was interrupted by a bellow from the open end of the alley.

"What the hell are you doing, Mary Nell? I told you to leave that damn dog alone." A hulk of a man barreled toward them. He had a patch of black hair on his chin and wore a denim jacket cut off at the arms.

"Oh, God," Mary Nell said under her breath. "I'm sorry, Boyd, I was just leaving—"

Boyd grabbed her arm. "You should have been leaving ten minutes ago. I been waiting for you, and it's fucking cold out there."

"I know. I'm sorry."

In a former life, Mitch would have walked away, leaving the two of them to sort it out. But the sin of indifference had come with a price too heavy to pay again. "You okay, Mary Nell?"

Just then, the back door opened and Neesy spilled into the alley. "Mary Nell, Boyd's—oh…" She stopped short. "Too late."

"You keep your nose out of this, Neesy. You and the new man over there."

"Happy to oblige," Mitch said. "When you take your hands off your wife. And apologize for the language."

Boyd's face turned blotchy with red. "Like hell I will." He yanked her close, and Mary Nell uttered a little scream of pain.

Neesy started toward them, but Mitch stepped in front of her. Mary Nell shook her head desperately.

"It's all right," she said quickly to Mitch. And in a lower voice to her husband, "Please, let me go, Boyd."

"Shut up," Boyd said to her. "I told you not to play with that shit-eating dog. When are you going to listen to me?"

"Maybe when you start treating her with a little respect," Mitch said.

Boyd turned his nasty, narrow-eyed gaze on Mitch. "What did you say?"

Mitch knew what was coming. But first he had to get Mary Nell out of the way. "You heard me. Or are you deaf as well as dumb?"

That did the trick. Boyd released Mary Nell to come after Mitch.

Out of the corner of his eye, Mitch saw Neesy run to the pregnant woman and gather her up and out of the way just as Boyd swung a massive fist. He was a wide-necked troll, and trolls usually weren't light on their feet, but Boyd moved faster than Mitch expected. He caught Mitch on the side of his chin.

The punch sent a shock wave up Mitch's jaw and into his neck and head. He stumbled back, cursing, but before he could engage again, the dog leaped, barking and growling and snapping his jaws. He latched on to Boyd's calf, and the monster man squealed in pain.

Mary Nell screamed, "Oh, no, don't. Don't!" and "Neesy screamed, "Give it to him! Give it to him!" and Mitch rubbed his chin, enjoying the sight of Boyd swatting, dancing, and trying to fend off the animal. Finally he landed a lucky punch that sent the dog flying.

The animal landed with a yelp, but he'd done enough damage. Boyd eyed them with malice, but he didn't budge, panting hard and clearly not wanting to start things up if it meant fighting the dog again.

Mary Nell ran over. "Bad dog," she scolded, and to Boyd, "Did he hurt you?" She bent down to look at the jagged hole in his pants, and he swatted her away, too. She put an arm around him. "Can we go home now?" She led him out of the alley, the dog growling behind them.

The minute they were out of sight, the dog began to whine. After the animal's heroism, Mitch gave in and kneaded him behind the ear. "Yeah, I know," he told the dog. "I'd follow her home, too, if I were you."

Neesy stared after the two of them. "God, I hate that man. He's always been a heavy breather, but ever since Mary Nell got pregnant, he's been meaner than mean. I offered her a place to stay, but she keeps finding excuses for him. One of these days, we'll find her at the bottom of the stairs and she'll lose those babies."

Neesy's words hit him with an unexpected wallop, and an image burst inside his head. Not of Mary Nell, but another woman. Lying on the floor, bloodied and broken. The sharp ripple of memory took him by surprise. He leaned against the back wall to steady himself.

"You okay?" Neesy reached up to finger his jaw. "You're going to have a nice bruise there."

A thrill of electricity from her touch gave him another

small shock. Man, it had been a long time since a woman's touch had set him off like that. Too long.

Casually, he ducked his head and stepped away. "Maybe Mary Nell should work a full day," he said. "Keep her away from that lout more."

"I tried. She wouldn't dare."

"Then maybe I should stop by now and again," he said grimly. "Check up on her."

"Boyd won't like that."

"We're not interested in what Boyd likes, are we?"

She looked him over like she was trying to figure him out. "What's in it for you?"

He gave her the same look back. "I don't know, Neesy. You offered her a place to stay. What's in it for you?"

She flushed, caught. "Nothing but trouble," she grumbled.

"I'm familiar with that."

"Hey, you two!" Loritta's voice came from inside the kitchen, shortly followed by her beehived head poking out through the back screen door. "We got lunch coming. Ketchup bottles to fill."

Neesy followed Loritta back inside, where the lunch crowd kept her hands and feet occupied. But while she took orders for BLTs and burgers, she couldn't stop thinking about the new grill man and what he'd done for Mary Nell. Neesy had known a lot of men in her day, but none of them would have stepped up the way Mitch had.

It intrigued her, and she kept finding excuses to go into the kitchen to see what else was behind the rugged lines of his face. Not that the face and body weren't reason enough. Mitch wasn't movie-star gorgeous, but he had nice, wide shoulders, and there was a solidity about him that was sexier than handsome.

But that wasn't it, either. It was what he'd done.

Not that he had to do anything to pique her interest. Neesy was famous for her men. Then again, after the last disaster, she'd sworn off the opposite sex. Practically taken a pledge.

And here she was sniffing around again.

She delivered a grilled cheese and fries, caught herself eyeing the kitchen door, and tore her gaze away. She should slap herself upside the head, that's what she should do.

Crick's closed at three, and by three-fifteen, the place was empty. Neesy and Loritta carried the last of the dirty dishes into the kitchen, but when they got there, Mitch was gone.

The two women exchanged glances. Loritta raised her brows. "That didn't last long."

Neesy dumped the plates and cups into the commercial dishwasher. "And to think, all afternoon I was fixing to pin a medal on him." She surveyed the mess he'd left—filthy grill included. "He couldn't wait to pop Boyd Collier one, but give him a dirty kitchen to clean and he runs like the Devil's chasing him."

How wrong could she have been about a man? Judging by the last couple, plenty. But after what happened in the alley, she thought Mitch was different. Then again, maybe there was no "different" when it came to men—they were all made of the same useless stuff.

With a sigh, Loritta handed her own stack of plates to Neesy. "Well, better get at it. Won't be the first time. And better get in touch with Old Man Crick. He'll need to find us a new grill man."

Loritta found the grill brush, but Neesy tried to take it from her. "Why don't I scrape and you phone?" Cleaning the grill was hard work, and Loritta was tired.

But the older woman elbowed Neesy away and began working on the grill. "I ain't dead yet."

"I wish you'd let me do that."

"I wish you weren't here at all. You know your mama wanted you to get out of this town. Go to college someday. Be something."

Neesy flipped through the book of numbers hanging by the phone, looking for Crick's. "I am something. Don't need no piece of paper to tell me that. And there's nothing wrong with this town."

"Ha!"

"Well, what do you think is waiting out there?" Neesy waved her arm in the direction of the back door. "Same old meanness and hurt. Only bigger."

She tried to shrug off Loritta's words, but they stung anyway. Since high school, Loritta had been friends with Neesy's mama, had seen her through her teenage pregnancy and the shotgun marriage to the man Neesy had called Daddy. Loritta had been through all the ups and downs—mostly downs—of her mama's life. When she got sick, she made Loritta promise to look after Neesy, and it was a promise Loritta never seemed to forget.

But Neesy had made no promises. Truth was, she didn't have big dreams. She never took to school; she liked mixing and mingling more than books. Was it a terrible sin to be nearing the big three-oh and still waiting tables?

She looked over at Loritta, who was doing the same at twice Neesy's age. But Loritta had family. Uncle Max might not be the best breadwinner in the world, but he was kind. He didn't drink, didn't hit anyone. If something needed fixing, he fixed it. It wasn't a grand life, but it was a good one. It was the kind of life Neesy had only known from the outside, and in her secret heart of hearts, it was all she really wanted.

Trouble was, the harder she tried to make it happen, the further away she got. She was always jumping in before testing the temperature or the depth of the water. But no more. She was off men for a while. Good thing, too. Lord, she was disappointed in Mitch. And grateful she hadn't made more of a fool of herself over him.

Neesy was on the phone with Crick when the swinging door between the kitchen and restaurant creaked. And who should appear but the man himself, hands on hips, glaring at Loritta.

"Back away from the grill, woman!" The bruise Neesy had predicted bloomed over his cheek, but the corners of his mouth were turned up, and beneath the glare was the gleam of humor. "What are you doing? Trying to take my job away?"

From behind him came a dark-haired sprite. The child—it was a child—was munching on a waffle smeared with jam. She strolled in like she'd been born there, hopped up on a stool by the prep counter, and said, "No one gets between Mitch and his grill."

Neesy was as shocked as Loritta. Both of them stood there like boobies, gaping. Mitch grinned, and Neesy quickly told Crick, "Never mind," and hung up the phone.

Mitch threw on his apron and took the grill brush away from Loritta. "Thought I'd flown the coop?"

"Well, you weren't here."

"Sorry. Had to pick up Jules from school. Julia, this is Loritta, who runs the place, and that is Neesy, her second-in-command. Mary Nell already went home, so you'll have to meet her another day. Ladies, my daughter, Julia."

Loritta beamed. "My goodness, no one said anything about... Well, good Lord, it's nice to meet you."

"Nice to meet you, too," Julia said through a mouthful.

Neesy couldn't think of anything to say. She couldn't think at all. She stood in the middle of the kitchen like an empty pot or a dry pan. If Loritta hadn't poked her in the rib with an elbow, she would probably still be standing there.

"Uh...Julia's a...a beautiful name," Neesy finally said.

The girl shrugged. "It's all right. But Jules is pretty good, too." She swung her feet and popped the last of the waffle in her mouth. "You have red hair. Does everyone in this town have red hair?"

Neesy shot Mitch a confused look.

"Sara Jean Blunt is one of Julia's few acquaintances," Mitch explained. "Another redhead."

"I see." And at last, she did. The whole town had heard about Mitch rescuing Sara Jean from the Forbidden River. And now he'd rescued Mary Nell from Boyd. He really was a hero—of course he wouldn't have left them in the lurch.

Just then, Mitch attacked the grill, his arm muscles expanding and contracting as he worked, making as attractive a picture of male beauty as Neesy had ever seen. Now that he'd redeemed himself, it seemed perfectly acceptable to stare.

And yet, there was something else in that kitchen that captured her attention.

A kid. The new grill man had a kid. A few of Neesy's exes had kids. But none they picked up from school. Or saw much, if at all.

"You live with your dad?" she asked.

Julia gave her a puzzled look. "Sure."

"Where's your mama?" Loritta asked.

There was a snag in Mitch's strokes over the grill, but the question didn't seem to unsettle Julia. "Oh," she said matter-of-factly, "she's dead."

A twinge of pity hit Neesy. "I'm sorry."

Another shrug. "It's okay. She died just after I was born, so I never knew her." As if to underscore her detachment, she jumped down from the stool, opened the big refrigerator, and helped herself to a glass of milk. She gulped down a third, leaving a white mustache on her upper lip, and eyed the adults over the glass as though waiting for someone to say something.

Neesy glanced over at Loritta, who raised her brows again.

Julia sighed, set down the glass, and crossed her arms over her small chest. "So...is someone going to tell me how my dad got that bruise on his face?"

Finally, Mitch spoke up. "That's enough, Junebug. Finish your milk and start your homework."

"But how long can it take to tell me what happened?"

"Too long," Mitch said. "It's been a tough day, and the women have work to do."

"Oh, we can work in here." Neesy had no intention of missing a second of whatever was going to happen now. She winked at Loritta, who took the hint, and in a flash the two of them had disappeared behind the swinging doors and returned with an armful of ketchup bottles and salt shakers.

"See?" Julia said to Mitch.

"I see plenty," Mitch said. "And don't think you're getting away with anything."

Despite the words, he wasn't really angry. Neesy was coming to appreciate the easy camaraderie between father and daughter—something she thought existed only in books. Or dreams. She wanted to step in, be a part of it.

"Like to help?" Neesy asked Julia.

"Can I?"

"Sure," Loritta said. "Many hands make fast work."

Julia climbed back on the stool at the counter, where Neesy was setting out the bottles. She showed Julia how to fill the shakers from the big box of salt.

"So when we're done, you'll tell me?"

"Oh, we can talk while we work," Neesy said. And despite the grumblings from the direction of the grill, she told Julia all about her dad sticking up for Mary Nell.

"So, you see, he saved the day," Loritta summed up.

Mitch shook his head. "I just did what anyone—"

"Well," Neesy interrupted, "he did have some help. Don't know what would have happened if the dog hadn't jumped in."

Julia's eyes widened. "Dog?"

"Now you've done it," Mitch said.

Neesy filled Julia in about the stray in the alley. If the girl had been interested before, she was totally energized by the mention of the animal.

She leaped off her stool. "Is he still out there?"

"No," Mitch said.

"Maybe," Neesy said at the same time. She flashed Mitch a smile. Now that he was back in her good graces, she could enjoy making him squirm. "Why don't we take a look," Neesy added.

"No," Mitch groaned. "Not a good idea. Please—"

But they ignored him and trooped outside. What could Mitch do but follow?

It was sheer pleasure to watch him watch Julia and that stray. He protested every step of the way, deflected all her "why can't we bring him home?" and "why can't we get a puppy?" requests. He made a face when the dog licked Julia's, but despite his protests, there was a secret joy in his eyes.

He loved that kid.

Better yet, the kid loved him.

The insight squeezed something inside Neesy, making her happy and sad at the same time. It was only later that she understood why: seeing Julia with her daddy made Neesy realize everything she'd missed growing up.

By week's end, Mitch's routine was set. He brought Julia to precare at school, then headed for Crick's. Morning setup included teasing Mary Nell and Loritta—who blushed and ignored him, respectively—and avoiding, not always successfully, flirting with Neesy. Then he fried his brain to a crisp on bacon, eggs, and pancakes. At lunch it was patty melts and fries with the occasional chef salad. On Wednesday, he introduced Big Apple dogs—he added grilled onions and kraut to the hot dogs—and on Friday he made egg creams. Both were a hit, and along with his cinnamon French toast, so, it seemed, was he.

At two-thirty, he left the shop, picked up Julia at school, and brought her back to Crick's while he finished cleaning up.

The first thing Julia did when she got to Crick's was go out back and feed the dog. She named him Huck, because she was engrossed in Mark Twain at the moment, and despite the billions of times he told her not to pet him, he usually caught her on the ground with the dog in her lap.

Which led to the inevitable—a trip to the vet and a bath. Mitch felt better about letting Julia hover over the animal after the dog had been shot up with hundreds of dollars' worth of vaccines and smelled like a greenhouse, but he still didn't want the responsibility of taking him home. They had to stay lean and light in case they had to leave quickly.

"Dogs make me sneeze," he told her in the truck on the way back from the vet.

"You haven't sneezed once," she rushed to point out.

"I will. We keep a dog around and I'll be sneezing like it's an eleventh plague."

"You're just making that up."

He shot her a glance. She was scowling out the windshield, her arms crossed stubbornly. He tried a different tack.

"Look, Junebug, I know the dog means a lot—"

"Stop calling him 'the dog.' He has a name."

He bit down on the angry response that came all too quickly—*yeah, and I told you not to name him*—and said instead, "Okay, okay. I know 'Huck' means a lot to you, but dogs cost money, and it's not like we have a lot of that floating around."

"He doesn't eat much. We can still feed him scraps from Crick's."

"Do you know how much he cost today? A couple of weeks' worth of paychecks. I had to arrange an installment plan to pay it off."

"What's an installment plan?"

He explained it to her.

"Oh," she said when he finished. She was quiet for a while, then, "I could get a job."

"You're eleven. There are laws against that."

"There is not."

"Google it if you don't believe me."

"On what?"

"There are no computers at school?"

"If it's true, it's a stupid law."

"You can still see him every day at the restaurant." She didn't reply. "Okay?"

She pursed her mouth but her shoulders sagged, and he knew he'd made his point, though he wasn't very happy about it.

"I guess," she conceded, then turned on him. "But no more yelling at me for petting him."

He lifted a hand off the steering wheel like he was swearing to it. "Vet says he's clean." At least for now.

It was hard taking Huck back to the alley, but Jules soldiered through it. The next day was Saturday, which meant she'd be at Crick's all day, so she knew she'd be seeing him a lot. Mitch suspected that helped.

To ease her over the hump, he offered to take her to Barrington, where there was a McDonald's and a movie theater, two of her favorite places.

"No, thanks," she said, surprising him. "We have to pay off the installment plan, remember?"

A twinge of guilt bit him. "We can afford a crappy burger and a movie."

She sniffed and raised her chin in the air like a little martyr. "Then I'd rather take the money and buy something for Huck."

He sighed. There was no winning with this one.

7

Special Agent Roger Carrick stood at the window of the FBI's Quad Cities resident agency, the satellite office for eastern Iowa. It was just after five, but outside it was dark enough to be midnight, except where the streetlamp stood guard over the parking lot. Snow fell through its narrow swath of light, then disappeared into the black.

Barely November and already the snow was falling. Not that Roger was surprised. After ten years here, he'd come to expect anything, especially winter. He had a fleeting thought for the farmers who might not have all their corn in yet. Funny, him thinking about farmers. He had grown up in Miami; farming was the last thing he ever expected to be worried about. But you couldn't live in Iowa without thinking about the key cash crop. Five minutes out of Moline and it was all around you. Green, gray, plowed under, or reaching for the sky. Corn was everywhere.

A knock on the door had him turning. The office manager held up a handful of envelopes.

"I'm taking off." She laid the mail on his desk. "See you Monday."

He said good-bye and scuffled over to the desk. The mail had landed on a stack of memos and reports, mostly about the Nebraska-Iowa Joint Terrorism Task Force. The JTTF was part of a huge revamping of the FBI since 9/11. Now over 40 percent of resources were devoted to counterterrorism. Unfortunately, Roger wasn't one of them. Someone else had handled the anthrax hoax and the series of pipe bombs planted in mailboxes outside Des Moines. The closest he'd gotten to counterterrorism were field exercises.

Wasn't much different with other major crimes. Eastern Iowa was as much a breeding ground for drug trafficking, child pornography, and armed robbery as anywhere in the country, but the special agent in charge in Omaha always had something else in mind for Roger when the big cases broke.

Nine times out of ten, he ended up chasing shadows. A drum of radioactive chemicals that could be used to manufacture WMDs goes missing? Give it to Carrick. Let him spend three days, over thirty man-hours, and who knows how many miles in a Bucar running that one down—only to find it had been inventoried incorrectly and had been sitting in the warehouse in Moline all along.

Was he bitter?

He laughed to himself as he sorted through the envelopes. Hell, yes, he was bitter.

Corn country had stolen his wife and kids—who were back in Miami—not to mention his career.

He paused in the act of slitting open one of the envelopes. Be fair, now. Can't blame the Midwest for everything. Some of it was his own undiplomatic fault.

He took out the letter and unfolded it. What he saw rooted him instantly.

A photocopy of a newspaper article, complete with picture. A picture he thought he recognized.

He rose and went to a cabinet against the wall, where he riffled through the files to the one he wanted and plucked it out. Inside were ten identical pages. On the top of each one, heavy black font spelled out HAVE YOU SEEN THIS MAN? and below that was a photograph.

Carrick compared the two. The one from the file was clean-shaven and carefree, the hair expertly trimmed, the smile jaunty, a bow tie from a tuxedo showing at the neck.

The one he'd just received was the face of a working man, stubbled and lined. The hair was shaggy, the expression sober—even a little annoyed—and the collar at the neck looked like plaid flannel.

He squinted. Looked at them both through a magnifying glass he kept in his desk. Were they the same? More than a decade separated the two photos. Did that account for the changes? Or were the men in these pictures only look-alikes?

He went back to the newspaper article. Read the story. Some guy who'd saved a kid when she fell into the river. He picked up a pen and circled the name of the local hero. Too similar to be coincidence?

He checked the date line. Two weeks ago. Checked the paper's name. *Crossroads Sentinel.* Never heard of it.

He did a computer search. There was no Web site for a *Crossroads Sentinel,* but there were several towns called Crossroads. One in Pennsylvania, one in Maine, and one in Tennessee.

He glanced at his watch. Five forty-five on the first Friday night in November. An hour later in Pennsylvania and Maine. Office hours were over, but the phones were always manned.

He drummed on his mouse.

Abruptly he rose, shut down the computer, and walked away from the desk.

He wasn't jumping on anything. The hotshot hot-rodder he used to be had been slowed considerably by his exile in corn country. He'd wised up. Learned how to think before acting. The weekend was coming up. He'd take the time to mull it over.

He put the article and its envelope in the manila file with the pages he'd received every year on the same day for the last ten years. Put the folder in his briefcase and snapped it shut. Then he grabbed his coat, his rubber boots, his scarf, his hat, and his gloves. As he headed out the door, he glanced at the window. The snow was coming down thick and heavy in the beam of the streetlight.

He hoped to hell his car would start.

8

Mitch's second week at Crick's ended on Saturday, the slowest day of the week for the restaurant. Mary Nell didn't work weekends, so it was just Loritta, Neesy, and himself. And Julia.

She wanted to go over to the Blunts', but he wasn't comfortable leaving her alone yet. So far, Crossroads had been quiet and friendly, the Blunts especially so, but Mitch had spent years looking over his shoulder, and he wasn't going to stop now. So he brought her to Crick's, thankful she was still young enough to enjoy filling salt shakers and ketchup bottles. After that, there was homework, and her latest book, so she had plenty to keep her occupied.

He made a batch of French toast, and Julia wolfed down two pieces plus extra bacon. He gave it to her even though he suspected that some of it would go out the back alley for Huck.

She thought she was pulling one over on him when she snuck past him, but he was wise to her shenanigans. He let her go, though, because Neesy stepped through the kitchen door and placed another order of fried eggs.

"Push the toast," he told her. "I've got a ton of it waiting."

"Don't know where everyone is this morning." She leaned against the inside of the swinging kitchen door. The position set off her breasts, and she seemed to know it. He could feel her watching him. Waiting. Looking for some hint of appreciation. "Must be the weather. Everyone's out in the yard." She shrugged, the little gesture moving that cleavage up and down.

He gritted his teeth, returned his gaze to the grill, and kept it there.

"You got plans after work?" Somehow, she'd snuck up behind him. "Because I was thinking." Her chest brushed against his elbow, and the egg he was cracking burst in his hands.

"Oh, geez." She ran for a towel and was mopping up his hand before he could protest.

"I'm fine." He pulled away, and when he trusted himself to look at her again, he found her smiling. The little . . . She knew exactly what she was doing.

But she did have a glorious smile. Her green eyes crinkled up, and a little dimple made mischief of her right cheek.

God, she was trouble.

"You're in my way," he said, easing around her to pop some bread in the toaster.

"Am I?" She looked around. "Well, I guess I am. Sorry." But she clearly wasn't, because she followed him to the toaster and back to the grill. "So, how about it?"

He was almost afraid to ask. "How about what?"

"A beer. You know, after work."

"Can't," he said automatically.

"Why not? You got a thing about dating in the work-place?" She leaned over to mock whisper, "I don't think old Crick would mind."

"It's not Crick; it's Julia."

"She'll be fine for an hour or two. Loritta'll watch her."

"I wouldn't wish that on Loritta."

She gave him a look he couldn't fathom. Part curious, part mystified, part determined. It made him nervous.

"You like girls, don't you?"

"Not in the morning when I'm trying to get my orders straight."

She balanced the plates on her arm, pursed her lips, and thought about it. "Another time, then?" She let loose that smile, leaned in, and spoke low, "I like a good challenge."

Despite his uneasiness, he almost enjoyed her resolve.

Until a high, piercing child's cry ripped through the screen door from the alley.

The scream startled Neesy so much, she jumped. The row of plates precariously balanced on her arm tumbled and smashed against the hard kitchen floor. The clatter coincided with the slam of the screen door as Mitch hurtled through it.

He'd moved so fast that Neesy was left standing there in a puddle of broken yokes and smashed crockery. She knew why, too.

His kid was out there.

Neesy had conveniently forgotten about Julia when she'd strolled in looking for a date. Of course she had. Can't be thinking about the kid when you're interested in the daddy. The pure selfishness of it embarrassed her. What the hell was wrong with her?

But she knew the answer. Much to her chagrin, she was doing what she always did, what she'd promised herself not to do. And without even realizing it, she'd gone ahead and broken that vow. She was chasing a man again.

Damn, she thought she'd learned that lesson.

Evidently not.

But this was different. Mitch was different. He was strong; he was decent—he loved his kid, for God's sake!

No wonder she just couldn't help herself.

Hell, maybe that was why he seemed less than fascinated by her. She didn't know what it was that attracted only the deadbeats, but the good men never seemed interested in her. An acute wave of shame ran through her, like she deserved what she got.

Quick as it came, though, she shook it off. She was done thinking badly about herself. Besides, how could she be worrying about her pathetic love life when there was clearly something wrong outside? Kicking herself, she stepped over the mess on the floor, bolted out the back door, and stopped short when she saw what was going on.

At the alley's far end, Mitch had swept up his child, whose face was buried in his shoulder. Neesy gasped when she saw why.

Against the alley's dead end was a bloody mess of flesh and bone. Its eyes were black sockets; its insides open fodder for the crows and vultures picking at it. It took Neesy a minute to realize the gore had once been the stray dog.

A spasm of revulsion twisted her stomach, and she had to force herself not to throw up.

Julia's shriek soon attracted a small crowd, most of them from Crick's. She heard gasps of shock like her own and expressions of sympathy as Mitch pushed through the crowd with Julia. Someone tried shooing the birds away, but they came back soon enough. The inevitable "who would do such a thing?" was carried through the crowd, and a few minutes after the door slammed behind father and daughter, a siren burped.

Someone had called the police.

Law enforcement in Crossroads consisted of a chief and two deputies. The slaughter of a dog didn't warrant a full-court press, and only a deputy, Nate Burgess, got out of the car. He left it blocking the mouth of the alley and headed to the gathering at the other end.

Clearing a path through the crowd, Nate took one look at what was left of the dog and then glanced back at the clump of people. "This what the screaming was about?"

"Little girl found him," someone said.

Nate frowned. "All right, folks," he said. "Show's over. Go on back, now."

Slowly, he cleared the area. "You, too, Miss Neesy." But he was walking around the carcass and not paying her much attention. "Sheesh. Looks like something had a good feed. You see anything back here? Another dog? A bobcat maybe? Been a couple of farmers complaining, but I wouldn't think you'd find one in the middle of town."

By now the shock had worn off, and Neesy was remembering the last time she'd been in that alley. "I don't think it was an animal," she said slowly. "At least, not the kind you mean."

He looked up from the body. "What are you talking about?"

She told him about Boyd's run-in with the dog. "One of these days, he's going to do the same to Mary Nell."

"Now, don't go all Rambo on me," Nate said. "More likely that bobcat."

"I'm telling you, it was Boyd."

"Okay, I'll check it out. Don't you be spreading rumors, though."

"Don't you be sitting on your duff telling yourself it's just a dog. Killing's easier once you start."

"Now, Neesy, I know you're upset, but ain't no call to get personal. I said I'd check it out."

"You find a reason to put Boyd Collier away and there's a week of free breakfasts for you."

He bristled. "Don't need no incentives to do my job."

She sighed. "I know. I'm sorry. I just don't like that man. He's dangerous. You come on in and I'll give you some coffee."

But he was already radioing in to the county animal control.

Back in the kitchen, Neesy saw Julia curled into Mitch's lap, her body hiccupping from sobs. Neesy wondered what it must be like to have a daddy you'd run to, not away from.

"She all right?" Neesy whispered.

"Of course I'm not all right," Julia said. She looked up with those amazing blue eyes, now red rimmed and sorrow filled. "Why would I be?"

"It's just something to say," Mitch soothed.

"Why do people need to say anything?" Julia asked.

"Because we want to comfort and don't know how," Neesy said.

"Oh." Julia hiccupped, and Neesy gathered towels to clean up the food and broken plates on the floor.

"I'll do that," Mitch said.

"No trouble." Seemed like Mitch was needed right where he was, and Neesy was no stranger to cleaning up messes.

Another hiccup. "Why would anyone do that?"

"I don't know, darlin'."

"Deputy thinks it was a bobcat," Neesy said, wiping up the eggs and bacon.

"A bobcat?" Julia looked up at Mitch.

"Could be," Mitch said. "Everyone's gotta eat, Junebug. Maybe he was starving, too."

That seemed to calm her, at least a bit. Knowing it was the natural course of things was easier to accept than human evil. Neesy suspected otherwise, but she didn't say so.

The rest of the day seemed interminable. Business picked up at lunch. Mainly rubberneckers finding excuses to go around back and examine the body for themselves. Took animal control most of the day to come by and pick up the carcass, so there was plenty out there for the sightseers.

"Bunch of ghouls," Loritta said under her breath. "Come in and eat first," she barked to one group who were arguing among themselves whether to go around back or have lunch. "You're not going to be too high on your appetite afterward."

Shelby Townsend was one with an iron stomach. She stopped by the alley with her camera, and when she was done outside, she came in for lunch.

When Neesy came to take her order, Shelby tried to

get her to open up about what had happened and eyed the kitchen all through the meal. Finally, Neesy told Mitch.

"She's finishing up, but she'll be asking questions in a few minutes."

Mitch looked over to the counter where Julia was playing absently with some pie dough. Bless her heart, she looked all worn out. "Not if I can help it," Mitch said.

"Why don't you call the Blunts? See if they can pick her up."

Mitch hesitated. He didn't like it when Julia was out of his sight. Then again, he liked her being questioned by Shelby Townsend even less.

He put in a call to Bitsy, but she and Sara Jean were at the mall, which was half an hour away. By the time they'd get back to pick up Julia, Shelby would have run all over her. Tommy was playing golf, so he was unavailable as well.

The sudden lack of options sent a rush of foreboding through Mitch. There was something about the savagery in the alley, something he refused to think about and didn't want Julia near.

The hell with it. He ripped off his apron and flung it over a hook. He'd leave. He'd put Julia in the truck and go.

"What are you doing?" Neesy said.

"Taking off."

"You can't leave. We've got people out there." She pointed toward the dining room. "Orders to fill."

"I'm not letting Shelby Townsend—"

Loritta pushed through the swinging door. "Shelby's wanting the check. And I need a grilled cheese and ham." She slapped the order on the counter, then seemed to notice something was amiss. "What's wrong?"

"Shelby wants to interrogate Julia about"—Neesy gestured with her head toward the back door—"and Mitch wants to leave so she can't."

Loritta glanced over at Julia and back at Mitch and Neesy. "And you've got a better idea," she said to Neesy. "Well, okay, go on. I can handle it. What do you think I did before you? Go on, scoot."

Neesy took down Mitch's apron and held it out to him. "Okay? Me leaving won't put Crick's out of business."

He didn't like it, but it was the best solution at the moment. He took the apron. "Thanks."

"Don't thank me, thank Loritta here. She's the one who'll be doing double time." Neesy gave the other woman a swift peck on the cheek. "You are a real peach." She flipped through her order book, tore out Shelby's, and gave it to the older woman. "I'll do your makeup for you—anytime you ask."

"I'll take you up on that," Loritta said.

"Junebug," Mitch said. "Neesy's going to take you to the mall to meet Sara Jean."

Julia frowned. "I don't want to go to the mall. I want to stay here."

Mitch lifted her down from the stool he'd put her on so she could reach the counter. "Do it for me, okay?"

"Come on," Neesy said, pulling her toward the back door. "We'll have fun."

"At the mall?" Julia said, as if Neesy might be crazy, but then the girl stopped dead as she saw where they were heading. "I don't want to go out there."

"Oh, God, of course you don't." Neesy looked around helplessly.

Loritta said, "Go on, I'll run interference for you. Just

give me a two count." She plodded through the swinging door.

"What's going on?" Julia asked.

"Shelby Townsend's out there," Mitch said. "She wants to ask you a lot of questions."

"About what?"

"About what happened in the alley," Neesy said.

"I don't want to talk about it," Julia said.

"Didn't think you did," Mitch said. "Which is why Neesy's going to take you to the mall."

Neesy peeked through the window in the kitchen door. Loritta was making her way to Shelby's table.

"Can't I just go home?" Julia asked Mitch.

"No, and if I'm not home when you get back from the mall, you stay over with Sara Jean."

"I'm not a baby. I can stay by myself."

"I'm sure you can. But not today."

"Come on, sugar," Neesy said. "I think we can make it now."

She grabbed Julia's hand, and just before she raced out with her, Mitch stopped her. "Don't just drop her off. You make sure she meets up with Bitsy. Personally."

She crossed her heart. "Yes, sir."

Then they were through the swinging doors. Loritta was at Shelby's table blocking her view. Neesy and Julia ran out the front and past the shop window without a word from the reporter.

"Slow down," Julia said.

Neesy stopped racing. "Sorry." She was breathing fast, and fanned herself. "My car's just ahead."

"You don't run much, do you?" Julia asked.

Wiseass. "Not if I can help it."

9

There were few times that Shelby Townsend missed her former life. She'd been happy to retire from the *Detroit News* and head back to her childhood home in Crossroads. Journalism—the kind she'd spent her adult life practicing—was dying. Newspapers were going digital, and she wasn't going with them. When she'd come back to Crossroads, she hadn't intended to run the *Sentinel*, but it was a natural fit when the previous owner wanted out. And it gave center and purpose to her life. If not a little amusement.

But her instincts for a story hadn't retired. And when she received a message from an anonymous caller a few days ago, those instincts kicked up. So when she heard about the dog in the alley behind Crick's, she headed to the restaurant. She'd been looking for an excuse to follow up on Mitch Turner. Wasn't every day someone walked into town out of the blue and saved one of their own. If she'd been curious before, she was downright suspicious now.

"Mr. Turner is not who he says he is."

All righty, then. Who was he?

The caller didn't say. He didn't leave a number, and she hadn't gotten around to replacing the old phones in the house, so she didn't have caller ID, either. She hadn't recognized the voice, not that she'd know everyone in town over the phone. But there was something about the speaker that made her think he wasn't from Crossroads. So, where was he from?

As much a mystery as Mitch Turner.

And she didn't like mysteries. She hadn't missed Mitch's reluctance to have his picture taken. Was he just camera shy? Or was there a reason for it?

She went to Crick's late in the day, just before closing, and she made sure to sit at one of Neesy's tables. Denise Brown was one of those women who was always hungry for what wasn't on the menu. And Mitch was definitely a blue plate special. Not particularly handsome, but strong-bodied and solid. Rugged, some would say. Hardy enough to tackle the Forbidden River, but not a muscle-bound lughead. And being a hero was always an attraction.

But the waitress was surprisingly closemouthed, and before Shelby could get anything out of her, she disappeared into the kitchen. It was Loritta who brought her check and hovered over the table wanting to chat. She stayed long enough to mention the bobcat theory and drop Boyd Collier's name before she was called away by another customer.

Shelby poured a river of sugar into her coffee and sipped it slowly. Boyd Collier was interesting, but not as interesting as the other name she was pursuing.

When her cup was empty, she paid her bill, then quietly slipped around the corner and through the kitchen's back door.

Since that anonymous tip, Shelby had spent a lot of time online but had come up with nothing. She'd tipped the *News* about the rescue, but the story had been reduced to a few lines on an interior page. She'd called a friend at the paper, told him about the phone call, and asked him to nose around. He'd called back this morning, saying he'd drummed up zilch.

Which in itself should alert her.

No bank accounts, no credit ratings.

What kind of man lives like that?

Shelby didn't want to jump to conclusions. They'd found no liens or bankruptcies. No criminal record, either.

Was he clean? She couldn't say what bothered her about Mitch Turner. Too good to be true? Most things were.

And, of course, there was that anonymous call.

She watched him through the screen door. He was cleaning the grill with strong, muscular strokes and complete concentration on his craggy face.

"Quite a day," she said.

Mitch turned, saw who it was, and for a minute seemed to freeze in place. Then he went back to cleaning. "What can I do for you, Ms. Townsend?"

She didn't wait for an invitation but marched right in. "Oh, call me Shelby. Everyone does. Just wanted to see how Julia was doing." She looked around. "Heard she was back here with you."

"She's spending the afternoon with the Blunts."

She frowned. "Oh. Well, hope she's okay. Hear she was fond of the dog."

He wiped his forehead with the back of his wrist. "She's fine. Thanks for asking."

Not what she'd call a talkative type.

"Hey, did you hear? Our story got picked up by the big-city papers."

"What story is that?"

"You know—about your derring-do. Told them I'd arrange an interview if they liked. Waiting to hear back. I'll let you know."

That got his attention. He put down the grill brush. "You do that."

She hadn't planned to throw that out at him; it had come out on impulse. But his reaction—or lack of one—was interesting. Maybe her suspicions were wrong. Maybe he *was* just camera shy. And maybe the caller was just trying to stir up trouble where none existed.

She examined Mitch for a moment. Something there she couldn't put her finger on. Something he wasn't saying or couldn't say. Or wouldn't. Something deep and dangerous and altogether darker than the good-deed citizen act he put on.

She shivered. "Well . . . just wanted to let you know."

She left through the alley again. Animal Control had shown up and was finally carting the remains away. She watched them absently. She wasn't satisfied. Not by a long shot.

Mitch did a half-assed job cleaning up the rest of the kitchen. First the dog, then the local Lois Lane. Which disaster to focus on first? If his picture had spread wider than Crossroads, he could be in big trouble. And if that dog wasn't killed by a bobcat . . .

All his muscles tensed.

The urge to run was bubbling inside him. But it warred with that other urge. To do right by Julia. The time would come when she would force his hand. Would leave him rather than leave with him. He'd hoped he had a few more years before it happened, but more and more the choice was staring him in the face. What would happen when her two months were up?

And then there was the other face he saw when he looked at the kid. The face that would have wanted a home with a yard and a tree swing. He owed that face everything—especially the well-being of her child.

Or had he already paid in full?

Truth was, he didn't know if that account could ever be paid.

He ran back over his conversation with Shelby. Innocuous. Small-town friendliness.

He'd have to keep a close eye. Just in case. He didn't want to do anything drastic, but he would if he had to. He'd done it before, God help him.

In the meantime, there was the other worry. The sight of that mutilated carcass was embedded in his head.

Was it coincidence that the eyes were missing? That it had been opened down the middle? Or did it look that way because the buzzards had gotten to it?

Finished at Crick's, he left quickly. Julia had been gone a couple of hours now, and he had that queasy, unbalanced feeling not knowing exactly where she was. But he had one more thing to do.

The nearest Walmart was forty minutes away, and though he wanted to get there immediately, he drove just under the speed limit. It was habit as much as anything—do nothing to attract attention was his personal Golden Rule. He couldn't afford a session with a cop. Not even for speeding.

When he finally got to the store, though, he raced inside. Quick as he could, he found a disposable cell phone and stamped his foot impatiently waiting to pay for it.

He drove fifteen minutes before the first sign of bars appeared. He pulled off the highway, found a secluded bend in the road, and parked.

His mouth went dry as he dialed the number. He let it ring once, hung up, and dialed again. Let it ring twice. Hung up and called a third time, hanging up after the first ring again. Then he waited. Watched the way the gray winter sky outlined a bare tree branch. Leaned against the truck, his arms tucked under his armpits, his leg drumming fast against the hubcap. He walked five steps, turned, walked another five back.

God, let him be there.

When the phone finally rang, he jumped like a startled bird. Cursed his skittishness as he punched in the connection.

"Aloha," said the voice on the other end.

"Same to you," Mitch replied with the prearranged signal.

A beat, and then the other voice said, "What is wrong?"

"We're fine. But there's a dead dog in the alley."

A pause. "A dog? You're calling me about a dog? Do you know what will happen if I am caught talking to you?"

"I know, I know, I'm sorry, and I appreciate it. But the dog is important. Where was he last night?"

"The hospital. He hurt his knee skiing. He had to get it cleaned out or something."

"You're sure?"

"I dropped him off in the morning, saw him go in, picked him up today, and he was on crutches. He has a whole schedule of physical therapy in a couple of weeks. He had to postpone the Ricci gallery opening and cancel several social events. Your mother would have been furious."

A picture of his mother's cool, severe face ran through his mind. She'd passed away four years ago, and it had been years before that since he'd seen her. Which, sad to say, was fine with him.

"Thanks," Mitch said.

"That's it?"

"That's enough."

"And the child?"

"She's fine. Better than fine."

"Good. I wish you well, Mr. Mitch."

"Goes double for me."

He disconnected, and the tension in his shoulders rolled away.

On the way back to Crossroads, he stopped at the Arby's on the edge of town and bought an extra-large coffee. He removed the lid and took a sip as he walked around to the back of the store. Once out of sight, he shoved the phone into the hot coffee, put the lid back on, and shook the cup. Then he tossed the whole thing into one of the two Dumpsters back there.

He strolled back to his truck, almost light-headed. The monster, the beautiful, gifted, sickly, twisted monster, was still in New York and nowhere near Crossroads.

10

Mitch expected Julia to come home with Bitsy. But later that afternoon, she burst into the carriage house followed by Sara Jean and a flushed, wind-whipped Neesy.

"Hot chocolate! Hot chocolate!" Julia raced for the kitchen.

"She has a convertible!" Sara Jean yelled, running after Julia.

Mitch glanced out a window. No wonder the girls had been so enamored. The car was long and lean, a red, white, and chrome boat that was older than Neesy. He was guessing late 1950s maybe. It suited her. She seemed like she was from some other time period herself. "You put the top down? It's practically freezing out."

Neesy laughed and shivered at the same time. "Actually, it's a breezy forty-nine degrees. And what could I do? They outnumbered me."

Mitch sensed she hadn't put up much of a fight. And after the way Julia had looked this morning, he could only be grateful that whatever it took—even pneumonia—was worth putting the excitement back in her face.

"Thank you."

"You're welcome."

There was a moment then. An unaccountable shift as they faced each other. Suddenly something between them was different. Neesy was still wearing her body-hugging Crick's uniform, but she seemed less the man-hungry hunter and more, well, softer, he guessed. Sweeter. And he'd always been a sucker for kindness.

He caught himself staring and tore his gaze away. "You...uh...you want that beer?" he asked.

Her face reddened, and she, too, looked away. "Beer? I thought I heard something about hot chocolate." She rushed after the girls, but it seemed more a way to put distance between them than anything else.

Which was strange, as up to now she'd done everything she could to bring him closer.

But that had been, what, flirting? Playacting? It had skimmed the surface. Whatever had happened a moment ago went deeper. It had been real. Intimate.

A ripple of dread ran through him, and he couldn't blame her for scurrying away. Intimacy was terrifying. Not the least because it meant uncovering secrets. And his were too dangerous to share.

Inside the kitchen, Neesy watched Julia stir the milk in a pot over the stove. With a wall between her and Mitch, Neesy could breathe again.

Only this morning, she'd been eager to see more of him. Suddenly, alone with him, looking at her with gratitude and kindness, was way too much.

Maybe it was the afternoon spent with Julia. That kid could break down any walls. Or maybe it was seeing

Mitch here, in his home, instead of at Crick's, where work made things between them less...personal? Real?

Intimate.

Less...intimate.

She'd been intimate before, hadn't she? Undressed, stark, raving naked. But that was only her body. That moment with Mitch...like he'd stripped her in a different way. Inside. As though every feeling she'd ever had before was false and shallow. Gave her a scary kind of thrill.

She shivered.

"The cocoa will warm you up," Julia said.

"Can't wait." Neesy rubbed her arms, encouraging the mistaken idea that she was cold.

"Sometimes Mitch makes it with real chocolate," Julia said. "He says it's not real hot chocolate without it."

"What is it, then?" Neesy asked.

"Cocoa," Julia said.

"My mom just opens a package and pours water over it," said Sara Jean.

"What did your mom do?" Julia asked Neesy.

She thought a moment, though why she took the time was a puzzle, since she knew the answer immediately. "Oh, she didn't."

The kids stared at her.

"Not even cocoa?" Julia asked.

"Not even."

They looked at her, mystified, and a little sad, too. Neesy shifted, uncomfortable. She didn't want anyone feeling sorry for her, not even these two. "We drank a lot of Coke, though," she said. "Breakfast, lunch, and dinner."

"Breakfast?" Julia said, and Sara Jean's mouth sagged open.

"Sure. Coke and a moon pie. Gets you off to a fine start—a sugar *and* caffeine high."

The two girls giggled.

They brought their cups of cocoa into the living room, and Julia handed Mitch one of his own. For a few minutes, the four of them sipped in silence. The girls sprawled on the floor, Mitch and Neesy on the couch.

It was a comfortable enough place. Or at least what Bitsy Blunt had done was comfortable. It was certainly three steps up the ladder from where Neesy lived across the river. This whole side of town was three steps up.

And yet, there was something nondescript about it. Not much of Mitch or Julia hanging around. No family pictures, no souvenirs of places they'd been. The coffee table was bare of magazines, and except for a few library books, the shelves were mostly empty.

Neesy had a cousin who'd gotten pregnant in high school. Neesy had felt betrayed when she found out and had told Trisha to get an abortion—better that than growing up the way Neesy had, the visible proof of her parents' teenage mistake.

But Trisha didn't listen, and the father was proud to marry her. They were still married and had three kids now, which only proved that happiness was made for other people. They'd moved to Lubbock years ago, and Neesy had visited a couple of times. The house had been full of their lives together—not only pictures, but also scribblings and drawings and all sorts of kid-created stuff on the fridge and the walls.

Here, the only purpose of the refrigerator door was to open it.

Chalk it up to male habits. Men weren't sentimental.

They didn't collect things. Although the men she'd known collected empty beer bottles and stolen license plates the way Trisha collected kids. The only thing Mitch collected were the two battered backpacks that sat by the door, waiting, it seemed, to be grabbed at a moment's notice.

"You always keep your bags packed and ready to go?" she teased Mitch.

"Doesn't everyone?" He laughed, making light of it.

"I *told* you to put them away," Julia said, rolling her eyes. "We don't need them here."

He shot Julia a sharp look, and she quickly busied herself with her cocoa. Neesy looked between father and daughter. What had just happened?

Mitch put his cup on the coffee table. "Anyone up for a game of backgammon?"

Julia waved her arm wildly. "Me!" She disappeared into one of the other rooms and came back with a collapsible case that unfolded into a game board.

Neesy had never spent an afternoon like that, playing games with two children. At least, not since she'd been a child herself. The game was easy but the strategy wasn't, and she made a lot of mistakes. But it didn't matter. She found herself laughing—at herself, at Mitch, at Julia. They all laughed. It was warm and amazing and like nothing she'd ever experienced.

After the fourth game, Julia invited everyone for dinner. But something moved behind Mitch's eyes: Neesy had stayed long enough.

Earlier, she'd been uneasy about that private moment with Mitch. After hours in his company, though, that keen, anxious closeness had expanded into real warmth, and she didn't want to ruin it. The old Neesy might have ignored his signals. But she'd promised herself—she didn't want to be that Neesy anymore. She'd like to stay. She would have stayed in a heartbeat. But only if he wanted her to.

"Oh, no. I couldn't. I don't think your dad is ready for dinner company."

"Sure he is. He's always ready. He can make food out of anything."

"I've got...I've got plans," Neesy said.

"I don't," said Sara Jean.

The two girls went over to the Blunts' to get permission, and Neesy gathered her purse and jacket.

Mitch caught her arm before she could head for the door. "You don't really have plans, do you?"

She looked into his eyes. They were pale blue, nothing like Julia's blazing color, but she saw sincerity there. "I do if you want me to."

"I should," he said ruefully. "I should hope you have plans from now until the end of the century."

What he said was unkind, but the way he said it... Encouraged, she asked, "But?"

"But if you don't mind potluck..."

She smiled. "It's my favorite."

Neesy was amazed at what Mitch whipped up from a couple of tomatoes, eggs, peppers, and onions. Julia was right—he could make food out of anything.

"What is it?" Sara Jean asked when dinner was put in front of her.

"Huevos rancheros," Mitch said.

"Wavos?" Sara Jean picked at the edge of the fried egg with its topping of salsa.

"It means 'eggs' in Spanish," Mitch explained.

"You have eggs for dinner?" Sara Jean was skeptical.

"Why not?" Julia said. "It's good. It tastes like a taco kind of."

That got Sara Jean to taste it, and once she did, she liked it. "My dad"—she flicked a glance over at Julia—"I mean, Tommy doesn't like spicy food. It gives him heartburn, and he says it's only good for the dogs."

The mention of dogs reminded everyone how the day began, and there was a small silence.

"Do you think they took him away?" Julia said in a low voice.

"I'm sure they did," Mitch said.

"What will happen to him?"

Mitch and Neesy exchanged glances.

"They'll give him a nice burial," Neesy said.

"Can I watch?"

Dang. "Uh...well, no, actually. It's private. Animal Control does it all, and they don't let anyone in. But you can have a memorial service right here," she added quickly. "Say a prayer or a reading. You know, tell doggie stories."

Julia nodded. "Maybe I will."

Later, Mitch walked Neesy to her car. It was dark by then, and the moon hung low in the sky. She shivered and Mitch pulled her jacket closer around her, holding it together at her throat. He was looking at her in a way she'd wanted him to from the first. The way a man who wants a woman always looks—like he was dying of starvation and she was the only food that could bring him back to life.

But the look went on, and he didn't do anything. Just pushed a strand of hair behind her ear.

"Thanks for that lie about the dog."

"Couldn't exactly tell her they were going to burn him up in the trash, could I? Kids take that kind of stuff to heart."

If Mitch had been another kind of man, she might have egged him on. Leaned a little closer, put her hands on him. But he was Mitch, and she liked him. Not in the way she'd liked Tommy Joe or Ed Pickett—because they'd wanted her, and it felt good to be wanted. But because Mitch didn't. Because he liked her without wanting her. Or, given that look, despite wanting her. And that was something more truthful and honest than anything she'd felt before.

His hand was still at her ear. It brushed the side of her cheek and sent a shiver of heat through her. "I had a good time tonight," she said.

He nodded. "Me too."

Do it again? The words were almost out of her mouth, but she swallowed them. Something powerful held Mitch back. Maybe one day she'd find out what that was; maybe she wouldn't. Either way, she'd promised herself, hadn't she? She was done chasing him.

"Thanks again for dinner." She started to get in her car, but his hand on her arm stopped her. When she turned back to see what he wanted, the question evaporated.

She knew what he wanted.

And when it came, when his mouth touched hers, she nearly stopped breathing. Her heart was thudding like she was thirteen again and this was her first kiss ever. But unlike then, the hands that held her face were strong and sure, and when he let her go, there was more than curiosity in his eyes.

For half a second, they looked at each other. Then every obstacle fell away and they were in each other's arms. He crushed her with his mouth, his lips. She inhaled him, swallowing his strength right down to her core and below. The winter night was cold, but there was a bonfire between them. His hands were on her back, her face, her hair, her butt. He pressed her into him, and she felt what he was feeling, and she went all liquid heat.

And as quickly as it had come, it was over. One moment his mouth was on hers, her soul in his hands, and the next there was only cold air between them.

She gasped, reaching for oxygen. Mitch's chest was rising and falling to a similar breathless rhythm. But he looked... horrified.

She opened her mouth to ask what was wrong, but he only shook his head and backed away.

"Mitch—"

"Go. Just go."

"But—"

He held up his hands like a traffic cop and shook his head again. One hand became a finger, which he put to his lips. The other fisted, white-knuckled and tight. "Get out of here." He growled it, a demand, not a suggestion. "Go!"

So she did. She got in, turned the ignition over, and gunned the engine. She was out of there so fast the tires squealed.

Inside the carriage house, Mitch leaned his forehead against the door. Christ. Sweet, holy mother of God. What had just happened? He'd wanted her worse than he'd wanted anything in his life. He wanted to wrap her up and let her seep into him like she was sunshine on a gloomy day. What the hell had he been thinking?

He shouldn't have agreed to dinner. If he'd been smart, he would have let her walk out the door.

But he hadn't been smart. And he had a terrible, appalling feeling that he wasn't going to be.

11

Mitch was distracted all day Sunday, but by Monday morning he was braced and tight and ready to keep Neesy at arm's length.

But when she walked into the kitchen at Crick's, all his preparation fell apart. He mumbled, dropped a container of maple syrup, couldn't even look her in the eye.

Not that she was any better. Her gaze remained somewhere around his knees.

"I, uh…I brought this for Julia." She held out a book tied together with two crisscrossed rubber bands. "It was Mama's. I thought Julia might…Well, you know, she does like to read. And I thought maybe it might help her get over…" She nodded toward the back screen door and the alley.

It was a hardbound copy of *Old Yeller*. The plastic film that had once coated the cover was peeling back, and when Mitch removed the rubber bands, he saw that the pages were brittle and brown.

He couldn't think of a nicer gift, one that was more thoughtful or heartfelt. Suddenly everything that had been there Saturday night outside the carriage house was back. The indescribable warmth that overtook him when Neesy was near. The choking need to touch her, hold her, devour her.

Jesus H. merciful Christ.

"Thank you," he said stiffly.

"You're...uh...welcome."

And then, thank all the powers in the universe, she disappeared through those swinging doors, and he could breathe again.

Somehow they got through the day. And the next. And the next. Neither one of them mentioned the kiss again. But whatever easiness had been between them before was gone. Mitch might regret it, but he was also grateful for it.

The month stumbled along. Julia practically swallowed *Old Yeller* whole. She talked about it for weeks, researched rabies, the Confederacy, and the Texas hills on Sara Jean's computer. She watched the movie over at the Blunts' about fifty times, and Mitch was so sick of it he was ecstatic when the science project reared its ugly head.

"Sara Jean says she'll help with it," Julia said.

Which would have been generous enough if the offer hadn't also come attached to sleepovers, which he wouldn't allow.

"You're being stupid," Julia huffed.

"I'm being safe."

"Safe? Do you think they're going to eat me or something?"

He poked her in the belly. "Wouldn't get much meat off you."

She stamped her foot. "*Why* won't you let me stay over?"

"Because."

"That's not a reason."

"I gave you my reason."

"It's a stupid reason! You're stupid! I hate you!" And she wheeled around and threw herself into her room.

Mitch sighed. But that night he made baked ziti, her favorite—with homemade sauce.

She frowned when she saw it. "You're trying to bribe me."

"Is it working?"

She sat at the table and spooned a huge helping onto her plate. "I don't know. I haven't tasted it yet."

"Why don't you invite Sara Jean here?"

"Because she has the computer. *And* the color printer." The last said like an accusation.

"You know, people did science projects before there were computers."

"They painted on cave walls, too," she said unhappily.

Crick's closed for Thanksgiving, and Mitch was looking forward to a long day of doing nothing. But the Blunts invited them for their traditional feast. From his personal experience, the holiday meal was cold, formal, and prepared by people other than family, so he was happy to bypass it. Besides, his Christmas deadline was fast approaching, and the more attached Julia grew to Sara Jean, the Blunts, and Crossroads in general, the bigger the brawl he'd have to fight when it came.

But Julia had never had a real family holiday, with the table sagging under the weight of food and family. He'd already denied her so much that he gave in to this.

Tommy's sister, Hannah, was there, of course, and she

greeted him with the same cold, lawyerly suspicion as the last time he'd seen her. It seemed that she wore the same shapeless dress, too, and he couldn't help comparing her to Neesy's warm familiarity. Not to mention her body-hugging wardrobe.

What was Neesy doing today? Who was she celebrating with? Quickly, he nailed the thought behind tightly closed shutters. They had arrived at détente, but the less he thought about her, the better.

Not that he was eager to talk to Hannah, either. Her cool wariness put him on edge, as though she knew he had secrets and she would make it her business to uncover them. At least he managed to keep their interactions confined to the table. She seemed less dangerous when everyone was there.

But leave it to Hannah to bring up the one subject Mitch would have gladly avoided. In the midst of passing turkey and dressing, Hannah said to Sara Jean, "I hear you're on quite an *Old Yeller* kick."

"Not me," said Sara Jean. "Julia. It's because of Huck."

"Huck? Isn't that a different book?"

"Huck's the dog in the alley that got murdered."

"I don't think that's a subject for conversation today," Bitsy said.

"Murdered?" Hannah's brows rose. "I didn't know anyone had determined what happened."

"Sheriff said it was a bobcat," Julia said. She'd piled her plate, especially the sweet potatoes, which she loved.

"A bobcat?" Hannah raised doubtful brows. "So close to town?"

Bitsy said, "Well, honestly, Hannah, what else could it be? And I really don't want us talking—"

"Do you think a person could have done it?" This from Sara Jean.

"Why would they?" Julia asked.

"Don't you believe in evil?" Hannah asked.

"Hannah!" Bitsy turned to her husband. "Do something!"

"It's just conversation, Bits," Tommy said. "And, for your information, I do believe there's a force for evil out there. It's called Satan."

"Satan?" Julia asked. "You mean, like, the Devil?" Julia turned to Mitch. "We don't believe in the Devil, do we?"

"People make choices," Mitch said quietly. "For good and for evil."

"Well," Bitsy said, spooning green beans on her plate, "if you insist on continuing, I did hear a rumor that Boyd Collier was behind it."

"Does that mean he's a devil?" Sara Jean asked.

"It means he's got evil in him," Tommy said. "And that could be the work of the Devil."

"Or he's just plain evil," said Hannah.

"You don't believe in the Devil?" Mitch asked her.

"I'm with you," Hannah said. "I believe in choice. Free will. And, of course, proof. I heard Boyd Collier was out of town that day."

"I think it was the bobcat," Julia said. "Did you know that bobcats can show their claws or pull them in?"

"Like Wolverine?" Sara Jean asked.

And the conversation turned to other things.

As was customary, Julia stuffed her face and ended up groaning on the floor with Sara Jean. The two of them went up to her room, but only after making the adults promise to call when dessert was served.

They were clearing dishes when Bitsy brought up the subject of Christmas.

"We're taking Sara Jean to Florida. It would be good for her to get away for a while." She dropped her voice. "You know, from all the...memories."

"She doesn't need a trip to Florida," Hannah said. "She needs a trip to a counselor."

Bitsy glared at Hannah. "There is nothing wrong with Sara Jean. It's just...growing pains. Anyway," she continued to Mitch, "we are going to Florida. To Disney World, actually. We rented a condo and there's plenty of room. I was hoping you'd let us take Julia, too."

Mitch almost dropped the plates he was carrying. "I don't think that's a good idea."

"See?" Hannah said. "Even Mitch doesn't approve."

He shot Hannah a "mind your own business" look. "That's not what I meant. I just don't want Julia going so far away."

"We'll take good care of her. I promise."

"I'm sure you will. It's just that—"

At that moment, Julia and Sara Jean came thudding down the stairs in a whirl of whoops and burst into the kitchen.

"Sara Jean wants me to go to Florida. Can I?" Julia was hopping up and down with excitement.

"Did you ask him?" Sara Jean said to her mother.

"Can I go?" Julia asked Mitch.

He wanted to strangle the Blunts. "I don't think so, Junebug."

"But—"

"The Blunts have done enough for us. A trip like that...
It's just too much."

"It would be our pleasure," Bitsy said.

"I could never repay it."

"You wouldn't have to."

"Dad—"

"I'm sorry, Jules. It's out of the question."

"But—"

Mitch could predict the coming explosion. "Dinner
was great," he said quickly. "I think it's time to go."

"I don't want to go," Julia said.

"We're going anyway. Say thank you to the Blunts."

She set her jaw but got out a frosty thank-you, and he
managed to drag her to the carriage house before the vol-
cano erupted.

"*Why* are you doing this to me?"

"We can't live off other people, Jules."

"But they *want* me to come. Sara Jean wants me to
come."

"We're living here rent free. Every stick of furniture
belongs to them. They feed us, gave me a job. We can't
keep taking and taking. It's not right."

She crossed her arms and flounced on the couch.
"Someday I'm going to be richer than rich," she shouted.
"I'm going to have six houses and hang out with whoever
I want and go to Florida whenever I want and sleep wher-
ever I want!"

She stalked off to her room, and Mitch didn't follow or
try to cajole her out of her bad mood. He couldn't blame
her for being mad. He wanted her to have everything she
deserved, too. The beach house, the ski chalet, the mansion on Park Avenue.

He closed his eyes.

Someday, Junebug. Someday.

But not this day.

Florida was just too far away. He couldn't watch her. And if he couldn't watch her, she would never be safe.

12

Roger Carrick spent the entire month of November and almost right up until Christmas working on a bank fraud case involving loans to two New Jersey men who wanted to start a turkey farm in Wilton, Iowa. When the men defaulted on their payments and vanished, both their identities and their ownership of the businesses used for collateral turned out to be false. It took Roger and an agent from Cedar Rapids nearly six weeks to track down the two men and arrest them as they were about to cross the Mexican border. But once the men had been processed and the investigative part of the case closed, he had time to think about the newspaper article he'd received from the *Crossroads Sentinel*.

He spent the day before Christmas tracking down the right Crossroads. He struck out in both Maine and Pennsylvania but hit pay dirt in the Memphis field office, where an agent put him in touch with the Crossroads police chief, Abe Marfield.

"Oh, sure," Marfield told him. "We got the *Sentinel* here. What's the FBI's interest?"

Roger dodged the question. "Who can I talk to about the paper?"

"Well, Shelby Townsend's the owner. She got herself mixed up in something?"

"No, no, just a few questions. Background stuff."

The officer paused. Roger could almost hear the frown forming on his face. "Nothing big coming my way? I'd appreciate any heads-up if you know of something. Drugs, gangs, anything like that."

"Nothing like that," Roger assured him. "But I'd appreciate any contact information you can give me for this Shelby Townsend."

Marfield put him on hold, then came back with a phone number. Roger thanked him and disconnected. He ran a computer search for the newspaper owner's name. Most of the hits revolved around her retirement two years ago. The accompanying pictures showed a box of a woman with a bulldog face. When he called, her voice barked at him through the phone.

"*Crossroads Sentinel,* Shelby Townsend."

Roger introduced himself. "A month or so ago, you wrote an article about the rescue of a young girl by a Mitch Turner."

"So the FBI is interested in Mitch, too."

"What do you mean 'too'? Has someone else asked about him?"

She told him about an anonymous tip she'd received shortly after the story ran. "After that, I had a friend up in Detroit do a search, but Turner came up clean. Almost too clean. But you can't write a story unless one exists, so I didn't pursue it."

"What's he done since he got to Crossroads?"

"He's a short-order cook at one of the restaurants in town. Takes care of his daughter. Keeps a low, law-abiding profile."

"What about the daughter?" Roger scanned the article. "Julia? That her name? How old is she? What's she look like?"

"Oh, I'd say she's maybe eleven or twelve. In the fifth grade, I think."

His interest quickened. "Anything unusual about her? Anything stand out?"

"She's eleven. Not been around long enough to do anything unusual. Unless you're talking about physical appearance. She does have very striking blue eyes."

Roger stilled. His hand tightened on the phone.

"I don't suppose you're going to tell me what this is all about?" Shelby Townsend asked. "What's the FBI's interest in a short-order cook and his daughter?"

"Appreciate your help, Ms. Townsend. Merry Christmas."

He disconnected. Stared at the opposite wall, where memos and bulletins were pinned to a corkboard. Was Mitch Turner the end of Roger's free fall? Or just wishful thinking? Should he check it out? Or should he follow procedure and alert New York? Faces wanted by the Omaha division stared back at Roger. Physical description, criminal caution, whether or not they were armed and dangerous. Mitch Turner wasn't up there. But it was still Roger's case. The case that had sent him tumbling into oblivion. If anyone was going to sweep up the pieces, shouldn't it be him?

He filled out a 302, requesting resources for a case, and picked up the phone to call Marbrue, the SAC in Omaha.

But Marbrue wasn't as eager to pursue as Roger. "First off, all you've got is a couple of maybes and a hunch. I'm not going to release Bureau resources on a wild-goose chase. And even if I was, it's New York's case. Let them pay for it."

Roger twirled a pencil maniacally. He hadn't expected to have to fight for this. "No one knows the case better than I do."

"Even after ten, eleven years?"

"Yes, sir."

"Is this why you've requested transfer back to New York twelve times in the last ten years?"

Roger frowned; his personnel file must be in front of Marbrue. "That and the corn, sir. I'm allergic."

"We're all allergic to the corn."

"Yes, sir."

"If you've got time on your hands, I just got a call from the Muscatine Police Department. They've got two skin-head yahoos in custody for beating up some black men at the Canterbury Pub in the Econo Lodge. Victims are calling it a hate crime. So head over to Muscatine, which *is* in your district, and see what you can find out."

Roger bit down on what he really wanted to say, murmuring only, "Yes, sir."

He hung up, crumpled the 302 on his desk, and threw it against the wall. Then he threw the entire contents of his pencil jar against the wall.

Then he yanked out another 302, barked at the office manager to give him a new case number, and filled out the form.

Ten minutes later, he was in his Bucar, heading southwest to Muscatine.

13

Mitch intended for Julia to spend the long Christmas break at Crick's, helping Loritta, reading, and doing whatever else he could think of to keep her entertained. There'd definitely been a cooling off between them. She didn't say she hated him and flounce off to her room anymore, but he could tell she was holding a grudge.

In other circumstances, he might even have resented it. But he could hardly blame her, considering what he'd asked her to give up. Not just a trip to Disney World, but also things she didn't even know she should have.

And it was Christmas. He hadn't mentioned it yet, and she probably thought he'd forgotten, but the promised deadline was upon them. Their stay in Crossroads was almost over, and Julia was not going to like moving on. He wanted to give her one lovely memory to take with her and hopefully ease her over the hump of leaving.

So on the day before Christmas, he snuck out of the restaurant while Julia was helping with the salt shakers and the customers hadn't come yet.

But Neesy burst through the swinging doors just as he was stepping through the back one.

"Going somewhere?" she said.

He took in a deep breath, braced himself not to feel anything, then answered her. "I'll be gone fifteen minutes. Got to set up a surprise for Julia."

Her brows rose. "What kind of surprise?"

He told her, and her whole face softened. "Well, the phone's for you. Want me to take a message?"

"Who is it? I've only got a few minutes to do this."

"Shelby Townsend. Said it was important."

Important? What the hell could she want? He hesitated, needing to get to the house but not wanting to leave without knowing what Shelby was after.

"If you want"—Neesy picked up a spatula and tapped it nervously on the counter—"I can run over to the house while you take the call. We got time, and Loritta is here in case anyone comes early."

"Thanks, but—"

"Look, if it's about…about what happened. I mean, about the—"

"It's not." God, he didn't want to talk about that kiss.

"You don't have to worry. I mean, it won't happen again." She gave him a little self-deprecating laugh. "I can keep my grubby hands off you."

"Your hands aren't grubby and I don't want—" *them off me.* He almost said it. Instead, he clamped his mouth shut.

She looked down at her hands. "I…I haven't gotten either of you anything for Christmas."

"It's fine. We haven't gotten you anything, either."

"Well, I'd be honored to help with this. Call it my Christmas gift."

Loritta stuck her head in. "You going to take that call or not? Can't keep the line tied up."

"Be right there." He turned back to Neesy. "You're sure?"

"Sure I'm sure. It would be my ... my pleasure."

He cleared his throat. "Maybe you'll stop by tomorrow?" What the hell was he doing? "For a ... a beer or something?"

She looked at him, her green eyes puzzled and pleased. "Maybe. Sure. We'll see."

He gave her the instructions, and she took off her apron and ran out the back.

Then Mitch went into the restaurant to talk to Shelby.

"Something's come up," she said. "I need to talk to you. Can you come to the house?"

Mitch had the afternoon all planned out, and a trip to see Shelby Townsend was not on the agenda. "Today? On Christmas Eve?"

"It's not Christmas Eve until tonight."

Which was true but beside the point. Especially when he had something special lined up. "What's it about?"

"I'd rather not go into it over the phone. But I will say it's about Julia."

Julia. What the hell did she have to do with Julia? The possibilities nearly gagged him, so he quickly arranged a meeting for later that afternoon.

Mitch was uneasy all day. He got two orders wrong, and when Loritta popped into the kitchen to bring one back, he snapped at her.

She eyed him with a sour expression. "What's wrong with you? Get bit by a Christmas troll this morning?"

"Sorry." Man, he had to calm down.

But then Neesy dropped off an order, and he did the same thing. "What the hell does that say?" He touched the order slip with a greasy finger.

"Eggs over easy," she said calmly, then pursed her lips and gazed at him thoughtfully. "You know you're being an ass. You got Loritta all whipped up. Mary Nell is afraid to come back here. There's nothing to worry about. Everything is lined up. She's going to love it."

As if pleasing Julia was his biggest worry. He flipped a sausage patty. He *was* being an ass. Truth was, he had no idea what Shelby wanted. Could be she wanted to announce the winner of the Christmas essay contest. Could be nothing at all.

He let out a huge breath. "Okay. Yeah, you're right. I'm being an idiot. Apologies all around. And . . . well, thanks for what you did. Appreciate the help."

She gave him the amazing smile that set off the dimple in her chin and made her green eyes sparkle. How could anything bad happen on a day that included Neesy's smile?

After Crick's closed, he and Julia drove over to Shelby's house. He left Julia in the truck where he could see her and knocked on the front door. There was no answer, and he tried the knob, but it was locked.

He knocked again. "Ms. Townsend?"

"Try the back!" Julia stuck her head through the window opening.

"Get inside," he yelled. "And lock the doors like I told you to."

Julia grumbled but did as he asked. Why was he so

weird about everything? Sara Jean said he was overprotective and that Julia had to break out one day.

Wouldn't take much. Just a pop of the lock and she could jump out and wait for him in the truck bed.

But she didn't.

Something was out there. Something Mitch never named or referred to, but something worse than the worst thing she could imagine.

Once, when she was little, she'd seen a miniature town in a store window. She still remembered the tiny stores and the train that went around and around. She'd let go of Mitch's hand to look at it. Next thing she knew, she was alone, surrounded by a swarm of strangers. It was interesting but not scary. Not until Mitch found her again and crushed her so tight he could have broken all her bones. And then he shook her.

"Don't you ever do that again," he'd said to her. His face was so scary she'd never forgotten it. She never let go of his hand again, either.

She talked to Sara Jean about what the awfulness could be.

"It's just that the world sucks in general," Sara Jean said, "and he doesn't want you to find out yet."

Julia sat in the truck pondering the suckitude of the world outside her window. It didn't seem so awful. It just seemed...ordinary. She almost wished there was a monster out there. At least that would be something different.

And now Christmas was here and Sara Jean was not, and they'd be going soon. At least, that was the deal. But Mitch hadn't said a thing about it, so maybe he'd changed his mind. She hoped so. She got all tight inside when she thought about leaving.

Julia kicked the front of her seat. Where was Mitch anyway? Miss Shelby must be talking his ear off.

Julia wouldn't have thought he'd have that much to say—not with the way he acted around her before. Like if he got too close he'd catch something.

Her stomach growled.

What was taking him so long?

Just as she was thinking of unlocking the doors after all and going in to get him, he finally—*finally*—came around the corner of the house from the back.

"So?" Julia barely waited for Mitch to get behind the wheel. "What'd she want?"

He started the engine. "She wasn't there."

"What took you so long, then?"

"Long? I was gone like five minutes."

"Locked up in here it seemed like a year."

He tried not to smile. "Well, your prison term is up, Junebug, and I've got a surprise for you."

Her jaw dropped. "What is it?"

He started the truck. "What kind of surprise would it be if I told you?"

"If I guess, will you tell me if I get it right?"

"No."

"No fair!"

He laughed and pulled away from the curb while Julia bounced in the seat, impatient to be home.

"Is it inside?"

"It is if Neesy did what I asked her to."

She was so excited she could hardly wait for him to turn off the engine when they got there. Before he set the brake, she was out of the car and racing up the walk.

Mitch watched her hurtle inside. She was going too fast to bother closing the front door, so he heard the scream as he was locking up the truck.

He smiled.

She ran back out and flung herself at him. He held her tight. "Merry Christmas, Junebug."

"It's beautiful."

"Do you like it?"

"It's the most beautiful tree in the world."

They walked inside, hand in hand. The evergreen filled the small house with the scent of thick, northern forests. He'd never paid much attention to Christmas before. They were often on the road or at a brief stopover. No place to put a tree let alone all the crap that went with it. So this was Julia's first, and it didn't disappoint. Her face was filled with awe and delight, her blue eyes sparkling.

"Want to decorate it?"

"With what?"

He held up a finger, went to the closet in his room where he'd hidden everything, and brought back glittery balls, tinsel, stars, snowflakes.

Julia spent a good hour taking everything out of the boxes, commenting on each ornament, separating the favorites from the less so. Then picking new ones and rearranging them.

He leaned over her shoulder from his perch on the couch. "Are you going to hang them or just look at them?"

"I haven't decided yet."

To further the process, he made them hot chocolate, the good kind, with cream and real chocolate melted over a double boiler. He remembered days colder than this one, skating on the frozen lake behind the winter house, and the thick, rich chocolate that was always waiting when they plunged back inside, breathless and freezing. Not to mention bruised—at least he usually was if his brother was there. They weren't allowed marshmallows, but Mitch threw a handful of the little puffs in Julia's and, to spite the past, his, too.

He made popcorn to go along with the cocoa, and still the ornaments were splayed out on the floor.

"Jules, you just have to start somewhere. If you don't like what you have, start all over."

She climbed onto the couch and snuggled up against him. "But it's our first tree. I want it to be perfect."

He put an arm around her. "It will be."

She sat there awhile, still undecided. So he gave her a little psychological push. "Want me to go first?"

"No!" She hopped off the couch, picked up a blue-and-silver ball, and hung it on a branch. Then she ran back to look at it.

"Pretty," he said to encourage her.

She was reaching for a snowflake when someone knocked at the door.

Julia's eyes widened. They didn't get many visitors, and Sara Jean was away. "Oohh, another surprise. You didn't say there was more." She rushed off, excited.

She loved surprises.

14

Like most people in Crossroads, Police Chief Abe Marfield liked to spend Christmas Eve at home. But over the long course of his career, he'd also had a growing family, and Christmas was holiday pay. So when the kids were little, they often spent the holiday without him. Now that his kids were grown and had families of their own, Abe was home more often than not.

There was a certain irony to that, which, if he had to confess, was not as enjoyable as it should be. His wife, Irma, was on the phone half the night with one grandkid after another. And ever since the doctor had mentioned the few pounds he'd gained, she'd cut down on the gravy and mashed potatoes, so Christmas Eve dinner wasn't even something to look forward to anymore.

He would have volunteered for holiday duty himself and spare the younger men, but now they were the ones with the growing families who needed the extra income. So it wasn't entirely without pleasure when he got the call from Nathan Burgess.

"You better get down here, Chief."

The deputy's voice was sober, even anxious. All the excuse Abe needed.

"Irma!" he called into the kitchen, where his wife was setting the table for the two of them. "Got an emergency!"

"Now?" she called back.

He was strapping on his service revolver when she came out of the kitchen with her GRANNY SANTA apron on.

He shoved his arms into his jacket and bussed her cheek. "Sorry. Gotta run."

She sighed, but they'd been married a long time, and this wasn't the first emergency to take him away. "Hope it's nothing too awful." She tucked his jacket closer around him. "Be safe now," she said. "And bring the boys around for apple pie if you want."

He nodded, ashamed to be so eager to get back to work, even if it was just another Crossroads nonevent.

Not that he was complaining. Crossroads was the bridge between the demanding work on the streets of Chicago and retirement, which Irma was endlessly harping on and which he wasn't ready for.

The town had been the perfect compromise. There'd been no murders, no gang shootings, and no armed robberies in the five years he'd been there. He'd had more than his share of drunk and disorderlies and domestic disturbances, but they paled in comparison to what he'd be doing if he stayed at the 07 in Englewood. And Irma had found her place among the church bazaars and the knitting club.

So Abe wasn't expecting much as he sped over to Shelby Townsend's house, where Nate Burgess was waiting outside with Shelby's brother-in-law, Lewis Keyes.

"Ms. Townsend was supposed to go to her sister's for Christmas Eve," Nate said when Abe had joined them.

"And when she didn't show up," Lewis continued, "naturally we were worried."

Keyes was a small, scrawny man whose aging red hair had paled to the color of the skin on his high, sloping forehead. A pair of steel-rimmed glasses accentuated his watery gray eyes, which looked up at Abe with grave concern.

"She's never late?" Abe frowned. Didn't seem like much of a crisis.

"Well, sure, but not without calling."

"And you tried calling her?"

"Yes, sir. No answer."

"So Lewis, here, took a ride over," Nate said.

"We've got a key, you see. For emergencies," Lewis said. "And when I got in . . . Well, that's when I called you."

"Okay," Abe said. "Let's take a look."

They escorted him around back and through the kitchen door. Nate led the way to the living room, which was evidently also Shelby's office. A desk with a computer sat against one wall. Didn't look like Ms. Townsend was much of a neat freak. But even still, the place was a mess. Pillows on the couch strewn on the floor. Chairs overturned. A bookcase disrobed of its contents. Abe scanned through the stuff on the desk. Announcements of Rotary meetings, a couple of births, the results of the high school holiday bake sale.

"And look." Nate pointed to a stain on the middle of the floor.

Abe crossed over, then bent down to examine it. "Get an evidence kit."

"You think it's blood?" Lewis knelt and reached out to touch the blot.

Abe swatted his hand away. "Don't touch it. In fact, don't touch anything."

"But who'd want to hurt Shelby?"

Abe thought about the call from the FBI agent asking about Shelby, but he didn't want to alarm anyone yet. "Now, don't go jumping to conclusions, Lewis. Could be a lot of explanations for this. We don't even know what the spot is yet."

Nate brought in the kit, and they both pulled on latex gloves prior to scraping up samples of the substance for testing. They were still kneeling on the floor when Nate drew his boss's attention toward the desk across the room.

Abe looked over and didn't see anything worth mentioning. The screen was dark. They'd already riffled through the papers, and it was all routine town stuff. "What?"

"Power light's on," Burgess said.

Abe homed in on a tiny green circle in the PC tower below the desk. It was right at eye level; if they'd been standing, Nate wouldn't have spotted it.

"Good eyes," Abe said. He rose and went over to the computer, where he pressed a key. The machine whirred back to life.

But when the picture resolved itself, Abe frowned.

Nate whistled. "Holy Christ."

Lewis said nothing. But he turned paler than a pack of bones bleached by the sun.

Hannah Blunt looked up from the briefs on her desk. Her eyes were tired, and her head was beginning to pound.

She opened a desk drawer, looking for the aspirin, and couldn't find any.

"Pammy!" Her paralegal didn't answer. She tried the secretary, but when Carol didn't answer, either, Hannah pushed back from the desk and flung open the office door.

"Does anyone know—"

If anyone did, they weren't saying. Largely because no one was there.

Well, of course no one was there. She'd given them the afternoon off, hadn't she?

She rubbed her temples and retreated back to her desk. The pile of briefs suddenly looked like the mountain of straw some silly girl was supposed to spin into gold.

The hell with it. It was Christmas Eve, and she'd worked a full day. Plus.

She grabbed her briefcase, quickly sorted through the pile and took what she needed, then left the rest where it was. She retrieved her coat from the closet and saw that someone had pinned a bright red bow to the black collar. She frowned, went to take it off, then left it where it was.

She gave the decoration a wry smile. "Merry Christmas, Hannah Blunt."

To celebrate, she'd go home and take a nice, long bath. The thought almost soothed her. Maybe she wouldn't need that aspirin after all. She let herself out of her office and headed toward the exit. But something on the floor in front of the door stopped her. Gifts wrapped in Christmas paper.

It took her a moment to remember what they were and why they were sitting on the floor. To remind her not to leave without them.

Bitsy was supposed to have taken them over to the carriage house but in the rush to get away had forgotten. She'd called from Florida in a panic. Typical Bitsy.

Hannah picked up the boxes and fingered the shiny green paper. What was it about Mitch Turner that made her so uneasy?

Good-looking men always made her uneasy.

But Mitch was more Rochester than Darcy. And like Rochester, there was something about him. Some dark undercurrent no one but her seemed to see.

She closed her eyes. Tried a deep breath. She could take the gifts over tomorrow.

But that's what she said yesterday and the day before and the day before that.

And she already had her coat on.

She gave the tub one last, longing thought. Then she grabbed the gifts and stalked off.

15

When the knock sounded, Julia dashed away like the puppy she wanted so badly.

Mitch ran after her. "Hold up, Jules! Ask who it is before you open—" Too late. He was rounding the corner when he heard the door open.

"Is your daddy home?" asked a deep, male voice.

"Miiiitch!" she cried.

When he got there, Mitch saw Chief Marfield and one of his deputies standing on the threshold, looking solemn and not at all in a holiday mood. A tall, wide-shouldered African American, the chief had a solid, authoritative air. This was a man you could trust to get things done.

Which didn't endear him to Mitch. Even more so when he was standing at Mitch's door on Christmas Eve.

His warning antennae, honed to perfection after more than a decade, went way up. The impulse to run suffocated him. But he had no chance. The deputy was already placing Mitch's hands behind his back.

"Mitch Turner," the chief intoned, "also known as Mitchell Hanover. You are under arrest for the murder of Alicia Ruiz and the kidnapping of her infant daughter."

If it was possible to lose every drop of blood in an instant, Mitch would have keeled over in a pool of red. Was he even still standing? He heard the official words from a distance as though said to someone on another planet. It took the snick of the cuffs and the chill of metal on his wrists to bring him back to this one. When he did, it was to noise and chaos.

Julia was hopping up and down and tugging at him and the deputy. "What are they talking about? What are they doing? What are you doing? Wait! Don't!" She gave the deputy a mighty push, and he expelled a puff of air but didn't move.

"Sorry, little girl," the chief was saying.

"Gotta do this," the deputy mumbled, and Julia butted him in the gut. And when that still didn't move him, she tried again.

Mitch reached out to stop her, but, of course, he couldn't. "Jules." She wasn't paying any attention. He swallowed. "Julia. Julia!"

"What?" she yelled back. "Are you just gonna let them take you away? It's Christmas Eve!" She glared at the two officers. "He didn't do what you said. You're lying."

He knelt down awkwardly, his balance off because of his hands behind his back. "Come here." When she did, he looked right into her stormy blue eyes. A pang of memory hit him, and for a brief minute it took him back, way, way back, all the way to the day this all started and the choice he'd made. The choice that had brought them all to this terrible moment. "It's going to be all right," he lied to her. "Just calm down."

She inched closer to him and put her arms around his neck. "I'm scared," she whispered.

If he could, he would have hugged her. "I know. But that's what bravery is all about. Being scared and going on anyway. And we both know how brave you are."

"I don't want to be brave."

"I'm sorry, Junebug. It's just for a little while. Until we get this straightened out." How he managed to sound so calm was a miracle even he didn't understand. Maybe it was all the times he'd imagined this happening. When it finally did, it seemed both inevitable and anticlimactic.

"Where were you today?" the chief asked.

He wobbled to his feet. "At Crick's, like always."

"And after?"

"After? Why?"

"Just answer the question."

But those antennae were quivering maniacally.

"We went to see Miss Shelby," Julia blurted out, her arms crossed, her face a thundercloud.

"Julia," Mitch cautioned.

"What? We can visit whoever we want, can't we? She wasn't even there."

The chief and the deputy exchanged a look. "Is that true, Mr. . . . uh . . . Hanover?"

"Our name's Turner," Julia said with scorn. "And I don't lie."

But the chief was waiting for it to come from Mitch. Julia was glaring at him. He nodded once, feeling like he'd admitted to a lot more than a visit. "She called me at the restaurant and asked me to meet her at her house."

"Did she say why?"

He cut a quick glance over to Julia. "Not really."

The chief seemed to catch the unspoken message. "All right, we can finish up at the station." He, too, looked at Julia. "Do you have someone you can call?" Both men knew without specifying what he was talking about.

"You know I don't," Mitch said.

"What about the Blunts?" the deputy asked. "They rent you the carriage house, don't they?"

"They're in Florida."

"She'll have to go into child services," the chief said.

His stomach flopped. "You can't do that."

"No other choice. Can't leave her here."

"If you're talking about me," Julia said with a scowl, "I can stay by myself. I'm not a baby."

All the men said no at the same time. For the chief and the deputy, that was common sense, if not the law. For Mitch, though, it was an absolute. Alone, she would always be in danger.

"Look," Mitch said, trying not to sound desperate and not succeeding, "you have to take her with us, right? Can't leave her here. Maybe we can come up with something." A thought exploded inside him. "Neesy! Uh...Denise Brown, from Crick's. Julia could stay with her." He knew instinctively that Neesy would do it. No matter what had happened between them, Julia was neutral territory. An enormous wave of relief washed over him. "Call Neesy." He gave them her number. "She'll come get her."

But when the deputy made the call, there was no answer.

"Okay, it's Christmas Eve," Mitch said quickly. "She's out. But you can track her down, can't you?"

"Maybe," the chief said. "In the meantime, kid's got to stay somewhere tonight. Burgess," he said to the deputy, "get hold of someone from the county and have them meet us at the station."

The relief Mitch felt a few minutes ago vanished into a new surge of panic. In the middle of the sickening, rolling, helpless swell, a new voice cut in.

"Abraham? What's going on here?"

Hannah Blunt stood in the open doorway. She was holding a couple of gaily wrapped gifts and had a red bow pinned to her coat. The sight of her, festive with the holiday, was incongruous to the point of bizarre.

"Police business, Miss Hannah," the chief said.

"Clearly," Hannah said. "What kind of business requires handcuffs on Christmas Eve?"

"They said he killed someone named Alicia," Julia burst out. "We don't even know anyone named Alice!"

Hannah looked from the chief to Mitch and back again. When she came back to him, her sharp eyes seemed to take in every shadow in his dark soul.

"I'll meet you at the station," she said crisply. "Julia, you'll come with me."

"Now, Miss Hannah," the chief said, raising his hand so the lighter brown palms faced them, "you don't want to get involved with this."

"I'm sure you're right, Abraham," Hannah said. "Come on, Julia." She held out a hand.

"I want to go with Mitch," Julia said.

"And I want to have a relaxing Christmas Eve. Doesn't look like either of us is going to get what we want."

"Grab your backpack and go with Hannah, Jules," Mitch said.

The fear in her face intensified. "I don't need my backpack."

"It's just for tonight."

"What about you?"

"I'll see you in a few."

"Promise?"

"You bet."

Still scowling, she picked up one of the backpacks by the door and gave him one last look. Then his girl, his child, the creature he'd risked everything for and whom he had no earthly right to, slid her hand into Hannah Blunt's and walked into the night.

16

Neesy sat at the bar at the River Road Café, nursing her Christmas Eve beer. Ron had made an effort to keep up with the season. A string of colored lights hung above the liquor bottles leaning against the back wall, and a tiny tree in one corner of the bar flashed on and off all night long. Other than that, it was business as usual.

Well...not quite usual. There was practically no one there. Everyone was off enjoying some kind of festivity. Or so it seemed. Maybe they were just celebrating at home.

Sitting in the café bar on Christmas Eve might seem depressing to some, but Neesy was exactly where she wanted to be. She didn't like spending Christmas at home. Too many memories. Daddy getting plastered. Wrecking the tree. Punching Uncle Henry until Henry stopped coming. Then punching Mama and, of course, her.

She shuddered. No thanks. Her parents may be gone, but their ghosts still lingered. She'd stay right here with Dolly and Shania and Mr. Cash blaring the same twangy Christmas songs year after year.

And tomorrow...

She smiled a small secret smile.

Tomorrow she'd go to Mitch's house. True to her promise, she'd stayed away from him. Well, mostly. She had done him a favor or two, but that wasn't the same as throwing herself at him, was it? And now he'd asked her over. She sipped her beer, pondering the invitation. Maybe she wouldn't even go. She might just let Mr. Mitch Turner spend the holiday without her lovely company.

Yeah, right. She shook her head at her own deluded self.

But if she did visit him...who knew what might develop? If she could keep her head on straight and her hands where they belonged.

"Hey!" The bartender tapped her shoulder. "That your phone?"

How he could've heard anything over the music she didn't know. But she checked, and sure enough there was a message.

She took it outside so she could hear and shivered in the cold. Maybe it was Loritta, checking to see if she'd stop by. She always invited Neesy over on the holidays. It gave her somewhere to go, but after a while she always felt a little smothered, what with Loritta shoving rolls and mashed potatoes at her and making sure she was all right every five minutes.

Neesy shook her head at herself. Little ingrate. That's what she was.

Not really. Just not used to being treated right. Worried over. Cared for. Made her feel uncomfortable.

You're a poor sick little puppy, Neesy Brown.

Maybe. But she'd skip Loritta's tonight and go

tomorrow. Save it in case the thing with Mitch didn't work out.

She punched into her voice mail, her story set. But it wasn't Loritta; it was Nate Burgess.

Something had happened to Mitch.

Because of the holiday, the small police station was empty when Hannah arrived with Julia. The minute they got there, Julia demanded to see Mitch.

"I'm afraid that isn't possible now," Hannah said.

"But he promised." The fear that crossed over the child's beautiful features was enough to wring even Hannah's heart.

"You'll see him later."

"Swear?"

Hannah opened her mouth, not sure what to say. A vague childhood memory swooped over her, and she raised a hand, gazing at the appendage as though it belonged to someone else. "I...I swear."

Julia looked doubtful but let herself be led to a bench along the wall. She drilled Hannah with a last warning look, then took a book out of the pack and settled in to read.

Or at least that's what it looked like. Hannah suspected it·was just a pose to get the grown-ups off her back. After all, how could she concentrate on anything given the circumstances?

But Hannah didn't check. She sat at an empty desk until the chief walked in from a back hallway, signaled to Hannah, and then let her into his office.

"You sure you want to mess with this? Pretty open-and-shut." He handed Hannah a stack of papers. "Found these on Ms. Townsend's computer."

"Shelby Townsend? What were you doing there?"

He explained the circumstances and Shelby Townsend's seeming disappearance.

Hannah blanched. "My God. You don't think Mitch—"

"Don't know what to think yet. We got a crew searching the woods behind her house, but it's dark and so far they haven't found anything. But your boy certainly has motive enough."

He nodded at the papers in her hand. She shuffled through copies of news articles dated over ten years ago. The woman Mitch was accused of killing, Alicia Ruiz, had fine, delicate features. Large, dreamy eyes, dark hair. She could see some of that in Julia's face. But more, much more, in Julia's face came from the other character in the tragedy: Mitch's brother, the fabulously wealthy, powerful celebrity artist Dutch Hanover. He had the wildly handsome looks that promised great beauty in Julia. And though none of the pictures were in color, many mentioned his startling blue eyes.

Then there was Iona, the cool, blond matriarch who was by Dutch's side in every picture. She always stood a little behind, as though ceding Dutch center stage. Yet Hannah's eyes were drawn to her icy patrician features as though Iona, and not Dutch, was the real power behind the Hanover throne. She must have been, since her husband, the late Henry Hanover, had succumbed to a heart attack, leaving Iona to raise their two boys.

While Dutch had the beauty and the talent—and clearly the family support—Hannah wasn't sure what Mitch had, or did for that matter. He had been on the Hanover Industries board of directors and several charity boards, but she suspected that was just window dressing.

As she read between the lines, it seemed as if Mitch didn't do much of anything. Which was strange because the man she knew—from the rescue of Sara Jean to the care he took with Julia to the hard work he did at Crick's—was anything but a deadbeat.

Had something changed him? Murder, for instance? Was the indolent rich boy now making up for the terrible crime he committed?

The news reports didn't say. What they did tell was a story as predictable as a soap opera. Rich family, poor girlfriend. An attachment no one wanted. According to the reports, Mitch saw her first. He took her out, bought her clothes and jewelry. But no one thought he meant anything by it. Evidently, he'd had dozens of women, and he treated them all the same: love 'em and leave 'em. The photos of Mitch seemed to substantiate that claim.

Hannah picked one up. It showed a younger, but still recognizable, Mitch. Dressed in black tie, with a golden-haired beauty on his arm, he sported a gleaming smile and a careless wash of hair over his forehead. The caption could easily have been "rich people at play." But the headline read HANOVER HEIR WANTED IN WAITRESS MURDER AND KIDNAP.

The article went on to imply that Alicia's relationship to the brothers became serious only when Dutch stepped in—perhaps to warn her of Mitch's fecklessness. Or the fact that the family would never accept her. But something untoward happened. They fell in love. And that love led to a child.

According to other articles, there had always been rivalry between the brothers, especially over women. When Mitch discovered Alicia was seeing Dutch, Mitch murdered her, stole her child, and left his brother grief-stricken and desperate to find her, the sole living remnant of his lost love.

Hannah sifted through the papers, giving herself time to take it all in. Usually, she loved being right. Not this time. This time she wished her instinctive suspicion of Mitch Turner had proved wrong.

Then again, all of this was pure speculation. Media churning to sell papers and raise ratings. Everyone loved a love triangle, but she couldn't get drawn into the sentimentality. This was murder and kidnapping. Nothing sentimental about that.

"This is just media spin," she said to Abe. "Was an arrest warrant issued?"

He slid over a sheet of paper. "NYPD faxed it over."

She reviewed the warrant.

"FBI's been notified, too." Abe told her about the phone call from Agent Carrick.

She pressed her lips together. "Well, then, I'd better have a word with Mr. Hanover."

Abraham led her to the interview room, where Mitch immediately jumped to his feet. "Where's Julia?"

"From what I've seen," the chief said, "you don't have the right to ask that."

Mitch's jaw tensed. "Whatever you think you've seen, I'm the only family she knows."

"She's fine," Hannah said. "She's outside in the office, reading." She turned to Abraham. "You can remove his cuffs."

"He's a murderer, Hannah."

"An *accused* murderer. And I don't think he's going to hurt me. Are you, Mr. Hanover?"

He gave her a short, bitter laugh. "What happened to 'Mitch'? And no, of course not."

The chief removed the cuffs, albeit reluctantly. "I'll be right outside." He gave Mitch a last warning look and left.

She sat in a chair across the table from him and shuffled through the articles and the warrant. "So, what do you have to say for yourself?"

"Promise me you'll take Julia."

She looked up. He was eyeing her with a hard, relentless gaze.

"Why don't we start with what you can expect to happen next."

Mitch leaned forward. "First promise me you'll take Julia."

Julia. That was the real tragedy here. Hannah didn't want to begin thinking about what Julia would do or where she would go. Not with her, that was for sure. She wasn't good with kids. They made her nervous.

"You're the one in trouble here," she said. "Do you understand the seriousness of these charges? New York is a capital punishment state. We're talking about your life here."

"It's you who doesn't understand," Mitch said. One leg was jittering up and down, a constant nervous twitch. "What happens to me isn't important right now. What happens to Julia is."

"We can talk about Julia later."

He grabbed her wrist. "Promise me." He squeezed.

She bit down on her jaw. "Let go."

"Not until you—"

"Let go; you're hurting me!"

The door punched open. "That's enough." Abraham wrenched Mitch back. "If you can't behave yourself, we'll make sure you do." He secured Mitch's hands to the table so he could cuff them to the anchor set in for that purpose.

Mitch didn't protest. He kept his gaze square on Hannah while Abraham chained his hands. "She won't be safe," he said to her. "Are you listening?" He started to stand up. "She won't be—"

"Sit!" Abraham pushed him back down.

"I'm telling you—" Mitch said.

"You need to calm down." The police chief dragged Hannah out of the room. "Let's give him a few minutes."

As they left, Mitch shouted after them. "She won't be safe! Listen to me! She won't be safe!"

The door shut on his ravings, but Hannah could still see him behind the one-way glass, straining forward, trying to break free, his face packed with fury, frustration, and something else.

Fear.

17

Neesy burst into the vacant police department at a run. "Mitch? Anyone here? Mitch?"

"Neesy!" Julia enveloped her in an embrace that was more terror than affection. It was a strange feeling, holding that little body close. Not unpleasant, but unexpected.

"My goodness, girl. What happened? Is your dad okay?"

"They said he killed someone named Alicia. I keep telling them we don't even know anyone named Alicia!"

The story shook Neesy up almost as much as it did Julia. Mitch Turner a killer? Ridiculous.

"Where is everyone?" Neesy asked.

"Ms. Blunt stuck me here and went down there with the policeman. I don't know where my dad is. And he promised I could see him."

"He never broke a promise to you, did he?"

She shook her head. Lucky girl.

"Well, I'm sure he wouldn't start now. Not if he can help it. Stay here, and I'll see if I can find him."

Julia hesitated, then slouched back onto the bench

against the wall. She wanted to go with Neesy, that was clear. But something else was going on, too. Like she was afraid of finding out more than she wanted to know.

Maybe not so lucky.

Neesy left Julia and went through an inner doorway in the direction the girl had indicated. She hadn't been here for years. Not since her daddy had passed. But the smell came back, familiar as ever. That overly clean, bleachy smell.

Picking up Daddy from the drunk tank never required her to go farther than the outer room, though, so this was new territory. The hallway was empty, and the chief's office was open. She hesitated in the doorway, told herself she probably shouldn't. But she did.

She went straight for the desk, saw a bunch of articles that looked like they'd been printed out from a computer. A picture of Mitch caught her eye.

She gaped. Man alive, he cleaned up nice.

A pang of jealousy went through her. That woman he was escorting in the photo was tall and thin and blond and expensively dressed—everything women these days were supposed to be. No wonder Mitch didn't seem too interested in Neesy. Not if this is what he was used to.

She checked the date. Eleven years ago. A long time to be holding out for someone like that.

Her attention was caught by the other photographs, too. The beautiful, dark-haired victim, the unearthly handsome father of her child. The accusation in the headline.

Shaken, she sank into the chair behind the desk. Was it possible? Could the man she knew—the devoted father, the short-order cook, the working-class hero—really be some kind of fugitive?

You couldn't argue with a picture. And that was Mitch all right. What did they call him? Scion. Scion of the Hanover family, one of the wealthiest in the country.

The beer swirled unhappily in her stomach. He'd played her. Played everyone. Pretending to be one of them, pretending to need a job, a home. He'd forced that child to live like a hobo when she could be living like the princess she was.

But why? Why?

The Mitch in the paper didn't seem like the Mitch she knew. She couldn't imagine that man doing any of the things he was accused of.

And yet... no getting around Julia. His own brother's child. If he'd kidnapped her, couldn't he have done everything else?

All this time, had she been hankering after a killer?

Then again, if a man caught her eye, you could take it to Vegas there was something wrong with him.

"What the hell?"

Neesy jumped. The police chief stood in the doorway, scowling. He marched up to the desk, and she quickly vacated it.

"What are you doing?"

"Nothing," she said. "I was looking for you. For someone. The door was open and—"

"These are official police documents." Abe swept up the papers on the desk. "They're not for public viewing."

"I don't mean to argue, but all I saw were newspaper articles."

"Good." He stuffed the papers in a drawer. "Now, what can I do for you?"

"I'm... I'm Neesy Brown."

"So?"

"Deputy Burgess called me. About...about Mitch?"

It took a moment for him to remember. "Oh, yeah. The little girl."

"What about her?"

"She's going into protective services unless someone is willing to take her."

Neesy blanched. "Me?"

"Wasn't my idea."

She bit her lip. "Can I...can I see him?"

"I have a few questions first."

They were mostly about Mitch—when she'd seen him last and things like that. But he also asked about Shelby Townsend, and she told him about the phone call that morning.

The chief drummed on the desk. Something she'd said—the phone call?—seemed important. "Do you know what she wanted?"

"No."

"And Mitch was at Crick's all day. Same as you."

"Well, yeah. Except, well, there was the fifteen minutes or so when I was at his house."

Abe's brows rose, and she told him about putting up the tree. "It was a surprise for Julia."

"So you and Mitch are friends?"

Her face heated, and silently she cursed her tendency to blush when she got flustered. Truth was, she didn't know what she and Mitch were. And now...well, maybe that was just as well. "I guess."

"You ever hear him talk about the *Sentinel* or Shelby Townsend?"

"What is this with Miz Townsend?"

"Just answer the question."

"Far as I can remember, he's never mentioned her. Well, except there was that one time with the dog. You remember. That dog that got killed in the alley? Shelby came by later that afternoon wanting to talk to Julia about it, but Julia was so upset that we snuck her out of there before Shelby could get hold of her." She explained rapidly, not wanting to dwell on that day, even in her mind. The lovely afternoon and the dinner that night. And after, outside on the curb in the moonlight… "Look, can I see Mitch now?"

He took her into a room with a two-way window. Hannah Blunt was there. Neesy didn't have time to glance at the window to see how things were going, but when Abe opened the door to let her in, the temperature inside was cold enough to freeze an Eskimo.

The minute Mitch saw her, though, his face warmed up. "Thank God," he said, trying to stand.

"Don't you dare," the chief said. "I only just let Miss Hannah back in here."

Mitch sat back down again.

"Can I talk to him alone?" Neesy asked.

"Don't see why," the chief responded. "Either you take the kid or you don't. Either way, I'll have to know."

Neesy didn't bother pointing out there might be other things she wanted to say to Mitch Turner or whatever the hell his name was. But she didn't. And even if they had been left alone, she probably wouldn't have said any of them. He looked awful. Like he'd aged a decade. His face had always been craggy, but now there were new lines around his eyes and mouth.

"Chief here says you want me to look after Julia," Neesy said.

"She'll go into the system if you don't," Mitch said.

"My life isn't exactly child-friendly."

"It would only be temporary," Hannah put in. "Until my brother returns from vacation. I'm sure he and Bitsy would take over then."

"Please." The word was soft and low, and it nearly broke Neesy's heart.

Damn her for a fool.

"You lied to me," Neesy said. "Hell's bells, Mitch, you lied to everyone. Making out like you were just folks when all the time you were anything but. I'll bet you laughed your head off every night thinking about us." *Thinking about me.*

"You know I didn't."

She looked him square in the eye. "Did you kill that woman?"

His gaze on her face didn't waver. "No."

"Did you kidnap her child?"

"What difference does it make?" he replied, and everyone could see it for the dodge it was. "It's not me you're helping; it's Julia. She hasn't done anything."

"Miss Brown, it's late," the chief said. "And my wife is home cooking up a low-fat Christmas Eve feast. Are you going to take the child or not?"

Neesy looked around the room. Everyone was staring at her. What did they think she was—some kind of heartless monster? "Well, if I'm the best choice that poor kid's got, she's in a bad way. Yes, yes, of course I'll take her."

Every muscle in Mitch's body unclenched. "Thank you."

Neesy nodded. "Does she have everything she needs, or should I stop by the carriage house?"

"She'll be okay for tonight."

"Well, then…" Neesy gave him a small, pitying smile, and the chief escorted her out.

When they were alone, Hannah said, "Now that we've got that out of the way, let's talk about you." She straightened, new strength in her voice. Strange how much more comfortable she was talking about life-and-death legalities than about what to do with a kid. "The first step will be a hearing to establish your identity. That should happen within ten days. Once the court is sure you are the Mitchell Hanover from the warrant, there'll be an extradition hearing. Of course, you can concede to the extradition and waive the hearing, which would save everyone—"

"Don't you want to know if I did it?"

"You already said you didn't. Besides, your guilt or innocence is irrelevant."

"Irrelevant? You'll be defending me."

"No, I won't. The crime took place in New York. That's where you'll be tried. I only have to get you through the extradition hearing."

He stared at her, reality getting colder and colder by the minute.

"Then what?"

"Then you'll be shipped to New York and—"

"What about Julia?"

"What about her? You took the child. Do you deny that?"

"How can I?"

"Murder aside, that's kidnapping. How do you think she's going to feel about that?"

He was silent. The twin terrors of discovery robbed him of thought. Not only did exposure put everything he cared about in danger, but it was also the beginning of Julia hating him. And that was worse than anything.

"What's going to happen to her?" he asked quietly.

Hannah pursed her lips, clearly not happy to turn the conversation back to Julia. "CPS will get involved. There'll be a hearing to determine temporary custody. If suitable relatives can be found, she'll most likely be placed with them. I imagine her father—"

"No!" His heart leaped into his throat. "You can't let that happen."

"There isn't much I can—"

"There is. There has to be!" He dove forward—to grab her, shake her, make her understand.

She jerked away. "Calm down."

"I won't ca—"

"You will or I'll leave."

His pulse hammered, his gut twisted, but he needed her. There was a monster loose, and he was coming for Julia.

Mitch closed his eyes, forced his breathing back to normal. Apologized. "It's just..." He searched for an explanation she'd accept. "Julia doesn't know him."

"Whose fault is that?"

The question felt like a punch, and he wanted to punch back. "Mine, okay?" Despite his promise to stay calm, he slammed a fist against the edge of the table. "Mine." He leaned in. "But if you knew what I know, you'd fight with every breath to keep Julia away from her father."

"What do you know?"

He opened his mouth. Closed it again. The truth was there if only someone would believe it.

"What do you know, Mitch?"

"I know my brother. If you want to know who really killed Julia's mother, ask him."

She frowned. "I've seen the reports. There isn't a shred of evidence against him. Whereas you—"

"Were stupid and impulsive—you think I don't know?"

"Well, you won't get very far pointing fingers at your brother. No one saw him in the area, there is no physical evidence against him, and he has no motive."

Mitch knew all this. By heart. But hearing the facts spoken so bluntly still chilled him. "You can't let him have Julia."

"Would you rather her go into the system?"

"Why can't she just stay with Neesy? Or the Blunts?"

"Any blood relative would have a better claim than either of them. And her father would have the best claim of all."

He sunk his head into his hands. He had no choice now. "I have to get out of here." He said it to himself, a vow, a plea, an entreaty to the universe. But Hannah heard him.

"That's not going to happen." She said it gently, with enough pity in her voice for him to know it was true. "You've been running for over a decade. No judge will set bail given the flight risk. Once extradition is set, the demanding state, in this case, New York, will send people down to get you. Two people usually. Detectives. With handcuffs."

"Then I'll just have to get out before they get here."

"Going to tunnel your way out?"

"I don't know!"

"Well"—she rose—"good luck with that."

18

The Ricci was the best art gallery in Manhattan. Even with the tightening of the economy and everyone pretending it was better to eat at home than out, Bernardo Ricci still sold paintings. Especially Dutch Hanover paintings.

Not that Dutch cared about selling. He didn't need the income. But he thrived on the adulation and loved the prestige.

And he did enjoy a party. Bernardo's openings always included Cristal and an elite list that had been winnowed down over the years to a select few. The show was invitation only, and art lovers killed for an invitation.

The thought made Dutch smile. He stood in the center of the gallery, surrounded by a respectful rabble. Words like *fascinating* and *insightful* swirled around his head, but he only pretended to listen to what was, after all, his due.

Instead he looked at *Priscilla,* the painting directly across from him. Bernardo had hung the work on a single white wall, and the woman it enshrined looked out at him humbly. Thankfully. He'd dressed her in rags, set her among an array of decaying cartons against a graffiti-strewn brick wall. And yet she looked regal. Pale, stark, and beautiful. The Princess of the Boxes. No wonder she was grateful.

His gaze caressed the beautiful carmine ruby around her throat. His mouth watered thinking of how he created that color. Nodding absently to whoever was on his left, he sipped his glass of wine. Dutch didn't drink champagne. He didn't like the color. So Bernardo always stocked a Barolo for him, preferably the '96 vintage. Not only did it taste like ambrosia, its burgundy tint was deep and rich.

Excitement buzzed inside him. He excused himself from the circle of worshippers to gaze fondly at another painting. In *Carolyn*, a woman huddled on a rooftop. A TV satellite dish, painted to look like some alien device, shielded her nearly nude form from the wind that was blowing the city's detritus around her. As pale and wan as Priscilla, Carolyn appeared alone and forlorn, and yet there was that same dignity in her face. And the same crimson jewel around her neck.

They were his signature, those pale, stark virgins with their scarlet rubies. It gave him a little shiver to think of them. They brought him millions he didn't need and the adoration he deserved. And no one but him knew their true worth.

Soon there would be another.

The thought stirred him so much he couldn't keep still. He dipped around a corner and behind a door that led to the gallery offices. Leaning against a wall in the dark hallway, he breathed heavily. He'd waited a long time for this one.

He'd already begun planning the painting. The setting

was nearly chosen. All he had to do was wait for the judge to sign the papers, and she'd be his.

It was too delicious.

The door opened suddenly, and the light popped on.

"Oh, Signor Hanover, I did not see you there."

"Just taking a moment to myself, Bernardo."

The curator continued down the hallway to his office. "You will be happy to hear we have already sold one."

Dutch followed him. "Oh?" Feeling languid and happy, he leaned against the jamb of the office door. "And who is the first to go?"

"As I predicted. Signorina Priscilla."

"Ah, yes, she is a beauty."

"You are never sad to see them go."

"Should I be? There are always more to paint. In fact, I am already working on another one."

"Buono, buono." Bernardo made some kind of note to himself and looked up. "I cannot wait to see it." He picked up the bottle of special reserve he kept for Dutch's exclusive use and offered to top off his glass. Then he poured some for himself. "To profit," he said.

Dutch smiled and raised his glass. "To art."

19

Julia didn't say much on the ride over to Neesy's. Then again, neither did Neesy. Just stuff like "Are you hungry?" and when they got to the house, which was so old it looked like it would fall down any minute, "This is the kitchen" and "This is your room."

The house smelled funny. Like old clothes piled in a dusty basement. But "I grew up in this house," Neesy said, so Julia didn't mention the smell.

Neesy made peanut butter sandwiches, and they ate them in a room she called the parlor, where they watched a stupid movie about Rudolph and Santa. Well, Neesy ate them. Julia had trouble getting it down, so she stopped trying. But Neesy didn't say a word about it. When the movie was over, she swept up the paper plates and disappeared into the kitchen. When she came back, she said it was time for bed.

Lying there in the pajamas that were always packed in her bag, Julia felt stranger than she'd ever felt in her life. She'd been in a lot of new places, but Mitch had always been there, and he'd made it feel like home.

She didn't like to cry. Only babies cried. But even though she told herself she wouldn't, tears leaked out anyway. They tracked down her cheek, over her ears, and onto the pillow. She wiped them away, and a few minutes later, more came.

Her dad had looked scary at the police station. His hands were cuffed to a table, and they made her sit on the other side instead of crawl into his lap and hug him like she wanted.

"Go with Neesy," he told her.

"I want to go home."

"I know, but this will have to do for now." He smiled. It wasn't his usual smile. This one looked like he wished he had something to smile about but didn't. "Everything's going to be fine."

She wanted to believe him. She really did.

"I've got your back, Junebug," he told her.

"I've got yours," she said. But she didn't know what that meant anymore.

When she got tired of crying and tired of remembering, she got up. Dully she roamed around the old house, touching and staring. The stove had clunky knobs and a tiny oven. It looked like something from the kitchen in *Old Yeller.* A light hung over a table in the room off the kitchen. The table had a whitish lace thing in the middle. When she flicked up the switch, the light didn't go on.

She missed the carriage house, with its clean wood floors and fireplace. Somehow she'd got it into her head that the deadline Mitch had set would come and go and they'd still be there.

But the year was almost over and now so was everything else.

She was poking around the bathroom when Neesy caught her. The older woman was wearing a purple night-gown that showed a lot of skin, and her red hair was all fluffy and wild. She yawned, which gave Julia a chance to study her. It beat thinking about Mitch, and besides, Neesy was different. Colorful. Nothing like Bitsy or Sara Jean's aunt Hannah. And her boobs were practically popping out.

"Do you know what time it is?" Neesy asked, yawning again.

Julia shrugged. "Nighttime, I guess." She braced for a scolding, because she knew it was the middle of the night and she should be in bed, but Neesy only sighed, gathered her gown around her, and plopped on the toilet.

"Can't sleep?"

Julia shrugged again. She didn't want to talk about why she couldn't sleep. She focused on the shelves across from the toilet that were filled with bottles and jars and tubes. She picked up a jar and unscrewed the cap. It smelled nice. "What is all this stuff?"

Neesy took the bottle from her. "Oh, I don't know. Lotions and things. Here." She scooped some into her palm and then rubbed it over Julia's hands.

"Why do you need so many?"

"Well, let's see. I need some for my hands, and some for my face, and some for the rest of me. And then sometimes I feel like spring is all inside me wanting to bust out, so I use this." She handed Julia a bottle. It smelled like flowers.

"And sometimes it's all dark and gloomy out, and I feel mad at the world. That's when I use this." She opened another bottle. It smelled dark and spicy. "I've got something for every mood just about."

Julia sniffed her hands. "What's this one for?"

"That's what I wear when it's three a.m., and I can't sleep, and I need something soothing." She smiled, and Julia's face got all hot. But she liked the way Neesy's eyes sparkled. Mitch's eyes did that when he was teasing her.

"I'll take some of the mad-at-the-world stuff, please."

Neesy handed her the bottle. "Want to talk about it?"

"No."

"Okay."

Julia was surprised at how fast she agreed. It made her want to talk despite what she said.

"Do you think...do you think he did what they say he did?" she asked.

"I don't know," Neesy said.

"He didn't!"

"I don't know if he killed anyone. I don't think he did, but..."

"But what?"

"But he does have you."

"He's my dad."

"Is he?"

That was the question Julia didn't want to hear, let alone answer. She ran out of the bathroom and raced back to the room she'd been given, slammed the door, and pounced on the bed. Burying her face in the pillow, she fisted her hands, and tried hard to hold back the tears.

But someone came in behind her. Someone soft, who smelled good. She gathered Julia up and held her, and suddenly it was no shame to cry.

20

They found Shelby Townsend's body on Christmas Day in the woods a couple of miles from her home. She was lying faceup, fully clothed, including shoes, and her eyes were missing.

It was a strange, grim sight in an otherwise normal facade. As Abe bent to examine the rest of the body, he heard the sound of retching behind him. Burgess was bent over, and the other deputy, Morris, looked like he was about to join him.

"Keep everyone, especially Lewis, away," he ordered Morris, referring to Shelby's brother-in-law, who had been with the search party. Looked like Burgess needed a distraction, too. "Nate!" Abe snapped. "Get the ME out here. Then set up a perimeter. Move!"

His deputies scurried to carry out his orders, and Abe knelt beside the body. Other than the jagged black holes that had once been eyes, there were no visible wounds, no ligature marks on her neck, no bruises on her legs or arms. She hadn't been roughed up first. And, given the surprising lack of blood, particularly around the sockets, she may even have been spared the horror of being sentient while the murderer worked. But if the extraction didn't kill her, what did?

She did seem unusually pale.

That could be explained by the fact that she was faceup, which meant her body's blood should have settled at her back. But when he lifted one side of her to check, there was no darkening of the skin there.

Had she been killed somewhere else and dumped here? The lack of blood made it seem likely.

Rigor was still present, so she'd been dead for at least thirty-six hours. The ME would give him an exact time, but Lewis said his wife had spoken to Shelby around noon yesterday, so that cut the murder window to within the last twenty hours or so.

Abe sat back on his heels. He already had someone with a clear motive sitting in his jail. Mitch admitted being at Shelby's house around three-thirty. If he did kill her, it was within that window.

But could he have killed her and moved her?

And if he did kill her, how?

The answer came within a few hours of the medical examiner taking control of the body. It came faster than expected, because one of the crucial forensic ingredients was almost entirely missing from the body.

Shelby Townsend had been drained of blood.

21

Because of the holiday, the New York Police Department took its time about sending a detective. Which, as it turned out, worked to Carson County and Abe Marfield's advantage. Once Shelby had been found, the chief was no longer as eager to get rid of Mitchell Turner. Instead, he asked the court to waive extradition and keep Mitch right where he was. That set up a legal fight between the two jurisdictions, which could take months, if not years, to settle. NYPD kept their guys home, and in the meantime, Abe continued building a case against Mitch for Shelby's murder.

First, he made sure Mitch was secure for the long haul. The Crossroads jail wasn't intended for lengthy stays, so on the twenty-sixth, Mitch was transferred to county.

The day began with a snowstorm. Tennessee didn't get a lot of snow, and they weren't prepared for it. The county owned neither snowplows nor snow tires, so Abe decided to wait and see if the weather improved. Channel 3 was predicting storms all day, but by two the sun was out and the snow melting, and it looked like they could make the county seat by four. He got Mitch ready for transport, shackling his hands and feet and putting him in the back of a police van.

Mitch went in docile enough. No use making a fuss because this was going to happen one way or another. But he had to keep constant rein on his thoughts or they would take him down a spiral so deep he didn't know if he'd ever get out again.

He hadn't seen Julia. After they found Shelby Townsend, everything hardened, and his lawyer was the only visitor he was allowed. Hannah told him Julia was fine, but the fear that she was coming to despise him grew. It was hard to believe he'd ever see her again, and if he did, that she would ever look at him the same way.

And yet what he did and why he did it was as important now as it was eleven years ago. Only this time he'd be far away and powerless to prevent the disaster he knew would come.

The chief had said it would take close to three hours to reach county. Hannah had told him what to expect when he did. The shower, the antilice spray. The mouth search.

It was cold, and the roads must have been slick. The driver—Nate Burgess—probably wasn't very familiar with navigating over snow and ice, because the van slid more than once. An hour out of Crossroads, they skidded again, only this time it felt like a runaway sled on ice. Mitch was jerked one way and then another.

"Steer into the skid!" Mitch shouted through the wall of perforated steel that separated him from the driver.

But like most inexperienced snow drivers, Burgess jerked the wheel away from the slide, and the van careened over the ice, spun, hit something, and flew into the air.

That's the last thing Mitch remembered until he came to. He was hanging upside down, imprisoned in his seat belt.

"Burgess!" Mitch called. "Burgess, you all right?"

No answer.

Mitch tried shifting in his seat, let out a cry of pain. Something had happened to his ribs. He waited for the throbbing to pass, then tried again.

It took him forever to maneuver himself out of the belt, and when he finally freed himself, he fell abruptly, smacking his ribs and knocking the life out of him. All that time, Burgess had said nothing.

He managed to get the van door open and slither out. It was already dark, so he knew it was after four, and his hands and legs were still shackled. He hobbled to the front and opened Burgess's door. The deputy's head was a bloody mess, but he had a pulse.

"Hang in there," Mitch said.

With his cuffed hands, it took a frustrating ten minutes to detach the keys from the deputy's belt. When he freed them, they fell to the ground and then he had to fish around for them. He finally got enough purchase on the ring, and using his teeth, unlocked his hands, then bent to free his legs. The position felt like he'd stuck a knife in himself. Breathing like a son of a bitch, he changed his angle and tried again. Finally, he got the shackles off, leaned back against the van, and took in some low, shallow breaths.

Jesus.

Moving was so painful he thought about staying right where he was until the county sent someone to look for them. But after a few seconds' rest, he gritted his teeth, found a flashlight on Burgess's belt, and used it to look around. He had no idea where they were. But he was going to need a lot more than a flashlight to make it through the night. He unbuckled the officer's utility belt and slung it over his shoulder. He wasn't big on firearms, but he took the deputy's anyway. A storage compartment revealed a blanket and an oilskin. He wrapped both around himself.

Another rest, another series of short, shallow breaths. Before he left, he tried the radio but couldn't get it to work, and there was no signal on Burgess's cell. Mitch almost took the phone, but he had a decade-long fear of phones being used to trace his whereabouts. Besides, if the weather improved, the signal might, too, and Burgess might need it. In the end, he left it where the deputy could reach it.

He closed the van door, staring at the man inside.

"Fuck," he said out loud.

Then he shrugged off the slicker and the blanket and draped them over Burgess. Mitch missed the extra heat but figured he'd make it up through exertion.

It would have been easy to follow the road, but that would have made it easy for the cops, too. So he decided to head into the woods. By that time, it was full dark. A cloud wall hid whatever moon there was, and without the flashlight, he wouldn't have been able to see more than a few inches in front of him. But he did have the flashlight as well as a feeling that the universe was with him. Why else engineer his escape? Gingerly, he took a single step and then another, found a rhythm where the pain was at a low throb, and set off.

22

When the weatherman predicted snow, folks in Tennessee acted like the end times were coming. Schools closed, factories let out early. Everyone raced to the Piggly Wiggly, and if you didn't get there early enough, all the milk and bread and bottled water would be gone. Half the time, the snow lasted only a day. The other half, the prediction never came true at all, and everyone ended up making tubs full of corn chowder and bread pudding.

The day they transported Mitch to county, Neesy made the ritual trip to the grocery store; she and Julia were set whatever the weather tried to do.

She'd decided not to tell Julia about the prison transfer. The child had had the god-awfullest Christmas, and Neesy didn't want to add to the mess. Not until she had to. So when the weather broke later in the day, she suggested they make hot chocolate. It would give Julia something to do, and it used up part of that load of milk Neesy had bought.

The knock on the front door came just as she and Julia were gathering what they needed to make the concoction.

They weren't making cocoa, mind you, but the "real" kind, as Julia put it. For that, she said they needed a double boiler. Which meant scouring every cabinet and cubbyhole looking for one.

"I think we're going to have to make our own," Neesy said when they heard the knock.

Julia immediately stopped rattling the cookware and shot a worried glance at Neesy. They'd had a few visitors in the time Julia had stayed there—Hannah Blunt, for one, Loritta, for another—and each time Julia had stilled and tensed until whoever was behind the door showed herself to be harmless.

Neesy flashed the girl an encouraging smile and gave her hand a squeeze. "It's probably just Mrs. Tilden from down the road. She always brings me a fruitcake for Christmas."

"A fruitcake?"

"Oh, my God, child. Don't tell me you've never had fruitcake before? Well, you are in for a treat." Neesy crossed her eyes and stuck a finger in her open mouth in the time-honored gesture used for anything nauseating.

Julia giggled, which was what Neesy was aiming for. She rose. "Go on, see if you can find the darn thing. I'll be right back."

But Mrs. Tilden wasn't at the door. Instead, the most gorgeous man she'd ever seen outside a movie screen stood there. He was tall and lean and wore a black wool overcoat that was the exact color of his hair. And his eyes— bluer than any Neesy had seen, except for one other pair.

"Denise Brown?" he said.

She looked over his shoulder. A long black limo was parked at the curb. "Uh…" For half a second, she thought it was the Prize Patrol coming to give her a million dollars.

"I'm Dutch Hanover."

It took a minute for the name to register. When it did, the realization came with a wallop. Neesy stepped outside and closed the front door, crossing her arms over her chest against the cool December air.

"You're Mitch's brother," she said.

"More importantly, I'm Julia's father," he said smoothly. "I've come for her."

Neesy wasn't sure she'd heard right. "Excuse me? You've come for... what?"

His smile was friendly and patient, but there was determination behind those blue eyes—Julia's blue eyes. "I have a court order." He handed Neesy a document from a leather wallet that looked like it cost half a year's wages. She scanned the official words with its authoritatively scrawled signatures.

"Look"—she handed the paper back to him—"Mitch left Julia with me. He trusted me. I can't just let her take off with a stranger."

"You don't have a choice. And I'm not a stranger. I'm her father."

"You're a stranger to me. And to her."

"Only because she's been kept from me all her life." The steel behind those eyes hardened. "Look, can I come in?" Suddenly his expression changed. He smiled, and that smile was a killer. His face had been handsome before, but now it was a thing of pure beauty. Neesy found herself gaping. In fact, she almost opened the door for him. But at the last minute, she remembered who was inside.

"I...I don't think so. I don't want to upset Julia. Wait here while I make some phone calls."

"There's no need—"

But she'd already stepped into the house and closed the door on him. And locked it.

Her heart was thudding and her mouth dry.

"Was it the fruitcake?" Julia called from the kitchen.

"Someone looking for a handout," Neesy called back to her, praying she'd stay in the kitchen.

"I found the double boiler," Julia said.

"Great. I'll be right there." But she found her purse and her cell phone and took it into the bedroom instead. She closed the door, leaned against the far wall, and punched in Hannah Blunt's number.

The receptionist at the office said Hannah was busy.

"I don't care if she's getting the Nobel Peace Prize," Neesy hissed into the phone, one eye on the closed door and the other peeking through the edge of the blinds at Dutch Hanover, who was sitting in one of the rockers on the front porch, no longer smiling and looking seriously put out. "This is life or death."

When she came on the phone, Hannah was equally annoyed. "What is it?" she barked. "I'm in the middle of a deposition, and—"

"Dutch Hanover is here."

"Who?"

"Dutch Hanover. Mitch's brother? Julia's...you know, her father. He's got a piece of paper with signatures and everything, and it says he can take her away, but Mitch left her with me, and she's making hot chocolate, and I don't know what to do."

"First of all, calm down."

"How the hell am I supposed to do that?"

"Take a breath, for one. Now, start at the beginning."

Neesy breathed, then recounted everything. "How do I even know this paper he's got is genuine?"

"I'm sure Dutch Hanover doesn't need to traffic in false documents. He's her father. Of course he wants her back. The man's been looking for Julia for eleven years."

"What kind of father just shows up like that? He should have called, let me talk to Julia first... something."

"Yes, well, he didn't."

"And I'm just supposed to let her go?"

There was a rush of sound on Hannah's end, like she'd pushed back her chair and was clearing papers off her desk. "Look, I'm coming over. I'll check the documents and make sure everything is in order. Would that help?"

"Can you talk him into leaving her here until she gets used to the idea?"

"I can try. But you'd better start preparing Julia."

Bleakly, Neesy disconnected the call and made her way slowly to the kitchen. Julia had set up the pot and was waiting for the water in the bottom section to heat.

"See?" she said proudly. "It was all the way in the back in the corner cabinet."

"Turn off the stove, sugar. I want to talk to you."

"We can talk while we're having hot chocolate."

"This isn't a hot chocolate kind of talk."

Immediately, Julia sobered. That worried look came over her face again. "What happened? Is it my dad? Is he okay?"

Neesy wanted to sink into the floor. "It's... it's not about Mitch. But it is about your... your dad."

Julia looked confused, and Neesy could hardly blame

her. She was making a hash of this. She dragged a chair out from her mama's ancient dinette table, sat down, and patted her lap. "Set yourself down, girl. Come on, now, so we can get cozy."

"I don't want to get cozy. I want to know what happened."

"Do it for me. I'll feel better with my arms around you."

Julia complied, but her body was stiff against Neesy's. "It's bad, isn't it?"

"Well, I don't know about that. It could be good. It could be real good." She stroked Julia's silky black hair. The similarity in color to the man's on the porch hadn't gone unnoticed. "You know that Mitch...Well, Mitch isn't really your daddy."

Julia pulled away. "He is, too!"

"He's the one who raised you, but the one who made you...well, that's someone else. His name is Dutch. Dutch Hanover. Do you ever think about him?"

Julia was all scrunched up and frowning. One hand drew an invisible picture on the edge of the dinette, and all her energy seemed focused on that. Without looking at Neesy, she gave a reluctant shrug. "Sometimes."

"Well he thinks about you. You're his baby girl, you see, and he's been looking for you a long time. And now he knows where you are, and he wants to meet you. What do you say? That be okay?"

"I don't know. I guess. Someday."

"Well, someday is today because he's right outside."

The child looked up from the table, an alarmed expression on her face. "Now?"

"Isn't that great?" Neesy tried to put as much cheer as

possible into her voice. "He's come all the way from...
well, goodness, I guess from New York. All that way just
to see you."

Julia looked at Neesy like a trapped rabbit. "I don't
want to."

Neesy's heart sank. "Not even for a couple of minutes?"

In answer, Julia ran out of the kitchen, and Neesy heard
the bedroom door slam just as someone knocked on the
front door.

Jesus H. Lord Almighty, that went well.

She unlocked the door and found Hannah Blunt outside with Dutch Hanover. She was already handing back
that leather wallet. Without asking, the lawyer barged in,
and, of course, Dutch followed.

"The papers are in order," Hannah said to Neesy. "I'm
sorry, but Julia will have to go."

Neesy turned to Dutch. It was funny how he changed
the room just by being in it. Made it more glamorous or
more...something. "Maybe you can come back? Give her
a couple of days. Let her get used to the idea."

"I've waited eleven years, Miss Brown."

Neesy glanced toward the hallway where Julia had just
fled. Dutch's gaze followed.

"Is that her room?"

"Yes, but—"

He smiled again, and it was truly mesmerizing. Neesy's
protest dribbled to a stop. "Just give me a few minutes,"
Dutch said. "If she still doesn't want to come with me,
I'll leave."

Neesy looked over at Hannah, who nodded.

"First door on the left," Neesy said.

She watched the man amble down the hallway and

disappear into Julia's bedroom. Listened for the explosion she expected. But none came.

In the silence, Hannah said, "He doesn't look much like Mitch, does he?"

"Mitch wouldn't have come at her like this."

"You don't know what Mitch would have done if he'd been separated from his daughter for years."

But she did. And she also knew it took more than a dazzling smile and a limo to make a good father. It took more than blood, too, if her own father was any indication. It took a special kind of gift. Mitch had the talent for it. Who knew what his brother had?

To her surprise, though, Dutch emerged a few minutes later with Julia in tow. He was even holding her hand. She still had that cornered look in her face, but there was something else there, too. Curiosity, maybe.

Well, it was a beginning.

"We're going for a ride," Julia announced a bit defiantly. "I can come back anytime I want."

Dutch gave her that stunning smile. "Go on—take a look. It's yours for the duration."

Julia went to the door and stared out at the long, shiny car.

Hannah rose. "Well..." She looked around as though searching for a way to prolong the moment and keep Julia there, but finally shot Neesy an apologetic look. "I'm sorry," she murmured. And then to Dutch. "I hope everything works out." She shook hands with him. "Good luck." On her way out, she bent to speak to Julia. "Enjoy your ride."

She left Julia at the door and Neesy alone with Dutch. He was taking out that leather wallet again. "I appreciate your taking care of Julia." He slipped out some bills and handed them to her.

Neesy held up her hands and stepped back. "Please, no need for that. It was my pleasure. And besides, I'm assuming she'll be back in an hour or so."

"Oh, that's up to her. I have high hopes."

"You work some kind of spell over her?"

He laughed. "Not at all. We just...connected." He gazed over at the door as though he hadn't doubted it for a minute, his face suffused with fondness. "I'm very grateful," he said softly. "More than you can know. To have my daughter back after all these years—" He stopped, unable to continue.

The emotion surprised Neesy, though it shouldn't have. No one under the sun would've felt any different. For the first time, she saw what Mitch had done to this man.

"Well," he said, gathering his composure, "I guess we're off." He took her hand, looked into her face with shining eyes. "I really can't thank you enough." He went to the door and put his arm around Julia. His long, lean frame towered over her. "Are you ready?"

"And I can come back whenever I want? You promise?"

"On my honor."

They walked out the door, and the two of them disappeared into the limo.

It was only later, after he left and the force of his beauty and those blue, blue eyes was gone, that she realized he'd left five thousand dollars on the arm of the sofa.

Dutch settled the girl on the seat opposite him so he could watch her, but she squirmed and fidgeted, making it difficult. If he could, he would give her a little piece of quiet. Something that would freeze her altogether so she was awake but could not move and he could stare freely and do what he wanted with her.

But that would be too much temptation, and though the urge had recently been satiated, just seeing those eyes and her hair and everything else that should have been his made his senses reel. He could feel the craving slither inside him, at the back of his throat, in the tips of his fingers. He would have to do something about it soon, but not yet.

Not now.

Now he let the child prattle about the shambles of a house and the dregs of a town he'd rescued her from. She was showing him the highlights of her pathetic little life, and he nodded and smiled at the appropriate points but allowed her words to became a drone inside his head. Something to endure until it stopped.

And it would stop.

He just had to get that drink down her.

Julia had never been inside a limousine before. She was amazed at how big it was. Dutch sat across from her and asked if she wanted a drink, and when she suggested a Coke, he didn't give her a lecture on the evils of sugar like Mitch would've done. He just opened a compartment stocked with bottles and glasses and even ice, and poured her a glass. She and Mitch had had plenty of drinks in the truck, but they usually came out of a cooler. She didn't even know you *could* have a refrigerator right inside your car.

For some reason, the drink made her feel better, like

all the bones in her body had turned into mush. She sat back against the seat and told the driver where to turn and gave Dutch a tour of Crossroads. She showed him the place on the bridge where Mitch had jumped into the Forbidden River for Sara Jean. She took him to the school and to Crick's and past the Blunts' and the carriage house. She told him about Sara Jean being in Florida and how Mitch wouldn't let her go. But then she started feeling like she was being disloyal to Mitch, so she shut up.

And that's when she decided it was time to go back. It was practically dark, anyway, so there was no point in showing off any more sights. Not that there were any more sights to show off. Besides, she was feeling sleepy and could hardly keep her eyes open.

"Why don't you lie down?" Dutch suggested. "When you wake up, you'll be there."

She didn't especially want to, but her head did feel heavy. And Dutch found a pillow behind another door—how many were there inside this car?—and laid it on the long seat. It looked soft and inviting, and before she knew it, she was stretched out on the seat.

"Close your eyes, Julia," Dutch said, and she did. His hand was on her head, stroking her hair. The last thing she heard was his voice crooning softly, "There, now. That's a good girl. A very good girl."

23

As much as possible, Mitch tried to stay parallel to the highway. But the roadbed had been hacked out of woods, and the land quickly rose under his feet. Before he knew it, he was above the pavement and surrounded by thick foliage.

By that time he was sweating from exertion, but his fingers and ears were hunks of ice, so he knew it was cold. Beneath the sweat he shivered, and after fifteen minutes, he felt the cold beneath the sweat.

He just hoped he didn't puncture a lung. He could think of better ways of dying than choking on his own blood.

Ten minutes later, the wind picked up and it started to snow again. It came down so fast the path was quickly covered, and the little he could see ahead was blurred by a whirlwind of flakes. He couldn't believe it. The powers that be had seen fit to let him escape only to have him die in the woods?

He should stop and find shelter, but when he turned the flashlight in a circle, all he made out were trees.

He trudged on. At some point his hand was so cold

it lost its grip on the light. He dove for it, but it crashed and rolled out of reach. He scrabbled after it, following the revolving beam, but before he could grab it, the light disappeared over a ledge Mitch didn't even know was there. He heard it bounce against rock, saw the beam go dark.

Disbelieving, he stared into the blackness. What now? Had anyone else heard the noise?

He stood in rigid silence for the sound of footsteps, but none came. His throat ached from inhaling icy air, his chest throbbed, and he couldn't feel his fingers. Should he go after the light? No telling where it had landed. Who knows where he'd end up if he tried to retrieve it in the pitch dark.

Instead, he stretched his arms ahead and crept forward, tense and desperate and keenly aware of the ledge at his right. Feeling with his feet before taking a step, he checked the air in front of him to make sure it was safe to continue. A few minutes later, he tripped over something small and hard, like a rock, and landed face-first in the snow. He wrenched back the scream that came up his throat so the sound wouldn't betray his position. It took a while to get up. He just wanted to lie there. Rest. Tomorrow he'd find his way. Tomorrow.

But a sharp voice rebuked him. The monster was loose. He would get to Julia if Mitch didn't. And to Neesy, who was sheltering her.

Dread spurred Mitch upward. Drove him forward. What seemed like miles later, his outstretched hands touched something that hadn't been there before. Hard, stonelike. He traced the shape.

A cliff or outcrop of some kind. Curved. Concave.

He shuffled closer, huddled in tight. The curve sheltered him from the wind. Almost instantly he felt warmer.

Shivering, he knelt down, wrapped his arms around his legs, and huddled there. The last thing he did was send up a prayer.

Please let me be alive in the morning.

Mitch didn't make it till morning. The sky was still dark when he opened his eyes. His feet were numb, which he knew was not good, and his whole body creaked as he rose. He gasped and stopped short as a keen pain stabbed into his chest and side. Groaning, he finished standing more slowly, taking in small gulps of air. He wriggled his toes, then gingerly stamped life into them. The snow had stopped and the sky was clear, leaving a gleam of moonlight to see by. Whatever rest he'd had was going to have to last until he could get Julia and find somewhere safe to sleep.

He set off at a lope, moving as fast as his frozen feet and his messed-up ribs would let him. The woods were thick but not high, and if the sky hadn't cleared enough for a little moonlight to shine through, he'd never have been able to negotiate them.

The slog was hard going. He traveled carefully, all too aware that if he accidentally moved in the wrong direction, his ribs screamed in agony. It didn't take more than fifteen minutes for the cold to disappear into a hot sweat of pain and effort.

He didn't know how long he'd been at it when a noise came through the trees. He stopped suddenly, straining to identify it. At first, all he heard was his own short, puffy breaths. Then the noise coalesced into sound.

Men thrashing. Animals huffing.

Fear shot up his chest. They'd found the van with his tracks and set the dogs on him.

Ribs or no ribs, he had to move. He took off, praying he wouldn't puncture a lung. Holding his side as best he could, he hobbled through the trees, only moonlight to guide him.

The freezing air felt good on his hot face, but the faster he went, the faster they seemed to come after him. He could hear shouting now, actual men's voices.

"This way!"

"He's over here!"

Groaning, he picked up the pace, running with what felt like an arrow in his side. The pain ran into his chest and up his arm like fingers squeezing the life out of him. He was breathing hard, and each breath brought a crack of torture.

He never knew what tripped him. A root, a rock, a random, invisible ridge. Whatever it was, he knocked right into it, went flying, and rolled down, down, down, unable to do anything except clench his jaw and hold on to his side.

When the long slide finally ended and his body came to a stop, he wasn't sure he was still alive. He had to get up and leave, but he couldn't manage it. He still heard the echo of the search, but now it was like a distant soundtrack drifting above him from an upper floor.

How long did he have before they figured out what had happened?

Braced against the coming pain, he made himself sit up. Miraculously, neither his legs nor his arms were broken. Taking care, he slowly made it to his knees and then

to his feet. He yelped in pain when he put weight on his
left ankle. Reaching down, he discovered it was already
swollen.

He wanted to scream at the Fates. Instead, he forced
his feet forward. First one step, then another and another.

He'd lost the equipment belt in the fall, but somehow
the deputy's gun was still with him. Terrific. What the
hell was he going to do with that? Other things on that
belt would have been far more useful.

A dozen yards later, the woods thinned, then stopped
altogether, and suddenly he found himself at the edge of
the highway.

Strong lights dotted the road. He limped into the shadows and gazed at the plateau high above. How far had he
fallen? He couldn't believe he hadn't broken his neck. But
at least they were taking their time getting down to him.

Keeping in the shadows as much as possible, he began
hobbling toward Crossroads. At the rate he was going,
he'd never make it before dawn. If he came to a house, he
could steal a car, but after fifteen minutes of walking, his
ankle was killing him and there were no houses in sight.

Suddenly, out of the dark, the horizon bloomed light.

He drew in a breath.

A police car?

In the dark he wouldn't be able to tell until the vehicle
was practically on top of him.

But if it wasn't the cops, he could miss out on his only
chance to get back to town quickly.

Then again, who would be stupid enough to pick him
up? It was the middle of the night. No way would anyone
in their right mind stop for him.

Unless...

His fingers closed around Burgess's weapon. It was hard and cool to the touch.

Mitch shuffled out into the middle of the road. The oncoming car's headlights washed him in light.

He waved his arms, then pointed the gun at the car.

And prayed he wasn't stepping right in front of the police.

Moses Dunn wasn't normally a man who took life lightly. But it was Christmas, and if you were going to have a good time, Christmas is the time to have it. So he'd maybe had a couple more eggnogs than he should have. Stayed a little later at the roadhouse than he should. But hell, Christmas only came once a year.

But when he saw the man in the road waving his arms, he couldn't help thinking it was punishment for that extra drink. Because of course he was seeing things. Then again, no telling what kind of ghosts walked the earth on Christmas. Shepherds. Kings. He slowed, not wanting to take a chance, then saw the gun aimed right at him.

Ghost or human, Moses wasn't going to argue with no gun. He put on the brakes and squealed to a stop. The apparition opened the door and slid right into the passenger seat.

"I need a ride to Crossroads," it said, sounding altogether real.

The ghost—or whatever it was—had him drive all over, and to tell the truth, the night was kind of a blur. What was clear as glass, though, was that gun. Moses didn't want to come face-to-face with it again. So he conveniently forgot to mention the incident to anyone.

. . .

When they got to town, Mitch ordered the driver up the hill to the carriage house, hoping to pick up his truck. But the police had gotten there before him. Two cars were parked outside the house, one with blue lights flashing.

"Keep going," Mitch said in a rush. "No! Don't slow down," he added as his driver started to do just that. Shit. Mitch ducked down in the seat and ordered the driver to go back over the river to the other side of town. Forget the truck; if he had to, he'd steal something. First, get Julia.

If there were police in front of his house, would there be more in front of Neesy's? He'd never been to her home, but he knew the street and house number from a letter Julia had sent via Hannah. He had the driver snake in and around the neighborhoods until they found Pearl Street and cruised by the house.

Sure enough, there was a blue-and-white sitting at the curb.

As much as Mitch didn't want to take another step on his bum ankle, he couldn't exactly pull up and waltz in. So he had the driver drop him off blocks away, but not before tossing away the man's cell phone. If nothing else, that would give him time before he called the police. He wouldn't need much. Just enough to get Julia.

As for transportation, Neesy had a car, didn't she? Not that he was happy about taking it. Not only was it showy and would get him noticed, it was her pride and joy. But he couldn't worry about that now. Someday he'd make it up to her.

When he was alone, he began the trek back. Weaving through backyards and alleys, he slunk in an uneven line toward Pearl Street. The houses were small and cramped and too similar in nature not to have been planned that way. With their old-fashioned porches and clap-board siding, they were too old for Levittown. They had a company-built feel. Railroad or factory. A place for the workers to come home to. Once upon a time, the Hanovers had built whole towns with those kinds of houses. Ones that were just big enough for the laboring classes.

Except there was no railroad anymore. And the factory was gone, too. So the whole area was run-down now. Some of the houses were abandoned with boards nailed over windows. Some, like Neesy's, slogged on, persevering despite the circumstances.

He'd counted down from the corner, so he knew which one it was even from the back. He took his time going into the yard, scouting it out first to make sure no one was stationed back there.

When it seemed clear, he limped between the line of hedge that separated Neesy from her neighbors. Bent low, he crept to the back door. Turned the knob and pushed. It was open.

He took that as a good sign, though no one locked their doors in Crossroads.

Inside, the dark shielded him. He stood still to orient himself, and the smell of limes and lemons wafted over him—the same citrus fragrance that sometimes floated past him at Crick's whenever Neesy whooshed by. It sent him tumbling back to a time when everything worked. When no one knew who he was, and Julia was protected. When he even dared to let himself do something men did every day—be attracted to a woman. Christ, things were fucked up. He'd spent enough time pushing her away; what the hell was he doing drawing her in now?

But he wasn't pulling her anywhere. With luck, she

wouldn't even know he'd been there. Except, of course, that Julia would be gone.

A light over the stove gave off enough glow to tell him he was in the kitchen. From there, he could see out to a dining room. Wide wooden blinds covered the front windows. He was pretty sure they would hide anything from the street, but to make sure, he kept low. From the dining room, he could pretty much make out the rest of the layout, and he headed for a promising hallway.

A night-light plugged into a socket lit the way. He passed a bathroom, so he knew he was on the right path. There were two other rooms, both with closed doors. He figured Neesy would take the one closest to the bathroom, so he skipped that and went for the second room.

Slowly, he opened the door. He couldn't see much from the doorway, so he stole in until he was at the bed.

He stared at it. Knelt down and patted the surface, even, to make sure.

Empty.

Was Julia sleeping with Neesy? If so, that meant he wouldn't be able to get away without waking her. And then what was he supposed to do? Leave her to call the police? His stomach knotted. Maybe there was another floor he didn't know about. One with a bedroom. A basement perhaps. But he could find no trace of stairs leading above or below that floor.

Which left the one door he'd skipped. Stealthily, he retraced his step. Put his hand on the knob. He had a bad feeling about this. A really bad feeling.

24

Neesy woke with a start. Someone was shaking her. Growling at her. It took a moment for her eyes to adjust to the dark and the words to penetrate the fog in her brain.

"Where's Julia?"

Mitch. Mitch was at the edge of her bed. Sleep left her in a rush. "What are you doing here? Abe Marfield has men all over looking—"

"Where the hell is Julia?"

She sat up, brushed the hair back from her face. "How did you get in?"

"No one locks their doors here."

"You should go. They walk around the house every few hours. They also come inside and check."

"I'll get out of here as soon as you tell me where Julia is."

Despite the snarl, he looked like he could fall over and sleep for a month. There was dried blood on his cheek and a cut on his lip. She'd never seen him so messed up. The car wreck was all over the news. Had he been hurt then, or later, during the escape?

"Neesy!" he barked. "For God's sake, what happened to my kid?"

And now there was something else in his face. Dread. What she had to say wasn't going to ease it. "She's gone, Mitch."

"I know she's gone," he said through clenched teeth. "I've been all over the house. What happened? Did the Blunts come back early?"

She shook her head. Didn't know how to tell him. "Far as I know, they're still in Florida."

"You didn't send her down there, did you?"

"It's..." She paused, searching for the best way to say it; then, when she couldn't find one, she just blurted it out. "Mitch, your brother came."

He tensed. "My brother."

"Tall, handsome? Killer blue eyes just like...just like..." She cleared her throat. "Anyway, he had papers, a court order—"

A line of flame leaped into his eyes. "You let him take her? How could you let him take her?"

"I didn't have a choice! I even called Hannah Bl—"

"I trusted you!"

"I'm sorry, Mitch, I—"

"Where did they go?"

"I—"

"Where did they go?" He turned on her, shouting it, shaking her.

"I don't know, Mitch. I don't know!"

They both heard the noise at the same time. Neesy grabbed on to Mitch and their gazes locked. Someone had come inside.

"It's the police," she whispered. Without thinking or

asking, she shoved him into the corner behind the door. "Don't move!" She shuffled out of the bedroom and met the deputy at the foot of the hallway. "Dammit, do you know what time it is?"

"Sorry, ma'am. Just doing my job."

She yawned. "I know." She patted his arm. "I'm just cranky. Coffee? I can have a fresh pot in a jiffy."

"Thanks, but I got some out in the car." She'd managed to make him look embarrassed. "I'll just...take a fast look around."

She stood in the hallway while he made quick work of it. He didn't bother going past her, which was what she was hoping for.

"Sorry to wake you," he said as he let himself out.

"No problem, Officer. I understand."

And he was gone.

Quickly, she returned to the bedroom. Mitch burst into more questions.

"When did Dutch get here? Why wasn't I told? Dammit. Dammit!"

He looked frantic, and she understood completely. She'd felt frantic herself. "He came yesterday. He just... showed up. You were being transferred, and there was no way to reach you. I even had Hannah Blunt check the paperwork, but it was all legal. Julia didn't want to see him, and then she did, and then..."

He grabbed her by the shoulders again. "What? Then what?"

She told him about the ride in the limo. "He promised she could come back whenever she wanted to. And I'm telling you, Mitch, it was a miracle he got her to go with him in the first place. I have no idea how he did it, but I swear, she had no intention of going off with him."

Mitch pressed his lips together in a grim line.

"I thought they'd be back in twenty minutes—thirty tops. A couple of hours later, he called and said she'd changed her mind and wanted to stay longer."

"Did you talk to her?"

Neesy shook her head. "I didn't think to! Hannah said he could take her. He's her father and he has every right—"

"Fuck that."

"I'm sorry, Mitch, really. If it makes you feel any better, he didn't seem so...so bad."

He laughed bitterly. "That's what all the little mice say. Right up until he rips their throats out."

Neesy stepped back. "Come on, Mitch, he wouldn't—"

"I don't know. I don't know what he'll do!" He paced away, and she noticed he was favoring his right leg.

"What happened to your leg?"

"My leg?"

"You're limping."

He waved the question away. "I screwed up my ankle. It's nothing."

"I'll get you a bandage." She started out the door, but he pulled her back.

"Why didn't you tell the cop I was here?"

She looked at his face, searching for an answer there. "I don't know," she said at last, "and that's the God's honest truth."

"Anyone finds out I was here, you tell them I forced you, okay?" He reached over to the nightstand and picked up a gun she hadn't even noticed was there.

Even though it was in his hand, the weapon didn't feel much like a threat. "Do you even know how to use it?"

He shrugged. "Point and shoot. How hard can it be?"

"Not hard at all…if you don't care about hitting what you're aiming at." She peered at him thoughtfully. He probably had a good couple of hours until the police made another round, and he looked like he needed a break. It wasn't her job to provide one, and she didn't know why she wanted to. Something about the despair in Mitch's face churned her own worry about Julia. It wasn't her fault she was gone, and yet it felt like it. Especially with him tramping around her room worrying.

She knew she should run outside and tell that nice deputy that Mitch Turner was in the house. She just couldn't make herself. "Look, I think I can find you some clothes. You can take a shower, even. You've got blood and cuts all over you. I'll make some coffee and get you something for that ankle. But then"—she took a breath—"then you have to go."

"I'll take the clothes and appreciate it, but the rest…" He shook his head. "There is one more thing. I don't like asking, but I need your car."

She'd opened the closet to unearth those clothes—leftovers from her exes. At the mention of her car, she turned and stared at him. "And let's say, for the sake of argument, that I let you have it—which I won't—but let's say I do. Where will you go? You have no idea where Julia is. Are you going to roam around in a 1959 Oldsmobile Super 88? Way to stay underground, boy."

"He's probably taking her home. To New York. I'll start there."

"And how are you going to look for her with your face

plastered all over the TV and your name blasted from every radio?"

"I don't know."

There was silence after that. She didn't have an answer, either, except the one circling inside her that was so crazy she immediately squashed it.

Instead, she ventured common sense. "Maybe you ... I don't know, Mitch, maybe you should give yourself up."

"I can't help her from inside a jail cell!"

"You can't help her if they catch you and kill you, either!"

He glared at her.

"You don't even know if she needs help," Neesy continued. "Granted, I didn't like the way Dutch implied they'd be gone for fifteen minutes and then never came back. And I didn't take to him leaving me all that money, though God knows I could use it, but—"

"He left you money?"

"Five thousand dollars." She rolled her eyes. "A little thank-you for taking care of Julia."

"Christ, he's smooth."

"I can't say I'm not a little worried about her, but he is her father, and he has been looking for her. Why would he hurt her?"

"You don't get it, do you?"

"Explain it to me."

"He'll hurt her because she's important to me."

"Well, aren't we the center of the universe...."

"It's what he does. What he's done all our lives. It's why I learned not to care about anything—school, job, career, and especially women."

She thought about the newspaper articles she'd seen

in the police chief's office—the picture they painted of a rich wastrel. It had never jibed with the Mitch she knew. Was that why? Because that wasn't the real Mitch—just some ghost of him, stripped of passion and enthusiasm, and anything except triviality?

"Is that what happened with Julia's mother?"

His gaze was a sharp, angry jab. "Are you asking me if I killed her?"

"No, Mitch. That's already been asked. And answered. But if she was important to you—"

"She was everything," he said in a fierce gust of emotion. "And, God help me, I should have known better."

25

19 February
Eleven Years Ago

Mitch woke with a groan. The lump beside him in the bed told him he hadn't spent the night alone, though he couldn't remember who he had spent it with. Her face was turned away, so the only clue was the tumble of expertly streaked blond hair. Which, given his proclivities, wasn't much of a clue at all.

Gingerly, he sat up, the blankets falling off his chest and exposing it to the cool morning air. Across the room, the floor-to-ceiling window would have let in the sun if there was any.

Another cold, gray, winter day. Christ, he was sick of them.

As if to echo that thought, the other body on the bed mumbled something and huddled deeper into the covers.

Whatever.

He'd find something to do. He always did.

He stumbled off the bed, picked his way to the bathroom through a trail of empty Taittinger bottles and plastic glasses, a puddle of glimmering cherry satin—which he took to be his companion's dress—his tuxedo jacket, his white shirt, and a pair of lethal gold stilettos. He knew he'd been at some charity thing for the Met—one of his mother's pet causes. The stilettos must have been there, too. He had a vague memory of staggering into the hotel's penthouse suite and the two of them laughing hysterically when whoever it was kicked off her shoes and suddenly shrunk by half a foot.

He did his business in the bathroom and crawled back to bed. She was awake by then, and he still couldn't remember her name, even when she rolled over and smiled seductively and he could see her mascara-smeared eyes.

"Hey, baby," she said.

He pulled her on top of him. "Hey, yourself."

She squirmed, and between the rubbing and the sight of her full breasts and jutting nipples, he had no trouble getting in the mood. But it was too early in the morning for exertion. So he rolled them over, and after paying a couple of seconds' attention to those nipples, he got her head down between his legs and could finally relax while her mouth did all the work.

After he came, he slept a little, then got up for a shower. She must have ordered breakfast, because it was there when he got out. She was sitting at the dining table in some kind of slip thing that showed the red straps of her bra and most of her legs. Objectively, he had to admit she was hot enough—no one could accuse him of bad taste—and she did give good head. So why did he wish she'd hurry up and go?

"I ordered you some eggs." She downed the last of her coffee and started gathering up her clothes.

Perversely, he stopped her. "Where're you going all of a sudden?"

She smiled—she did have a pretty smile—and pushed him away. "I have work to do."

"On Sunday?"

"Yes, on Sunday." She slid into the red satin, and now he remembered eyeing her from across the ballroom.

"Can't you do it here?" He put his arms around her. A minute ago he couldn't wait for her to leave; now he was practically begging her to stay.

She untangled herself. "No, Mitch, I can't. I want to write up the event while it's still fresh in my mind."

Write up the event. Was she a reporter?

"How about tonight, then?"

"Got plans."

"Cancel them."

She laughed and slipped into those killer shoes. "Look, here's my card." She took a sober-looking business card from a tiny, glittery purse and handed it to him. "Call me." She kissed his cheek. "Thanks for breakfast."

And she was gone. He looked down at the card he was still holding. Well, at least he knew her name now.

The rest of the day stretched in front of him. He ran through a list of things he could do, found reasons not to do any of them. The eggs were cold, so he ordered more, and while he was waiting, he called Carlo and had him bring over a pair of slacks and a shirt so he wouldn't have to put the tuxedo back on.

"I'm in the penthouse. Just bring them up."

"Sure, Mr. Mitch."

The eggs and the clothes arrived the same time as the phone rang, so he was waving the food in, telling Carlo to throw the clothes on the back of a chair, and answering the call all at once. Which is why it took him a moment to recognize the voice on the other end. But when he did, he went cold. Not frozen, the way a rabbit does, but a small shiver of recognition as though greeting a past he never thought to hear or speak of again.

"Just a minute," he said curtly into the phone. Then he told the waiter to leave the food on the cart and told Carlo to help himself to coffee.

"Mitch? Are you there? Mitch? God, please don't hang up."

The last time she'd called—he counted back, a year ago?—he'd heard similar desperation in her voice, but he'd refused to talk to her.

"What do you want?" he demanded.

Carlo was sitting at the edge of the couch, his chauffeur's cap parked precariously on one knee. Blank-faced, he was staring straight ahead as though not listening, though there was no way he couldn't hear every word. Mitch could have excused himself or ordered Carlo to wait in the car, but deep in the heart of his black soul, he was glad Carlo would hear him blow her off. He wanted the entire world to hear.

"I'm in trouble, Mitch."

"That's what you said last time."

"I know, and I'm sorry," she said swiftly. "I had no right to call you. But it's worse now."

"Call Dutch, then." He banished the picture of his brother that rose in his head. "You had no trouble calling him when you were sleeping with me."

"I know." Her voice cracked. "I made a mistake. I'm sorry. I'm so sorry."

But ever since Dutch had taken the first girl Mitch had showed any interest in, he'd made it a strict policy not to fight his brother for who or what he wanted. The minute a woman looked his brother's way, Mitch was over her. This one was no exception.

Except she was.

She wasn't educated at Chapin or groomed at Foxcroft, and she didn't attend debutante balls. Her mother's English still wasn't very good, and her father had long since disappeared. The only thing she had going for her was an incredibly fragile beauty and a smile that used to take his breath away when she blessed him with one at the coffee shop where she worked.

But he steeled himself against the memory. "Sorry doesn't cut it, babe."

"He's going to kill me, Mitch. I know he is."

She started crying, and despite his determination, the wall around his chest cracked a little. "Jesus, Alicia, cut out the drama."

"I'm not. I mean it. Oh, God, you have to help me. I don't know who else to ask."

"Okay, calm down. Who's the big bad wolf this time?"

"Dutch." Her voice trembled on the name.

He stilled. "Dutch," was all he managed to get out.

"He wants the baby."

"The—" The rest dried in his throat.

"He can't have her." Beneath the tremble of threatening tears, her voice took on a hard determination. "I don't care if it is his. There's something…something wrong with him. Oh, God, if only I'd—" She stopped, inhaled a huge, shaky breath.

If only she'd what? Hadn't been mesmerized by Dutch's face? By his whispered promises? His legendary charm?

Stronger men had been swayed by his brother. The entire world fell at his feet. Why should a little Latina from the Bronx be any different?

"If I could go away," she was saying in a rush, "somewhere he couldn't find us. All I'd need is a little money. We'd never bother you again. I promise. Just help me this once." She broke down completely now. Great gulping sobs came over the phone.

He swallowed. "All right, all right!" It took her a while to hear him, but when she calmed down enough, he said, "Where are you?"

She told him, and he looked over at Carlo. Still straight-backed and blank-faced.

"What car did you bring?" he asked the driver.

"The Bentley."

He debated. Too showy for the Heights?

"Can you meet me at the Cloisters?" he asked her.

Her breath hitched, but she spoke eagerly. "Sure. Yes. Anywhere."

The Cloisters was a museum on the northern tip of Manhattan, above Washington Heights. Dedicated to the art and architecture of Europe in the Middle Ages, it was composed of covered galleries that were once part of five different French churches.

Its calm, peaceful atmosphere usually eased Mitch's tension, but when he arrived, he barely noticed the arched and columned walkways or the sun glinting off the stained glass.

No one was waiting for him when he got to the West Terrace. He perched on the low stone wall circling the space and stared out at the Hudson. John D. Rockefeller had donated a couple hundred acres on the opposite shore to make sure the views would be spectacular, and they were, especially in spring and summer. Today, the trees were bare and the river looked as gray as the stone. Mitch waited half an hour, then spent another half hour combing the gardens, the chapel, and the art-filled interior.

He was furious by the time he got back to Carlo and the Bentley. The chauffeur opened the door, and Mitch slammed it shut without getting in.

"She wasn't there," he bellowed. "That fucking bitch wasn't there."

"I'm sorry," Carlo said, infuriatingly calm. "Would you like to go home now?"

"I'm going to kill her," Mitch fumed.

"Before or after I take you home?"

He looked at the chauffeur. He'd been working for the family as long as Mitch could remember, yet he didn't seem that old. Maybe it was the way his face never reflected his thoughts, so it remained relatively unlined.

"I'm not going home," Mitch said.

"Where would you like me to take you?"

"I don't know." Mitch paced a little circle beside the car. The thought of getting in made him even more angry. "I'm going to walk," he said suddenly.

"It's a long way back," Carlo said dubiously.

"I'll take a cab if I have to."

Carlo left, and Mitch shoved his hands in his pockets

and marched off. Why was he always the fall guy for his brother's sick games? When he warned Dutch not to go onto the ice pond behind their winter estate, and Dutch went out, anyway, Mitch was the one punished for not watching him. When Dutch stole things—an emerald ring or a silver dessert spoon—they always managed to be found in Mitch's drawer. When Mitch told his mother about the room with Dutch's weird drawings, she accused Mitch of jealousy and selfishness.

Mitch may have been the eldest, but it was the baby she doted on. Maybe it was because he'd been born after their father died, making Dutch the last living link between Iona and her dead husband. Maybe it was because Dutch was too beautiful to be anything but perfect in her eyes. Appearance was everything to her, and heads literally turned when Dutch walked into a room, even as a child. To admit there was something deeply wrong with her baby was something Iona couldn't do. So she denied and hid and kept up the fiction that Dutch was as beautiful inside as he was out. And if that meant paying off the occasional witness to the contrary, or donating an extra-large gift to the school he attended, so be it. By the time Mitch was fifteen, he'd learned not to fight with his brother; Dutch always won.

So why was it that years later he was still caught in his brother's mess?

He almost turned around and called Carlo back. Almost. Then he reminded himself of the panic in Alicia's voice. The way she whispered Dutch's name, as though saying it aloud would call an evil spirit closer. The anger at her duplicity turned to concern, and when he went over their conversation, it turned to worry. He began to walk faster. Harder. He knew where he was going now.

By the time he got to the edge of Washington Heights, he was running. And by the time he reached the address she'd given over the phone, he was breathless and sweaty. He pushed the button to the apartment, and while he waited for the buzz to let him in, he bent over his knees to catch his breath. Just then, someone came out and he slipped in while the door was still open, then ran up the stairs to the sixth floor.

He knocked on the door and got no answer. But it gave way under his fist, so he walked in.

The mewing sound of a cat hit him immediately. He called out, and again, no answer. But the cat kept on, an aching, endless squall.

Jesus, someone should let him out, Mitch thought.

He walked in farther, looking for the animal, and that's when he saw Alicia. There was blood everywhere. Her eyes were gone, her body cut down the center like she'd been dissected. Her initial was carved into her forehead, a jagged, bloody brand.

He sank to his knees. Jesus, sweet Jesus.

Mitch recognized Dutch's handiwork. He'd seen it before. On rabbits and birds and the neighbor's dog. Mitch had thought—had hoped—Dutch had outgrown it. Their mother had not only been sure of it, she'd refused to discuss any other option.

And, of course, there was never proof. Just as Mitch was sure there wouldn't be any now.

He should have taken Alicia's safety seriously. But the minute she'd looked at Dutch, Mitch had left her to live or die at his brother's whim.

Sorry. So sorry.

He staggered into the bathroom, nausea throttling him

in such violent spasms that he almost didn't get there in time. He emptied his stomach and everything else he had. After, his throat was raw and his head pounded. He wiped his mouth with the back of his hand, ran the water in the sink, and rinsed out his mouth. Then he sat on the edge of the tub, shaking in the silence.

Except it wasn't silent. The mewling was all of a sudden on top of him. It increased and turned into screams, and he realized it wasn't a cat making that noise.

He looked around. Ripped open the shower curtain. The tub was empty. Then he noticed the hamper in the corner behind the door. He flipped up the top, and there, lying on a pile of white underwear, was a dark-haired child.

26

When he finished speaking, Mitch was appalled. He'd never told that story to anyone. It was like the secret heart in the center of the hidden temple, and here he was pulling back the curtain and showing it to the world.

No, not the world. Only Neesy.

They were sitting side by side at the edge of the bed. She reached over and squeezed his hand. There were tears in her eyes. The empathy pushed him forward again.

"If Julia hadn't been crying, I would never have found her. It was a sign—or at least I took it as one. She hadn't cried for Dutch or he would have got her. Maybe she'd been asleep when Alicia hid her there. Maybe she'd slept through...through everything Dutch did to her mother. All I know is that she was crying—for me. So I picked her up. The minute I did, she stopped and looked at me. Like she was desperate for help and there I was."

What he didn't say, what he could hardly articulate even in his own mind, was the way that moment had coalesced into a tiny, diamond-hard pinprick of light. And that small radiance had flickered over his detached and aimless life and given it meaning and purpose. This was what he was meant to do. Shield and protect this life at all costs.

"Why didn't you go to the police?" Neesy asked. Her hand was still in his, and it felt warm there.

He shook his head. The question made sense, but only if you lived outside his deformed world where the appearance of things won out over truth. "Would anyone believe me? How could I take that chance? If I lost, I'd be handing her over to Dutch and that would have been obscene."

"So you just walked away with her?"

"I didn't exactly walk. I called Carlo and took the Bentley from him. Traded it for my truck and some cash to get me started."

"Do you really think Dutch will hurt her? She's his daughter."

"Do you want me to wait and find out?"

She didn't reply. What was she thinking? That he'd been a selfish son of a bitch to abandon Alicia? That he'd been stupid and impulsive to take Julia and run? That despite what he knew his whole life, he should have trusted the truth more?

There was a long silence. Why did he even care what she thought?

But he did.

He sat like a prisoner in the dock waiting for some kind of judgment, but all he got was a thank-you.

He hadn't expected that. "For what?"

"Telling me." She looked down where their hands were touching on the bed. Her finger traced a pattern over the back of his where the veins stood up. It sent a shiver of feeling through him. "You have strong hands," she said.

"It takes a strong man to do what you did. Abandon everything for someone else." She looked up. "But it takes an even stronger one to talk about it. So...thank you."

He didn't know what to say to that. She was looking at him with those marvelous green eyes, and for once there was no teasing in them. There was no judgment, either. Only warmth. And kindness.

And he wanted more of it. He wanted to sink into that warmth and surround himself with it. He touched her face, where the glow seemed to shimmer. "Thank you for listening," he said softly. And by listening he meant so much more. For understanding. And believing. "Thank you," he said. And again, and once more, leaning in and meeting her lips.

She accepted him without objection, without murmur, without rebuff. There was only consent as she put her arms around him and drew him down.

She had a lush body, round and full and all soft curves. Her nightgown was gone in an instant, and he luxuriated in the opulent swathe of her skin. Next to her, he was ashamed of his own clothes, still smelling of incarceration and escape. But they, too, were soon gone, and this act, this coming together of two beings that he'd kept only in memory, was suddenly real, the heat and the wet and the welcome he'd almost forgotten.

But his body remembered. And even if he wanted to stop, or if he could have heard the voices in his head telling him to stop, he wouldn't have been able to. The long, luscious pulls that made him shiver and her groan, the pleasure of watching her face tighten in an agony that was bliss, the frenzy, the need, the animal want, until the awful, final explosion of rapture.

And the slow, soft fall. His breath easing. The floating down onto a pillow of after.

And even then, when the blurred edges of the world were gone and all the lines were straight again, and he knew where he was and what lay ahead, even then everything was different.

He opened his arm and drew her to him. "Do you think we're crazy?"

"Yes." Catlike, she settled against him.

"How much time before the next house check?"

"Time enough to do it again."

He laughed. And he hadn't thought he would ever laugh again. "Give me ten."

She reached down and stroked him. "Bet you'll only need five."

27

The arrest of Mitchell Hanover by the Crossroads police gave Roger Carrick the necessary leverage to finally talk Omaha into letting him work the case. Then the second murder introduced the jurisdictional fight, which mucked things up again. It took Roger a week before Omaha, New York, and Tennessee came to an agreement that gave him time and money to take charge.

He left Moline on a cold, gray morning and arrived in Crossroads ten hours later in the middle of a freak snowstorm. Looked like he'd brought the weather with him.

The long drive had given him plenty of time to review the case. There had never been much doubt that Mitchell Hanover was guilty. He'd left hand- and footprints in the blood around the victim's body that matched prints they took from his home. They also matched samples of his vomit to DNA they took from a used tissue. He'd been careless about being seen, and they found witnesses to his entry into the apartment building and his exit with the bloodstained baby. And from what Roger had learned from friends of the family, the rivalry between the two brothers was legendary, so there was clear motive. They never found the murder weapon, but they had enough for an arrest. Especially since both Mitchell and the child were gone.

But Mitchell had a good twelve-hour head start before police discovered the body, and if he had been stupid about the murder, he was clever about the getaway.

He never showed in any of the places he used to frequent. There was no trace of him in Martinique or South Beach, the Hamptons or Aspen. He made no ransom demands and never contacted anyone from the family. He'd taken the Bentley from the family chauffeur and traded it for a pickup and a boatload of cash and... vanished.

Walking to the small Crossroads police station in what looked like a new municipal building, Roger tried to picture the man he'd come to know through his investigations. Mitchell Hanover was a man who had been born into wealth and who had never appeared to resent it, and who now lived a poor, cramped life away from the haunts of the rich and pampered. The murdered newswoman had told Roger that Hanover had been working as a short-order cook in a local diner. Roger had to hand it to him—it was a smart way to disappear. Into the ordinary. Away from the loud and into the quiet.

But that meant nothing to the rest of the Hanovers— the ice-queen mother, Iona, and, of course, the distraught father of the missing child, her younger son, Dutch. They blamed Roger for bungling the case, and the Hanovers neither forgot nor forgave.

Every year, on the anniversary of Alicia Ruiz's death, he received the same reminder. Every year he added one more to the collection in the manila folder. They were postmarked New York, and he suspected they were sent by Dutch Hanover. Which didn't endear him to Roger.

Not that Dutch and his freeze-dried mother had done much to engender sympathy. They couldn't have cared less about the dead woman, Alicia Ruiz. And to hear them talk, you would have thought the missing child was a valuable family heirloom. And they were eager, perhaps too eager, to believe in Mitchell's guilt.

When Mitchell's trail went cold, his brother's fury turned vengeful. Dutch Hanover had the kind of connections that kings and princes have, and he used them. Within a week, Roger found himself in Iowa. And he'd been there ever since.

So he couldn't wait to get his hands on Mitchell. To dump his ass at his brother's feet and watch Dutch Hanover squirm with appreciation. More than that, though, more than seeing Dutch's face when he delivered Mitch, he wanted justice for that poor girl who'd been caught between two sets of powerful jaws and devoured by them both.

A lone deputy whose name tag said MORRIS manned the intake desk inside the Crossroads Police Department. When Roger introduced himself, the deputy looked stricken.

"Oh, geez," he muttered. "Thing is, Chief's not here. Tell you the truth, forgot you were coming. We got us a... a situation."

Roger didn't like the sound of that. "What kind of situation?"

Deputy Morris scratched the side of his face in what appeared to be an effort to stall his answer.

"Deputy?"

"Well, I'm sure the chief would rather tell you himself, but he's not here and..."

Roger raised his brows, waiting.

"Prisoner escaped," Morris finally admitted.

Roger wasn't sure what he was hearing. "The prisoner? You don't mean Mitchell Hanover?"

"Yup, that's the one. Took off last night on the way to county lockup."

"Any sign of him?"

"We sent the dogs out, but none so far. Figured he hitched a ride somewhere. Chief's about to wrap up the search."

Roger stared. He thought of all the wheedling he'd had to do. The favors he'd called in and the plans he'd been making for transfer once he redeemed himself by finally bringing Mitchell Hanover to justice.

And the man had got away?

Again?

He slammed a hand on top of the intake desk. "I want every piece of paper you have on Mr. Hanover. Every file, every document, every note written on a napkin."

"Yessir."

"I want to speak to your chief. Now. And I want an office."

Morris showed him to an empty cubicle and dumped a pile of folders and interview DVDs on the desk. Several things caught Roger's attention. First, from beginning to end, everyone in town said Mitchell Hanover—Turner— was a great father. Second, Roger saw the proof for him- self when he viewed the interview of the child, Julia Turner. Watching that interview brought his own kids back to him. It was Christmas, and he missed them. Did they miss him? Would his own children defend him as robustly as Julia Turner did the man who'd raised her? A smidgen of envy went through him. And, oddly, admiration. Roger had lost his family on the altar of his career. Mitch had lost everything but that child. No wonder he was suspected in the murder of the newswoman, Shelby Townsend. He not only had opportunity, but he also had a whopping big motive.

It was only when he got to cause of death in the ME report that Roger paused. The victim had been exsanguinated, a method that was beyond bizarre. And the one thing Mitch had never been in all this time was bizarre.

28

Julia woke in a giant bed in a tangle of pillows. She tried to sit up, but her head felt all woozy, so she plopped back down again. Where was she? How did she get here?

She'd never been in a bed like this. There were like twenty pillows, and everything crinkled when she moved. The sheets smelled like one of Neesy's lotions, and she might have liked that, but right now, with her head all funny, it made her a little sick.

To get away from the smell, she sat up again, this time more slowly. The rest of the room was as big as the bed. And there were a ton of boxes in one corner, all wrapped with shiny paper like presents.

Gradually, she got out of bed. She was wearing a nightgown—where had that come from? She'd never had anything like it in her life. Mitch always bought her sweats or pj's. This was white and soft with lacy ruffles down the front. She didn't remember putting it on. She didn't remember anything except drinking a Coke with Dutch in the limousine.

Drapes covered the window, and she squeezed between

the opening. Sunlight made her squint, so she shielded her eyes until they adjusted. What she saw made her gasp. Stretched out below her was a wide blue sea, so big she couldn't see the end of it. Was it the ocean? Was she trapped in a tower like Rapunzel?

A knock, and the door opened. Julia stilled, hidden by the drapes.

"Julia?" The voice was low and strange. She heard whoever it was moving around. Another door opened and closed. "Julia, I don't enjoy games. Come out, please." This time the voice was cold enough to make her shudder. "I don't think you'll enjoy the consequences, my dear. I suggest you come out immediately."

The drapes swished open, revealing Dutch.

He was wearing a red robe that was so dark it was almost black. It shimmered as he moved. He was amazingly handsome, and he had her same blue eyes. Was he really her father? Did Mitch really steal her?

She didn't want to think bad things about Mitch.

"Well, I see you're awake." Dutch tugged her out into the center of the room, not caring that he practically pulled her arm off.

She jerked away, rubbing her shoulder. "I see we're not back at Neesy's."

"Very astute of you."

"You promised."

"I think it's time you learned one of life's most important lessons: promises are made to be broken. Now, get dressed. We've got a big day ahead of us."

"I don't want to get dressed. I want to go home."

The eyes that were the same color as hers narrowed. "Do you have a car or an airplane?"

"No."

"Enough money to buy a bus ticket?"

"No."

"Then you can't go home, can you?"

She glared at him. Now who was playing games?

"Where are we?" she said at last.

"Chicago."

She wasn't very good with geography, but she knew that was north of Tennessee. "Chicago isn't on the ocean."

He laughed and waved an arm in the direction of the window. "Let me introduce you to Lake Michigan."

She'd seen lakes before but never one that big. Was he lying again? Mitch never lied to her.

Well, except for the biggest lie of all. That thought widened a little hole inside her.

"Are you...are you really my father?"

He waved the question away as though it wasn't important. "Have you looked in the mirror lately? Genes don't lie."

"But you do."

He slapped her. Right across her face. It stung and brought tears to her eyes. "Enough!" He pushed her toward the boxes in the corner. She stumbled and fell. "Find something suitable to wear." And he swept out of the room.

Julia sat where she fell, too shocked to move. No one had ever hit her before. She stared at the festively wrapped boxes with a sinking certainty: having one dad in jail was nothing to having another one roaming free. Everything was going to be different. Everything. No one was looking out for her now. She'd have to do it for herself.

Aggrieved and guarded, Julia shredded the gift paper and dumped out the stuff in the boxes. Velvet dresses and skirts in super-soft corduroy spilled out, blouses with tiny pearl buttons and stockings (stockings!), all of which she tossed aside, looking for a pair of jeans.

When she couldn't find any, she decided to wear her old ones, but they weren't in their usual place—on the floor by the bed. They weren't in the huge bathroom or in the wide closet or in any of the drawers, either. She looked around the stupid room. Mitch probably—

She caught herself. Mitch wasn't there.

Another knock reminded her who was. "Decent?" Dutch called through the door.

"Uh…just a minute."

She pawed through the clothes, found the least objectionable thing—a plain black wool skirt—and tugged it on. Another pass, looking for the closest thing to a T-shirt she could find, which turned out to be a soft wool sweater in the palest of blues, like the sky on a cloudy day. It was sleeveless and she looked for something to toss over it. But there were no long sleeves anywhere. She shoved her head through the neck of the sweater and opened the door.

Dutch stepped into her room, quickly surveyed the open boxes and tissue paper and clothes on the floor, then came back to her. "Well," he breathed, "don't you look beautiful."

She eyed him resentfully. She still felt the sting of his hand on her skin. And Mitch never called her beautiful. He called her Jules, or Junebug, or kid.

"There weren't any jeans."

"No?" His eyebrows rose, like he was surprised. But she got the feeling he wasn't surprised at all. "Oh, well, you don't need jeans, do you? All of this"—his eyes swept over the clothes—"is so much nicer, don't you think?"

She held out her arms. They were covered in goose bumps. "I looked for a sweater. Couldn't find one."

He smiled, and the expression made her feel like a baby or something. "A woman's arms are beautiful and should never be covered."

She didn't know what to say to that. Before she could even try to figure it out, he sat on the bed.

"I owe you an apology, Julia. I shouldn't have struck you. It was terrible of me, and I hope you can forgive me."

He seemed to expect her to respond, so she said, "I don't know."

"I'd like to start over." His voice was soft, his eyes pleading. "And to prove it, I thought it would be fun to have breakfast up here." He had a dark, melty voice, nothing like Mitch's easygoing tones.

"I guess."

"We could go downstairs if you prefer. The restaurant is decent enough."

She shrugged. "Whatever."

He paused. She could tell he was trying to figure out what she'd like, but she wasn't going to help him.

"Well, we'll have it here, then." He stood, rising like some kind of slow, twisting dancer. "I hope you like bacon."

She *loved* bacon. "It's okay."

Another one of those smiles, like he knew exactly what she was thinking. "Good. I'll let you know when it arrives." He disappeared behind the connecting door.

Breakfast came with a waiter in a tuxedo, who wheeled in a table with a white cloth and a ton of silver plates and covers. Her stomach grumbled. She never knew breakfast could smell so good or look so pretty.

Dutch pulled a chair out for her like she was a princess. He told her the thick, puffy thing piled to the ceiling with raspberries and whipped cream was French toast. Mitch made good French toast, but it was nothing like this. He would have a fit if he knew she was having whipped cream for breakfast.

There were eggs, too, sitting on an English muffin and covered with some kind of lemony sauce—the best Egg McMuffin she'd ever tasted.

And no one rationed the bacon, so she could have all she wanted. She hadn't been going to eat anything, but it smelled good and she was hungry, and before she knew it, she had pretty much stuffed herself.

Suddenly she noticed Dutch's plate was empty. "Aren't you going to have anything?"

"I never eat breakfast."

"My da—Mitch says breakfast is the most important meal of the day."

"Does he, now?" Dutch eyed her coolly over the rim of his coffee cup.

"You don't like him, do you?"

"Not especially. Not after what he did."

"But he's your brother."

"Sad, isn't it?"

She pushed around the leftover whipped cream and the maple syrup. She didn't know what it was, and that made her mad and miserable and confused and—

"Julia." Her full name vibrated low in his throat. She missed someone calling her Jules. But the longing made her feel guilty, too. "Come over here."

She didn't want to. She didn't want to get too close to him. But she looked up into his eyes. They were so blue and so beautiful, and they looked so soft that she hardly believed he'd hurt her earlier. She stood and went around the table to his chair.

"Closer," he said, putting an arm around her and pulling her in. His hand was long and narrow, his arm bony but strong. It encircled her tightly, not at all like Mitch's familiar embrace. "There, now," he crooned, "that's better." She could smell the shaving cream on him, sweet and metallic. He touched her neck, tracing a line down her shoulder and over her arm. He turned her hand to examine the inside of her wrist. It made her feel all quivery inside. "We won't talk about Mitch, will we?"

She didn't want to agree, but she couldn't help herself. "Okay."

"It's just the two of us, now, all right?" He found a spot below her elbow crease where a blue vein showed beneath the skin. He stayed there, softly rubbing over the faint blue line with his thumb, staring at the spot like there was something special about it. "We're going to have a whole new life together. And nothing that happened before will matter. Just you. And me. Forever."

She shivered, and abruptly he released her. A knock on the door startled her, and she jumped, which made him smile. He rose, and the mood shifted, lightened. Without knowing why, she felt...relieved.

He ushered in a big man. He looked like a football player, except he wasn't wearing any pads. Those were his real shoulders under that jacket.

"Julia, this is Gus," Dutch said. "He's going to watch out for you."

"Hey," Gus said in a deep, deep voice.

"I don't need a babysitter," Julia said, though she'd never seen a babysitter that big before. "Besides, what are *you* going to do?" Mitch never needed help watching out for her.

The shadow of a frown touched his face. "I have business to attend to."

"What kind of—"

"Gus?" Dutch cut her off.

"Yes, sir?"

"Is the rest of the team assembled?"

"Yes, sir."

"Good. You have your orders?"

"Yes, sir."

He turned back to Julia. "Get ready," he said. "We have a press conference in fifteen minutes. I want you to smile and look your best. Your grandmother always said nothing could go wrong when you looked your best."

Then he disappeared into his own room, leaving her there with a giant whose shoulders were so big she didn't know how he managed to cross his hands in front of him.

Dutch could barely wait until dark. He'd been angry with himself for losing his temper with the child, but he'd managed to smooth things over. It was his special gift, getting people to do what he wanted—even though what he really wanted was to let the sacred music swirl out of Julia's veins until she gave up everything inside her.

It took great effort to suppress that craving. Soon it would be too strong to resist, and he would have to satisfy it. But not with Julia. Not yet. He had far bigger plans for Julia.

Tonight he'd find some other sweet soul ready for sacrifice. Until then, he'd resist.

The press conference went enormously well, even with that thirst slithering up his throat. But then there were the long hours until he could give in to it, and the constant temptation of the child.

To stave it off he kept to his room, preparing himself for the night's pleasure. Excitement rising, he unlocked his briefcase, flicked the tiny lever, and opened the hidden compartment. Just looking at the hallowed tools took the edge off. The vials of flunitrazepam, the syringe, the collection tubes. He took his kit with him everywhere, for just the reason he'd need it later. To slake that keen hunger.

In the meantime, he ordered Gus to keep Julia in her room. To ensure she'd remain, he dosed her with a little more soda. Ordinarily he might have been appalled at her low-class taste, but her eagerness for the stuff proved useful.

As it was with the runaway he eventually found, once the dark had taken hold of the sky.

Usually he preferred his brides to be fair-haired if possible, and thin. His mother had been slim and blond, and he liked to be reminded of her. While she was alive, he'd kept the two promises he'd made to her: to be discreet and to not hurt his brother. As long as he upheld those vows—more or less—she kept hers: to remain silent and to smooth his way.

When the mess with Julia's mother was discovered, Iona had been furious. He'd apologized, of course. Explained how upset he'd been. But she hadn't been in an understanding mood. He'd had to make it very clear that a lot could happen on a single night in a large mansion. His next adventure might be much closer to home if she didn't stand by him.

And she did. She was, after all, his mother.

But now that she was gone, he was free to use his powers in any way he chose. And sometimes he chose to remember how she harnessed and constrained him. That's when he enjoyed watching the life seep out of those who looked like her.

But this night he needed a substitute for something else. For someone else. So he took his time, a hat pulled low over his head—cruising in a nondescript car he kept for this purpose—until he spotted one with dark hair.

She was shivering and hungry, and when he pulled up to the curb, lowering the window enough for her to hear his offer of a meal and shelter from the cold, she leaped at it. Once inside the car, she told him she was sixteen, but he suspected her age was closer to fourteen.

As promised, he fed her. One of those awful messy sandwiches from McDonald's, a large batch of greasy French fries and an extra-large Coke. While she was busy with the food, he slipped the drug into the drink. Within ten minutes, she was dizzy and within another ten, she was immobile.

Fulfilling the second part of his promise, he took her out of the cold—to an abandoned warehouse he owned. He had these buildings stashed here and there, bought under false names or companies, places he'd purchased and dedicated to his art. This was one of his favorites. Chicago was easy to get to from his base in New York, and the structure was in an ailing industrial part of town with many old and derelict buildings. It had a delivery ramp he could drive right up and inside so he didn't even have to worry about being seen with the girl.

Reverently, he carried her out of the car and onto the table he'd placed there long ago. He hummed as he stripped her, noting her small, budding breasts and the small thatch of hair at her crotch. He ran a hand over her smooth, warm skin. Once the clothes were gone, she seemed quite virginal. Except for the makeup. Lovingly, he wiped that away as well, using remover pads from his kit. Now she was ready.

He stretched out her arms at her side, palms and wrists up so she looked like she was welcoming him. She had told him her name was Stephanie, but he called her Rose. His sweet, winter Rose.

From his kit, he took out all the tools he'd need for the ritual. He found her vein and rubbed it with a finger, prolonging penetration. Then when he could barely stand it, he pierced the skin with the needle.

The sacred liquid flowed out, and a familiar power filled him. He could do anything, be anything. Create, destroy, it was all one, and he was master.

He remembered his first glimpse of Rose, chattering from the cold. Thanks to him, she'd never have to worry about staying warm again. She was free from want and need. From whatever pain had brought her to the streets. Because of him, she would be immortal.

Rose didn't linger. She was a petite thing, and it didn't take long to deplete her. Soon enough, her heart stopped. He waited for the final few drops to leak out of her, then slid out the needle. A bubble of blood rose over the tiny hole in her vein. He licked it clean, lingering over the taste and feel of her.

He kissed her forehead like a father. He kissed her lips like a lover. Then he took out a new scalpel—he always used a new one; it would be disrespectful not to—and carefully cut out her eyes.

29

The day after Mitch showed up at Neesy's, the chief called off the car in front of her house and abandoned the search in the woods. All of which would have been good news, except it meant that state authorities had taken over. They widened the search south to Nashville, west to Memphis, and east to Knoxville, and they called in the FBI. Because he had taken Deputy Burgess's gun, Mitch was considered armed and dangerous, but every news anchor assured the public that he wouldn't be able to leave the state.

Which was why Mitch was still lying low in Neesy's house, and why the idea Neesy had had ever since Mitch had appeared, the one she'd quickly squelched, came roaring back with ferocious drive.

It had started early that morning when Loritta called about Crick's. The old man always shut the place down for two days around Christmas, but this year he decided to stay shut.

"Says he got a cousin in Bowling Green whose oldest is going with a man whose brother is a fry cook looking to move. But he doesn't want to start until the new year, so with Mitch gone..."

No point opening a restaurant if there was no one to cook. Days past, Crick would've done it himself, but he was over eighty now.

"Looks like we're going on vacation," Loritta said. "Hope it don't last too long. My pocketbook can't take it."

Neesy agreed but the thought of time off, right when she needed it, was too much to dismiss. "Might take a ride up to Lubbock and see Trisha and the kids."

"Not me. I'm going to sleep 'til noon, watch TV the rest of the day, and just plain do nothing. But you have fun. Watch out for the weather, now. Travel safe."

Neesy assured her she would and hung up. Then she went to the kitchen to start coffee, all the while her brain screaming, *What the hell was I thinking?*

She was thinking about Julia. And Mitch. And what might happen to the two of them. And how much nicer things might have been for Neesy if someone had been on the lookout all those years of her growing up.

Once the coffee was started, she sat at the dinette table to wait for it to finish. It was the same table she'd eaten every meal at for as long as she could remember. Her mama had gotten it from her mama, who had bought it shiny and new once upon a time. Neesy imagined the gleam of the chrome edge before the gunk of generations had dulled it, the swirls of yellow Formica before the drunken rages had nicked it.

She should have gotten rid of it long ago. She'd heard there were nuts out there who would pay good money for a vintage 1950s kitchen table, cracks and all.

But she'd hung on to it. Like she'd hung on to everything else. At least the pain of the past was familiar. If she sold the table, she'd have to buy a new one. And who knew what they cost these days? Could she afford it? Would anything else look right in this tumbledown kitchen?

She picked at a scratch near the edge. Who said she had to stay here anyway? She had no ties, no one holding her back. Couldn't she come and go as she pleased? She should have left years ago. Right after Mama died and before Daddy got sick. Before Tommy Joe, before Vernon and Ed Pickett. Before the entire line of worthless men paraded in and out of her life.

Was she stuck on another one?

After what Mitch had told her, she didn't think so. He'd done a terrible thing, taking that child, but it was also a good thing. A brave thing.

But she was sleeping with him. And that kind of taints your judgment.

But if Julia had needed Mitch then, she also needed him now. Maybe more than ever. Neesy still couldn't think about that child without an anxious queasiness and a squeeze of guilt. Julia had been her responsibility, and she'd let her walk right out of the house. Neesy hadn't even hugged her good-bye. If anything happened to Julia, Neesy wouldn't be able to live with herself.

She must have drunk ten cups of coffee that morning while she figured things out. The cop at her curb was gone. Crick's was closed.

All the signs were pointing in one direction.

She went into the bedroom where Mitch was holed up. He was wearing the jeans she'd given him and an unbuttoned flannel shirt, studying a map he'd asked for. She stood in the doorway and watched for a few minutes. Just the sight of him made her feel like something was crushing her, creating a languid, liquid heat inside. He had a beautiful body, hard and muscled, and she still hadn't had enough of feeling it beneath her hands.

But more than that, something happened to her when she was around him. Like a new skin was papering over the old, and it was fresh and warm and beautiful.

He looked up, saw her there. The lines in his face softened. "I heard the phone. Everything okay?"

She nodded and glided over to him, slipping her hands beneath the loose shirt. The bruise from his cracked ribs was angry and broad, and she tried to stay away from it. "It was Loritta. Crick's is closed 'til after New Year's."

"I'm sorry." He sounded genuinely regretful, and she nodded, accepting his remorse.

He didn't say anything more, just looked at her for a long time, then ran a hand down her cheek. "I have to go."

She leaned into his palm, her heart and her head battering her. "I know."

They stayed that way for whole minutes, leaning into each other as though neither wanted to admit an end was coming.

"You're going to need help," Neesy said at last.

"I'll manage."

"Every cop in the state is looking for you."

He didn't respond. How could he? It was true.

"Old Man Crick isn't reopening for a while, so I have time. I told Loritta I was going to Lubbock to visit my cousin."

He gazed at her, the implication sinking in. Then he shook his head and stepped away. "No."

"Yes."

"Helping me will get you in trouble."

"I'm not helping you. I'm in Lubbock. Besides, I can always say you forced me, right?" She went after him, taking his face in her hands. "It's not for you. It's for Julia. I've seen you with that girl, and she couldn't ask for a better daddy."

"Even if it's not her real one?"

"I would have traded my real daddy for a fake one like you any day of the week."

They left that afternoon around four when it was dark enough that only the outline of Mitch's body could be seen. To disguise it during the walk from the front door to the car, he'd put one of Neesy's long summer skirts over his jeans and a wool beret over his head. If any of the neighbors were watching, he and Neesy hoped he looked enough like a woman to pass.

Earlier, Neesy had made a fast batch of brownies, put them in a Christmas tin, and ran over to Mrs. Tilden's with them. The older woman was thrilled, and Neesy managed to reveal that she and a girlfriend were off to see her cousin that afternoon.

She spent twenty minutes conspicuously packing the car with bags of empty boxes wrapped to look like Christmas presents and Tupperware containers of what could have been cookies or Chex Mix or both.

Neesy took the first driving shift. To keep up the fiction, she started west out of town, and when they'd gone a good ten miles, she turned around and headed east to New York. From what they could gather from news reports, the authorities were concentrating their search for Mitch on the bigger population centers, so he devised an alternate, back-roads route.

When it was safe, he divested himself of Neesy's clothes, laid back his head, and closed his eyes. It was a long trip to the East Coast, and once they switched drivers, he'd be up most of the night.

A piece of luck came later that evening when they pulled into a gas station. Mitch had dozed off, and when the rhythm of the car stopped, he woke. Neesy wasn't there, and he guessed she'd gone inside to the bathroom. He rubbed the sleep out of his face, hoping she'd come back with coffee.

She came back with a newspaper. The front-page headlines were all about him, but Neesy said, "Page three."

He opened the paper as she drove off. There, on the right side of the page, was a picture of Dutch smiling that Tom Cruise smile, his arm around Julia.

"They're in Chicago," Neesy said.

Inset into the column was also a picture of Mitch. He looked hulky and dangerous in the police photo, but he only skimmed over it, devouring the picture of Julia instead. Did she look all right? He couldn't tell. Something was...wrong. Or different. It took him a minute to figure it out.

She was wearing a dress.

His heart clenched in a stab of pain. He was changing her. He was already changing her.

"Look at the hotel," she said. He peered at the marquee over the entrance, which was partially obscured. "I think it says...Is that Drake? Do you know a Drake hotel in Chicago?"

He smiled grimly. "Oh, yeah, I know it." For four

generations, the Drake had been the Hanover place of preference—the same grand hotel that ambassadors, presidents, and movie stars chose. His grandparents had dined there with Jimmy Stewart, his mother with Margaret Thatcher. He could show her where Marilyn Monroe and Joe DiMaggio carved their initials in the Cape Cod Room or the suite where Princess Diana stayed when she'd visited. The Drake was expert at handling high-profile guests. If Dutch wanted to avoid the press, he could have.

Mitch stared down at the picture. A mistake? Or deliberate?

"What are you thinking?" Neesy said.

But he was done thinking. "Pull over. I'll drive."

They switched places, and after a few minutes studying the map, he pressed down on the gas with his good foot. But even speeding, it would take most of the night to get there, and he had to stick to the legal limit—he didn't want to give the police any excuse to find him.

The junction north turned out to be nearly half an hour away. It was maddening to turn around again. Every minute lost seemed a notch in whatever protection the publicity had given Julia, and it infuriated him to know he'd already wasted so many.

They found the right road and got a couple of hours in before the flurries started. By ten they were in a solid snowstorm, and by midnight it had turned into a full-fledged blizzard. The only way to know they were on the road was the faint blur of the preceding taillights. Traffic slowed and finally stopped. Edgy and anxious, Mitch drummed on the wheel.

The snow was coming down so heavily, neither of them

saw the state trooper until he was practically upon them. Mitch froze, and Neesy grabbed his arm.

"What should we do?"

For half a second, Mitch thought about bolting, blizzard or no blizzard. But it was already too late. The cop was at their car.

Mitch's whole body tightened, ready to be dragged out, arrested, cuffed, sent where he could never get to Julia again. Next to him, Neesy's breathing was a nervous wheeze of apprehension. Rigid with tension, he gripped the door console and at the last second remembered the gun hidden under the seat.

He rolled down the window.

30

A ferocious blast of wind and chill roared over them through the opening.

The cop leaned in. "We're clearing the highway," he shouted over the storm. "Got lights set up. You're only a few miles from Felton. Follow the markers and they'll take you to a Red Cross shelter, where you can stay 'til the storm passes." Then the trooper was gone, disappearing into the white swirl and onto the next car.

Mitch sat there with the wind and snow exploding into the car. Then the realization of what had happened washed over him, and with a shaky hand, he rolled up the window.

He laid his head back against the seat, a little light-headed. When he looked over at Neesy, she was swatting away tears. They caught each other's gaze, and without warning, they burst out laughing.

And then she was crying, and suddenly he was holding her, swamped by guilt.

"I'm sorry," he soothed. "It's all right. We're all right." He smelled that sharp lemony fragrance in her hair, and it sent him back to that hot, searing kiss outside the carriage house and how he had ended it. As he looked back, his attempt to keep her at arm's length seemed doomed, and the reality of her here, in his arms, inevitable.

He held her tight. "Want me to take you home?" He'd do it, too, much as he needed to keep heading north.

"No. I'm all right. I'm fine." She pushed him away. Hiccupped. "Oh, geez, I'm not usually such a crybaby."

Mitch wasn't sure he believed her, but he didn't have time to probe. The cars had started moving, and it was all he could do to stay on the road from marker to marker.

It took them half an hour to get off the highway and into the Felton High School gym. They rumbled into the crowded parking area, barely able to make out the school's backlit sign. No one was directing traffic or parking, so once they got there, it was every man for himself. The chaos gave Mitch his first chance to separate from the highway caravan.

He eased around cars that were stuck, at odd angles, or waiting for a place to pull in. Eventually he found a rear entrance and drove back into the storm.

"What are you doing?" Neesy asked.

"We can't go to the Red Cross. They might want IDs."

The whirl of thick snow in the headlight beam was the only clear sight as they left Felton behind. Neither one of them breathed. Mitch leaned forward over the wheel, squinting into the night.

How much longer could they go on like this? He had a good half tank of gas left. If he stuck to the road, could they outrun the storm?

Easier said than done. There were no taillights to follow, and visibility was down to nil.

"Maybe we should pull over until the snow stops," Neesy said.

"We could freeze here," Mitch told her. He slowed to less than a crawl, making his best estimate on the curve of the road.

"We could also drive off a cliff," Neesy said.

They remained on solid ground, but twenty minutes later the street turned bumpy and rutted; despite his best efforts, he'd turned off the pavement and onto something else. A gravel drive? A dirt track?

He stopped. Turned to Neesy. "Got a flashlight?"

She opened the glove compartment and handed him one. "But it's probably dead. I never remember to change the batteries."

He switched it on. Dim light flooded the car.

"Wow," she said. "Lucky us."

"Stay here. I'm going to see if I can figure out where we are."

He didn't have much of a coat; Neesy had given him a sweater and a denim jacket. He pulled up the collar, opened the door, and set his shoulder into the wind.

He'd forgotten about his ankle, though; so the first time he put his weight on it, pain shot through him. But he set off at a slow limp, trying not to let Neesy see. In a minute the snow covered the sight of the car, so she wouldn't have been able to see him in any case.

Because of the blur, he was reluctant to go far. The flashlight was a cheap one without a lot of power, so even with it he couldn't see much ahead. He counted his steps, took ten, then flashed to his left. Nothing in that direction. He turned the light to the right. Made out a darker shape in the darkness.

Scuttling back the ten steps, he used his hands as well as the light to find the waiting car. He cracked the door. "There's something over there. A house, a barn. I want to check it out. Take the wheel and follow me."

She slid over the console, and he placed himself in the headlight spill. Using the flashlight, he picked his way to the building.

The wind was a literal pain, burning across his unprotected face, but it was lucky in one thing: it blew the snow so the drifts were growing only on one side. It would have been impossible to get through otherwise.

When they were close enough, he saw two shapes. The closer one was a barn, or the remnants of one. Shielding his face with his arm, he ran the flashlight over the structure. The roof was intact, more or less, and most of two sides still stood. He signaled Neesy to take the car in.

Once there, it was still colder than it had any right to be. Between the open end and the gaps in the other walls, there was small hindrance to the wind.

He left Neesy to check out the other building, and returned as quickly as he could. "It's a house," he told her. "Abandoned, looks like. But it's got four walls and a roof. It'll be warmer there than here."

"Think it's okay to leave the car?"

"Any car thieves out in this weather would have to be as crazy as us."

He took her hand and led her through the snow. His feet were soaked by now; hers soon would be. The doors were all locked, so he had to break a window to get in. He used the butt of the flashlight to knock out the glass, then hoisted himself through and unlocked the front door to let in Neesy.

Once inside, she shuddered and held herself, hands working up and down her arms while she looked around. "Well at least it has walls."

The window Mitch had broken was letting frigid air into the room. "Come on, let's see what else it has."

They found a kitchen and two small bedrooms in the back, all empty of furniture. Ancient wallpaper peeled away from the walls, showing layers of even older paper beneath.

He led her to a back room as empty as the rest. "We can stay here. It seems as warm as any."

He was already attacking cobwebs in a corner of the room. Outside, the wind battered the room's single window, which was thick with the fog of snow. At this rate, it seemed as if it would never stop.

Neesy wondered what it would be like to be trapped here forever. Her own little island of want and can't have. Because there was still a world beyond the storm. A world that could explode with a twitch. That moment in the car when the trooper was at their window—what would she have done if he'd been there for less innocuous reasons?

Like the aftermath of a punch, the risk she was taking rolled over her. She was in the middle of nowhere, stranded in a blizzard, alone with a fugitive—a situation anyone in their right mind would never have gotten into in the first place. Why had she jumped in feetfirst?

With a wince of pain he tried to conceal, Mitch slid into the corner and waved her over. He got between her and the wall, and she settled with her back to his chest and his arms wrapped around her.

"Okay?" he asked.

"Uh-huh."

She was more than okay. The hard width of his chest shielded her. His mouth was at her ear, his breath a warm, soft wind. She entwined her fingers with his and found the answer to her question.

Getting onto the floor and into this position had hurt him. But he did it, anyway, to keep her warm. Just like he'd gone after Boyd Collier in the alley—and taken a cuff to the face for it. This was a man who cared more about the right thing than the easy one.

She snuggled against him, and her doubts faded.

It was nice leaning against him. No furious blaze, but a slow, steady burn.

"What took us so long?" she murmured.

"What do you mean?"

"You know what I mean."

He took a beat before answering. "Isn't it obvious? I'm carrying the kind of weight that would crush anyone who gets too close. The last woman I was interested in ended up dead."

"Julia's mother."

The conclusion was so obvious he didn't bother corroborating it. "You believe me," he said instead. It wasn't a question; it was confirmation of what he already knew. But there was an edge to his voice. As though he didn't understand why or was suspicious of her conviction.

"Why shouldn't I believe you? That's what you told me, and I choose to trust you. Can't say it was especially smart because trusting usually means I end up getting screwed—and not only in the usual way. But I think... I think I'm through being smart. I think I'm through being a lot of things." She turned around in his embrace so she could see his face. "I'm cold, Mitch. I don't mean just here, in this run-down place. I've been cold all my life. I can't explain it, but there's something about you. About me when I'm with you. I suddenly feel like there's real warmth in the world, and if I can only grab it, I'll never be cold again."

She stopped. Had she said too much? Her face heated, and she tried to look away. But his hand was there, lifting her chin. There was heat in his eyes and a strange, crooked tilt to his mouth.

And that was all she saw, because those lips covered hers and blocked out everything else.

Mitch wrapped her tight against him. Once again, he couldn't get enough. Not of her mouth, her tongue, her hair, her smell. But it wasn't just her body. It was the awe she inspired in him. It was cold where he lived, too. Cold and lonely without a single soul to confide in. He'd lied his way through the last ten years, kept the world and everyone in it on the other side of a thick wall. And now this woman was blowing it up—bricks, barbed wire, everything—exposing something he didn't even think he had anymore. His true self.

It filled him with a raw kind of tenderness. With a boundless, freeing gratitude. And, as she opened her body to accept his, with the first green shoots of a barely recognizable love.

Neesy was no sloe-eyed virgin. She'd been ridden hard and put up wet a time or two. But when Mitch touched her, it was like none of that had happened. Like this was her first time.

And maybe it was.

She'd had sex before—even with him—but had never made love.

The chill, the hard floor, none of it mattered. She shucked her jacket, unbuttoned her shirt, let him see her, feel her. She straddled his lap, and his tongue lapped her nipple through the violet lace of her bra. Then her bra was gone, his face burrowed between her breasts, sucking her soul through her skin.

She reached beneath his collar, rubbing her hands over his shoulders. He had such fine, muscular shoulders.

Then he pulled her arms away, took her head in his hands, and kissed her slow and deep. She was giddy with the feel of him, and when they got their jeans off and he was inside her, she felt bound to him in a way she'd never been bound before. Not because she needed him, but because he needed her. Like a pledge, a vow to always be there. To believe in him the way he believed in her.

His hands on her hips, he guided her to an achingly sweet climax. And when it was over and they'd calmed down, she nestled against him and didn't care that they were in a bare, ugly room.

She understood why they called it falling in love. She felt like she'd plunged off the tallest building in the world, jumped off the highest mountain, dropped off the sharp edge of the earth. And if she never hit bottom, if she stayed in the clouds, floating and flying forever, it was fine with her.

Mitch closed his eyes, and despite the fact that he had every cop in the neighborhood after him, that he was charged with murder and kidnapping, that if he wasn't careful, he'd be caught and his child, the one person in the world he'd given his life to protect, was at risk, despite the fact that he'd foolishly, selfishly, lovingly added another vulnerable soul to his load, he slept.

31

It took Roger a couple of days to trace information on exsanguination, and he wasn't surprised to learn there had been others. He mapped out the similarities between each murder on a whiteboard in the office loaned to him by the Crossroads PD.

All the victims were women, mostly marginal, like runaways and prostitutes, which made Shelby Townsend an exception. The eyes were always removed postmortem, and none showed signs of a struggle. There was never much mess at the crime scenes, which meant the murderer was neat and precise and had removed the blood.

It was a strange crime, requiring very specific phlebotomy equipment—vacutainer needles, pipettes, tubes or bags, refrigeration of some kind. Which meant it couldn't be done randomly. They'd found no evidence of this kind of equipment in Mitchell Hanover's home or truck. On the other hand, no two murders were committed in the same place, which led to the conclusion that the perpetrator moved around a lot. Which Hanover did. In fact, according to the interview with the minor child, Julia, he had even been in some of the same places they'd found victims. She wasn't able to confirm times and dates, so they couldn't know for sure if he'd been there at the time of the murder, but it meant he was still high on the suspect list.

Roger went over all of this with Abe Marfield, who stared at the whiteboard with its pertinent information. "What would anyone want with all that blood?"

"Maybe a good cocktail," Roger said.

"You think someone is trying to convince us that vampires really do exist?"

"I doubt it, but whatever the murderer wants it for, it's probably ritualistic. Plenty of religions and cultures see blood as sacred."

"You're thinking, what, voodoo, Santeria?"

"Possibly. What do you know about it?"

"I ran into some Santeria practices in Chicago. They use blood sacrifice, but strictly animal, not human."

"Anything can be corrupted within a twisted mind."

"Well, I've been in Crossroads for five years now, and there's never been even a hint of Afro-Caribbean religion here. We don't have the population. Same thing for voodoo."

"And Hanover?"

Abe shrugged. "Nothing showed up in the house search. But I still like him for this. At least he has a motive."

"Still, if Shelby Townsend had her nose in this story, maybe she was working on other stories that made enemies."

Abe looked at him closely. "Let me get this straight. You're thinking Mitch isn't responsible?"

"Not ready to make conclusions."

"And the other? The murder and kidnapping?"

"Oh, that's open-and-shut. We just have to find him."

"Well, take a look at this." Abe handed over a copy of a newspaper article. A picture of Julia with her father, Dutch. "They're in Chicago. From everything I know about Mitch and his kid, that's where he'll be."

32

Mitch wanted to fly straight to the Drake, but Neesy wasn't happy about going there looking like a hillbilly. Over his protests, she stopped at a JCPenney on the outskirts of the city. There, she bought herself a black suit, which Mitch assumed was supposed to look dull and professional and looked anything but on her ample curves.

She also bought him a coat and a pair of gloves, along with a change of clothes. By the time she was satisfied, he was wired and tense, and could hardly wait the twenty minutes it would take to get to the Drake.

They worked out a rough plan, and he parked in a public garage a few blocks from the hotel. Before Neesy left, she pulled a bag from their impromptu shopping spree and took out a handful of curls. "Everyone notices red hair." She tugged the wig on, checked for stray hairs in the mirror, and turned to him. The color, a medium brown, did what the suit couldn't: it took the luster out of her face. She looked almost...ordinary. A pair of drugstore glasses he hadn't even known she'd purchased completed the transformation. "Okay?"

"Not how I'd like to remember you."

She laughed. "Hopefully no one will remember me."

He took her face in his hands, sober now. "Be careful."

"Like a mouse with a hawk circling overhead."

He kissed her, and when it was over, she still had her eyes closed. "Besides," she said with a shivery sigh, "I need more of that."

He stroked her cheek. God, she was soft. "Gotta come back for it."

Neesy felt Mitch's gaze on her back all the way out the parking garage. She didn't mind the heat of it. Not the part that was a man looking at a woman. What she felt was the responsibility of it. Like she was a soldier sent to the front with a message that could win the war.

She couldn't mess up. Mitch was depending on her.

Not to mention Julia.

This was Neesy's chance to repair what she'd done when she let Dutch take Julia. And in some ways it was a chance to repair what she could of her own childhood. To make sure that no other little girl was mistreated by those who were supposed to love her.

She spotted the hotel a block away. A gold canopy over the entrance was trimmed with lights. Had it been dark enough, it would have glittered and shone. Even in the day, the entrance had a gilded glamour, with its bellhops and uniformed doormen. A discreet flag with THE DRAKE printed in medieval script fluttered in the knife-cold air.

A doorman with gold braid on his sleeves held the door open for her. "Welcome to the Drake," he said, as though she were the Queen of England.

The impression of royalty persisted inside. She didn't

want to appear out of place, so she raised her chin, not gaping but trying to take it all in nevertheless.

From the doorway, she went through a foyer and up a set of stairs lined in sapphire and gold. She was almost afraid to step on it.

She nearly gasped when she got to the lobby. A huge floral arrangement was the first thing she saw. Above it, a heavy crystal chandelier made the one over her mama's dining room table seem sad and shriveled, even if it had worked. Under her feet, the thick, crimson carpet was topped in places with blue rugs that absorbed most sound. The place was as hushed as a library.

Another set of stairs took her to the front desk. She squeezed her fingers around the chain handle of her purse, hoping the clerk couldn't spot a fake Chanel from behind the desk.

"Can I help you?" she asked.

Neesy braced herself and smiled. "A hotel phone?"

He directed her to an alcove with a small brocaded ottoman and a phone with nothing but a receiver. She and Mitch had rehearsed what to say, but she had no idea how Dutch would respond and whether he would buy her story that she missed Julia and wanted to make sure she was okay. Neesy took a breath, picked up the receiver, and, when the operator came on, asked for Dutch Hanover.

The two minutes she waited seemed like two hours. Hotel guests walked by, all of them appearing to have a greater right to be there than she did. Were they staring at her? Would anyone be able to identify her? Self-conscious, she turned her back to face the alcove instead of the expansive room. Where in the great salt mountains was that operator?

When the hotel operator finally got back to her, she spoke in an impersonal voice. "Mr. Hanover is no longer a guest at the hotel."

Her heart stopped. "He's...he's checked out?"

"Yes, ma'am. I do see he left a message for anyone who inquires about him."

She swallowed. "A message? What kind of message?"

"I'm sorry. You'll have to check with the concierge for that."

She disconnected, mystified and a little uncomfortable. Was the message for Mitch? The operator had said "whoever inquired." Who had Dutch expected?

She found the concierge desk, and the man behind it was as solicitous as a diplomat. "Mr. Hanover? Yes, of course." He removed an envelope from a drawer and handed it to her.

Neesy examined it. No address, no note. Just clean and white. "And Mr. Hanover said to give this to whoever asked for him?"

"Those were my instructions," the concierge said.

"And has anyone asked?"

He smiled. "Only you."

She opened her mouth to say something, then didn't know what to say.

"Is something wrong? I hope the message isn't of an upsetting nature. I had the impression he wanted to change a meeting time."

She waved his concern away with a little laugh. "Oh, no, it's nothing at all. In fact, he said he might have to do that. So...thank you." She held up the envelope and took a couple of steps back. "Thank you."

"Careful!"

She started, turning just in time to miss nicking a settee. "Sorry," she said to the piece of furniture, then thanked the concierge again.

"You're quite welcome."

She turned and fled.

33

Mitch was pacing in front of the car when Neesy returned.

"Let's get out of here." She slid into the passenger seat, and Mitch climbed in behind the wheel.

"Why? What happened? Where's Julia?"

"I have no idea. They'd already checked out."

Mitch slammed his door shut. He'd been waiting like a man set for execution or deliverance, and the last thing he wanted to hear was that neither option was viable.

Neesy pulled off the wig and shook out her hair. "Sorry."

"Screw that," Mitch said. "Not your fault."

"I hope not. But that place—the hotel—gave me the creeps."

Instantly Mitch was on alert. "Did something happen?"

"Kind of." She told him about the message. "It was like he knew you'd be coming."

"What's in the envelope?"

She grimaced. "I was afraid to look." She fished in her purse and handed it to him.

He examined it, shot her a thin smile. "Too slim to be a bomb." Then again, there were bombs that exploded only inside a man's soul. The contents of the envelope could be nothing, a message intended for someone else. But he knew his brother, and inconsequential wasn't his style. He went in for pitch-perfect cruelty, the subtle kind that only the victim understood. So he braced himself for a picture of his Junebug, hurt, pleading, even, God forbid, worse. His mouth dry, he slid open the envelope.

And pulled out...a brochure.

Across the top it read DISNEY WORLD RESORTS.

"What the...," Neesy said. "Why would he leave that for anyone?"

The words blurred in front of him, relief and fear vying for control. "Well, at least we know where we're going next."

"But...if he expects you to follow him, he's setting up a trap."

"Maybe."

"Maybe? If you go there, every cop in the world will be waiting."

"So will Julia."

"Yes, but—"

"Look, I'm going." He gripped the wheel, not wanting to say the rest. The buts multiplied in his head: it was too soon; they'd just started; he needed her, wanted her. But he'd known all along what would happen in the end. "You've been...great," he said slowly. "I appreciate it. But maybe it's time to say good-bye to your cousin."

She stared at him. "I've been great? You *appreciate* it?"

"What I'm trying to say is—"

"I know what you're trying to say. *Get lost.*"

"No! That's not what I meant."

"Hey, I've heard 'wham bam thank you, ma'am' a million times. I just didn't think I'd hear it from you."

He reached for her hand, and she jerked it away.

"Neesy..."

Her jaw tightened, and her eyes filled. She snapped her head away so he couldn't see.

For half a second, he looked out the windshield into the depths of the garage. The concrete was crude, heavy, and unadorned, protected by its hard functionality.

And there was Neesy. Soft, pretty, and easily hurt.

He placed a hand lightly on her shoulder. When she didn't jerk away, he slid the hand around her back and pulled her toward him. She came stiffly, but she came.

"It's enough," he said gently. "You've done enough. I couldn't bear it if anything happened to you, too. Go home. Go back to Crick's. Live your life."

"I'm not sure I want to live that life anymore."

"Living with me is no life at all."

"Julia did okay."

"She's a kid. It's all she knows."

Neesy was silent, but his shoulder was damp where her head rested.

"How would I even get there?" she said at last.

"I can put you on a bus."

"I leave in the coolest car in the world and come home by bus? How am I supposed to explain that?"

"Just say you totaled your car."

"Uh-huh. And what do I do about a new one?"

"I'll figure something out. What do you want? Porsche? Cadillac?"

"Oh, yeah, me and a Caddy. I can just see everyone in Crossroads taking that in stride."

"So I'll buy you a used Honda. Whatever. Just—" He untangled himself to turn over the engine, but she grabbed the key out of the ignition before he could.

"What are you doing?"

"I told you. I'm taking you to the bus station."

"The hell you are. I've had my ass frozen off in a blizzard and my face cut up by the wind in this damn city. If Florida doesn't sound good to you, it does to me. Sun and sand—"

"—and cops and killers."

"Yeah, well...nothing's perfect."

"You're nuts; you know that?"

"Exactly why I need a vacation." She gave him a hard-nosed look. There were tearstains on her face, but her green eyes glittered as sharp as cut emeralds. "Get out. I'm driving."

34

The Chicago division of the FBI was housed in the glass-and-steel federal building. Roger Carrick had been there a couple of times for meetings, so he knew where it was. He presented his credentials, but the special agent in charge who headed up the division wasn't keen on helping.

"We've already contacted New York. You're out of Iowa. What's your interest?"

Roger explained, and after a few moments' consideration, the SAC said, "You're too late. Hanover's already gone. But I'll let you talk to Dyson. He kept the lookout."

Dyson proved to be a trim, competent-looking man who had moved on to other things. "We were on the hotel from the minute Hanover got here with his kid," Dyson told him. "The brother never showed, and Hanover and the girl have already left."

"What about the staff? Did you talk to anyone at the hotel?"

"No reason to. Nothing happened."

"Did Dutch say where he was going?"

The other agent shook his head. "Truth is, we tried to

keep a low profile. He has his own security, and he wasn't all that cooperative. Seems he wasn't happy with the way the original investigation had been handled." He eyed Roger, who eyed him right back. "Anyway, he's gone and so are we."

"Mind if I talk to some of the hotel staff?"

"Knock yourself out."

Roger didn't expect to find much but was surprised when he spoke to one of the concierges, who told him about an envelope Dutch had left.

"Who picked it up?"

"A woman," the concierge said. "In a suit. Light brown hair. She seemed a little, well, surprised. Like she wasn't expecting it, though she said she was."

"Do you know what was in the envelope?"

"I got the impression from both Mr. Hanover and the woman that it was something about a meeting."

"And when was this?"

"Yesterday. I'd say around two."

"And you're sure Mr. Hanover didn't say where he was going?"

"Only that he had a car take them to the airport. I believe he had a jet waiting for him."

Roger thanked the man and got the number for the airport. If Dutch flew out of Chicago, he would have had to file a flight plan. Easy enough to find out where. And if he could find out, so could Mitch.

Roger scowled, waiting for Flight Service Station to pick up. If he were Dutch, the last thing he'd do would be to pose for the press. And if he posed for the press, he'd never divulge his whereabouts. It was like daring Mitch to find them.

But maybe that was the point. Dutch wanted his brother caught. What better way than to hold out as bait the child Mitch had raised?

It took FSS a few minutes to look up the flight plan and for Roger to check out a map of Florida. What was in Orlando that would take Dutch there so soon after winning back his long-lost daughter?

On his way to the airport, he called Abe Marfield in Crossroads. "Can you think of any reason why Dutch Hanover would take Julia to Florida, specifically Orlando?"

"Not for sure," Abe said, "but that's where the Blunts are."

"The Blunts?"

"Tommy, Bitsy, and their daughter, Sara Jean. You remember—it was in the reports. Mitch fished Sara Jean out of the river after she fell in. They gave Mitch a place to stay, and I understand the two girls became friends. Maybe Dutch is taking Julia there to spend time with Sara Jean."

Roger stared out the car window as the city passed around him. "You have kids, don't you, Chief?"

"Three boys, all on their own now. Good kids."

"I've got one of each—a boy and a girl. Also good kids. Would you say Julia is a good kid?"

"Don't know her well, but from what I and others observed, I'd say yes."

"And if something happened to your boys, say, one of them was kidnapped and you didn't see him for years, and then suddenly—*poof*—he's returned to you, what's the first thing you'd do?"

"Don't know exactly," he said slowly. "Take him home, I guess. Make him feel safe."

"You wouldn't go gallivanting to a ritzy Chicago hotel and have your picture taken by the press?"

"The hotel, maybe. If I could afford it. The press? No, sir. Not on your life."

"And what about Disney World? That be your choice?"

"No, I'd want to get him out of the public eye and someplace secure and safe, where he could settle in and get to know us again."

"So why is Dutch Hanover dragging that child all over the country?"

"The rich are different."

"Not that different."

"What are you thinking? That he wants everyone to know where he is?"

"Not everyone."

"Just Mitch."

"For all the trouble he's gone to over the years, Dutch Hanover seems more concerned about luring in his brother than he is about the welfare of the child he's been so desperate to find."

There was a small silence. Roger hadn't seen Dutch Hanover since the original murder investigation, but he was a hard man to forget. When he had walked into New York's FBI headquarters, a hush had fallen over the office. For a second or two, everyone stopped what they were doing to stare. He was rich, he was famous, and he was ridiculously good-looking. He could smile even the toughest agents into submission. A couple of them made excuses to talk to him and murmur expressions of sympathy. One, a woman with years of experience, even asked if he'd like coffee. She never asked Roger if he wanted coffee. In fact, if he had asked her to get him a cup, she'd have told him to fuck off in a lot more colorful language.

Dutch had been gracious about the fawning, almost as though he expected it. Even during this awful crisis, he'd joke with the small crowd that inevitably gathered around him, charming them all.

But something else lay beneath Dutch's graceful exterior. Roger never figured it out, and his concerns were chalked up to the tension over his lack of progress on the case. And then, of course, he was shipped off to Iowa.

But whatever had bothered him back then was resurfacing now. Maybe it was just that he didn't trust good-looking people. The rest of us tripped over ourselves to do things for them, and they never had to fight for anything. Life was too easy for them.

"Did you ever see the crime scene photos of Alicia Ruiz's murder?" Roger asked Abe.

"NYPD faxed them over to me."

"What do you make of that letter carved into her forehead?"

"The *A*? It's her name—Alicia."

"You ever read *The Scarlet Letter*?"

"In high school, way back in the day. Don't think I paid much attention, though. What's it got to do with the Ruiz case?"

"*A* for 'Adultery.' That's the scarlet letter in the book. And that's what closed the case on Mitch. That *A*. It gave substance to the motive. Jealousy."

"Well, he's cooled down since then. Never flew off the handle here, didn't romance the ladies, never seemed the possessive type. Except when it came to Julia."

"Exactly."

"Always comes down to the kid, doesn't it?"

They were pulling into the airport drive. "How's that deputy of yours?"

"Nate? Oh, he's hanging in there. Just took him off the critical list."

"Glad to hear it." They disconnected, and Roger got out of the car.

Something about that *A* had always bothered him.

He just didn't know what.

35

Julia stared at the computer screen. She'd never had her own computer before, and ever since her dad—since Dutch—bought it for her, she'd been scouring the Net for news of Mitch...and other things.

Dutch thought she was playing some stupid Barbie dress-up game, and she'd decided to let him go on thinking that. He hadn't hit her again, and though neither of them ever mentioned it, she hadn't forgotten.

She hadn't forgotten anything—including what Dutch or Mitch had done. Not the guards posted everywhere or the questions she'd answered over and over. Like she was some expert on her dad.

Her uncle.

Her...whatever.

Besides, the Mitch she knew would never have run away. Not without her.

Turns out, ha-ha, she didn't know Mitch at all, did she? So how was she supposed to know where he was? She was just a kid. No one told her anything.

Which is why the computer was so cool.

Outside her room, someone fumbled with the door-knob. Quickly, she pulled up the Barbie screen.

"Julia! Open this door!" Dutch.

"Just a minute." Her cover in place, she didn't need more time but pretended anyway. Then she waited for the explosion. One, two...

"Not in a minute. Right now!"

Right on time.

She opened the door. "Okay, okay."

Dutch's handsome face was mad and glaring. "I told you not to lock this door."

She put on that goody-goody expression he liked so much. "A lady needs her privacy," she reminded him.

He smoothed out the frown as if it had never been there, and she sprawled back in her chair in front of the laptop. He always did that—went from boiling to...well, to nothing. To a scary kind of calm, like those wax people in a museum where Mitch had once taken her. When Mitch was mad at her, it took him, like, a whole day to get over it. Sometimes she even had to crawl. But Dutch... Sometimes she annoyed him just to see if he could stay mad. He never did.

Did that make him better than Mitch, or just strange?

As if to prove it one way or the other, he braced himself on her shoulders, leaned over, and kissed her cheek. He did that a lot—touching her, kissing her. She couldn't decide if it gave her the creeps or if she just wasn't used to it. Mitch chucked her on the chin and ruffled her hair, but he wasn't big on all the kissy-kissy stuff.

"Your friend is in the lobby," Dutch said.

She jumped up, as much to get away from him as from excitement. Ever since he'd told her Sara Jean was coming,

Julia had been planning. Now that she was here, a shot of nerves suddenly rocked Julia.

"Shall I have her come up?" Dutch asked.

Why did he always talk like he walked out of a cardboard-doll book?

"Or I could just meet her down there." They'd been in Florida how many days now and the closest she'd been to Disney World was the hotel suite.

"I think it would be better if you played up here. I wouldn't want you to get lost."

Right. Like the lobby was some kind of jungle. Truth was, he didn't want her to go anywhere unless he was with her. Or one of the guards. She should be used to that by now—Mitch was always watching out for her. But Mitch did things with her. Fun things. Dutch's idea of fun was room service.

How was she ever going to get away from him if he didn't take his eyes off her?

"You could come, too," she said hopefully.

"Far easier for her to come up, don't you think?"

She shrugged, not hiding her disappointment. "Sure. Okay."

"Don't pout, Julia. It's so unattractive in a woman."

She flounced over to one of the couches and threw herself down. He was always criticizing her.

"Shall I cancel the visit?" Dutch's voice was so quiet and calm it gave her the shudders. She'd learned not to ignore that tone. She sat up and took the frown off her face, and he smiled that movie-star smile.

"That's better."

While she waited for Sara Jean, she thought about what she'd learned from her Net search. Mitch had escaped and there were cops all over looking for him. A "manhunt," one article called it. She pictured slathering dogs and nasty men with shotguns.

She knew she shouldn't, but she hoped they never found him.

A knock on the door had her jumping up again. She ran to answer it, but Dutch got there first.

"Mr. Hanover?" Bitsy Blunt's voice cut through the initial awkwardness. "My goodness, here we are."

Dutch stepped aside, and Sara Jean and her parents came in.

"Well, look at you," Bitsy said to Julia. She held out her arms for a hug. Julia was enveloped, and for the first time in an eternity, she felt normal. Then Bitsy let her go, holding her at arm's length. "Don't you look a picture," she said. "Doesn't she look sweet, Tommy?"

Behind her mother's back, Sara Jean rolled her eyes.

"You look very pretty," Tommy Blunt said.

"It's the dress," Julia said, feeling awkward enough in the fluffy thing.

"I think a woman should look like a woman," Dutch said, waving them in.

The adults sat on the couch, and Julia dragged Sara Jean into her bedroom.

Sara Jean looked the same—tall and lanky with her red hair all scraggled up. Lucky her, she was wearing shorts and flip-flops. She sat on the bed and examined the room. "This is amazing."

Julia straddled the chair by the desk so she was facing the bed. "It's okay."

"We're not even staying at the park."

"Well, I haven't been inside it yet."

Her jaw dropped open. "How come?"

Julia shrugged.

"What's he like?" Sara Jean asked, gesturing with her head toward the door and the adults behind it.

"Weird."

"My mom says he's rich."

"He's still weird."

"She says you'll be rich, too."

"I guess." Right now, she hardly had pocket money. Well, except for what she'd lifted, bit by bit, from Dutch's wallet, and that she needed for later. "He has this thing about arms." She held out her bare arms in the sleeveless dress. "Fine in the summer, but it was freezing in Chicago."

Sara Jean wriggled onto her stomach, her feet on the pillows, her head propped in her hands. "What about Mitch?"

She frowned. "What about him?"

"Do you miss him?"

She'd rather be fried in Crisco than admit it. Especially since he'd left her here. "Why should I?"

"Think he did it? My mom says he must have because he has you."

"Well, at least he's not weird."

"Killing someone and stealing their baby—that's pretty weird."

Julia couldn't argue that, and Sara Jean didn't seem to expect her to.

"Your dad," she said. "I mean your real one—he is *gorgeous*. My mom says you have his eyes. She says you'll be gorgeous, too. She *never* says that about me."

"Mitch did. He likes red hair."

"How do you know?"

"He told me. He was talking about Neesy, but I could tell he meant it in general."

"He was cool."

Julia didn't want to agree, but she didn't want to disagree, either, so she said nothing. They drifted into silence. Sara Jean began waving her feet in the air. Her flip-flops came off. One slipped onto the floor. "What do you want to do?" she said at last.

Julia had it all planned out, but now that the moment had come, she was scared. "I don't know," she said, prolonging the moment. "Want to play poker?"

"Poker? That's gambling. I'm not supposed to. Daddy says it's Satan's tool."

"Since when do you listen to your father? Besides, we don't believe in Satan."

"I don't know how to play."

"Me neither. But I downloaded a game that teaches it."

Sara Jean crawled off the bed and wandered over to the desk. "When did you get the computer?"

"Dutch bought it when we got here."

"See? Rich, rich, rich. We could still trade places, you know. I wouldn't mind being rich."

"You'd have to wear sleeveless dresses all the time."

"I guess it would be okay if I could shop in New York. That is where you're going to live?"

"I don't know. Dutch doesn't talk about it."

"You haven't asked?"

"Don't have to." Julia's heart began thumping. She lowered her voice. "I'm running away."

Sara Jean's eyes widened. "You are not."

"Yes, I am. I've got it all planned out, too." She turned around to face the computer. Sara Jean dragged a chair over.

"Check this out. Did you know there's a whole, like, city underneath Disney World? It's how Mickey and Goofy get where they're supposed to be." She showed Sara Jean what she'd found.

"But how do you get down there?" Sara Jean asked.

"There's doors all over the place. Look." She clicked over to a video on YouTube.

As the piece played, Sara Jean gasped, covered her mouth, and then started giggling.

"Shhh," Julia said, and started giggling herself.

They both checked to make sure the door was closed.

"I can't believe you," Sara Jean whispered.

"It'll work. You just sneak off, open one door, and disappear into the tunnels. When you pop up, it's miles away and no one knows where."

"But what about food and stuff?"

"What good is having a rich father if you don't have money?"

Sara Jean's eyes widened. "He gives you money? How much?"

"I wouldn't say he gives it to me. At least, not on purpose."

"You stole it?"

"You said it'll all be mine someday. I'm just getting a head start."

"Oh, my God, you are so bad. You know they'll find you." She covered her ears. "Don't tell me any more. They'll torture me and I'm not good with pain. I'll tell everything."

"Not if you come, too."

"What?"

Julia yanked Sara Jean's hands down. "Not if you come, too." She repeated it a little slower and more emphatically.

Their gazes locked.

"I couldn't," Sara Jean said.

"Yes, you could."

She covered her mouth again. Then, scrunching her shoulders and leaning close to Julia, she said, "I could, couldn't I?"

"But first we have to get into the park."

It took Julia two days to get Dutch to agree to a trip to Disney World. First he refused because he didn't want to go.

"I'd rather be dead," was how he put it.

"Oh, you don't have to go," Julia assured him. "I can go with Sara Jean and her parents."

But he managed to find reasons against that idea, too.

He gave in only after Bitsy made two phone calls and implied it was strange that he'd taken Julia to Disney World but she'd hardly seen anything except the hotel.

In between asking herself and having Bitsy call and ask, Julia collected gear. She'd managed to hang on to her backpack, even though Dutch had tried several times to get rid of it. But she didn't feel safe without it. All her life she and Mitch had a just-in-case bag packed and ready to go. It felt wrong not to have one now.

By the time permission for the trip was given and arrangements made, she'd hoarded bottles of water and PowerBars from the vending machines and had stuffed in a change of clothes. After more Net research, she added a

book of matches she found on the floor. You never knew
when you might need to start a fire. One of the packages
Dutch had bought her came wrapped in pretty red string,
and she kept it for emergencies. A knife from room service
would be handy, and because it might rain, she collected
every plastic bag she could find. Along with the shampoo
and soap the hotel provided was a small sewing kit, and
she took that, too. In case she or Sara Jean got hurt and
needed stitching. And at the last minute, she threw in the
lotion, too. It smelled nice and reminded her of Neesy.
She and Sara Jean IM'd like crazy; Sara Jean was going to
bring crackers she'd been stealing from restaurants.

Julia had snuck out one afternoon and stashed the
backpack with the bellhop. First thing that morning, she'd
called down to have it ready at the desk.

She had one more thing to do. She'd never asked Dutch
for money, but the morning of her escape, she asked him
for fifty dollars.

"For food and stuff at the park," she said.

"You won't need money."

"But—" She shut up. He was staring at her with that
cold look in his eyes. He didn't like it when she argued
with him, and she'd learned not to defy that blank chill.

A knock on the door interrupted. "The Blunts are in
the lobby," Gus said when Dutch opened it.

"All right. She's ready. Enjoy your day, Julia. And don't
wander away from Gus."

Julia opened her mouth in alarm. "He's not coming
with us, is he?"

"Gus is to be with you at all times," Dutch said sternly.
"Unless I have your word you won't wander off, I can't
let you go."

So not fair! "What about my money?"

"As I said, you won't need any. Gus will take care of it. She can have anything she wants," Dutch said to Gus.

"Of course," the big man said.

Julia glowered. "Well, come on," she said to Gus.

"Yes, ma'am," the big man said, and out of the corner of her eye, she saw him wink at her.

That made her scowl even harder.

36

While Neesy slept, Mitch pored over the map in the darkened hotel room. Disney World covered forty-seven square miles, which was twice as big as Manhattan; no way could he check it all out. Not without a couple of centuries. Or an army.

Or a crystal ball.

He crumpled the thing in frustration and stomped away.

The hotel room felt like a prison. It had been a bad idea to come. They should have stayed in some other place. Someplace where he'd be less likely to run into Dutch or his goons.

But that meant he'd also be less likely to run into Julia.

He looked at the bed, where Neesy was out cold. They'd driven nonstop from Chicago, and Neesy was so exhausted she'd dropped like a stone. He'd pulled the drapes and turned off the lights—all except the one by the desk—but she'd already been asleep and didn't notice.

He couldn't join her. Every time he closed his eyes, he

dreamed of the dog split down the middle. Or the holes where Shelby Townsend's eyes should be. Or Julia.

So he studied the map they'd picked up at a gas station and tried not to let panic overtake him.

Think. He had to think.

If Julia could choose, what part of the park would she go to?

He smoothed out the crumpled paper and stared at it again. There were six major areas, four theme parks and two water parks. But anyone coming to the park for the first time would probably start at the heart.

The Magic Kingdom.

But Julia had long outgrown Mickey Mouse. Would Cinderella's castle draw her? Besides, how long had Julia been here, and how many times had she visited the park already?

Just then, his gaze caught something he hadn't seen before.

Tom Sawyer Island.

A pinprick of hope. Julia had just read Tom Sawyer. She'd named that poor dog Huck, hadn't she?

If there was a Tom Sawyer Island, maybe there was an Old Yeller Farm, or a King Solomon's Mines. He found a pad of hotel paper on the desk and started a list.

An hour later, Neesy was still sleeping. A faint flush showed beneath her milky skin, and her hair tumbled around her face and the pillow. He sat at the edge of the bed and brushed a few strands back from her cheek. She murmured but didn't wake.

He wished he could give her this peace forever. He wished he could give it to himself. Just looking at her soothed him. A hot rush of feeling ran from his belly up to his throat. He was crazy to have brought her. Crazy and selfish. But, Christ, he was glad she was here. Glad and grateful and falling deeper and deeper into her light-filled world. He hardly remembered what it was like to be alone, and he didn't want to.

He kissed her cheek, and her eyes fluttered open. "Hey, you," she mumbled. She gave him a sleepy smile, put her arms around his neck, and pulled him down for a real kiss.

The heat expanded inside him, expanded and melted into every nerve.

But it would have to wait. "Go back to sleep."

She smiled sleepily. "Come to bed." She rolled over, taking his hand with her.

He spooned around her, whispering in her ear, "I will. Gonna check out the park for a while first."

"Mmm," was all he got in response.

Just in case she didn't remember their little conversation, he left a note, then slipped out of the room.

He bypassed the elevator, taking the stairs instead. Few people used the stairs, so he was less likely to run into anyone, especially Dutch.

It had been four days since he'd messed up his ribs and his ankle, not nearly time enough to heal. But when his foot was taped tight like it was now, he could put a little weight on it. And his ribs...Well, they only hurt when he laughed....Gingerly, he hobbled down the steps and was almost at the lobby floor when voices and footsteps echoed up from below.

"Never work with kids and dogs. Whoever said that got it right." Radio static, and the footsteps stopped. Another voice said, "We're at the south staircase. Over."

Mitch ducked through the door leading to the lobby. Leaving it open a crack, he glimpsed two men dressed like any other tourist in slacks and golf shirts. Except the walkie-talkies and the earpieces gave them away.

Hotel security or Dutch's employees?

He snatched a ball cap off a table outside the gift shop and a pair of sunglasses off a rack. He hadn't shaved in days, but he didn't trust any of that to mask his identity. Head down, he stuck to the perimeter.

Was that bellhop staring at him?

Behind the registration desk—was the clerk watching him?

Mitch's pulse rose and his mouth dried. The journey from the stairs to the door seemed the work of months instead of minutes. When he finally burst into the sun, he was shaking.

He wiped sweat from his forehead and found the stop for shuttles into the park. Merging with a large group, he shuffled onto a bus with them.

The Magic Kingdom was a hallucinatory experience. Snow White had a crowd of giggling, pointing children around her. A scowling Queen of Spades and a blond-haired Alice were having their picture taken with a pair of lanky twins in jeans. Strollers and diaper bags were everywhere. And people. All shapes, all ages. Wherever he looked, Mitch saw a blur of happy color. Nothing could be more ordinary and safe than right here in the middle of this fantasy.

Yet it left him bereft. Nauseous almost. His girl, his child, the person he'd pledged his life to protect, was in more danger here than anywhere. Because no one would believe anything bad could happen in a place like this. It was designed to make dreams come true, not nightmares.

Heading west to Frontierland, he dodged a couple speaking Japanese, a wide stroller for two, and a father with a squiggly toddler in his arms. Continually scanning the crowd, Mitch looked in vain for that one familiar face.

Then he came to a wooden footbridge over a river.

There on the other side was Julia.

Mitch stopped. Everything he'd been through—every fear, every ache—it all disappeared in a rush of joy. Even from the back he'd know that dark head anywhere. She was here; she was safe. He'd found her.

Ignoring his bum ankle and bruised ribs, he ran the rest of the way. Breathless with relief, he spun her around into a hug that nearly squeezed the life out of her.

She screamed. It wasn't a happy scream, either.

Suddenly, a heavy hand yanked him away. "What the hell are you doing?" An angry man pushed him back.

Julia rushed to the man, who put his arm around her.

Except it wasn't Julia. It was some other dark-haired little girl.

Mitch blinked as if that would clear his vision and miraculously morph the strange child into his own. "Sorry. I...I'm looking for my daughter. I thought..." He backed away. "Mistake. Sorry." Mitch left quickly. Jesus, God, he couldn't make an error like that again.

In less than a heartbeat, he'd gone from delight to distress, and the swift spill of emotion shook him to his core.

He bought a bottle of water from a vendor and swallowed most of it in one gulp. The rest he splashed on his face and neck to cool down even further. Then he continued with more caution, trying not to stop breathing every time he saw a dark-haired girl around Julia's age.

The only way to get to Tom Sawyer Island was by raft, and a long line waited to board. Mitch examined the crowd from a distance, but no one familiar stood in the long, snaking queue. What he did notice were a lot of folks scurrying around it with walkie-talkies. They dressed as tourists, but they looked—from posture and expression—more like security.

Something was up.

Was it him? Were they looking for him?

He bolted around a corner and behind some trees, but there was no privacy in a theme park. An elderly man was also taking advantage of the shade. When he saw Mitch, he stepped out of the shadow and nodded toward the commotion. "You notice that, too?"

"What's going on?" Mitch asked.

"Don't know exactly. They've been running around like that for half an hour now. You ask me, someone's lost."

Or found? How could they have known half an hour ago not only that he would be in the park, but where?

A pair of kids dragged the older man away, and Mitch took a few steps out of his hiding place to squint toward the huddled group. They seemed to be waiting for something.

A speedboat came around a bend in the river and headed toward the raft dock.

Not something. Someone.

Dutch.

Mitch jerked back under the trees. The urge to stay out of his brother's sight was as instinctive as breathing and honed over years of avoidance.

Dutch stepped out of the boat and went straight for the huddle of men and women.

From somewhere Mitch couldn't see, another group appeared and joined with the first.

Bitsy and Tommy Blunt.

Mitch's pulse began to chatter. What about Julia and Sara Jean? Were they on a ride? Having fun somewhere else? If so, why was park security swarming around the adults? He remembered the men on the staircase. *Never work with kids and dogs.*

Kids.

The blood pounded faster. Had something happened to the girls?

Dutch moved among the group like a swan among frogs. His thick, dark hair was brushed back from his forehead, and, as always, he looked horribly, sinfully handsome. Mitch thought about Shelby and Alicia and what he knew but couldn't prove. Bitter resentment swirled through him, and it mixed with ferocious dread.

If Dutch had hurt Julia, too . . .

Every second of the last ten years, every tie Mitch had cut, every lie he'd told, every hardship he'd forced Julia to endure, it all exploded outward. He charged forward and toppled Dutch, his hand around his brother's throat.

"What did you do, you monster? *What did you do?*"

Around him screams and shouts erupted. Hands tried to drag him away.

But he hung on, squeezing, pressing. *God, let him die, let him die.*

Strong arms ripped him away, but he didn't go easily. He swung and howled and jerked to escape, but he was caught between two men.

"What did you do?" he shouted at Dutch. "Where's Julia? What the fuck did you do to her?"

Dutch dusted himself off. As always, he was cool and calm. But Mitch didn't miss the gleam of angry satisfaction in his eyes. "This man is a fugitive," Dutch announced. "He should be taken directly to the police."

"I am the police," said one of the security detail in khakis and a Disney ball cap. "Deputy, Orange County Sheriff's Department." He turned to Mitch. "Sir, can I see some ID?"

"You don't need ID," Dutch said. "He's Mitchell Hanover, also known as Mitch Turner. He's wanted for murder and kidnapping. Call it in."

Neither Tommy nor Bitsy said anything, but the look on their faces confirmed it.

"Call it in!" Dutch repeated.

"I don't need to. We have a BOLO on him from the FBI." The deputy gripped Mitch's arm and herded him away.

Over his shoulder, Mitch called to the Blunts. "What happened? Where's Julia?"

"Sir, I need you to come with me." He pulled Mitch, who was forced to stumble along.

Tommy jogged alongside them. "They went to the restroom. They never came back."

"That was almost an hour ago," Bitsy wailed.

Rage surged through Mitch, pulsing with enough vehemence to break the deputy's hold. He hurtled back, grabbed Dutch by his pristine white shirt. "Where are they? *Where are they?*"

"You should be restrained like the mad dog you are."
Dutch snatched himself away and pushed Mitch, who lost
his footing.

The deputy and the other guards dove. Tackled, Mitch
landed with a shock wave of pain. He tried to get up, but
something shoved against his back, and whatever he'd
suffered before was nothing compared to now. He arched,
yowling in monstrous agony. Before the waves could sub-
side, his hands were yanked behind and secured. Someone hauled him to his feet.

The deputy was aiming a bulky weapon at him. A
Taser.

"Move." The deputy shoved Mitch forward.

His back and side still throbbing, he couldn't do much
else.

"Don't let him hurt her!" he shouted to Tommy and
Bitsy, and got another hard shove for it.

"Shut up."

The last thing he saw was the smirk on his brother's
face.

The deputy pushed him through a door half hidden
behind trees. Inside, the magic vanished into a service-
able steel stairway. It led down to a concrete hallway lit
with fluorescent lights. The walls were painted blue halfway up from the bottom, and a big square sign outlined in
red told him he was below Liberty Square. Given the fact
that his hands were tied—literally and figuratively—and
he was a phone call away from prison, he was in no mood
to appreciate the irony.

The corridors turned and merged with others. They
passed utility carts, some parked, some hauling material

down the corridor. Other directional signs pointed to Frontierland and Tomorrowland. The paint changed from blue to red to brown. A costumed woman held Mickey's head in her hands, her own head looking odd and tiny in the mouse costume. They passed a cowboy and a Cinderella and lots of employees dressed in slacks and Disney vests.

"Where are we?" Mitch asked.

The cop eyed him warily. "Utilidors," he said finally. "It's how cast members get from place to place without having to go through the park. So you don't see a cowboy walking through Tomorrowland," he added. "And it's where all the controls for the shows and parades are. Not to mention a nice locked room for people like you."

A bend in the hallway took them past a cafeteria. Inside, ordinary joes shared tables with Aladdin and Snow White. They passed a huge smiling Mickey painted on a wall. Rows of lockers marched by. There were break rooms, vending machines, offices, and finally, one marked SECURITY.

The cop pushed Mitch inside, where he thrust him into a chair against the wall. Several other men were milling around. A couple had on uniforms with military-style caps and silver badges. They looked a little like the rest of the costumed characters in the park. The others looked like park visitors.

The cop who'd captured him gestured to one of the latter. "Keep your eye on him," he said, nodding to Mitch, then disappeared behind an inner door.

The guys stared at him, and he stared back. Eventually, they returned to whatever they were talking about before his entrance interrupted them.

The position of his arms behind his back was awful,
and he shifted around trying to get comfortable. A useless
undertaking. Just like his attack on Dutch. Ill-conceived,
unthinking, stupid, stupid, stupid. He would never find
Julia now.

And she was here. He could feel it. As much as the
park itself was fascinating, seeing the inner workings was
even more so. Julia would have found the real part of Disney World far more interesting than the fantasy.

Which gave him an idea.

"Hey!" he called out to the group. "Is there a bathroom
around? I gotta go."

"Dwayne will take you when he gets back out," one of
the men said, evidently referring to the cop who'd brought
him in.

Mitch laid his head against the wall, closed his eyes,
trying to look like he was in pain. He didn't have to fake it
much. "I don't think I can wait." He squirmed and jiggled
his leg up and down.

"Oh, go on," someone said. "Ease up a little."

Mitch opened his eyes. A young security guard was
standing over him. "I'll take you." Mitch had hoped the
request would get him out of the security office, but the
guard escorted Mitch to a bathroom deeper in. On the way,
he scanned the hallways for a way out. No windows, no
doors. Nothing but a narrow corridor that led to the bathroom and back. Frustrated, he wanted to kick something.

The guard cut off the Flex-Cuffs so Mitch could use
the urinal, but even if he took the chance to run, he could
only escape back to the room with all the other security
men. Still, he did his business as slowly as he could, trying to figure his best move.

When he could delay no longer, he washed his hands and dried them under the hand dryer. It was one of those new ones with jet-engine air propulsion. It heated fast, and the force rippled his skin for the few seconds he held his hands under it.

When Mitch was done, the guard pulled his arms back to run the plastic around his hands again.

The guard was young, a kid really. He'd already revealed a soft side by taking Mitch to the bathroom. Mitch appealed to it again. "I busted my ribs a couple of days ago. Mind putting them in the front?"

The guard laughed; young or not, the kid was no pushover. "As a matter of fact, I do mind." He continued rebinding Mitch's hands just the way they'd been. And to prove he was in charge, he gave the cuffs an extra tug, wrenching Mitch's wrists. Then he pushed Mitch out the bathroom door and returned him to the central room.

Back in the chair, Mitch's leg still twitched up and down. He had to get out of there, but his best chance had already proved no chance at all.

A radio crackled. "We found the girl. Bringing her down to security."

Mitch stilled. *The girl.* His girl? His mind raced to the rhythm of his fast-beating heart. He'd have to get them out of here before Dutch showed up. Now he was glad he hadn't made his move yet. Now Julia would come to him. He could see her, talk to her. They could run then. Together. He pictured their escape, Jules laughing, the wind of freedom washing over their faces.

But when a security guard came in, he carried a towheaded child much younger than Julia. And she had a mother who rushed in to claim her.

The air inside Mitch's lungs whooshed out like he'd been punched. He watched the reunion as though it weren't real. How could it be? That was supposed to be him and Julia.

The guard transferred the child to the mother. Her smile made Mitch want to snatch it right off her face. He wanted that smile, those arms around his neck. He wanted to steal that relief and fly away with it.

The office broke into applause.

"You got lost," the kid said, and the room erupted in laughter.

No one was watching Mitch. They were all fixed on the mother and child who were blocking him from sight.

He bent down, slunk off his chair. Crept to his left.

A second later he was out the door.

37

The escape lasted maybe ten seconds. Long enough for half a hallway's head start.

Behind him, Mitch heard shouting.

"Hey! Stop him!"

A couple of people stared as he tore by, but they were too surprised to do anything. A corner up ahead.

He turned. Flew down the red corridor.

His hands behind his back made running awkward. Couple that with his less-than-perfect ankle, and he made a jerky, stumbling path down the hallway. Any moment they'd catch him.

He had to get his hands free.

A utility cart sat against the wall. A fast scan—was there a knife or a pair of scissors in it?

No such luck.

He peeked over his shoulder. The cop and a couple of other security men turned the corner. Rushed down the hallway toward him.

He raced off. Zigzagged around people.

Another corner. He took it.

Dove behind a float labeled WISHES COME TRUE.

He stifled his breathing, which was loud enough for the whole planet to hear. God, his chest hurt.

Flashes of color that were the security men raced by. Mitch closed his eyes. Counted to ten. Crossed his fingers.

He peeked out.

The corridor was clear.

He doubled back at a fast walk and passed a restroom. On impulse he dove inside. Maybe a maintenance man had left something—anything—he could use to cut off his cuffs.

Lucky, lucky, it was empty. Desperate, he banged open stall doors. Peered into every corner. Nothing.

On his way out, he noticed the hand dryer, the same kind he'd used earlier. On impulse, he backed up to it. Stuck his hands beneath it. Like before, the thing heated up instantly, blowing hot air with force enough to take off his skin.

But it wasn't just his skin that heated up; the plastic cuffs did, too. While they did, he stretched them, pulling hard against the outside of his wrists. All the while, he watched the door. How long would this take? Would he be caught before he finished?

The heat was singeing his skin, but finally the plastic gave, widened just enough, and he slipped his right hand out of its loop.

Quickly, he worked the left and got it off, too.

Then he was out the door and back in the hallway.

Where were the cops? He had no idea.

He went left, away from the security office, then turned down a random corridor and ended up at a dead end. He retraced his steps, but before he could get out, he heard shouting and the noise of the chase.

A rapid pivot. Dead end. The other way? Cops. He was trapped.

Two doors down, a man exited a room. Mitch dove inside before the door could close.

Julia and Sara Jean sat in the red hallway behind one of those yellow car things. As long as no one took it for a drive, they were out of sight. At least for a while.

"What are we going to do?" Sara Jean asked.

"I don't know."

"We need to get back to the park."

"Duh." She knew she was being a total crabhead, but she couldn't help it. She did not want to get caught.

"Hey, this is your plan," Sara Jean said.

"How was I supposed to know you're only allowed down here if you're sixteen? What's so great about sixteen anyway?"

"It's older than thirteen."

They'd already been caught once, which is how they found out about the sixteen rule. And why they were hiding.

"We're going to have to run," Julia said morosely.

"I don't like running."

"Would you rather go back to security?"

"I'd rather go back outside like we planned."

Julia was beginning to regret including Sara Jean. She paraphrased Dutch. "Whining is so unattractive in a woman."

"I'm not whining."

"Whatever." Julia crawled to the edge of the cart and

stole a look outside. A bunch of men were running down the hall. Quickly she ducked back, her heart hammering. Were they looking for her and Sara Jean?

The thought of going back to Dutch made her dizzy. And she didn't know where Mitch was. Not that she cared. He'd stolen her. Lied to her. Worst of all, he'd left her. Even if she could find him, she wasn't sure she wanted to.

"What's going on?" Sara Jean said.

"Shhh."

Sara Jean crawled up to Julia. "What's happening?" she whispered.

"Some men. Running."

"Running where?"

"I don't know!" Julia peeked out again. The men were gone. The hallway was empty. "Come on."

Slowly they stood up. Looked right and then left. Julia grabbed Sara Jean's hand, and they scooted off and around the corner.

They ran smack into a woman with a name tag. From where Julia stood, all she could see was the gold rectangle, winking in and out in the light.

"What are you two doing here?" she asked.

Julia said the first thing that popped into her head. "Oh, my dad works here." She squeezed Sara Jean's hand for support.

"He does," Sara Jean added, which somehow made them seem less truthful rather than more.

"We were just going to the cafeteria," Julia added in a rush.

"It's the other way," the woman said. She looked at them suspiciously. "Are you sure your dad works here? What's his name?"

"Uh...," Sara Jean said, but the last half of the word ended in a squeal as Julia yanked her away at a run.

"What are you doing?" Sara Jean stumbled, then righted herself and bobbed along.

"What does it look like?" Julia said.

"Come back here!" The woman started after them, but she was wearing heels.

They rounded another corner and slowed to catch their breath. Closed doors stretched up and down this hall. "What do you think's here?" Julia tried a couple of doorknobs.

"I don't know, but hurry! She's coming!"

Julia looked up. The woman was turning the corner. Julia sped up, zipping from door to door.

They were all locked.

Mitch tumbled into the room, closed the door behind him, and leaned his forehead against it, eyes closed.

It hurt to breathe.

He stood absolutely still, rigid, every cell tuned to the noise outside the door.

Silence. Pure, blessed silence.

No one challenged him from outside, and no one challenged him from within, either.

Relieved, he exhaled a slow, careful breath. Turned to see what he'd gotten himself into. And came face-to-face with...

Goofy.

And Donald. And a couple of the seven dwarfs.

Or at least their decapitated heads.

He gaped, the sight not registering. Then he realized what he was seeing and where he was.

A costume room.

The heads were stacked in front of him, each character's name labeled on a shelf. The bodies hung from special hooks on either side of the room. Again, each character had his or her labeled area. It was all very neat and efficient.

He started breathing again. Laughed. God almighty, he was due for a break. *Thank you, thank you, thank you.*

How much time did he have before someone came in? He skimmed quickly over the selection. The only one that looked like it would work with his height was the Goofy outfit. Hurrying, he took one down from the wall and pulled up the pants. He was reaching for the head when a noise interrupted him.

He froze.

Someone was at the door.

His gaze snapped to the knob. It turned one way, then the other.

He held his breath.

His eyes burned from staring at the silver handle.

But no other sound came.

No one burst in.

Even so, he tucked Goofy's head under his arm and waited. A minute. Two minutes. How long did he have? Was anyone out there?

Julia and Sara Jean backed down the hallway. The woman with the name tag headed toward them. Somehow she'd found a helper. Now there were two of them.

Julia's stomach was tight. She wanted to burst into tears. The adults advanced steadily.

"What are we going to do?" Sara Jean squeaked.

"I don't know." Julia was frantic. She looked right and left. No exits. And she'd taken a turn down a dead end, so there was no way out there, either.

They backed up until they hit the wall.

Inside Julia's head, *No, no no!* wailed over and over.

The two women cornered them. Just as they lunged to grab them, Julia shouted, "Run!" and ducked under the reaching arms.

But it was too late for Sara Jean. The second woman got hold of her before she could bolt.

Julia was just as unlucky. Heels or no heels, the first woman managed to grab hold of Julia's shirt. "No, you don't," she said, pulling Julia to a stop.

With a firm grip, they marched the girls back down the hallway and around the corner just as Goofy opened the door and stepped out of the costume room.

38

Roger Carrick got to the Disney World security office, trying to contain his excitement. He'd come to Florida on a hunch and had only been there a few hours when the call came.

He flashed his credentials at the man behind the intake desk. His badge said his name was Walsh. "You have Mitchell Hanover here? I got a call from a deputy"—he checked the piece of paper he'd written the name down on—"Dwayne Sever."

Walsh shifted. Looked beyond Roger to another man who was standing at the door. Both men looked decidedly unhappy.

"What happened?" Roger asked instantly. "Where is he? Where is Mitchell Hanover?"

"Gone," Walsh said. "Ran."

Roger glared at the man. "How the hell could you let him escape? Didn't you restrain him?" The man opened his mouth, but Roger cut him off. "Never mind. How long ago? What was he wearing? Write this down." He gave them his cell number. "He turns up, you call me immediately.

You hear? Immediately! Better yet—do you have a radio, a walkie-talkie? How do you communicate?"

Walsh gave him a walkie-talkie and told him the channels to follow.

"What direction did he take?" Roger asked.

The man at the door pointed it out. "Got a whole squad looking for him," he said. "He'll turn up."

Roger wasn't as confident. This was the second time Hanover had escaped just as Roger was about to snatch him. Mitch had managed to stay underground for a decade. He was good at disappearing into the crowd.

And in the bowels of Disney World was quite a crowd to vanish into. Roger dashed down the hallway and rapidly saw that finding Mitch was not going to be easy. There were countless people combing the corridors—many in costumes that included wigs and hats and full head coverings—and numerous places to hide.

"Walsh," he barked into the walkie-talkie, "I'm outside the cafeteria. Bring me a master key to the rooms and offices."

While he waited, Roger realized one thing in his favor: most of the costumed actors were in dishabille. Those with heads—like the donkey from *Pinocchio* and the mice from *Cinderella*—carried them under their arms like dozens of Ichabod Cranes. It was certainly true of the cafeteria. Anyone in a full costume had their heads off—it was the only way they could eat.

Suddenly, the search got easier. He scanned the busy hallways for one thing—anyone in full regalia.

Walsh came jogging down the hall and handed him the master key. "Should open everything. Let me know if you have trouble."

Roger took off, this time going slow, careful to examine all the characters coming his way.

Suddenly the radio crackled. "He's in Fantasyland," someone said.

"No, I just saw him near the Haunted Mansion," someone else said.

"Shit!" came a third voice. "Get your fingers out of your ass."

Roger ignored the chatter and focused on his own hunt. Ahead of him, a tall, costumed figure came into the main corridor from a side hall and began walking away. From the back, all Roger could see was the big, floppy ears and the long, costumed head. But he was the only fully costumed character Roger had seen so far.

He picked up speed. Assessed the figure's height and weight. Even under all that extra stuff, it was possible. Very possible.

He crept up. Now he was within arm's length.

He pushed his suit coat back so he could get to his weapon.

He gritted his teeth, braced himself, and reached out.

Mitch turned down a hallway and merged with the crowd. He'd been up and down these corridors already, but maybe he'd missed something. He was prepared to search them a hundred times if he had to.

Suddenly, a hand reached out and grabbed him.

Roger spun the character around.

"FBI. Don't move!" He whipped out his weapon. The figure froze. Held up his hands. Around them, people slowed, stopped.

"What's going on?" Roger heard someone whisper, but he concentrated on the person in front of him, not the small crowd that was forming.

"Take off the head," he said. "Slowly!"

He wasn't immune to the ridiculousness of the picture he made. Holding his weapon on one of Walt Disney's beloved characters.

The dog lifted the costume upward. It was bigger than Roger had expected and took longer than he liked. Was that Mitch inside there, stalling?

"Keep it coming, Hanover," Roger said grimly. "Nice and steady."

Finally, the human head appeared.

"I'm Goofy," the actor said, "not Hanover." The crowd giggled, and Roger scowled.

Mitch froze.

"Hey, where have you been?" A man wearing a headset turned him around. "Goofy Two is ready to come out and you're supposed to go in. They're already prepping for the parade."

Mitch nodded his big Goofy head and signaled a salute. Luckily the questioner pushed him forward, so Mitch had a general idea what direction to take. Of course, he had no intention of getting involved with a parade, but the staging area was central and he couldn't avoid it. And when he tried to shy away, another handler with a headset tugged him back.

"Come on, we're starting."

Without meaning to, he found himself marching out with the rest of the cast. He sweated and waved those pudgy white hands with their swollen fingers. On the sidelines, kids screamed and pointed excitedly while their parents held up videocams to capture the parade. In other circumstances, Mitch might have enjoyed the color and commotion, but at the moment he was more aware of being exposed and in the open. If he ran, he'd have to do it in front of the whole world.

Just then he spotted security with their walkie-talkies. They dotted the mob of onlookers, keeping a constant lookout. If he did anything out of the ordinary, they'd notice.

The parade music was loud and tinny and seemed as encroaching as the ticking of a bomb. As he was forced forward, his legs moved without him being conscious of it. His attention was fixed on a way out. He scoured his surroundings. Left. Right. Ahead.

Endless minutes plodded by. Then the parade curved to the left, and he saw it. A gap in the crowd. A building to hide behind.

He edged closer and closer, still waving. At the last moment, he darted through the opening and ducked behind a wall.

His hands shook as he ripped off the costume.

Mitch had to walk out of the park, no easy task on a bum ankle even if it was taped, but he didn't trust the monorail or the tram. Plainclothes security with walkie-talkies was everywhere.

By the time he got to the hotel, he felt as though he'd covered all twenty-five thousand acres. Already exhausted, he was dismayed to discover security at every entrance. As always, he had no cell phone, so he couldn't call Neesy to come get him.

Stuck, he limped into a thick stand of trees and found a place on the ground where he couldn't be seen from the road. As the sun went down, it grew cool, but he was so tired he fell asleep despite the chill.

He didn't know what woke him—a car horn, a bird cry. Suddenly he was awake and wary. The sky was dark, and the little forest he'd chosen even blocked out the moonlight. But the pitch suited him. No dogs, no men with flashlights. And after a few hours' rest, even his ankle seemed better.

What now? Hike into the nearest town, find a phone, and call Neesy to come get him? That would get him out of his present jam.

But it would get her into it.

The authorities now knew he was in Florida. If she showed up, wouldn't they make the connection to him? Aiding and abetting was serious business.

He thought of her pluck and her smile. Her eyes glowing with an affection he didn't deserve but cherished. She'd proven she wasn't afraid of a fight, but did that mean he had to lead her into one?

Besides, the closer he got to Julia, the closer he got to Dutch. Which endangered any woman around him. And he already had enough lives on his conscience.

But how could he just go off—no explanation, no good-bye? Just thinking about it gave him a cold, dark sensation, not only for the callousness of it but also for the barrenness it would leave behind. He'd be on his own again, isolated, solitary. Could he even go back there?

He thought of the night he'd confessed the one thing he'd never shared with anyone—how he'd taken Julia. Neesy had opened her arms to his past, and he loved her for it. Loved her then, and later, during the blizzard, when she'd confirmed her trust and belief in him. And now. Just picturing her filled him with a billowing warmth he ached to grip tight.

And yet, he'd never told her. Never said those words women liked to hear. He said them now, inside his head.

I love you, Neesy Brown.

Fat lot of good it would do her now.

He searched for excuses: it was unkind to leave; Neesy would worry. She'd be furious. She'd be sad.

But worry, anger, even hatred, were better than prison or, worse, death.

And that was the final hand. Game over. All his chips gone.

So he didn't call Neesy. Not then. Not ever.

He pictured her free and heading back to Crossroads. Telling the new grill man about cinnamon in the French toast batter.

It gutted him. Like someone had taken a hot blade and seared through every sinew. And when it was done, he was dead to everything but rage.

He made it outside the park on foot. At a gas station, he bought a few supplies and shaved his beard in the men's room, leaving a thick mustache. He dyed it and his hair blond at a hooker hotel off the highway, and when he was done and checked himself in the mirror, it stirred up memories. Only this time, he didn't have an infant gurgling at him from an open drawer.

He took a bus to Orlando, where he saw the press conference on a TV in a run-down bar with a HAPPY NEW YEAR garland draping the counter.

Dutch wore that smooth smile. He had an arm around Julia, who stared straight ahead.

"Turn it up," Mitch said quickly to the bartender.

Dutch was in the middle of a sentence. "—has had enough excitement. It's time she got settled into a normal life in New York."

Reporters threw questions at him, but Mitch didn't listen.

The bastard was taking her home.

39

New Year's came and went while Neesy waited for Mitch to show up. She lived on peanut butter crackers and Coke, afraid to leave the hotel room for fear he would call, yet worried he was outside somewhere waiting for her to appear so he could signal her.

At ten in the morning, two in the afternoon, and again at ten at night, she rushed downstairs when the lobby was the least crowded. She wore the wig and stuck a pair of sunglasses on her nose, and sat for half an hour. She took a side entrance and loitered outside, slowly cruising the property in hopes he was out there. Then she raced back to the room, hoping the phone's message light would be on.

It never was.

She cried on the third night, sure he'd dumped her, and again in the morning, sure he was dead.

Either way, he was gone without a word.

There'd been no fights, no hard words or rough treatment leading up to it. In the end, though, it was the same: she was alone again. Why did she think Mitch would be different? She'd placed her trust in him, and he'd betrayed it like every other man she'd known. He'd walked off without telling her. Without a word of explanation. Without a single good-bye.

Dully, she thought about slinking back to Crossroads. Returning to the life she thought she'd left behind. It just about killed her. But she couldn't stay here—this place was draining her dry, and Mitch had left her to pay the bill, damn him.

She turned on the TV so she didn't have to think about it. That's when she saw the press conference. If Mitch had left to look for Julia, he hadn't succeeded. There she was with her real father squeezing her tight. God, he was a gorgeous man. How could a man who looked like that do such terrible things?

In the middle of the news report, she snapped off the TV. She was done. With Mitch, with Dutch, with feeling sorry for herself. The whole sad, sorry mess could go on without her.

But that still left Julia.

She powered up the TV again. The program had moved on to other stories, so she switched channels. And again.

There it was. The same snippet. Dutch joyous and triumphant; Julia safe.

Neesy muted the sound and stared at the girl. Not much expression on her face. She looked...dazed. Not bruised or roughed up. Just diminished. Dulled down. Where was the smart-mouthed, Mark Twain–quoting kid she knew?

Was it stage fright, having all those cameras and lights and voices shouting at her? Or was it something else?

Amid all the self-pity came a clear, sharp memory: Dutch coming down the hallway with Julia in tow. Julia staring out at the long black car at the curb.

"You promise?"

"On my honor."

Mitch said his brother had no honor.

What would Neesy have given for someone to have made sure she was okay? How many times had she wished for a fairy godmother to sweep in and take her away?

She would never call herself a fairy godmother. With these hips and cha-chas, light on her feet wasn't one of her best qualities. But how could she go home not knowing if Julia was all right? Mitch had trusted his child to her, and she'd let someone walk right out the door with her.

And what about Mitch? Was she going to spend the rest of her life wondering if he was alive or dead?

If he was alive, eventually he'd make his way to wherever Julia was. Did Neesy want to be serving up ham and eggs when he did?

She thought of that old, scratched-up table in the kitchen. That was her, sitting and sitting, waiting for someone to come along and fill in the cracks and polish the chrome. Well, she was done with that. Done with waiting for someone to rescue her. Time to rescue herself. Not to mention a child and her daddy.

She fished in her purse, found the phone, and dialed Loritta.

"Got some bad news," she told the waitress. "Trisha wrecked her car and broke every bone in her body. I'm going to stay down here for a while longer. Don't know when I'll be back. If Crick opens, better not hold my spot."

Neesy had never been to New York. She had all sorts of images in her head—mostly from the movies—about what it might be like. But the reality of it, the hordes of people, the buildings so tall they blocked out the sun, the sheer noise of everything—the screech of the subway echoing in her ears; the car horns; the grinding of gears; the shouting in Spanish, Korean, and who knows what—was more than she could absorb in a year, let alone a day.

Plus it was bitter cold, especially after the Florida sun. The air rushed down between buildings, turning them into Arctic wind tunnels. Her ears nearly froze off her head.

So it wasn't surprising that she spent her first night deeply regretting her impulsive decision to come.

But she regained her sense of purpose by morning, especially after she found a tiny doughnut shop and had a chocolate glazed and a cup of coffee for less than a fortune.

The stay at that Disney money pit had nearly wiped her out, even with the cash Dutch had left. She had two assets: her car and the gun under the driver's seat. She didn't want to mess with the latter, so she removed the clip, tossed it in one Dumpster, and threw the gun in another.

As for the Olds, it took a while, but eventually she found someone who'd buy it without papers. She thought it would kill her to sell it, but in the end it was less painful than she thought. It was just a car—nothing compared to the human lives at stake. And she got enough money to buy a plane ticket and keep her in coffee and doughnuts for a while if she was careful. She was staying at the cheapest place she could find, but her money wouldn't last long if she didn't find a job real quick.

New York was full of restaurants, even the kind she was used to, with grills and eggs over easy. But there were fewer up where she needed to be. She'd done her home-work, knew that the Hanover mansion was on the Upper East Side between Madison and Fifth, where the super-rich had built massive homes at the turn of the last century. Most of them had long since been co-opted into apart-ments, condos, schools, and businesses. Some, like the Frick, were now museums. Hanover House stood alone, one of the few mansions that still housed a single family in much the same way it had when it was built in 1908.

She tried to reconcile what she knew about Mitch with what she learned about Hanover House, and she couldn't keep the two images in her head at the same time.

And what about Julia? Was she in there? Did her bed-room have fifteen-foot ceilings and a fireplace? Did the wealth and the luxury and the toys compensate for the loss of the father she'd always known? Was she happy?

Was she safe?

Hanover House was a city landmark, and Neesy took an architectural walking tour that included it. She'd set off with the insane hope that when they got there, she'd run into Julia on the street. Or coming out of the house. But Neesy almost fell over when she first saw it. The sheer mass of the place made a casual meeting seem as impos-sible as flying to Mars.

The huge limestone façade looked more like a bank than a home. The tour guide said it encompassed nearly 20,000 square feet, contained thirty rooms, seventeen of them baths, plus a hotel-sized ballroom. Neesy couldn't imagine growing up there, coming home from school, flinging books on the kitchen table, sitting down to milk and cookies. Maybe people like the Hanovers didn't fling their stuff around or sit at the kitchen table.

As the tour continued, she scouted the area for coffee shops. She found five within walking distance, one on the corner of 68th and Madison. She had lunch there one day, watching the tired faces of the women behind the counter and wondering if any of them remembered Alicia Ruiz.

She chatted one up, mentioning she was looking for a job, and said she would check back. She repeated this in all five restaurants, telling stories about Crossroads and Crick's and generally sympathizing with whatever they had to say. And she tipped generously.

It took her longer than she'd hoped, but eventually she got a bite at the place on 68th. One of their waitresses had fallen and broken her arm. It was strictly fill-in till the other girl healed, but Neesy was there the next morning, uniform pressed and ready to go.

Food was culture as far as Neesy was concerned, and there were a few things to get used to here. The bagels were hard and chewy, neither grits nor biscuits were on the menu, and when it came to tuna, there wasn't a sweet pickle in sight. And what was a knish? Or a nosh? Luckily she was a fast learner, and customers seemed to get as much of a kick out of her accent—which she swore she didn't have—as she got out of theirs.

She was bone tired that first night, but tips had been pretty good. Not enough to keep her in MetroCards over the long haul, but enough for now. Until she could figure out some kind of plan.

Until she'd actually seen Hanover House, she'd had some vague notion of snatching Julia off the street. Or finding some pretense to waltz in. But once she'd seen the place, she realized how foolish that was. Ain't no one getting inside that building unless invited.

Every day she walked to and from the subway along a route that took her past Hanover House. She scanned the stone, staring at the windows, hoping to catch a glimpse of Julia, trapped and waving haplessly to anyone who could scale the walls and free her.

Neesy tried not to think too much about Mitch, her feelings still raw over the way he'd abandoned her. But every once in a while, she found herself dreaming about him taking her to the fancy places she saw on her way to work. Restaurants with Italian and French names, shops where a single blouse cost a month in tips. And at night? What would it have been like at night? She'd imagined him moving above her, the width of his shoulders, the cut of his jaw strong in the streetlight spilling through the window. Sometimes, to make it more real, she even brought herself to climax, pretending it was him.

But when the alarm went off in the morning, she woke up alone. Took the subway alone, squished between all the other nameless people going to work. On those days, when she felt sorry for herself and longed for her spring-time lotion to brighten up her day, she reminded herself why she was here. For Julia, not her daddy.

Then, three weeks after Neesy first clapped eyes on the Hanover House, she was walking to the subway after her shift, and there she was, that small, familiar form, getting out of a long black limo in front of the mansion. Neesy stopped short, her breath clogged in her lungs.

She would have killed for a pair of binoculars, because from where she was across the street, she couldn't get a good look at Julia. Except to note that she was bundled up for the weather in a scarf and hat and the kind of coat you go to church in, not the kind you play in. The scarf hid half her face, and besides she was mostly looking down. Two giant men, one white, one black, towered over her. They wore suits and ties and looked respectable enough. But they kept to either side as they walked her through an iron gate. Bodyguards? Prison guards? Julia disappeared into the mansion before Neesy could cry out.

After that, she grew impatient. Mitch had disappeared. Who knew if he was even alive? There was no one but her to make sure that child was protected. But the house was too big and too intimidating to just march up to the door and knock, much as she wanted to.

Instead, she wrote a letter. She told Julia she'd read about her going to New York with her new father. She told her about Trisha and her accident and how Neesy missed Crossroads and wondered if Julia missed it, too. She gave Julia her cell number and told her she could call anytime, especially if she was feeling down and needed the name of that mad-at-the-world lotion. She signed it "love," bought a stamp, and mailed it.

She waited a few more weeks for Julia to call. It was well into February, and school was under way. But she never saw Julia coming or going again. If she hadn't glimpsed her that one time, Neesy might have thought she wasn't even in New York, and all this spying was for nothing.

But she had seen her. And those two brutes, who had grown exponentially ever since in Neesy's imagination.

When another week went by without hearing from Julia, Neesy took a risk. She sent another message. She didn't sign her name, didn't put a return address, and didn't even mail it. She just folded up a take-out menu from the restaurant and slipped it into the handle of the iron gate she'd seen Julia walk through.

That day she got a couple of orders wrong, spilled a cherry Coke all over a customer, and gave incorrect change. When the manager screamed at her, she blamed it on getting some bad news from home. Truth was, she hadn't gotten any news—good or bad—because Julia never called.

She repeated the same trick with the menu the next day and the day after that. By the fifth day, she had stopped being nervous. In fact, by closing time she almost forgot to take a menu with her for the morning. It seemed silly and useless anyway. But she gave herself one last day of trying and plucked the single sheet of paper out of its holder by the cash register.

She was folding it so she could fit it in her purse when she was stopped outside.

"Miss Brown?"

One of the giants stood in front of her.

She froze.

"Miss Denise—Neesy—Brown?"

He had a deep, buttery voice and smooth black skin with small, precise features that contrasted sharply with the size of his neck. As he waited for her response, his expression was polite enough, but there was something cold in the center of his eyes. She swallowed and nodded.

"Come with me, please?"

Not on your life. "Uh . . . where exactly?"

"I understand you'd like to see Julia."

She blinked in surprise. "Is she all right?"

"Come with me and see for yourself."

Could it be this easy? She studied him, hoping to probe his true intentions. But all she could fathom from his face was cool courtesy.

She hadn't forgotten what Mitch had told her about his brother. Was this a trick? She pictured herself in one of those movies when the heroine is standing at the top of the basement steps and everyone is yelling at the screen, "Don't go down there!" and, as if she didn't have a lick of sense, she does.

But if Dutch wanted to hurt her, why bother going to all this trouble to get her inside the house? Those giants could take her out anytime, anywhere. This was her chance, maybe her only chance, to see Julia. Risky or not, did she really have a choice?

"All right," she said, and he gestured with an open arm for her to precede him into a waiting car.

She was on her guard as she got in. Hanover House was only a few blocks away; there was no need for a car. But maybe the rich never walked anywhere. In the meantime, she watched the route carefully, making sure she knew where she was going, one hand on the door so she could jump out if she needed to.

The giant, who introduced himself as Gus, said nothing. In a few minutes they'd gone around the block and were at the curb in front of the mansion. Gus opened her door, stood until she got out, then used some kind of electrical device to unlock the iron gate. With a slow, ponderous arc, it widened on its own.

"This way," Gus said when she'd walked through.

Behind a stone abutment was a door hidden from the street. He held it open for her.

Neesy held her breath and stepped inside.

40

It took Mitch over a month to get to New York, and when he finally arrived, it was by way of St. Louis and craigslist.

At first he had to lie low because his face was on every newspaper and news show in the area, and even with the new hair, he wasn't sure he could keep off the grid. When things finally died down enough for him to move around more freely, his escape options were limited. Flying out of Florida would have been suicide, and the cops were watching the bus routes. Walking was too slow, especially on his ankle, though he was prepared to hike if he had to.

He was gearing up to hoof it when he got an idea from overhearing three high school rock and rollers discuss buying a drum kit on craigslist.

Using a computer at the library, he scrolled through the rideshare section of the list. Anyone looking for him would expect him to go north, so he found someone heading west who wanted company. He told the driver he had a construction job waiting outside St. Louis, and in the three days before the trip he cut his hair down to a Marine Corps buzz, then added a pair of steel toes and a hard hat to his disguise.

From St. Louis he took a Greyhound, which arrived in Manhattan the next day around four in the morning. Not an auspicious time but it suited Mitch's mood. He disembarked into the fetid atmosphere of the Port Authority, where the noxious smell of fuel combined with the lingering fragrance of piss and vomit. The terminal smothered him in heat, and he quickly shed the jacket he'd picked up at a rest stop in Ohio.

An obese rat scurried across his path as Mitch walked from the gate into the station. Farther on, a silver-haired woman wearing a tattered bridal veil was singing a warbling version of "Tonight" from *West Side Story*. Like a decrepit Beatrice leading them through the gates of hell instead of heaven, she waved the oncoming line of passengers from his bus toward her. No one paid attention.

A few people with luggage and backpacks were camped out on benches, waiting for buses they had missed, but so were the ragged fringes of humanity trying to keep out of the cold. Those homeless and drug-addicted souls not asleep against a wall or crunched into filthy corners eyed Mitch as he moved across the terminal. One woman, a girl, really, approached him for money. A walking skeleton, she had sores on her mouth, and when he shook his head, she approached someone behind him. Then she came back to him, and from the way she looked at him, he could tell she didn't remember already asking.

Outside, he sucked in the cold, a fleeting relief from the suffocating heat inside. It smelled better out there, too, even if the cleaner air was washed with exhaust. The respite was soon gone, though, as the wind came down between the buildings on 42nd Street. He shrugged into his jacket, pulled up the collar, and huddled into it.

Dawn was still several hours away, and as well as the streets were lit, they were also rimmed in shadow. Times Square glittered, and the AMC and Amsterdam theaters blasted movies and musicals in glaring neon. But these were just desperate bulwarks against the darkness.

He found an all-night coffee shop and slid into a seat at the counter. He hadn't eaten dinner, so he ordered a couple of eggs. But he couldn't get them down. Would he, like Persephone, be stuck in the underworld forever if he consumed even so much as a spoonful?

He was stuck now, wasn't he?

And so was Julia.

He paid his bill, hoping he wasn't too late, and pushed that thought aside. Until he could contact Carlo, worrying about Julia was unproductive.

Instead, he walked over to 8th and from there downtown. Twice he was stopped by prostitutes who were willing to get him out of the cold and into their panties.

He pushed on, though the thought of a woman was not an unpleasant diversion. Especially if she had red hair and a handful of curves. But Neesy was gone now, out of his life. He hoped she was back in Crossroads, hoped she was safe.

He stopped at a corner. The thought of Neesy so far away sent grief splintering through him. He missed the dimple in her chin, her milky skin, and the devil in her green eyes. Most of all he missed her hand in his. The sense that he'd never be alone again.

When he got to 24th, he turned down the street and examined the line of art galleries and cafés. They ran the gamut from sedate to outrageous. Furniture made out of cardboard and cinder blocks. Pictures of bare-chested men in wide crinolines made out of newspaper. A Cindy Sherman retrospective showed dolls with their legs splayed and their heads gone.

Bernardo Ricci occupied the corner. In the window, a poster of a Dutch Hanover painting heralded the new show. The setting was as violent as any Dutch had drawn as a child. Dark, malevolent, the wind whipping trash around a decaying, graffiti-marred alley. And in the center of the maelstrom, the fragile, bloodless woman. Graceful and otherworldly, she was also calm and composed, placed among the refuse as though she had called the storm down on herself. Not an earthy whore, but an ethereal Madonna.

Alicia had been like that, quietly beautiful.

But it wasn't her beauty that had drawn Dutch to her. It was the sheer fact that she had been Mitch's.

How many girlfriends had Dutch lured away from Mitch? By the time he was in college, Mitch didn't have commitments. He had sex. If Dutch wanted in, no skin off Mitch's back.

Alicia was different. She was a woman who demanded caring just by breathing. Sweet, simple, traditional. The kind who expected a ring and a ceremony in a church.

If Mitch had stayed away from the coffee shop, she'd still be alive. But he'd haunted it. He came so often, always sitting at Alicia's table, that the staff started to tease them. It began to seem rude that he never did more than flirt.

So though he knew it was dangerous, he took her out.

She wore a white dress that floated on the breeze and showed off her olive skin and long legs.

It didn't take long for him to become besotted. One weekend he took her to the Dominican Republic, and they stayed at the best hotel on the island. She, in turn, took him to visit Tia Amelia, and the day they spent surrounded by her close-knit family was the best.

But when they returned, Dutch was in the limo with Carlo, and the future had already begun.

Dutch teased her gently, got her to laugh, and Mitch could see she was flattered. It was hard not to be when Dutch turned on the high wattage of his charm. Then he asked her to model for him. She agreed, and Mitch later caught them in bed together. Well...he washed his hands of her. She was spoiled, like rotten fruit.

So when she called him for help, he hung up on her. Even though she was crying and begging him to forgive her. Even though he knew she was pregnant and Dutch was hurting her. That's what Dutch did. Even though he knew she had no one with the power or the financial resources to take on a Hanover. Even though he knew all that, he'd abandoned her to it. He went back to having sex and shut Alicia up in the same place he shut up anything else that mattered to him.

Until she called that gray February morning.

So even though Mitch hadn't used a knife, he had killed her all the same.

By seven, a few hardy souls were rolling up the iron security gates over their storefronts, and the sound of the clashing, clanging steel rang sharp in the early morning. Mitch headed back to midtown.

He had purchased another disposable cell phone before he left Florida. Now he took it out and punched in the number. Once again, he let it ring, hung up, and dialed again. He went through the whole prearranged routine.

Then he needed a place to wait that was out of the cold and where he wouldn't be noticed. He headed for Penn Station.

A step up from the Port Authority, Penn was already busy with commuters from Connecticut, New Jersey, and Long Island. It was filled with shops and restaurants, though most hadn't opened yet. Still, the smell of popcorn hovered over the air.

He found an empty bench in the waiting area across from a gate that said PORT WASHINGTON and listed the stops along the way. His knee jerked compulsively up and down as he watched a swarm of commuters come through the gate and disappear into the station. He sat through four more arrivals and departures. All the stores had opened, and the station was crawling with people before the phone finally rang.

This time, though, the voice on the other end didn't stick to the script.

The first thing out of Carlo's mouth was, "Are you crazy? I can't help you anymore, Mr. Mitch. He's got guards in the house. The police are in and out. I can't do it."

"I'm sorry. If I had anyone else, I'd use them. But all I've got is you."

"Look, the kid is fine. She's home; she's okay. Leave her be. Let her get settled."

"She's going to school?"

The chauffeur paused.

"She's not, is she?"

"She will," Carlo insisted. "These things take time."

"Does she go out?"

Another pause. "Once."

"When was that?"

"Two, three weeks ago," Carlo said reluctantly.

"How did she seem? Happy? Was she laughing? Smiling? What's she reading?"

"She's a kid. Sure, she's happy. And reading? Kids, they don't read anymore."

"This one does. Has she been to the bookstore or the library yet?"

"No."

"Anyplace else?"

"No." The answers were as good as an admission.

"So she's a virtual prisoner."

"Which is exactly what I'll be if they find out I helped you."

"And if you don't, I'll let them know anyway."

Carlo said nothing.

"I don't want to hurt you," Mitch said. "You've been good and fair to me. But I can't let Julia stay there."

"You won't get anywhere near the house."

"You let me worry about that. First, I can't keep walking the streets. I need a place to stay."

"A place to stay? Where are you?"

Mitch debated. He was putting himself in Carlo's hands, and he didn't know if he could trust him fully. "Let's just say I'm close."

"How close?"

"Close enough."

Carlo muttered something in Spanish, then sighed. "Okay, Mr. Mitch. I'll see what I can do."

Carlo called back just before the evening rush hour. Mitch had spent most of the day in the movie theater in Times Square, going from one show to the other and waiting for the call that would give him a more permanent base.

But when Carlo finally called with an address in Spanish Harlem, Mitch still bided his time. He was expected shortly but the timeline was too predictable. He didn't know if Carlo would betray him, but why take a chance? So he sat through two more movies, sleeping in the back despite the noise of the film.

He left the theater at eight and made his way uptown. He didn't phone ahead and tell Carlo he was coming. Hands in his pockets, head down against the cold, he approached the address. Streetlights and store lights spotted the area, but Mitch kept to the shadows. When he could see without being seen, he stopped to tie his shoes. Watched for abnormal movement, for cars that shouldn't be there, people who shouldn't be there.

A woman rolled a baby stroller up the block and then down. She didn't seem to have any destination in mind. She passed a derelict-looking guy hanging out in front of the apartment building. Shook her head so slightly Mitch might not have seen it if he wasn't looking. But he was looking. He also saw a delivery van at the curb across the street, parked under a NO PARKING sign. Was it making deliveries, or was it watching for him?

He went into a bodega and pretended to scan the shelves while looking out the window. He ordered a half pound of chorizo, which they sliced for him, and bought a couple of loaves of bullet-shaped bread and some beer. All in all, he was in the bodega maybe twenty minutes. When he got out, the woman was still pushing her stroller and the van was still parked at the curb.

Mitch turned and walked away.

He roamed the streets until he found an abandoned building. Someone had already broken in, and Mitch stepped through the opening in the wood over the doorway. He ate some of the chorizo with the bread. Drank a beer. Settled himself in to wait for the long night to be over.

Sometime before dawn, a squeaking noise woke him. A few feet away, a family of rats were feeding on what was left of the bread. Beyond them, the shadow of a man loomed.

Mitch crept to his feet, intending to back into a corner to hide. He backed into a man instead.

"Yo, look who we got here."

Before he could move, the man had him by the neck, a knife at his throat. "We don' like junkies here, man."

Two other men dissolved out of the shadows to watch. They were grinning. Mitch tried to tell them he wasn't a junkie, but the one who had his neck only squeezed tighter. "What's he saying? Hey, 'Tonio, what d'you think he's saying?"

"I think he's trying to tell you something," 'Tonio said.

"That true, man? You trying to tell me something?"

Mitch didn't reply.

"See what he's got," the one with the knife said. The other two approached and started fishing in his pockets. Mitch gritted his teeth, struggled, making it difficult to search him. But the thrashing loosened the grip on his neck and gave him an opening.

With a powerful heave, he broke the grip around his throat. He struck out, bloodied a nose, landed a few good hits, but it was still three to one. They took turns restraining him and beat him until his legs wouldn't hold him. They lifted his phone, his cash, and his jacket. And they left him curled in a ball on the cement floor with the rats and the roaches.

41

Mitch didn't know how long he lay there. Only that eventually he came to groaning consciousness. It took every effort he had, but he managed to crawl to his feet and get away from that place. Outside, it was still night.

Jaw set, head groggy, he shuffled away. He had to stay alive long enough to get where he was going. It was a long walk, and if it hadn't been so frigid, he didn't know if he would have made it. But the keening of the cold wind kept him awake until he got where he was going. He made no secret of it, either.

Leaning heavily against the wall, because he would fall down otherwise, he banged on the building door loud enough to wake every cop in the neighborhood.

"Carlo Diaz!" he shouted. "I want Carlo Diaz!"

If someone called the police, so be it. He was going down one way or the other.

But Carlo got there soon enough.

"Mr. Mitch!" he whispered. "What are you doing?" He pulled Mitch inside, a sick, agonizing move for Mitch, who settled against the entry wall in the small foyer for support.

"Why are you here?" Carlo said. "You were supposed to be—"

"I know where you wanted me," Mitch said. "I saw the cops waiting."

Carlo had the decency to flush. "I am sorry. I just couldn't do it anymore. And Mr. Dutch—" He got a closer look at Mitch. "Oh, my God. What happened? Wait here. I'll get some water and ice. You should go to the hospital. A couple of those cuts look bad."

"I'll take a couch instead."

Carlo shook his head. "I can't. My wife, my kids—I can't."

Mitch held up his hand to stop him. "Fine. But there's one thing you can do. And after that I will no longer require your services."

"What is it?" He looked over his shoulder. "Hurry. Please. I don't want my wife—"

"No, no. No wives. I just need the limo."

"What?"

"Bring it here."

Carlo looked around like he was surrounded by madmen. "Now?"

"Now, tomorrow. I'm not leaving until you do, so it's up to you."

"It's the middle of the night. What am I going to tell Sofia?"

"Whatever it takes. That Mr. Hanover has it in his head to go for a midnight movie. That there's an emergency at the house, which there is. Tell her anything you like—just get it here."

"And what will you do?"

"Wait."

"You can't wait here by the front door."

"Your apartment, then."

"No!"

Mitch closed his eyes. He was having trouble staying upright.

"There is a bar halfway down the block. You can stay there."

"I think it would be better for everyone if I stayed with Sofia. Just in case you decide to talk to the police again. Or Dutch."

Carlo was about to protest, when Mitch started shouting again. "Carlo Diaz! Let me speak to Carlo Diaz!"

"All right! All right!"

Carlo escorted him into his apartment and sat him on a couch. It was warm inside. Cozy. It smelled of onions and tomatoes and rice, the kind of food Alicia had once made for him.

Carlo disappeared into a back room. Mitch heard the soft whisperings of words exchanged. Then Carlo was back, this time in his chauffeur's uniform. He left Mitch a bowl of water and a washcloth.

"You should clean those cuts. You probably need stitches."

Mitch said he would, but the minute the door closed behind the chauffeur, Mitch shut his eyes. It should have taken Carlo three-quarters of an hour round-trip, but it seemed like five minutes between the time he left and the time he shook Mitch awake.

"I am back," he said. "What do you want with the car? You're not going to sell another one, are you?"

Mitch tried to get up, but Carlo had to help him. "No, I just need a lift." He limped out of the apartment, onto the elevator, and down to the first floor. Carlo had parked at a side entrance to keep as out of sight as possible. He slung Mitch's arm around his shoulder and helped him outside.

"Open the trunk," Mitch said, and when Carlo only stared at him, Mitch said, "Just do it. Open the trunk." Carlo did as asked. "Now help me in."

"Mr. Mitch—"

"Help me in, dammit!"

Between the two of them, they got him inside the compartment. "Now take me home." Mitch explained what to do when they got there, and then Carlo shut him in. Once again, Mitch closed his eyes. Then snapped them open. He couldn't fall asleep now. God, he hurt. And the jolting of the ride didn't help.

When the car stopped at last, he waited for the snick of the latch to unlock. Two quick raps on the car told him Carlo was leaving. He counted to fifty, then slowly, carefully opened the lid.

Like all wealthy people at the turn of the last century, the owners of Hanover House needed a place to store their carriages and the horses that drew them. The house and stables were often situated in the back, somewhere downwind of the main dwelling.

When the carriages were sold and replaced with automobiles, the Hanovers of the time sold the carriage house and converted the stables into a garage. And, because he was a little automobile mad, he had a tunnel built so he could get to the garage whenever he had the urge to get behind the wheel and take his latest obsession for a spin.

The car collection was long gone, but the tunnel and

the garage were still in use. And, as Mitch hoped, quiet and empty.

Carlo was gone, and Mitch was only a few yards away from Julia and safety.

It took more than he thought it would to climb out of the trunk. Actually, *fall* would be a better description. The best he could do was roll himself out. He landed with a wallop of pain.

The piercing agony reverberated through him, and he lay crumpled on the ground for precious minutes, sweating and nauseated. Then, using the back end of the car for leverage, inch by raw inch, he struggled to his feet.

The tunnel was only a short walk away, but it seemed like miles. To test himself, he let go of the car. Swayed. Caught himself. Blinked away the dizziness. Tried again.

One step. Then another.

He could make it. He had to.

Body burning, vision unsteady, he dragged himself forward in a ragged line, concentrating on one thing and one thing only: the door that led from the garage into the tunnel.

When he finally reached it, he was breathing as hard as a marathon runner at the end of a race. He grasped the knob, leaning against it with all his strength. He managed to turn it. Managed to swing open the door.

Bright, white light hit him smack in the face. Instinctively he shielded his eyes against it. But in doing so, he let go of the door. His legs wobbled, and the last thing he thought as he tumbled to the ground was what Dutch would do when he found him.

42

Neesy stared at the top of the canopy bed in the middle of Hanover House. She was trying to stay calm, to stay focused, and, most importantly, to stay awake. It was the middle of the night, she'd been at Hanover House for hours, and she still hadn't seen Julia.

What she had seen was Dutch, and plenty of him.

And though he was steadfastly polite, unhumanly beautiful, and, yes, magnetic, she could not forget what Mitch had told her: he was dangerous.

In the face of his presence, though, it was often hard to remember. He'd greeted her like an old friend, like it was perfectly natural for her to show up in New York, expected even.

"I'm delighted to see you," he'd said, beaming.

Meanwhile, she'd sat at the edge of a stiff armchair, her legs crossed at the ankles the way her mama told her was proper and which she almost never did except once in a while at church. Then again, it felt kind of churchy in the huge room—all dark wood and stuffed furniture from a previous century and a large, showy fireplace.

He offered her a slim glass of something or other, and when she accepted it, the stem was cool to the touch, delicate and spare. Neesy had the feeling if she wasn't careful, she would snap the thing in two. She put it down, hoping the round table next to an armchair wasn't just there for the fun of it. She'd looked, but there were no signs saying "do not touch."

"Would you like to see the rest of the house?" Dutch asked. She was in her uniform, and it was streaked with ketchup and grease, and probably smelled that way, too. Yet he'd asked the question as though she were wrapped in mink. "It's quite a showplace."

"Right now, I'd like to see Julia." No point wasting time; it's why she was here, after all.

"Of course. But first, I have a proposition for you." He smiled, and she couldn't help catching her breath. Gorgeous wasn't a strong enough word. Sexy didn't say it at all. Lovely sounded too feminine, and stunning wasn't descriptive enough. He was all those things. Tall and lean, and when he turned that smile on, with those ocean-blue eyes and that pitch-black hair, any woman worthy of the term would have stopped breathing.

Which is why Neesy had to force herself to look away. Remind herself that he'd turned on the charm in Crossroads and ended up walking out her door with a promise to return. A promise he didn't keep.

"What kind of proposition?"

He had his own glass, and he rolled the stem between his thumb and forefinger. "I know you've come to New York to make sure Julia is all right. And I know your accommodations are less than desirable. And I know Julia would enjoy spending time with you while you're here. So I'd like to solve all those issues in one stroke. Stay here as long as you like. You'll have a comfortable room, all the resources of my home at your disposal. And, of course, Julia."

Her heart began to hammer. Coming over for an hour or two was one thing. Agreeing to stay was something entirely different. "I don't know..."

"Oh, come, Neesy—you don't mind if I call you Neesy? Do you know how many people would kill to get inside this place? It's never been photographed—did you know that? No reporter has ever set foot in here, and here I am, laying it at your feet."

"Can I see Julia first? Maybe she doesn't want any reminders of—"

"Oh, she will adore having you here. And so will I." He swooped her out of the chair and onto her feet. "Let me show you the room I've picked out for you."

Ignoring her protests to slow down, he pulled her through a dizzying maze of hallways that suddenly emptied into a jaw-dropping foyer. Wide-eyed, she took it all in—the marble floor, the chandeliers, the winding Rhett-and-Scarlett staircase.

Geez Louise.

As if she wasn't giddy enough, he raced her up the grand staircase and down a stately hall. Thick carpet, inlaid wood, and sculpture dotted the way. Despite the fact that it was January, there seemed an endless array of porcelain vases with blood-red roses.

Finally, he swept her through a door and into a room that seemed designed especially for her.

A white ruffled canopy shaded the bed. Floral chintz covered the armchairs and the bedspread. A mirrored vanity sat in a corner with its own ruffled skirt. A white brick fireplace took up one wall, and there was even an adjoining bath with a deep spa tub. It was so pretty, she gasped.

"It's . . . it's lovely." Was this how he got Julia to go with him? Did he promise her something amazing, something she'd never had or done—like a ride in his modern chariot? "Is Julia's nearby?"

"She's going to be so surprised to see you!" He took both her hands in his and gazed at her, his blue eyes warm and pleading. "Say yes. Please. Don't disappoint me or Julia."

She could see why Mitch thought no one would believe him. Dutch was so charming and eager to please she hardly believed it herself. But if she asked Dutch if she'd be free to leave anytime, would he swear on his honor that she could?

Then again, if she refused his offer, would she get to see Julia? She suspected not.

She was trapped. She couldn't go, and Lord knows she didn't want to stay.

He shook her hands. His fingers were warm and insistent. "Don't keep me waiting."

"Yes," she said. "Yes, all right. But only for the night. Just until I see Julia."

"Wonderful! Now, let me get you something to change into. I'm sure you're eager to get out of that uniform."

"Oh, that's okay. I don't need—"

He waved objections away. "Don't worry your pretty little head about it. Just go and take a nice long soak. Fresh clothes will be here when you get out."

He was gone before she could say another word.

Without him in it, the room seemed smaller and darker. She could think again. What in the world had she just agreed to?

She sank onto the bed, trembling. Yes, she'd come for Julia, and, yes, she wanted to help, but she wasn't crazy. Sticking her foot in the middle of a viper's nest...Surely there was some other way to help.

She jumped off the bed, bolted out the door, ran down the hallway to that outrageous staircase, and flew down the steps to the foyer and the massive front door.

And came face-to-face with the other giant.

Like Gus, he was broad-shouldered, thick-necked, and well dressed. His suit coat bulged around his hip where a weapon would be. And he stood right in front of the door.

"Can I help you?" Like Gus, he was polite, but he was also unmoving.

"Uh...I thought I'd get some fresh air."

"Perhaps Mr. Hanover will take you for a walk," he said. "Would you like me to call him?"

God, no. "Thanks. Maybe later."

"Would you like me to escort you back to your room?"

"I...I think I can manage."

But he came with her to the foot of the staircase and stood there while she trudged back up, his gaze burning through her back all the way.

Like a prisoner returning to her cell, she returned to the room with the canopy bed, closed the door, and leaned against it. Now she was truly stuck.

Or was she?

When he'd brought her, Gus hadn't taken her through

the front door. That meant there was another way out. Maybe more than one. All she had to do was find them. One way or another, she could sneak out—take Julia with her if it came to that—even if it meant waiting until the middle of the night.

In the meantime, she'd play along.

Admittedly, she did enjoy the bath. There were candles and French soap, and she stayed in the warm water until her skin wrinkled. When she finished, she wrapped herself in a fluffy robe and stepped into the bedroom.

True to his word, Dutch or one of his minions had laid out clothes for her on the bed. A silk and cashmere skirt with an Italian name on the label and a sleeveless sweater, also cashmere. A pair of leather pumps that added four inches to her height. They were like the clothes she'd seen in the fancy boutiques on her way to work. Clothes she'd never dared to try on, let alone wear. Everything was tailored expertly and fit surprisingly well. How had Dutch managed that? It was almost as though... as though he'd been expecting her.

A sudden quiver made her hand shake as she drew up the zipper on her skirt. But she finished and smoothed down the material. She couldn't think about that now. Worry would only fuzz up her mind, and she had to concentrate if she was going to get herself—and Julia—out of there.

She looked for a matching cardigan but didn't find one. What she did find was a handwritten note on heavy cream paper with an embossed *H* on top. Dutch requesting her company at dinner.

She fluffed her hair and adjusted her makeup with the small collection laid out on the vanity. Good looks could work two ways, couldn't it?

At last there were no more clothes to put on and nothing to prolong her stay in the room. Pulse pounding in her throat, she opened the door and stepped into the hallway.

She made her way down the staircase, this time at a slow, sedate walk. The man at the door nodded as she passed, but somewhere she made a wrong turn, because she found herself in a narrow back hallway with a jumble of empty rooms that Dutch later told her was for staff and servants to come and go without being seen. By sheer luck, she managed to unearth a way into the mansion's main section and finally stumbled upon the dining room by accident.

Getting lost had made her anxious and breathless, but Dutch didn't seem to notice. He gave her an admiring stare.

"You look quite beautiful. I knew that color would set off your eyes."

She held out her bare arms. "I think you forgot the cardigan."

"Not at all." He ran a hand down her skin, stopping to caress the crease at the elbow. "Your arms are so beautiful. Why not show them off?"

He was giving her goose bumps, so she pulled away. That was when she noticed the table set for two. Alarmed, she said, "Isn't Julia coming?"

Dutch was profusely apologetic. "She wanted to spend the night with a friend. You understand . . . She's just starting to make connections, and I didn't want to ruin her fun. She'll be here in the morning. You'll see her then."

How Neesy managed to get anything down at dinner was a miracle. She nodded and smiled and pretended it was fine that Julia wasn't there. But inside she was quaking.

Before she'd finished, she pushed back her chair and rose. "I think I should go. I can come back tomorrow."

In an instant, Dutch was at her side. "Of course you're not going." He tucked her hand into a crook in his arm. "But if you're done, I have something to show you."

Her arm firmly locked in his, she was forced to follow him to the top of Hanover House, where he kept his studio. It seemed an odd space for a painter, as it was dim and eerie under the eaves. A small lamp emitted a pool of sickly yellow light. It cast sinister shadows on the unfinished walls with their dark, open beams. Cobwebs grew unfettered in the corners, and she shuddered. The place was as creepy as a pharaoh's tomb.

He must have seen her discomfort. "Something wrong?"

"I don't like spiders."

"Really? But they're such marvelous creatures. Patiently weaving and spinning. Waiting for their prey to come to them."

"Marvelous or not, I'd take a dust mop to all these webs."

"Oh, I find great beauty in them." His voice was soft, admiring, and the tone made her shiver again. She changed the subject, asking about the orderly niches fashioned between the rafters lining the perimeter.

"Oh, those were for the beds," Dutch explained. "For the maids and staff. At one time or other, the Hanovers employed dozens of people."

She'd hardly seen anyone in the time she'd been there. Then again, there was only Dutch to look out for now, and how many were needed for that? But someone must have cooked the meal she'd just choked down. And someone must vacuum all those rugs. Dutch must not let them get near this place. She'd bet they wouldn't like spiders, either.

"See that?" He pointed to the central peak above their heads, the place where the main beams crossed. "Family legend has it that one of the maids hung herself there. Although some say she was murdered for carrying the master's child."

Was he deliberately trying to scare her?

The hell with that. She pushed past him to a table with paint, brushes, and other gear. It stood against one wall not far from a draped easel.

She reached for a corner of the drape. "May I?"

"Don't touch that!" He said it with such force and fury that she immediately dropped her hand and jumped back as if bit. He laughed at his own vehemence. "Sorry. I never let anyone see a painting until it's finished."

"Ah. And this one? How much more is left to do?"

"Oh, quite a bit, I think." He sidled up close to her. Tucked a strand of hair behind her ear. "Perhaps you'll let me paint you one day." He slid a hand to her jaw, slowly moved her face in one direction, then another. "Very nice," he said softly. He seemed reluctant to let her go, and she held her breath while his fingers skimmed down her neck to where her carotid pumped madly. "Very nice." He seemed fixed on the spot, and before he went all Dracula on her, she stepped away with a small laugh.

"I don't think I'm ready to be immortalized. Besides, I'm not staying that long." She made her way to the door, and after a beat he followed.

And that night, she waited until the house was still— past midnight, even past one. But when the clock in the hallway struck two, she crept out of bed. Dutch had been as generous with the night things as he was with the day. She slid out of the silk gown he'd provided—she'd checked the label, so she knew it was real and not that fake stuff she got at Walmart—and slipped the cashmere clothes back on. She already knew her uniform and coat had disappeared; they were the first things she'd looked for after dinner when she got back to the room. But uniform or not, bare arms or not, she was dressed and ready to go. She grabbed her purse, peeked out the door, and tiptoed into the lit hallway.

She wasn't sure what she'd find—a way out if nothing else. But the story Dutch had given her about Julia staying with a friend...It didn't ring true. She couldn't say why; she just had an awful gut feeling.

The house was a maze, but at least she knew where the bedrooms were. She crept down the hallway outside of hers. One by one, she quietly, carefully turned knobs and opened doors.

There were eight rooms on her floor. All were richly furnished like a museum display, but a quick scan of wardrobes and drawers revealed neither clothes nor books nor belongings of any kind.

She stole up to the next floor and its additional four bedrooms. All were as devoid of a human presence as the ones on her floor.

By now she was genuinely afraid. Even if Julia was over at a friend's house, where did she sleep when she was here?

She remembered the servants' hallway that had confused her earlier. Those rooms had been empty, but might there be others? At the far end of the hallway, she found a door leading to the back stairs. Stealthily she headed for it, reviewing routes and paths in her head.

A noise.

Were those footsteps on the stairs?

She looked wildly around. Lord, she didn't want to get caught. Not by Gus or his light-skinned twin, and especially not by Dutch. She ducked into a room, all the saliva in her mouth suddenly turned to dust.

"Neesy? Is that you?"

Dutch.

She groaned silently. What in the blue moon was she going to do? Frantic, she saw one of those big wooden wardrobes in the corner. She knew from her own home that closets were a luxury most people didn't have when the mansion had been built. Instead, they had these big, wooden pieces of furniture to hold their stuff. She ran to the one in the room, flung open the door. Empty like all the others. Quick as she could, she slipped out of her heels, crawled inside, and held the door closed behind her.

"Is someone there?" He was inside the room now.

Oh, how she wished she was one of those skinny things that were all bone and no flesh. Her purse and shoes squished against her chin, she folded herself as small as possible. But if she breathed out, she would burst through the walls. She closed her eyes, sent up a prayer for luck, and held her breath. The wardrobe reeked of old wood, varnish, and mildew. She was so close to it that the smell could have choked her.

She fisted her hands and waited. Was that the room door closing? Still, she huddled inside, afraid to reveal herself. Slowly she counted to fifty, then to a hundred. Then, for good luck, she counted to fifty again.

Finally, she cracked open the wardrobe door. She intended only to peek out, but her position was so precarious that the minute the door opened, she tumbled down and landed on the carpet.

She nearly swallowed her heart.

Collecting herself, she scanned the room. Empty, thank the Lord. She slid the heels back on, picked up the purse, and stole a glance into the hallway. It, too, was empty.

She slipped out of the room, again heading for those back stairs. A door hid them from view, and when she opened it, she found herself in darkness. She looked for a light switch and couldn't find one. Surely the entire house had been electrified at one time or another? Seeing how there was no staff anymore, maybe Dutch had cut the power to this part of the house. Man, even the rich like to save money on electric bills.

If she was going down there, she'd need a flashlight, but where in this monstrosity of a house was she going to find one?

Stymied, she was about to go down those stairs, anyway—if only to prove to herself she would not be defeated—when she remembered something.

Taking off her shoes, she raced back to her room and into the adjoining bath with its spa tub. Thick white pillar candles sat in all four corners of the tub, each atop its own glass holder. She lit one and returned to the stairs.

Creeping down was like creeping back a hundred years or more. Was this what it was like to be a servant to these Hanovers? Maybe this was how the other Mr. Hanover got to that poor serving wench who'd hung herself after he knocked her up. Or maybe she'd gone to him. Sneaking around by candlelight in her nightie.

Had they been caught? Would she?

What would she tell Dutch if he found her? Would he believe her?

Shadows bounced off the walls like ghosts. At the bottom of the stairs, the hallway loomed black and baleful, her candle a flimsy shield against whatever menace lurked ahead.

But it was only the dark. Only more empty halls and more empty rooms—even more so than the ones she'd inspected earlier. Those at least had been furnished. These were starkly unadorned, stripped down to pale walls and wood floors.

And yet the lack of human presence didn't settle her uneasiness. The floors squeaked as though protesting her footsteps. The house sighed and moaned around her. It felt as though unspeakable things had been done back here. Lives lived and snuffed out, out of sight and mind.

She progressed slowly, staying within her small spool of light. Every sound sent a warning through her; every nerve ending grew frayed and raw. And still, she found no sign of anyone, and especially not Julia.

She also saw no sign of another way in or out of the mansion.

But there had to be another exit. She'd come through it, hadn't she? Truth was, she had no idea where she was in relation to that door or any other. She was completely turned around. She was pretty sure the staircase was toward the left, but she'd been going to the left and it had taken her nowhere.

So she turned to the right and the nearest door. It opened, not to anyplace familiar, but to a long, light-filled hallway. It was the only lit hallway she'd seen for hours, and it blinded her at first.

But she was grateful, so grateful to be back in the twenty-first century. She snuffed out the candle and practically ran down the passage toward a door at the far end.

That had to be the way back to the core of the mansion.

All at once, she slowed. A heap of clothes blocked the door.

She squinted, peering hard. No. Not clothes. At least, not clothes by themselves.

Someone was inside them.

Julia.

She drew in a sharp, fearful breath, raced the last few yards, and skidded to her knees.

But it wasn't Julia.

43

Neesy was so shocked she could only sit on the floor and stare. The absolute last person she expected to see was conked out in front of her.

And, oh, God, he looked...well, awful wasn't awful enough. The right side of his face was a swollen mess of blood and bruises; his mouth was cut and twice the size it should be. Even if he was conscious, she doubted he could open his right eye.

But he was breathing. That was something.

Unbidden, her eyes filled. What in heaven had happened to him? He disappears whole and hearty and reappears like a ship torn against the rocks. Had he been here all along, hidden away like Julia? She cracked open the door he was crumpled against, saw the garage. Was he coming or going? And what should she do? She didn't want to move him, and she couldn't leave him there. But if she did move him, was she thwarting his escape or helping him infiltrate?

Roughly, she scrubbed her eyes, trying to figure out

what to do. She wasn't even sure where to touch without hurting him.

So she just bent over, close to his ear. "Mitch! Wake up! Wake up, Mitch!"

That didn't do a whole helluva lot of good.

She shook him as gently as she could. "Dammit, Mitch, open your eyes!"

She kept at it, scared now that he'd never wake up. Suddenly he groaned.

"That's it," she encouraged. "Come on, open your eyes, wake up."

Slowly, like it hurt to do it any other way, one eye opened. The other, as she'd predicted, was swollen shut. He took one look at her and the open eye rolled back into his head.

"Oh, no, you don't." She nudged him hard enough to hurt, and the pain did the trick. He opened his eye again.

"Neesy?" His voice was a rough grumble, like he was drunk on gravel.

"Yeah, it's me."

He paused. "I'm not...not seeing things?"

"No, but you can't stay here. Come on, let's get you up."

He closed that good eye again. "You've got to be kidding."

"If only."

He braced a hand against the floor and tried to push himself up. "Jesus fucking Christ."

He ground his jaw, hard enough for her to see the muscle working. His knuckles were white with intensity. She went around the other side and tried to give him leverage. He cursed every move, but with her help and the wall, he finally managed to get to his feet.

And swayed there.

"Whoa." She steadied him against the wall.

He closed his eyes and breathed hard. "Have you seen her? Is she okay?"

He didn't have to say who he meant. She knew. "Look, we have to get you out of here. I'll tell you everything then." She put his left arm around her shoulder to take his weight. "Were you trying to get in or out?"

"In."

She stopped suddenly.

"Christ, what now?"

"The candle. I blew it out."

"My head is kind of spinning. Did you say you blew out a candle? Dutch not pay his electric bills?"

She explained about the back hallways and needing a light and getting lost.

"What the hell were you doing back there? Better yet, what the hell are you doing here, period?"

"I said I'd tell you everything once we get you out of sight. But unless you want to go through the main rooms, we'll need a light."

"Just go to the kitchen. There are always matches there."

She opened her mouth to ask how he knew that, then remembered. He had lived there.

"The thing is—"

"I don't know how long I can stay upright."

"The thing is, I don't know how to get to the kitchen."

"Go through the door at the end of the tunnel, make a right, then a—" He closed his eye. "Better idea. I'll take you there. Or, you can take me."

Then they were both silent as the struggle up the

hallway began in earnest. He wasn't a huge man, nothing like Gus, but he had plenty of height and weight on her. Why she thought she'd be able to hold a candle and help him at the same time was a mystery. In the end, they had to go in darkness. But Mitch knew the way, and though they stumbled several times, which elicited a sharp gasp and an equally sharp "fuck," or "holy fuck," or "holy motherfuck," they made slow, slogging, curse-filled progress.

By the time they arrived, he was panting and grunting in pain. "To the left," he eked out through gritted teeth. "Behind the utility closet."

There was no "behind" at the back of the closet, just wall. It took Neesy several minutes to figure out she had to move the thing. Now it was her turn to curse. But with a lot of heaving and not a little swearing, she finally managed to pull it away from the wall. Behind it was a rough, spare door that looked like it hadn't been opened in years. She had to shove it ajar using her shoulder, but after several attempts, it gave with a screech of protest.

Oh, God, it was rank. A cramped little hidey-hole. There were water stains on the floor and Dutch's beloved cobwebs in the corners. Clearly it hadn't been aired in years, and the accumulated mold and dust and remains of other inhabitants she didn't want to think about made it smell like a tomb. But there was a small, ancient bed and a crooked washstand with a pitted white bowl.

Had someone actually lived here?

She returned to the kitchen, where she'd left Mitch leaning against a wall. "What is that place?"

"For the scullery maid."

"Geez, you people treated the staff so well."

"Help me in."

"It's a mess."

"Is the bed still there?"

"Yes, but—"

"Help me in."

"All right, all right. But first let me clean it up a bit."

"Do it fast. I think I'm gonna fall down pretty soon."

She ran back to the little maid's cell and swung a kitchen towel to swipe away the cobwebs. There was nothing but a thin mattress on the bed, which was closer to a cot, and she managed to wriggle the thing off and whomp it a couple of times to get the dust off. She coughed and waved the powdery stuff away from her face. She hated the thought of putting him on that filthy thing without something between his wounds and the dirt, but there were no bedclothes and no linen closet. In the end, she covered the mattress with more dishrags. At least they were clean.

She had to widen the space behind the pantry a few more feet to make enough room for him to squeeze through. He collapsed on the bed, mussing the towels she'd so carefully placed.

"Here." She handed him a package of frozen peas. "Put that over your eye." Then she left him to tackle the washstand, which was broken but still usable. She cleaned out the bowl in the kitchen sink, filled it with fresh water, and brought it back to the room.

He fell in and out of sleep as she cleaned him up, and she was constantly having to put the peas back in place. After she got the blood off his face, she tackled the rest of him. She gasped as she opened his shirt. His chest and sides were red and beginning to bruise up. The sight of them sickened her, and she had to force back the tears and the growing fear. Was there more damage under the skin where she couldn't see it?

"Mitch. Mitch!"

He grunted.

"I think you should see a doctor. You've got cuts on your face that probably need stitches. And your ribs are a mess. You could be bleeding internally."

"No doctors."

"But—"

He grabbed her hand, hard and fast. "No doctors."

Given the state he was in, she was surprised he could move that quickly. But she nodded, and he let go.

"Tell me about Julia."

She sat on the edge of the cot and told him everything she could, intertwining that story with how she came to be in New York and then at Hanover House. By the time she'd finished, he'd fallen asleep, or so she thought. But when she stopped, he reached for her hand. "Thank you." Both eyes were still closed, and speaking seemed like a huge effort. "Sorry. Shouldn't have left you."

Gently, she brushed the hair back from his forehead. "Damn right you shouldn't have," she whispered.

"Wanted you safe. Now, too. Dutch...dangerous. Go."

"Who'll take care of you if I go?"

He squeezed her fingers. "Not important. Get out."

"But—"

"Out." His good eye opened with a ferocious glare, and he crushed her hand.

She pulled out of his grip. "Okay, okay. Geez."

"Go."

She rose. "I'm going."

"Promise." He tried to get up to enforce the vow, and sweat broke out on his forehead from the agony. She jumped to ease him back down, but he wouldn't let her. "Promise."

She couldn't bear it. "All right. I swear. On a stack of Bibles. Will you lie down now?"

"Go first. Back door." He told her how to get there, and continued to sit up until she left.

The minute she was out of sight, she slumped against the pantry. His poor, tortured face. The tears welled up then, but she didn't care. How was she supposed to leave him like that? He needed to be fed and cared for, and she didn't have a clue how to do that without alerting Dutch. But she would. Somehow, she would.

In the meantime, she grabbed an armful of apples and oranges, found some cheese and bread, and a couple of bottles of water. She shoved everything into a shopping bag, fished around her purse for a bottle of Midol, and added that. Then she tiptoed back to the room, prepared for another battle. But luckily, Mitch was out cold.

After she shoved the pantry into place, she hurried through the house, ignoring Mitch's directions to the rear door and trying instead to find the back stairs that would return her to the bedroom. She was scurrying down a hallway when a door opened and Dutch stepped out.

She stopped short. All the blood in her body went straight to her toes.

"Going somewhere?" Dutch lounged against the wall.

Neesy's breath clogged and her brain jammed.

"Perhaps you couldn't sleep," Dutch said.

She nodded, relieved to be given an excuse. "New place, new bed. You know how it is."

"I do, indeed. And I have the perfect remedy." He smiled and slithered toward her. She would have stepped back, but he was beside her before she could. Like he'd done after dinner, he slipped her arm through his. "There's nothing more relaxing than a little brandy."

She tried to pull away. "Oh, no, I'll be fine. I'm really tired now."

But he had her fast and refused to let go. "Nonsense. You'll be surprised at how quickly the brandy will help." He pulled her along, and in seconds they were in the room with the fireplace where she and Dutch had first talked. A glass cart trimmed in gold sat in one corner. It held glasses and decanters and a variety of mixers. A snifter holding an inch of russet liquid already sat on top. He ushered her to an armchair, handed her the drink, and poured another for himself.

"I was just about to have a nightcap. So glad you could join me."

She sipped at the brandy. Truthfully, she could use it. She couldn't stop thinking about Mitch and how close he was and what would happen if the brothers came face-to-face.

She swallowed the last of the drink and set down the glass.

"Better?" Dutch asked.

"Much." She rose, too quickly it seemed, because she nearly fell over. "Oops," she said as Dutch ran to support her. "Sorry." She straightened herself.

"That's perfectly all right."

She put a hand to her head. "I think...I think I should go to bed now."

"Of course you should."

She headed for the door, but it wasn't where she thought it was.

"Here," Dutch said, "let me escort you."

He walked her back to the room with the canopy bed, and it seemed to take forever to get there. Waves of hot and cold scuttled over her, sometimes together. Where was he leading her? Why was it taking so long to get there?

She tried to ask him, but her mouth wouldn't work. She tried again and still couldn't make her jaw move. Terror and panic rushed through her. What was happening?

All of a sudden, whatever had happened to her jaw spread to the rest of her body. The last thing she remembered was Dutch, catching her as she fell into darkness.

44

Mitch opened his eyes to an old-fashioned light fixture on the ceiling above his head. It took him a few seconds to recall where he'd seen it before. When he finally did, and realized where he was, bits and pieces of the night before tumbled back.

Neesy. He'd seen Neesy.

Either that or he was going out of his mind.

But if he wasn't, and he had seen her... He rocketed upright and nearly screamed aloud.

His body pulsating pain, he sank back against the thin mattress. If that had been Neesy, she had to get out of here. He had to make sure she was out of here. But he could barely move.

A minuscule octagonal window told him the sun was up. How long had he been there? He spied the washstand with a towel over the bar. A bottle of water on the floor next to an open bag of food. And a bottle of... He squinted. Midol?

Definitely Neesy.

Gingerly, he rolled over, snagged the bottle, read the

label. Mostly ibuprofen. He shook out a small handful of tablets and washed down the pills.

Slowly, he lay down again. Christ, that was hard. He was going to need a couple of days to get his strength back. But he didn't have a couple of days; he had to move now. He tried again, and again didn't make it. But the pills should help. He gave himself twenty minutes to let them do their magic.

He didn't intend to sleep, but he did. The little window was dark when he woke again. He cursed when he saw it. Had he slept all day? Or was it the day after?

He took another dose of Midol, downed half the bottle of water, and ate an orange. He still hurt like a son of a bitch, but moving was less torturous and getting vertical no longer felt like a crawl up a high, rocky mountain.

He tried his sea legs, shuffling around the perimeter and holding on to the walls.

It was ironic, hiding out in that freak show of a room. The walls had long ago been painted over, but he'd never forget what they'd looked like before. Like someone had gone crazy in there. Precise but insane drawings in heavy red ink. Circles around circles around eyes dripping blood. Things that looked like spiders with huge teeth crushing bodies. No one could ever accuse Dutch of not having talent. Some of it had even been painted in blood, or at least that's what Dutch said when he crept up to Mitch's bed the night after he'd showed the room to their mother. That was what the washstand had been for. Mice, birds, cats, even a small dog.

"I can do the same to you," Dutch had whispered in the blackness of Mitch's room. "And no one would care."

Mitch believed him.

When he showed the room to Iona, she'd gone as white as the walls were now. She'd dragged him out, shock and fear on her face.

"Don't you ever, *ever* mention this again," she'd said, her hand a claw on his arm. "Not to anyone, do you understand?"

Within the hour, she'd dismissed one of the help, a girl who'd come to them recently and who was categorized as "slow" and who probably didn't even know the room existed. Painters were there that afternoon, and the pantry moved in front of the door the next day.

He'd had years to think about his mother. From the distance of time and the occasional news photo, he saw how brittle she'd become. As though keeping her beautiful son's secret had turned her into a pillar of ice—one with faults and fissures she was desperate to conceal. The strain must have been enormous; no wonder she was barely sixty when she died.

Had she thought about him in those last moments? When he'd read about her death, he'd had a short-lived hope that somewhere inside her had been a softer place, a place that was sorry and wanted forgiveness. But reality soon surfaced. She'd probably been too focused on Dutch to worry about her firstborn. That had always been the pattern—Dutch consumed every ounce of her energy; she simply had no room for anything or anyone else.

Now he carefully lowered himself onto the cot. He hadn't lasted long, but just the fact that he lasted at all gave him hope.

For the first time, he heard noise from outside the room. It must have been there all along—pots and utensils banging in the distance—but he hadn't been focused enough before. If it was dark outside and the kitchen was being used, it probably meant dinner. So it was sometime in the late afternoon or early evening. He wouldn't be able to sneak out and look for Neesy and Julia for hours.

He spent the time alternating between sleep and exercise, trying to rest as much as possible but also keep his muscles from forgetting what they were there for. By the time the cooking noises beyond the door had stopped, he felt as ready as he'd ever be to find what he'd come for.

The biggest obstacle was going to be pushing that pantry away. Ordinarily it would have been no problem, but he was not at full strength. He used his back and his legs, the least compromised parts of his body, and was gratified to hear the scratch of the wood on the floor. He rested, pushed again, a little wider this time. A third push gave him enough room to slip past. The exertion left him breathless, so while he waited for his heart to slow, he went over the plan in his head.

Neesy had said she'd checked the upstairs bedrooms and some of the servants' quarters, too. But she also said she'd gotten lost, so there were parts of the back hallways she might have missed. Not to mention a few nooks she'd never find unless she knew where they were.

When he'd regained his strength, he slipped through the door, past the side of the closet, and into the kitchen. He didn't remember coming through with Neesy, so it seemed as though this was the first time he'd been there in over a decade. The smell of lavender hit him immediately. His mother had abhorred cooking smells and insisted on a fresh bouquet at all times. He also recognized the long prep table with the pots hanging above it. There was a new stove and refrigerator, both stainless, wide, and professional-looking. Other than that, the kitchen looked exactly as he remembered.

Except for one small detail.

Dutch lounged against the counter.

45

Neesy woke slowly. The light was so strong she flinched and slammed her eyes shut. God, her head...It was so huge and so heavy it must have grown ten pounds overnight.

She groaned, tried to raise an arm to shield herself from the glare seeping through her lids.

Her arm didn't move.

She tried again.

Icy heat raced through her. She bolted up, her eyes jerking open.

But straps across her chest and waist, her thighs and ankles, kept her still. She was in some kind of chair—not unlike what the dentist used—and with horror saw that on either side, her arms were cradled in some kind of support, her palms and wrists up like a sacrifice. A needle was inserted in her vein just below the elbow fold. It was attached to a tube that was taped down the length of her arm. The tube disappeared into a bag that was slowly filling with blood.

Her blood.

Her stomach cramped. She gagged.

What was happening? Where was she?

Forcing herself to calm down, she looked around. Above her, open timbers formed the ceiling. The three walls she could see were completely transparent, and they went all the way up to the roof. Beyond them, everything was white—walls, floor, all lined in white tile. A set of chrome shelves held boxes of syringes, tubing, scalpels, packages of sodium citrate, and something labeled FLUNITRAZEPAM.

Was she in the hospital?

Her heart thudded desperately.

No hospital looked like this.

She searched her memory for something to hold on to. Her mind was fuzzy, and it took a while for a solid recollection to surface. The mansion. Hanover House. The name slipped into her mind like a victory. Yes. The last place she'd been was Hanover House.

Another memory surfaced. Mitch. She'd found Mitch and he'd been hurt. She'd helped him to that room off the kitchen and then...

And then...

She tensed. Dutch. Something had happened with Dutch.

Had he brought her here? When? Why couldn't she remember?

She stared at the thing in her arm. Forget the where and why—she just had to rip that thing out of her arm.

She wriggled, trying to dislodge herself. When the wriggling didn't work, she pulled and jerked, twitching herself into a crazed, spastic dance.

The straps didn't budge. Neither did the needle in her arm.

A haze of icy dread swirled around her as she realized with growing terror that she was too securely bound to escape.

How long had she been there? How much blood had she lost?

She started screaming. She screamed until she was hoarse. Until she wore herself out.

No one heard. No one came.

Exhausted, her muscles went lax. All that effort and she was exactly where she'd been when she woke—lashed to a chair.

And bit by bit, with inevitable and relentless detachment, the blood slowly drained out of her.

46

Shock rooted Mitch to the floor.

"What took you so long?" Arms crossed in front of him, Dutch looked unflappably relaxed in a pair of charcoal trousers and a crisp white shirt open at the neck. Exhilaration gleamed from his baby blues. "I left you enough breadcrumbs. That poor dog." He shook his head, but it was more mock sorrow than the real thing.

Warily, Mitch kept his distance. "Heard you'd busted your knee."

"Amazing what medical science can do these days, isn't it? People see what they want to see, what the true artist frames for them. A man on crutches? Surely he was in the hospital all day."

Sick knowledge swirled inside Mitch. "And Shelby?"

"Just another body to add to your long list. A little incentive to get you moving. I've been expecting you daily."

"You should have sent a car."

Dutch grinned. "Now, where's the fun in that?"

They stared at each other. Mitch fisted his hands; the

memory of his brother's throat beneath his fingers was potent. But he was acutely aware of the knives in the block within Dutch's easy reach, and of his own weakness. Given his current physical state, his younger brother could grab a blade and thrust it through his heart before he could evade, let alone disarm, him.

Dutch seemed to know it, too. "This what's bothering you?" He slid out a large butcher knife and waved it provocatively between them. "I don't think I'll be needing this, big brother. At least, not yet." He rammed the knife home. "You want Julia and I have her. That's really all the leverage I need."

Mitch growled, and Dutch held up an open hand. "First, a few ground rules. Disney World was exciting, but I don't relish a repeat. You will neither attack nor interrupt me, and you will do exactly as I say. Finally—now, I want to be clear about this—you can have Julia or you can have Miss Brown. But not both."

"Miss Brown?"

"Oh, come on, Mitch. You're not very good at deception. You know Miss Brown. Neesy. Your...companion in arms, so to speak. You really should have told her to clean the floor when she moved the pantry. She left a mark even a blind man could see."

Mitch looked down. A slight discoloration in the wood showed where the pantry had stood for decades and where it stood now, an inch over.

"The devil is in the details, isn't it?" Dutch said.

A cold, slimy film coated Mitch's mouth. He wanted to spit in Dutch's face. Skewer him with a knife himself. Silently, he flung a dozen curses at him. But out loud all he said was, "Fuck you, Dutch."

His brother threw back his head and laughed. He held out a trim arm, still burbling. "Shall we?"

Dutch produced a flashlight and directed Mitch through the back hallways. They met no one on the long, dark route.

"No thugs today?" Mitch asked.

"Family matters are best left to family, don't you agree?" Dutch smiled amiably and opened the door to the attic. "Up you go."

"Neesy said Julia wasn't there."

"Can't believe everything you hear. Or see."

Mitch gazed up the narrow, winding steps. Dutch had given his thick-necks the day off—a sign of supreme confidence. He thought he could handle Mitch alone, without help or witnesses. But that worked both ways. Climbing those stairs would be difficult for Mitch. He'd have to go slow and stop often. But the pace might give him a chance. One chance only, when he got to the top ahead of Dutch. For a second, maybe two, he'd have Dutch off balance with the sweep of the stairs behind him and Mitch in front. Even with his injuries, Mitch thought he could shove Dutch hard enough to topple him down the stairs. And hopefully break his neck. And there were no bystanders to deny it was an accident.

He started up, hopeful, planning, braced for the coming struggle.

"No, no," Dutch said. "Wait a minute. I think I'd better go first this time."

Mitch stopped dead. Didn't move.

"Unless you'd rather not see either of the women," Dutch said.

Wordlessly, Mitch shifted to one side so Dutch could

go ahead of him, then slogged the rest of the way, holding on to his side and gritting his teeth.

The attic was as naked of humanity as Neesy had said it was. If anything lived there, it was the spider, the rat, and the roach. Then again, that was how Dutch liked it. Always fodder for his little hobbies.

"Well?" Mitch demanded.

"Patience, brother," Dutch said. "Perhaps you'd like to see my latest project?" He uncovered an easel that sat off to one side.

"I'd rather see..." But the words died in Mitch's throat. On the easel was another of Dutch's strange child-women. She was lounging on a glass slab, half naked and half covered in fur and animal skins. Her face had no features yet, but her hair was short and dark like Julia's. That alone set alarms clanging, but there was more. Something Mitch couldn't name, an innate evil that jumped out at him from the canvas.

"Of course, it's not finished," Dutch said. "In fact, I may never finish it."

"Where is she?" Mitch scuttled over to his brother like an injured crab, limping and jogging and dragging one leg.

Dutch easily avoided him. "All right. So you're not an art lover."

"You tell me what I want to know or I'll shove that thing down your throat and watch you choke on it."

"You do and you'll never see Julia or Miss Brown again." His eyes were blue flint, hard and cold, and Mitch wanted to hack out those beautiful orbs. His thoughts must have shown on his face, because Dutch's lethal glare immediately softened into amusement. "No need for hostilities. A deal is a deal." A table near the easel held a variety of painter's tools, and Dutch reached for one.

Not a brush. A remote control.

He held it toward the center of the attic ceiling. "You remember Agnes, don't you?"

"Agnes? What are you talking about?"

"Family lore, Mitchell. The girl in the attic."

"The one who hung herself? That's just a story."

"Actually, it's not. I looked it up. Her name was Agnes Deare, and she was probably murdered. Of course, the authorities covered all that up. And I'm sure they were well paid for it, too." He pressed a button on the remote. "I just thought it appropriate to carry on the family tradition over the spot where she died." Above their heads, the ceiling opened like the heavens dividing. From the groaning split, a set of stairs slowly descended.

When they were in place, Dutch gestured Mitch up, and once again, Mitch had a chance to break free.

But when he got to the top and saw what was there, all thought of escape evaporated.

The stairs led up through the center of a new room. In front of him was a glass prison, its transparent walls built up to the ceiling. Inside, Neesy was strapped to a chair, a needle in her arm.

"So," Dutch hissed behind him. "What shall it be, the lady or the tiger?"

47

With frenzied intent, Mitch scanned the room, looking for something, anything, to use on the glass.

Dutch opened a door that was flush with the tiled walls. He brought out a baseball bat. "This what you're looking for?"

Mitch wrenched the bat away and used every ounce of strength he had to attack the glass.

Dutch watched, an amused expression on his face. "You're wasting your time. It won't shatter. I know because right after I had it installed, I tried to break it myself."

Mitch tossed the bat away, and it landed on the tile with a crash. He grabbed Dutch by his shirt.

"What the hell are you doing to her?"

"Remember our deal," Dutch warned.

Shouting, Mitch shook his brother. "What are you pumping into her?"

"I'm not pumping in anything. I'm withdrawing."

"What the fuck does that mean? Withdrawing what?"

"Her blood, Mitchell."

Mitch was so stunned he relaxed his grip, and Dutch

stepped away. "It's a relatively painless way to die." He straightened his shirt. "Eventually there won't be enough left for her heart to pump and it will simply...stop."

"You're even more of a monster than I thought possible."

"Sticks and stones, brother." He brushed his hands together, ridding them of invisible dust. "Now, I should count that as a deal-breaker." He smiled. "But I won't."

That smile enraged Mitch. He swiped a scalpel from a shelf of medical supplies and sprang at Dutch. "The keys, *brother*! Where are the keys?"

But even with a knife inches from his jugular, Dutch only looked amused. "Do you think I would resort to something so mundane?"

"Give me the key or I'll cut your throat—I swear I will. I might even do it anyway." Mitch nicked Dutch's throat. Droplets of blood landed on the collar of his pristine white shirt.

Dutch flinched. "Kill me and she'll bleed out before you can open the door."

"The key, Dutch!"

"There is no key! The cube can only be unlocked by a code. And only I know what it is. Kill me, kill her."

Mitch looked over at Neesy. She was watching with stark, bloodshot eyes.

"I'll take that." Dutch grabbed the scalpel. "I see you can't be trusted to hold up your end of a bargain." He played absently with the blade. "But I won't have it said that I'm a hard-hearted bastard." He picked up the remote and quickly punched in the number on the keypad. "There. Go ahead. Take her."

One of the walls began to slide open. Mitch ran to it,

but it halted before it was wide enough to slip through. He whirled. Dutch was watching him closely.

"Of course, I do keep my end," Dutch said. "So, if I let you take Miss Brown, you'll have to leave Julia with me."

Mitch took a step toward his brother, and Dutch smiled again.

"I thought you might change your mind."

"What do you want from me, Dutch? Do you want me dead? I'll die for you, but you have to let Julia and Neesy go."

"Very noble of you. But I want you very much alive. I want you to watch them die. I want to see your face when the life goes out of theirs. And I want you to know your choice made it happen."

"Why?"

Dutch laughed. "Why? Why not? Because I can, brother. So, what will it be? The woman or the girl?"

"Where is she? Where's Julia?"

"Is that your choice, then? Julia over Miss Brown?"

Mitch looked at Neesy. There were tears in her eyes. "Let me see her," Mitch stalled. "Let me make sure Julia is all right and then I'll decide."

Dutch shook his head. "I don't think so."

"She's your own flesh and blood for God's sake!"

"Is she?"

"What's that supposed to mean?"

"What's that supposed to mean? *Après moi le déluge*, you stupid little man. You think there could ever be one like me?" Mitch saw the warning in Neesy's eyes a split second before Dutch swung the baseball bat with such force, it laid Mitch out flat. "You think I, the unique and glorious I, would deign to reproduce even if it was biologically possible?" He kicked Mitch, shouting, "Look at you, crumbs under my boot heels." He pushed his foot on Mitch's windpipe and pressed.

Mitch struggled beneath the force of that foot. It was crushing the air out of his lungs. He was pinned, choking and gagging. The room was turning red; bursts of light popped in and out of Mitch's peripheral vision. He was going to black out. He was going to die. Unless...

Dutch's stance, strong as it was with his weight behind it, was also an unbalanced one. At the last second, Mitch seized Dutch's ankle and yanked. His brother fell.

Still half strangled, coughing, Mitch rolled onto his side in an effort to stand. Before he could, Dutch bared his teeth and leaped on him like a rabid dog.

They scrambled on the ground, inches away from the center where the floor opened into a wide square for the staircase. Dutch pounded Mitch, forcing his head into the opening. He was healthy and strong, and Mitch was wounded and weak. But he was also possessed by adrenaline fever. The madness fueled his body. He pushed Dutch back, hand on his brother's chin, and Dutch gave, inch by maddening inch. Soon, Mitch was able to flip positions and force Dutch onto his back. Mitch sat on him, smashing his brother's beautiful face. Again. And again.

And again.

Dutch was mashed and bloody and finally, finally still. Sick but satisfied, Mitch crawled off him, stumbling to his feet. He dragged himself to the glass wall. Neesy's eyes were closed. Her skin was pale and stretched tight. She looked smaller, shrunken. How much time did he have?

He was looking around for something, anything, to get

him inside, when a hot searing pain shot into his back. He staggered, turning.

Dutch was conscious, standing, and holding a bloody scalpel. His face was raw and smeared with blood, but his teeth gleamed white. "I'm going to turn you into art."

He lunged, and Mitch barely managed to sidestep him. But as he did, Dutch's knife arm came within reach. Mitch snatched it, raised his leg, then cracked the limb backward over his knee with all his might.

The sound of bone breaking splintered the room. Dutch dropped the knife and screamed in agony. Holding his shattered arm, he reeled backward, lurching and tottering, and Mitch watched in horror as his brother lost his footing, stepped unawares into the room's open center, and fell.

In an eyeblink he was gone.

48

Mitch was shaking, his whole body quivering uncontrollably. He wanted to stop, think about what had just happened, but he couldn't. Neesy was still losing blood. And when he thought about Julia, a river of molten terror ran through him.

The ceiling wasn't terribly high, maybe eight feet. He grabbed the metal shelving and pulled it down. Everything on it fell and scattered on the floor, but he ignored that. Instead, he dragged the shelving close to the back wall of the glass room, unpended it, and with a grunt of pain, started battering the ceiling. It took him an eternity to pound a hole wide enough to crawl through. Every inch of him hurt, but he couldn't think about that now. His mind was a frantic web of fear. Hurry, hurry, hurry—his only objective. When he finally made it through, he didn't even know if Neesy was alive or dead.

The minute the hole was wide enough, he let the shelving crash to the ground. He turned it right side up and shoved it against the wall. Praying it would hold his weight, he used it like a ladder, pulling himself up the few feet necessary to reach the ceiling.

The crawl space was warm and damp and smelled of mice. He lay on his stomach, reached back through the hole, and pulled up the shelving. Then he repeated the entire routine, this time on the floor several yards away.

By the time he managed to crack though the beams, the shelving was dented and deformed. Then the bottom shelf fell out of its housing. He set the unit aside before more of it broke, then scrabbled with his bare hands, ripping out wood and nails. His fingers were bleeding, but finally he yanked open a big enough hole. He threw down the now-distorted shelving, then dropped down after it.

He was beyond despair when he saw Neesy up close. She hadn't flinched at the noise he'd made. He felt for a pulse at the side of her neck and could barely find it. With a frenzied jerk, he pulled out the needle. Blood spurted everywhere. He ripped off his shirt, wrapped it around the needle entry, and bent her arm over it.

He was undoing the last of the straps when her eyes fluttered open.

She stared at him. "Hey, you," she whispered.

"Hey, yourself." He stroked her face.

"Am I dead?"

He kissed her forehead. "Not dead."

"Am I dreaming?"

He kissed her lips. "Not dreaming, either."

Tears leaked down her cheeks. "Are you sure?"

He took her good arm, the one that hadn't been used for bloodletting, and guided it to his face. "Feel real enough?"

"You need a shave."

He smiled. "Will you be all right for a while? I undid all the straps but you should lie here and rest until I can get you out."

"What about... what about Dutch?"

Gently he said, "You don't have to worry about him anymore."

"And... and Julia?"

He shook his head, hoping she couldn't see his fear.

"Oh, God."

"I'll find her."

She nodded. "I know you will." But the tears welling up in her eyes betrayed her own fear and misgivings.

"Don't Neesy," he said. "Please don't."

She closed her eyes as though trying to hold them back, but it didn't work. "I won't," she said as they slid down her cheeks. "I'm not."

"Stay here?"

"Too tired to move anyway."

He left her, unsure if he was doing the right thing. Did he get there in time? Would she die anyway? But the other drumbeat inside his chest gave him no other option: he had to find Julia.

He climbed out the way he'd come, the choice haunting him. The makeshift ladder held most of the way up, but it buckled just as he reached the crawl space. He was left hanging, his arms clutching the crawl space, his feet dangling over the glass room. If he fell, there'd be no way out for either him or Neesy.

The thought gave him the extra strength he needed. At the last second, he managed to heave himself up and over the lip of the hole he'd carved. He lay on his back, breathing hard and fast.

A few seconds' rest, and he jumped down into the room below and jolted down the stairs. His brother still lay at the bottom, his body twisted, his neck at a skewed angle. For the first time in his life, Dutch looked graceless.

Something pierced Mitch—sadness, relief, the overwhelming knowledge of talent wasted. If lives weren't at stake, he might even have stayed with his brother's body longer, but he didn't. He flew down into the heart of the mansion. In his mother's room he found a landline, the phone itself an old-fashioned rotary, cream colored with gilt trim.

For a half second he paused. What he was about to do would be the end of everything. But better that than the end of everyone he loved.

He picked up the receiver and dialed 911.

While he waited for the police and EMTs to come, he tore the house apart searching for Julia. There were several places that had been special to Mitch when he was a kid—an old garden shed that had survived the sale of the gardens, a butler's pantry with a pulley compartment that went between floors, an ancient laundry chute that snaked down to the basement. At one time or another, he had escaped to all of them. Now he hustled from one to the other, each time sure Dutch had stashed her there, and each time shattered to find it empty.

By the time he got to the basement, he was in a frenzy of hopelessness. The police would be there any minute, and he wasn't under any illusions about being arrested. He'd never be able to find her, help her, heal her when they took him away.

He punched the end of the metal laundry chute. The old steel was fragile, and the thing collapsed in a cloud of dirt and dust. Mitch inhaled a lungful and backed away. The broken chute seemed to represent himself—stuck in the mess of the past and looking at the collapse of the life he'd made to escape it.

He trudged out of the basement. For the first time, he felt a stinging throb at his back where Dutch had sliced into him. He was shirtless and cold, and the adrenaline was wearing off. How deep was the cut? If he never found Julia, it couldn't be deep enough.

His pace slowed to a limp, and fear rose to a clanging crescendo. What if he never found her? He pictured her curled into herself, her small, helpless body lifeless and hidden where no one would ever find her. A keening moan escaped his throat. What had Dutch done to her?

A knock boomed through the house. Mitch ignored it.

The knock turned into pounding. It battered at the huge front door, thudding with the beat of his heart.

The police had arrived.

Mitch plodded from room to room. Every cell in his damaged body seemed to cry out in pain. Not that it mattered. Nothing mattered.

The police were still trying to get in. Their efforts had become a steady report that echoed like a soldier's drum on the way to the gallows. Mitch entered the portrait gallery with the rumble of that drum in his head. It seemed to be sounding out the beats of a lifelong battle. A fight that had ended in loss and was now nearly over.

A small door on one wall led directly to the foyer. He looked toward the door, acutely aware of his failure, wanting, almost needing, the cuffs and the chains and the bars.

Halfway there, he halted. Inhaled a huge, panicked breath.

Above the door was a picture frame, but there was no painting inside. A small body hung in the center. Lifeless, head drooping, arms limp.

Julia.

Now the sound of heavy, galloping feet echoed through the house. But all Mitch heard was the bellow of grief that roared up from his throat, flew out his mouth, and swelled like a noxious demon to fill every corner of the room.

49

Once Mitch was in custody, Roger Carrick flew to New York and undertook a complete search of Hanover House. Among other things, the search turned up a specially designed chamber hidden in the walls of Dutch's secret attic room. It contained a stockpile of blood, all carefully packaged, stored, dated, and labeled. It was those labels that brought Roger to Rikers Island, where Mitch was being detained.

Despite what they'd found at Hanover House, the New York prosecutor's office wasn't ready to drop the original murder and kidnapping charge—there was still no evidence to support any suspect other than Mitch. And with his evasion of prosecution for over a decade, plus his recent escape from detention, no one was willing to release him on his own recognizance. Even house arrest had been denied.

So he stewed in jail, and if Roger couldn't connect Dutch to the murder of Alicia Ruiz, Mitch was going to be there a long, long time.

But the scarlet letter theory made sense only if Mitch

had carved it. And though Alicia's eyes had been taken like the other victims, she hadn't been exsanguinated, so there was no blood evidence to connect Dutch to her death. And the best connection—her eyes—unlike those of the other victims, had never been found, even after several top-to-bottom searches of the mansion.

But Roger had come to Rikers for another reason, which was why Mitch sat across a bare table from him, along with Hannah Blunt and Mark Cascio, a member of the New York firm she'd hired to represent Mitch. Roger still wasn't sure why Hannah Blunt was there, since she wasn't licensed in New York. But perhaps, since she was someone Mitch knew and seemingly trusted, he was more comfortable with her help.

He certainly looked uncomfortable in his orange jail clothes and floppy slippers. Underneath the jumpsuit, he had a ten-inch cut across his back where Dutch had sliced into him. The scars from the beating he'd received while on the run made him look rough and coarse, a river rock instead of the polished gem the ten-year-old pictures from the original investigation showed. Certainly nothing like what you'd expect from the heir of a great fortune.

Not that Mitch seemed overly interested in the wealth. The only thing he ever seemed to care about was the kid and the woman from Crossroads.

Roger had debated bringing charges against Denise Brown—aiding and abetting, accessory after the fact.... He didn't have any proof, though he was sure he could get some if he looked. He didn't. Mitch swore he'd forced her to do everything, and though he had been armed, Roger suspected that was a dodge to protect her. In the end, though, he let the story stand. Any help she gave Mitch was to protect the girl, who, it turned out, really did need protecting.

Roger hadn't been there when the police bludgeoned their way into Hanover House. But he'd read the reports and talked with the first responders. Mitch had been demented with grief, howling like a mad wolf and trying to crawl his way up the wall to the girl. His fingers and knuckles were bloodied from punching and scratching handholds into the plaster, and even after the police were able to cut her down and tell him she was alive, he had to be Tasered in order to restrain him. He'd been on suicide watch for the first two days in jail, and even now, weeks later—when Dutch was no longer a threat, and Mitch was receiving daily progress reports from Hannah Blunt and knew the girl was recovering—her health and safety as well as that of Miss Brown was the first thing he asked about.

"I understand they're both doing well," Roger said. "That's not why I'm here."

Mitch visibly relaxed.

"Why are you here?" Hannah Blunt asked.

"It's about the blood." Roger told them about the stored blood they'd found. "Each sample was carefully named—"

"They have names on them?" Mitch looked down at his hands as though the thought was incomprehensible.

"Yes. But they don't correspond to the victim names. We were hoping you could help us figure out why."

A dark, angry scowl crossed Mitch's face. It was a look Roger had seen many times in the past weeks as the full story of Dutch's crimes took shape and still Mitch was held accountable. "Me? Why the hell should I—"

Hannah Blunt put a hand on his arm. "You've told us Mr. Turner is not a suspect in these murders," she said to Roger. "Why would he know anything?"

"Mr. Turner and his brother moved in certain circles. Perhaps the names would be familiar."

"The crimes happened all over the country," Cascio said. "I don't think those circles stretch that far."

"Besides, Mr. Turner has been out of that world for years," Hannah said.

Roger knew this was a long shot, but it was the only shot he had. He'd been able to place Dutch in each respective city at the time of each murder—he'd been in each town for an art show. But why change the names? It couldn't be a way of covering his tracks—Dutch would have known a simple lab test could tie the samples to the victims. FBI profilers and psychiatrists had floated a lot of theories, but none of them had satisfied Roger.

He turned to face Mitch directly. "If you could tell us something, anything…"

Mitch took a deep breath. He looked at the two lawyers. Both gave him a small nod.

"Okay. What are the names?"

Roger removed a list from his briefcase and ran down it. "Viola, Cecilia, Nancy, Priscilla, Rose—"

"Wait," Mitch said. He looked stricken, almost sick. "Viola…"

"Cecilia, Nancy, Priscilla…Do those names mean anything to you?"

"Oh, my God."

"What?" Roger said. "What is it?"

"The paintings," Mitch said. "Dutch's portraits. Those are the names of his paintings."

Roger was dumbfounded. "Are you saying he...he painted his victims?"

"I don't know. But...we're talking blood here, right? You said these were the names found on the blood he collected?" Mitch looked even worse now.

"What is it?" Roger said. "What do you know?"

"I know that as a kid, my brother liked to paint with blood." He told them about the room off the kitchen.

Now Roger understood why Mitch looked so terrible. "Are you telling me that those portraits were painted in the victims' blood?"

The room was stunned into silence.

"Well..." Roger sat for a few seconds. He didn't know quite what to say. "I guess I'd better get a warrant for the paintings so the lab can get on it. Thank you. I...appreciate your help." He rose.

"Does that mean you'll expedite the other tests?" Hannah Blunt said. "It's been weeks and we've heard nothing."

"I'll make some calls," Roger assured them.

"Don't strain yourself," Mitch said.

"Mitch," Hannah scolded. Then to Roger she said, "These last few weeks have been very difficult, as I'm sure you can imagine. My client has cooperated fully with every aspect of this investigation, and he's still incarcerated."

"I know," Roger said, gathering up his papers and his briefcase. "And I'm working on it. I'm doing everything I can." He signaled that he was ready to go, and a corrections officer let him out.

After Carrick left, Mitch turned to Hannah and Mark. "You might as well take off, too."

Mark was already stuffing his briefcase. Mitch never had to tell the guy twice to shove off. He was always halfway out the door, onto the next case, the next meeting. "I'll see that he makes those calls," Mark said. He snapped the case shut. "I'll make a few myself."

Mitch nodded. At this point he wasn't counting on anything. The system was large and vast and moved at its own pace: slow and slower.

After Cascio left, he turned to Hannah, who hadn't made a similar move to leave. "You staying for lunch? I think it's a delicious bologna today."

She drummed on the table. It was metal and fake wood, and it was bolted to the floor. "I want to talk about Julia. She wants to see you."

He shook his head. "We've been over this."

"Neesy is picking her up from the hospital today. They can come right after."

"Did you get the hotel room? I don't want Julia going anywhere near that house."

"She won't. I promised, didn't I?"

Mitch breathed out a huge sigh. It should be him picking her up, him taking her back to Tennessee. But it never would be. Not now. And five years from now? Ten? He stared at the lock on the heavy electronic door that closed them in. Every milestone, every step in Julia's life, he'd only experience second- and thirdhand.

"Mitch, look at it from her point of view. If the situation were reversed, would you care where she was or what she'd done? And besides, what have you done? You protected her and took care of her. That's no crime."

"Not according to the prosecution."

"We're going to straighten that out."

"I'll see her then."

Hannah's brow furrowed and she pursed her lips.

"What now?"

"She's threatened to come on her own if I don't take her."

Christ.

"She'll do it, too," Hannah said. "You know she will."

A wave of affection for his girl washed over him. She was a stubborn little thing. "All right," he said. "All right. But not today. Let her get settled a little after the hospital. Take her to Serendipity for ice cream, if it's still there. Neesy will know what to do. If Julia still wants to see me in a few days, fine."

Hannah rose and gathered her things. "I make no promises, but I'll try to hold her off."

"What about the plane tickets? Are those bought?"

"I don't want to rush things. The doctor said to let her feel as if she has some control over what happens to her. I was thinking of letting her book them herself."

"I don't want her in New York any longer than necessary. She'll be better off in Crossroads."

"We'll get there. But it will be on her timetable, not yours."

He sighed in frustration. "What about Neesy? Did you get her car taken care of?"

"I did. It's sitting in front of her house even as we speak."

"Well, hallelujah. Something I asked for finally got done."

"Yes, and it will be a nice surprise for her."

She signaled the guard to open the door. "Don't wallow," she said crisply, then walked out.

The guard came for him, too. Cuffed him and took him back to his cell.

"Don't wallow."

Ha.

Easier said than done.

50

Neesy sat next to Julia in the cab on the way to the hotel. A glittery green garland hung from the back of the seat in front of them. Hard to believe it was nearly St. Patrick's Day.

For weeks she'd hovered over Julia's hospital bed, sleeping in a cot in her room. It had taken Neesy little more than a couple of days to recover, but Julia had floated in a haze of illness far longer. When Mitch had found her, she was malnourished, heavily drugged, and near death from blood loss. The doctors had brought her back slowly, but as Julia's body improved, her mind worsened. She began to wake up screaming in the middle of the night. The hospital had hooked her up with a therapist, but the process was slow, and Neesy was worried and exhausted.

She looked over at the girl. She'd been quiet ever since they got into the car. Then again, she hadn't been her old talkative self in the hospital, either. It was as though Dutch had drained her personality the same way he'd nearly drained her of blood. Her body was back now; would the rest of her return to life?

She put her arm around Julia and drew her close. It seemed important that Julia feel someone's touch at all times so she'd know she wasn't alone. Not that she seemed to care. She let Neesy embrace her, but her little body was unresponsive.

On Mitch's instructions, Hannah had made reservations for them, and when they arrived at the hotel, Neesy expected Julia to continue sitting there, listless, while she paid the driver.

Instead, she sat up and looked out the window. "Where are we?"

"The hotel, darlin'. Where did you think we were going?"

"To the house."

"The house?"

"You know, Hanover House."

"Oh, God, baby doll, you don't ever have to go there again. Ever. Your daddy—Mitch—he made us all promise. You'll never have to see that awful place again."

"Never?"

Neesy drew an X over her chest. "Cross my heart."

Julia sighed. Did she seem reassured? Neesy hoped so. She paid the driver and they got out. The doorman opened the hotel doors for them, and Neesy went to register. Julia dragged behind, running a hand over the surface of all the furniture. Finally, she plopped onto an upholstered armchair. The chair swallowed her, but she snuggled into it, her legs sticking straight out because they weren't long enough to reach the ground. When Neesy finished with the desk clerk, she turned around and saw Julia swinging her legs.

It sent a rush of warmth through her. That was the first carefree thing she'd seen Julia do in a long time.

"Come on." Neesy held out her hand. "Let's go see what our room looks like."

"Not yet," Julia said.

Neesy was taken aback. "Not yet? Are you hungry? Want to grab lunch first?"

Julia shook her head.

Neesy knelt so she was almost eye-to-eye with the girl. "Well, missy, what do you want to do? You just say the word, you know, and I'll make it happen."

"Promise?"

"Shoot, yeah. Of course."

Those gorgeous blue eyes looked right at Neesy, and sent so many horrific memories through her she had to force herself not to look away.

"I want to go to Hanover House," Julia said.

"You want to do what?"

"You promised."

"But..." Neesy examined the child. She had that stubborn look, but there was fear there, too. "Look, shove over." Neesy squished her way onto the chair and slung Julia's legs over her lap. "I know you've been having bad dreams. Why would you want to go back there?"

"I don't."

"Well, you don't have to."

"No, you don't understand. I do have to. I need to. I feel like I'm going to be scared forever if I don't."

Neesy stroked Julia's hair. "Okay, but you don't have to do it right away. We can wait a few days. You'll feel stronger after a few days."

"I want to get it over with."

Neesy sighed. "Did you talk to Jilene about this?" Jilene was the therapist Julia had been working with at the hospital. She and Julia had talked every one of the last ten days. Sometimes twice a day.

"Kind of," Julia admitted.

"So this is her idea?"

"No!" She found a loose string on the edge of Neesy's sweater and wound it around her finger. "But we talked about the house a lot. She asked me about it, and I pretended to go inside with her."

Neesy shuddered. "Were you scared?"

She nodded. "But after a while, the scary part went away. And then I could go in more. And more. And now I want to do it for real."

Neesy didn't know what to do. Julia was capable of all sorts of antics, some of them entirely unhealthy. "Well, let me make a phone call and see what I can do."

She left Julia in the chair and walked away to call Jilene. When she explained what Julia wanted to do, the therapist gave permission. "I didn't expect her to be ready so soon, but if she wants to, go ahead. Just proceed slowly and if she expresses any anxiety, stop and wait. She'll tell you when the anxiety goes away and if she's ready to continue. And the minute she wants to leave, go. Take your cues from her. Let her be in control."

Neesy had her doubts, but she took the advice. She called Hannah, who had the codes and house keys and who was also aghast at the idea.

"Mitch will have my hide if he finds out," Hannah said.

"Well, he doesn't have to know, does he?"

"Are you sure the therapist said it was okay?"

"I wouldn't even think about it if she hadn't."

"Well, all right. I'll meet you there." She paused. "You have to hand it to her—that child's got guts."

· · ·

Julia swung her legs back and forth again. How many times could she swing them before they fell off?

It was a stupid thing to think about, but it was better than thinking about Hanover House.

"Okay, we're all set." Neesy said it like she was saying something exciting and happy, even though they both knew she wasn't. Why did people do that?

She held out her hand, and though it was babyish, Julia took it. Sometimes it was okay to be a baby. At least, that's what Jilene had said.

She held on to Neesy all through the cab ride uptown, and even after they got out of the car. Hannah was waiting for them outside, but it was the iron gate that started Julia's heart racing. She paused on the sidewalk to watch it open.

"We don't have to go in," Neesy said.

"I know." Julia waited. Jilene had said that after a while, her heart would stop beating so hard and all she had to do was breathe and go slow. So she did that now, and eventually Julia saw that it was just an iron gate and she had the choice to walk through or not.

She walked through.

Hannah had already unlocked the door, and it stood open, like the entrance to a dark cave. Neesy squeezed her hand and waited for Julia to go first.

They made their way to the fireplace room. That was where Dutch had taken her the first day. He never said a word to her from the time the cops turned her over to him in Florida. If it hadn't been for Gus, she probably would've starved to death before he put her in that . . . that—

She wasn't ready to think about that room. Not yet.

"This is where I met Dutch the first time," Neesy said.

Julia looked at her. "Really? Did he make you sit there for hours, too?"

Neesy looked stricken. "No, baby doll, he didn't. He gave me a drink, and I was afraid to touch it because I might break the glass."

"Gus brought me a sandwich and some water, but Dutch yelled at him."

"Are you sure you want to keep going?" Hannah asked. "There aren't any pleasant memories here."

"Dutch is gone, isn't he? So he can't hurt me anymore, right?"

"That's right," Neesy said. "Where else did he take you?"

"Nowhere. Just . . . just upstairs. You?"

"Not at first."

Neesy had a funny expression on her face—like they shared a secret. Julia had been so busy thinking about herself she hadn't thought at all about what had happened to Neesy. It wasn't very nice, but Julia was glad she wasn't the only one who understood what Dutch could do. Suddenly she wanted to know everything. "Where did he put you?"

"In a room."

"Was it awful?"

"No, it was pretty."

Julia hadn't expected that. "Pretty?" Dutch hadn't given her a pretty room.

"He had to persuade me to stay," Neesy said gently. "He didn't have to do that with you."

"Show me." Julia grabbed her hand and pulled her out the door.

Neesy looked over her shoulder at Sara Jean's aunt. Hannah shrugged, and Neesy said, "Okay, I'll try. I got lost a lot, though. It's a big house."

On the way, they passed through the narrow room with all the pictures in it. Julia knew Mitch had found her in this room. Dutch had hung her up in a frame, like a picture, but she didn't remember any of it. No one said anything as they walked through. The old paintings stared down at her, and she was glad they were all strangers. She didn't want to know any more Hanovers.

Eventually Neesy found the hugest staircase Julia had ever seen. Her mouth opened, and she wondered what Sara Jean would say. "He never showed me this."

"He didn't have to," Hannah said. "Remember that, Julia. He did only what was necessary to get what he wanted. He wasn't being nice to Neesy. He was manipulating her."

"My room was up there." Neesy nodded up the stairs.

A flame of fear ran up Julia's back, and she pulled away. "How far up?"

"Just to the next floor. There's another floor above it and another above that."

"And above that?"

Neesy put an arm around her shoulder. "That's where he put you and then me."

"I don't want to go there yet."

"You don't have to go anywhere you don't want to. We can leave right now."

"No. I want to see your room."

They climbed the stairs and went down the hall. The carpet hid the sound of their feet, and in the quiet, Julia was afraid everyone would hear her heart making that

awful sound in her ears. She concentrated on the statues
and curlicues in the wall and all the dead flowers drooping in their vases.

"I'll get someone in to clean this all up," Hannah
murmured.

Julia was relieved to see that Neesy's room wasn't
scary at all. It was just a room. A pretty room, like Neesy
said. The flowers and ruffles and stuff went with Neesy
and her lotions and floaty purple nightgown.

"He gave you the perfect room," Julia said.

"For a while," Neesy said.

Julia looked around. "Where else did you go?"

"Do you want to see how I found Mitch?"

"Is it upstairs?"

Neesy shook her head. "But it's dark and I was scared.
Sure you're up for it?"

Julia nodded, and Neesy got some candles from the
bathroom and gave one to each of them. She lit them;
then they all went down a back stairway where there were
lots of small, empty rooms that made Julia feel sad for
the people who had lived in them. Neesy explained about
the servants and how they had to run around behind the
pretty rooms and make sure everything was nice for the
Hanovers.

The Hanovers.

It gave Julia a shivery feeling to be one of them.

If she lived here, she wouldn't make her servants stay
in the back behind everything nice.

Finally, Neesy opened the door into a hallway that had
lights on it.

"Mitch was here, all the way at the other end."

"He came to find me, didn't he?"

"Didn't you know he would?" Neesy asked gently.

But Julia hadn't been sure. She'd been so mad at him. And now he was in jail and might never get out. Jilene said Dutch had given her a drug called a roofie. It made her unable to walk or talk, so nothing was her fault. But sometimes, she couldn't help thinking it was. If she hadn't run away, if she hadn't gotten caught...

She took a deep breath. "I want...I want to go upstairs now."

"Are you sure?" Neesy asked.

"We can come back," Hannah said. "Do that some other time."

"I want to do it now. I don't want to come back. Ever."

She slid her hand into Neesy's, and the older woman led them into the kitchen and from there to the doorway that led to the attic.

A freezing feeling swept over Julia at the bottom of the stairs. The last time she'd been there, she had refused to go up. Dutch had slapped her so hard she fell down. And when she woke up, she'd been alone in that glass room.

But this time no one forced her up. She stood at the bottom of the steps, her hands and feet tingling.

There is nothing scary up there, she told herself. It's just a room. Just like with Jilene. It was safe. She could leave anytime she wanted.

She put her foot on the first step. Then the second. Behind her, Neesy and Hannah climbed the stairs, too. She was glad they were there with her.

By the time they got to the top, Julia was gasping for air.

Neesy bent down to look at her. "Are you all right?"

Julia nodded. Waited. Like Jilene said it would, her

breathing slowed, and she could keep going. Neesy got up, and Julia looked around. It was bare wood up here. Old and musty. The metal stairs in the center blocked most of the view.

"He took me here also," Neesy said. "Showed me all the cobwebs. He liked spiders."

"I hate him," Julia said, and the words weren't enough to cover all the hatred inside her.

"Me too." Neesy squeezed her hand again.

"Well, now that we're all agreed," Hannah said, "can we go home?"

"There's one more room," Julia said.

Hannah sighed, and Neesy said, "Oh, baby, are you sure?"

But Julia had to see everything. She dragged Neesy to those metal stairs. But when she got there, she could see the part of the attic the stairs had blocked. And against the far wall was an easel covered with a sheet. "What's that?"

"One of Dutch's paintings, I think," Neesy said.

"Can I see?"

"You can do whatever you want," Neesy said. "You're safe and in charge."

"I'll pass, if you don't mind." Hannah stayed at the foot of the metal steps while Julia and Neesy approached the easel.

"Do you know what it's a painting of?" Julia asked.

"This was one thing Dutch wouldn't let me see," Neesy said.

"How come?"

"He said it wasn't finished. He seemed very protective of it."

"Like he cared about it a lot?"

"Just like that."

Julia thought about Dutch caring more for a painting than for her. "Then maybe we should finish it for him."

Slowly, Neesy grinned. "Maybe we should."

Near the easel was a table with a bunch of stuff on it. Paints and brushes and scissors and cans of turpentine and pencils and boards with licks of paint on them. Neesy found a tube, squeezed it onto the table. Bright blue gushed out. She stuck a brush in it and got a gob of paint. "Go ahead. What color do you want?"

Julia picked up a tube that said BURNT UMBER and squeezed some out. It was a dark blackish brown. Perfect.

"Would you like to do the honors, or should I?" Neesy said.

"Oh, I think you should," Julia said.

Neesy whipped off the cover, revealing a strange, half-finished sight: a woman lying on a piece of glass. She wasn't wearing regular clothes; she was mostly naked, and the parts that weren't were wrapped in furs. She had short dark hair but no mouth or eyes. Her face was just a creepy blank oval.

Around the lady's throat was a necklace. Only it wasn't painted; it was like a real necklace. Or at least, the jewel part of it was. The chain was painted, but hanging on the chain was a real...something. It looked hard and plasticky, a tiny, ugly, grayish box. There was a small depression in the canvas, which made a little place for whatever it was to sit.

"What the...," Neesy said. "Hannah, come look at this."

Julia peered closer. "What is that?" She poked at it with her brush. A gob of paint stuck to the thing, and when she tried to rub off, the box got loose and fell. It hit the floor and cracked open, splashing water and letting out a bad smell. Something rolled and landed at Hannah's foot.

"Oh, my God," said Hannah.

Julia and Neesy ran over. "Lord in heaven," said Neesy.

Julia said nothing. She just stared at the thing lying at the end of Hannah's shoe.

It looked like someone's...eye.

51

Mitch felt as though his skin could peel off; he was that nervous. The last time he saw Julia was months ago. She was near death, her pale, dessicated body hanging loose-limbed and unconscious in the portrait gallery. She was alive, thriving even, according to Hannah, but until he saw it for himself, he would never be free from the familiar swirl of fear that had always been his constant companion.

But to see her, he had to face her. Face the lies and the life he'd forced on her. He ran his tongue around the inside of his sandy mouth. Would she understand? Forgive?

He took in a huge breath, glancing around at the crowd streaming in and around the steps and the huge stone lions that anchored them. Some might say the New York Public Library was an odd place for a reunion, but Julia had always been comfortable around books. And he wanted her to be comfortable. He wanted her to feel natural enough to say whatever she wanted, even if it was "I hate you."

He checked his watch. He was ridiculously early. But after Rikers, he couldn't stay in the hotel room, pacing between the walls. He had to get out in the air, walk, adjust to the simple freedom of going where and when he pleased.

And yet, would he ever be truly free? He'd hoped his release would ease the memories, but there were still times when he could hardly move without thinking about Alicia and all the other victims of Dutch's madness.

His paintings—his masterpieces. The creations he'd given to the world. Every one was tangible proof that he could get away with murder. God, how he must have enjoyed that. The shows, the renown. The sick satisfaction of knowing that every owner of a Dutch Hanover portrait paid hundreds of thousands to hang a forensic tour de force on his or her wall.

He'd mixed blood into all the paint. Blood dosed with sodium citrate to keep it from coagulating. And every painting contained an eye, each one preserved in a sac of formaldehyde, placed in a special box inserted into the canvas, and then painted over. *Impasto,* the art experts called it. A special layering technique that gave oil paintings three-dimensionality. Except Dutch's jeweled necklaces had only enough layers to disguise what he'd hidden. The gruesomeness of it staggered Mitch, but he was also grateful for it. He'd never have been cleared without it.

And perhaps the truth about Julia would never have come out, either—at least not enough for the courts. But they had a solid DNA sample with Alicia's eye, which was taken from Dutch's unfinished painting. That, plus a cheek swab from Julia and Mitch, was all they needed. Dutch's mad ramblings about never reproducing proved to be the one sane thing he'd said. He was sterile, a fact brought out by a second autopsy.

Julia had been Mitch's child all along, and a paternity test proved it with a 99.9 percent certainty.

Which is why Dutch had carved that letter into Alicia's skin. The saddest thing was, he'd been wrong. She hadn't cheated on him. She'd just slept with Mitch first. She was probably already pregnant when Mitch caught her with Dutch.

"Then why the hell didn't she say so?" Mitch demanded when Hannah brought him the news. He'd still been in jail, still waiting on the slow pace of justice.

"Maybe she didn't know."

"Right. How can you be pregnant and not know?"

"I understand it's possible."

"Only in soap operas."

"I spoke with several doctors, Mitch. You can carry the baby in such a way that you hardly show. You can even have your period—or what you think is a period. If that's what happened to Alicia, she could have misread the signs and the month of conception. She could have thought Julia came early. Was she a small baby?"

Mitch shook his head. "I don't know."

"She had no reason to lie to you, did she?"

Mitch slumped in his seat, suddenly drained. He propped his elbows on the table and hung his head between his hands. "No. She begged me to help her, and I refused. If she knew the baby was mine, she would have told me."

"But Dutch knew," Hannah said softly.

His arms fell, and his gaze met Hannah's. She reached over and squeezed his wrist. "She's yours, Mitch. Concentrate on that."

"Concentrate on that." Like he could think of anything else.

It had taken the lab a month to do the DNA work, and then he'd had to wait another two weeks for the court schedule to fit him in. He'd been out two days, and it felt like two minutes. There was a .jackhammer inside his chest, and he almost ran. He needed more time, another hour, another day. He hadn't figured out what to do with her, what to say to her.

Just then, his gaze caught a bobbing burst of bright auburn in the crowd. Strangers parted like the Red Sea, and there was Neesy walking down Fifth Avenue toward him. At her side was Julia.

His breath caught. They looked good. Both of them. But it was the child who held his attention. Underneath her open jacket, she was wearing shorts, which made him frown because it was the middle of May and hardly warm enough for shorts. At least her legs were covered, even if it was with red-and-white-striped tights. Neesy had warned him that Julia had discovered Pippi Longstocking and was growing out her hair so she could braid it. Mitch understood the attraction. Pippi lived in a house with a monkey and a horse and no adults to screw up her life.

He watched Julia march forward on the biggest, clumsiest pair of black clodhoppers he'd ever seen. God, she looked silly. Silly, weird, and wonderful, and he had trouble keeping that boulder in his throat from choking him.

He was planted at the foot of the lion where he'd arranged to meet them, and they stopped the minute they saw him. Neesy bent down for a conference, but she was too far away for him to hear what she said. Instead, he watched her zip up Julia's jacket and kiss her on the cheek. She rose, gave him a small wave and an encouraging smile, then turned back the way she'd come, leaving Julia alone on the sidewalk facing him.

The first thing she did was unzip the jacket. Then she stood there, clearly as unsure of what to do as he was. But he was the adult, after all, so he braced himself and started forward.

"Hey, Junebug," he said, because that was all he could think of now that she was there in front of him.

She smiled, and it was so full of everything he remembered it nearly broke his heart. He knelt down to her level, and the minute he did, she burst into tears and threw her arms around him.

He lifted her up, holding her tight. "It's okay, Jules. Everything's going to be okay now."

"I...know," she said between tears. "It's just...it's just..."

"What? It's just what?"

"It's just..." She sniffed. "No one's called me Junebug in, like...forever."

He carried her to a stone bench in the shadow of a lion and set her down, then sat beside her.

He handed her a crumpled tissue from his pocket. "You'll always be my Junebug."

She scraped the tears away with the back of her hand, then loudly blew her nose with the tissue.

"Better?" he asked when she was through.

She nodded.

"Want to go inside now?"

She looked down, playing with the tissue. "I know you don't have to...I mean...I know you're not really—" She took a deep, shuddering breath and looked at him bravely.

"If I'll always be your...your Junebug"—she gulped a breath—"will you always be...be my dad?"

That boulder in his throat turned into an entire mountain range. He lifted her chin. Her blue eyes were red-rimmed and filled with worry.

"You don't have to decide right away," she said quickly, and hiccupped. "You can think about it. I know I'm kind of a pain and—"

"I don't have to think about it, Junebug." He brushed a strand of hair behind her ear. Her bangs were long and raggedy, but he didn't care. "I already know the answer. It's yes. Unequivocally. And, anyway"—he tried grinning at her, though it wasn't easy since his face wanted to crumple up with emotion instead—"I don't exactly have much choice." And he told her about the DNA test.

Her eyes widened, but a speck of wariness mingled with the hope he saw there. "You're sure? You're not... you're not just saying that to make me feel okay?"

There was a time when she trusted him to tell the truth. That time was over now, and he was sorry for it. "No, I'm not just saying that. It's the truth. I'll show you the papers."

He wanted her to say she believed him without proof, but she didn't. "Okay."

He'd been carrying the test report with him ever since he got it. Now he took it out of his wallet and handed it to her. Carefully she unfolded it, then took her time reading it. Mitch waited silently, his jaw clenched, a cold wind roaring inside him. When she was done, she folded it up again and handed it to him.

"Thanks," she said solemnly.

Tentatively he put an arm around her, half expecting

her to pull away. "You know it wouldn't matter either way. I've got your back, Jules. I always have. I always will."

"That's good." She leaned into his embrace, snuggling close. "Because I've got yours."

Hanover House sold for 95 million dollars, setting a record in New York for the sale of a single-family dwelling. Mitch put half the money aside for Julia and the other half he donated to the Innocence Project, an organization dedicated to exonerating the wrongfully convicted.

Along with the deed of the mansion and the many legal papers he'd had to handle, Mitch was given a letter from his mother. As a condition of her will, it had been kept secret from Dutch. Had he not been underground, Mitch would have received it years ago. It was a short letter, in her own hand.

If you are reading this and your brother is still alive, I am no longer here to stand between you. Beware, Mitchell, dear. Be careful. And most important of all, be warned.

I've loved you the only way I could and kept you safe—from a distance. I don't ask for forgiveness, only understanding.

She'd signed it with a wobbly flourish that indicated her poor health. It was dated the week before her death.

The letter set everything he'd known and experienced on its side. From that perspective, he was forced to look back with new eyes. He could see now that his mother might not have been simply favoring one brother over the other. Her behavior could have been strategic and deliberate. She'd isolated herself with Dutch and steadily drove Mitch away to keep him out of his brother's reach.

The necessity of the sacrifice sickened him. But for the first time—ever—he wished his mother were alive so he could talk to her. Recapture a little of what Dutch had taken from them. But she was gone and so was Dutch. Much as he might regret what could have been, Mitch could not forget what was. His brother was out of his life now, and Mitch wanted him out of his head, too.

So he didn't dwell on the letter and its revelations. As soon as he could, Mitch took his girls and left New York. They flew to Bermuda, where he bought a boat, hired someone to teach him how to run it, and took Neesy and Julia around the world. For six months they went where they wanted, stayed as long as they wanted, and left when they got restless. Julia's skin turned a golden tan, and Neesy's freckles went wild. And in all that time, no one mentioned Dutch or New York or murder or death. Silently, separately, each of them buried the past at sea.

One warm and glorious night, Mitch was out on deck. The moon glittered on the sea and the only thing on the planet seemed to be their ship and the stars. He was leaning over the rail enjoying the solitude when Neesy's tart, lemony smell drifted over, and the woman herself slipped beneath his arm to lean against his chest.

She stayed there awhile, not saying a word. He didn't think he could ever explain how good it felt to have her beside him. To know there would always be someone he could confess anything to and she would believe and understand.

"Missed you," she said at last.

"Couldn't sleep."

"Anything I can do? Warm milk? Shot of Jack?"

He turned so his back was against the railing and she was facing him. He brushed back her hair and took her face in his hands. "How about a shot of you?"

He leaned in and she met him halfway. Her lips were soft and familiar now. Welcoming, loving, a place he could always come home to.

The boat rocked gently, and the kiss went on. It led to another and another. He was fine to stay out there all night in the dark with the scent of the ocean and Neesy mingling together.

But footsteps interrupted them.

Julia came up on deck and stopped, clearly not expecting to find anyone there. "What are you guys doing here?"

"What are *we* doing?" Mitch kept his arm around Neesy. "What are *you* doing, Junebug? It's late. You went to bed hours ago."

She shrugged. "I know."

"Something wrong, baby doll?"

She shrugged again.

Mitch didn't like the ambivalence. She didn't used to be so cautious.

"Tell you what," Neesy said. "How about you sit there and keep your daddy company while I make us all some hot chocolate?"

"Not the powdered kind," Julia said.

"You're pushing it, kid," Neesy said, and disappeared down below the deck where the galley was.

Mitch dragged a couple of deck chairs together, and they sat in them side by side looking up at the stars.

"You got something on your mind, Jules?"

"Kind of."

"Well, go on. Spit it out."

"Well, I like the boat and the ocean and, well, you know all the stuff we've been doing."

"Uh-huh."

She took a deep breath and kind of scrunched down in her chair like she was afraid he was going to hit her or something. "The thing is..."

"Julia..."

"Okay, okay. Don't be mad, though."

"When do I ever get mad?"

"Right."

"Come on, you're killing me here."

She got out of her chair and climbed onto his lap. "Are we *ever* going home?"

Mitch opened his mouth and closed it again.

"All this floating around—it's not some kind of...of punishment, is it?"

"Punishment? Why would you think that?"

"I know I shouldn't have run away. I'm sorry. I'm really, really sorry. If I hadn't run away, he wouldn't have been so mad and then maybe he wouldn't have—" Her voice cracked, and he put his arms around her.

"Aw, Jules, no."

"But then he put me in that room and you had to call the police and take me to the hospital and that's why they caught you and—"

"Listen to me." He hugged her tight against him. "Dutch wanted to hurt me. And he knew he could do that by hurting you. It was never about what you did or didn't do. It was only about me and him. It's not your fault."

She sagged against him. "Really?"

"Really."

She sniffled. "Then why can't we go home?"

Mitch paused. He didn't know what to say. "I...I didn't know you wanted to."

"Don't you?"

"Well...by 'home,' what do you mean exactly?"

"Home. Crossroads. The carriage house. I miss Sara Jean. And it's summer now and school will be over, and she's going to camp, and I've never been to camp, and there's this boy she's been e-mailing me about, and—"

While she chattered on, he looked back at the golden weeks on the ocean. Suddenly they seemed less a refuge of healing and peace and more a retreat—part of the same pattern he'd been following for years. Never staying in one place too long. Never making more than superficial contact with people. Always moving, always changing.

But Julia had thrown away her backpack. Was it time for him to do the same?

He held up his hand, signaling a stop to her lava flow of words. "Okay, okay."

"Okay what?" Neesy came on deck carrying a tray with three cups. She set it down on the deck and handed out the cups. "Put a little something extra in ours." She winked at him, and he tasted the Baileys with the chocolate.

"Okay, we're going home!" Julia cried.

Neesy looked at him. "Home?"

"Crossroads," he said. "She wants to go back to Crossroads."

Neesy shot Julia a look full of reproach. "Baby doll, I thought we decided—"

"You said to wait until he was ready. But I've been waiting and waiting, and it didn't seem like he would ever be ready."

Neesy turned to Mitch, examining him carefully. "Are you sure? Because if you're not..."

He looked at his two girls, their faces glowing in the starlight.

The lies were over.

The loneliness was over.

Most of all, the running was over.

He'd had a lot of endings; maybe it was time to begin something.

He smiled and opened his arms, embracing them both. "I've never been more ready."

THE DISH

Where authors give you the inside scoop!

♥ ♥ ♥ ♥ ♥ ♥ ♥ ♥ ♥ ♥ ♥ ♥ ♥ ♥ ♥

From the desk of Jill Shalvis

Dear Reader,

When I started this series, about three estranged sisters who get stuck together running a beach resort, I decided I was out of my mind. I have a brother, and we like each other just fine, but I don't have sisters. Then at the dinner table that very night, my three teenage daughters started bickering and fighting, and I just stared at them.

I had my inspiration! "Keep fighting," I told them, much to their utter shock. I've spent the past fifteen years begging them to get along.

After that night, it was a piece of cake to write the sisters—Maddie, Tara, and Chloe—with their claws barely sheathed, resentment and affection competing for equal measure.

All I had left to do then was find the three sexy guys who could handle them.

It just so happened that, at the time, my neighbor was having an addition put on her house. For six glorious weeks, there were a bunch of guys hanging off the roof and the walls, in a perfect line of sight from my office.

Which is really my deck.

So I sat in the sun and wrote while in the background cute, young, sweaty guys hammered and sawed and, in general, made my day.

And on some days, they even took off their shirts. Those were my favorite days of all. But I digress . . .

I was working very hard, planning out conflicts and plot pacing and trying to nail down my hero. And given what I was looking at for inspiration, it shouldn't be any surprise at all that the hero for this first book in the Lucky Harbor series, SIMPLY IRRESISTIBLE (on sale now), turned out to be a master carpenter.

And a very sexy one at that.

I'm actually writing book two right now. I keep going out on the deck, sitting and patiently waiting, but my neighbor hasn't hired any more sexy carpenters. Darn it.

Enjoy!

Jill Shalvis

www.jillshalvis.com

♥ ♥ ♥ ♥ ♥ ♥ ♥ ♥ ♥ ♥ ♥ ♥ ♥

From the desk of Jennifer Haymore

Dear Reader,

When Jack Fulton, the hero of A SEASON OF SEDUC-TION (on sale now), first entered my office to ask me to write his story, I was a little confused about his motives.

"Okay." I stared at him dubiously. "From what you've said, it sounds like you met a woman and fell in love. What's the issue here?" Honestly, I couldn't figure out why he'd come to me in the first place. I'm here to write about characters with real, serious problems, and his seemed straightforward enough. Actually it didn't seem like a problem at all.

"For one thing, she's the sister of a duke, and I'm a sailor."

Hmmm . . . a Cinderella story in reverse. There might be something here. Yet . . .

Frowning, I skimmed through the application he'd laid on my desk. While I had to admit that when he'd walked in I'd gotten a brief vision of the rolling sea, the guy didn't comport himself like a salty seaman at all. I tapped the papers. "Says here you're from a distinguished family. Your father and brother both sit in Parliament. You're a gentleman."

Fulton sighed. "By blood, maybe."

"Hmm." I know how thick bloodlines ran in nineteenth-century England. The fact that he was a gentleman from a reputable, wealthy family with noble roots would go far in aiding his bid for a duke's sister. If he were a chimney sweep or something, it might be different. But I didn't feel this was quite enough.

He leaned forward in his chair. "Lady Rebecca doesn't trust anyone. She doesn't trust me. And because of that, she pushes me away."

"Why doesn't she trust anyone?" I asked.

"Because of her previous husband."

"What about him?"

A muscle twitched in Fulton's jaw, and his hands gripped the chair arms so tightly I could see his knuckles whitening. "William Fisk was a bastard," he gritted out. "He didn't love her. He married her for her status and her money. He planned to steal it all away from her."

I had to agree, this Fisk dude *was* a jerk. Poor Lady Rebecca. Still, I couldn't see the relevance of any of this. I shook my head. "Look, I don't think this is the story for me. The lady might have some issues with trust, but don't we all? If she loves you and you love her, you can work it out. I guarantee it."

Clearly agitated, Fulton thrust a hand through his brown, sun-streaked hair. He rose and began pacing my tiny office, from one end to the other and back again. I watched him patiently, but secretly hoped he would leave soon. I had a lot of work to do.

Finally, he spun around, pinning me with dark eyes. "You don't understand."

I shrugged. The issue seemed clear enough to me.

"There's a problem. An *insurmountable* problem." He stalked toward me, placed his hands flat on my mahogany desk, and leaned forward until his nose was an inch from my own.

"You see," he began, his voice quiet but with an edge of something hard and brittle, like a thin sheet of glass about to shatter, "she shouldn't trust me. She shouldn't believe a word I say."

"Why's that?" I murmured, staring up into his narrowed, dark eyes.

"Because," he said very, very quietly, "my motives when it comes to Lady Rebecca Fisk are exactly the same as her first husband's."

Once I heard that, I was hooked. I knew I had to take this story on. I invited Fulton back into his chair, and after some arduous work and heavy arguing, we finally hammered out the fair solution to his problem, and A SEASON OF SEDUCTION was born.

Please come visit me at my website, www.jennifer
haymore.com, where you can share your thoughts about
my books, sign up for my newsletter and some fun freebies,
and read more about the characters from A SEASON OF
SEDUCTION.

Jennifer Haymore

♥ ♥ ♥ ♥ ♥ ♥ ♥ ♥ ♥ ♥ ♥ ♥ ♥ ♥ ♥ ♥

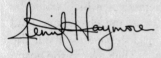

From the desk of Annie Solomon

Dear Reader,

One of the most interesting things I did for TWO
LETHAL LIES (on sale now) was the research. Nor-
mally, I don't enjoy that part of the writing process, but
I had some interesting experiences with this book.

In one scene, for example, I wanted my heroine,
Neesy, to disable a car. But she had to do it quickly—
before the bad guys could get her—without tools, and in
a way that could just as easily be reversed so the car
would start once the evil ones were gone. Sound easy?
Well, the car was a 1959 Oldsmobile, and I couldn't find
any reliable source, online or off, who could help. So I
went to the only experts I knew: Click and Clack, the
Tappet Brothers from the radio show *Car Talk*. We had
a great time on the air, and they came up with a good
solution. But after all that? The scene was cut!

Although the Net didn't help with that problem, it
was a godsend for others. When I decided to do a section

of the book at Disney World, I was a little nervous. I'd been to the park once, but it was years ago; I had only vague memories. But when I went online to see what information I could find, I was amazed. I discovered not only maps and the pictures from the Disney site, but lots of videos taken by visitors themselves, which would be much closer to the experience of my characters. And then I hit the jackpot—a mini-documentary about the secret tunnels beneath the park. That shaped the entire section. And it was so cool to write about something most people don't know.

I found lots of other things that helped me set the story of Mitch, his daughter, Julia, and his love, Neesy, in reality. The Drake Hotel is a well-known hotel in Chicago—and Princess Diana really did stay there! Hanover House in New York City is based on the Sloan Mansion, a turn-of-the-century home with fourteen-foot ceilings and seventeen bathrooms. I put Roger Carrick in the Omaha-Nebraska section of the FBI so I could write about Muscatine, the small town on the Mississippi that I visited last year. I met lots of great folks and had a wonderful time. And it's true, as Roger says—corn *is* everywhere.

If you'd like to see pictures of the places I've been, watch the videos, hear me on the radio—even take a gander at the scene that bit the dust—it's all on my website, www.anniesolomon.com. Stop by, check it out, and say hello. I'd love to hear from you!

Happy Reading!